# Dawnblaze
# Saves Summer

GW00578211

## Daisy Meadows

ORCHARD

# To Ida Mason

# Special thanks to Conrad Mason

ORCHARD BOOKS

First published in Great Britain in 2019 by Hodder & Stoughton

5 7 9 10 8 6 4

Text copyright © 2019 Working Partners Limited
Illustrations © Orchard Books 2019
Series created by Working Partners Limited

A CIP catalogue record for this book is available from the British Library.

ISBN 978 1 40836 585 4

Printed and bound in Great Britain by Clays Ltd, Elcograf S.p.A.

The paper and board used in this book are made from wood from responsible sources.

Orchard Books
An imprint of Hachette Children's Group
Part of Hodder and Stoughton
Carmelite House
50 Victoria Embankment
London EC4Y 0DZ

An Hachette UK Company
www.hachette.co.uk
www.hachettechildrens.co.uk

# Contents

# Meet the Characters

Aisha and Emily are best friends from Spellford Village. Aisha loves sports, whilst Emily's favourite thing is science. But what both girls enjoy more than anything is visiting Enchanted Valley and helping their unicorn friends who live there.

## Dawnblaze

Dawnblaze is the Fire Unicorn. She loves to swim in the hot springs on Firework Mountain with her dragon friends!

The Air Unicorn, Shimmerbreeze, is in charge of making sure the air in Enchanted Valley is fresh and clean. She likes to use her magic to create little breezes, so her friends can fly their kites.

**Shimmerbreeze**

**Glitterhoof**

Glitterhoof is the Earth Unicorn, who makes plants grow strong and beautiful. What she likes best is being part of a team ~ there's nothing she won't do for her friends!

Sparklesplash has so much fun playing in the rivers and lagoons of Enchanted Valley. This Water Unicorn wants everyone to love the water, just as much as she does.

**Sparklesplash**

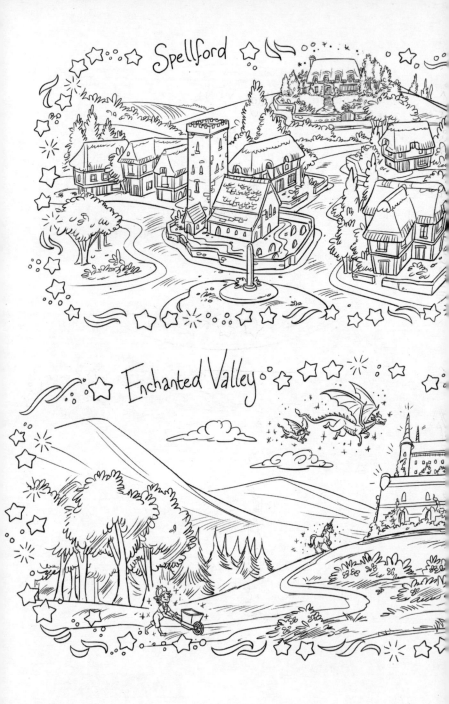

An Enchanted Valley lies a twinkle away,
Where beautiful unicorns live, laugh and play
You can visit the mermaids, or go for a ride,
So much fun to be had, but dangers can hide!

Your friends need your help – this is how you know:
A keyring lights up with a magical glow.
Whirled off like a dream, you won't want to leave.
Friendship forever, when you truly believe.

## Chapter One
# A Horse in the Attic

"I can't believe we're really going to live here!" said Aisha Khan. She stared up at her new house, clutching a cardboard box full of her belongings.

Enchanted Cottage had a thatched roof, neat little windows and walls the colour of summer sunshine. The front

garden was bursting with red and blue
flowers. A rose bush grew on either side of
the doorway, spreading over it in a leafy
green and pink canopy.

Aisha's dad threw an arm around her
shoulders. "Home, sweet home!" he said.

"It's perfect," said Aisha, grinning.

The Khans walked up the cobbled path, and Aisha's mum got out the keys. The front door was bright red, with a silver door knocker. It was shaped like a horse's face, with a single silver horn on its forehead.

"A unicorn!" said Aisha's mum, fitting the key in the lock. "I never noticed that before."

The door creaked open, and Aisha raced up the stone stairs to find her bedroom.

The summer sun shone through the window on to the old floorboards.

The slanted ceiling had wooden rafters, and there was a soft, cosy bed in the corner. Through the window, Aisha could see the big green lawn of the garden. In the middle was a statue of a magical bird, flying out of a fire. A phoenix, her dad had called it.

She put her box down on the bed. Inside were a tennis racket, swimming goggles, a cricket ball and a big collection of football stickers. Aisha loved sport more than anything.

Just then, the doorbell rang. "I'll get it!" shouted Aisha, and she raced down the stairs.

When she opened the door, she found a girl about her age standing before her.

The girl was wearing a stripy T-shirt, shorts and trainers. Her hair hung loose and curly round her shoulders.

"Hi!" said the girl. "I found a football on the road outside." She held it out. "I thought it might be yours."

"Oh, thanks!" said Aisha, taking the ball. "It must have fallen out of the removal lorry."

"I'm Emily Turner, by the way," the girl said. "I haven't seen you before!"

"We've only just moved to Spellford," said Aisha. "I'm Aisha Khan."

Emily looked around the front garden in awe. "I wondered who was moving into Enchanted Cottage. I've always wanted to see what it's like inside!"

"Why don't you stay for a bit?" said Aisha, smiling. "We can explore the cottage together!"

Emily clapped her hands with excitement. "I'd love to!"

Aisha led Emily through to the kitchen. Her mum and dad were unpacking pots and pans, and Aisha introduced them to Emily.

"It's lovely to meet you, Emily!" said Aisha's mum.

"How about we make some tea and get the biscuits out?" said her dad.

"Thanks!" said Aisha. "And I'll show Emily the cottage."

Aisha's mum smiled. "You girls have fun exploring the place. We'll call you when it's time for tea."

The two girls raced upstairs to Aisha's room.

"Let me guess," said Emily, picking up Aisha's tennis racket. "You really love sport!"

"That's right!" said Aisha with a grin. "What's your favourite hobby?"

"Science!" said Emily. "I love it. I've got a science kit at home with test tubes and safety goggles." She grinned back. "But I love magic too. That's why I always thought Enchanted Cottage looked so cool. You know, with the unicorn knocker and everything."

"Me too!" said Aisha. From somewhere above, they heard a distant thumping. Emily frowned. "What was that?"

"It sounded like … hoofbeats!" said
Aisha.

They both listened hard. Again, the
thumping sound echoed above them.

They stepped out on to the landing. A
ladder stood at one end, going up into
darkness above. Emily shivered. "There

can't be a horse in the attic, can there?"
she said.

"Come on," said Aisha, stepping on to
the bottom rung of the ladder. "There's
only one way to find out!"

## Chapter Two
# Queen Aurora

"I can't see a thing!" said Aisha, as Emily climbed up into the attic after her.

"If we wait, our eyes will get used to the dark," said Emily.

Sure enough, as they stared into the darkness, they began to see piles of dusty cardboard boxes, and an old sofa with the stuffing falling out.

Aisha frowned. "There definitely isn't a horse up here!"

"So where did the hoofbeats come from?" wondered Emily.

"Whoa!" Aisha crossed the attic to a low table beside the sofa, making the floorboards creak with each step. "Look at this!"

Emily went to join her. Sitting on the table was a little glass model. It was twinkling despite the dim light.

"It's a unicorn!" cried Aisha.

Emily carefully picked it up. The unicorn fitted perfectly in her palm. It had a delicate crystal horn, and its two front hooves were raised. Even in the darkness,

the unicorn glittered.

"What colour is it?" asked Emily. "It's hard to tell."

Aisha glanced around for a light switch and spotted a skylight covered over with a blind. She stepped on to an old stool, stretched up on tiptoes and pulled a cord.

*Swish!* The blind flew open and beams

of sunshine flooded through the window into the attic. The girls blinked and covered their eyes from the bright light.

When Emily looked again, she gasped.

In the sunshine, the girls could see swirls of colour glowing inside the unicorn, in every colour of the rainbow. The colours swirled faster and brighter. Then – *whoosh!* – they exploded around the unicorn in a shower of sparkles, like a firework going off.

The girls gasped as the sparkles flew around them, whirling past so quickly their feet were lifted off the floor.

"We're flying!" said Emily, as a blur of colour whizzed past their faces.

Suddenly the sparkles disappeared, and

the girls drifted on to solid ground.

Aisha looked down at their feet. They were standing on soft grass. "This can't be right!"

"What happened?" said Emily. "Where are we?"

"I've no idea," said Aisha. "But I don't think we're in the attic any more!"

Emily pointed up ahead. "Aisha, look!"

On a hillside stood a glittering golden palace. Flowers climbed up the walls, swaying slightly in the breeze, and windows glinted in the sunlight. The palace had lots of tall turrets rising against a bright blue sky.

"They look like unicorn horns!" said Aisha in amazement.

"It's incredible," Emily whispered. "What is this place?"

Aisha shivered with excitement. "Let's find out!"

Hand in hand, the girls walked up the grassy hill towards the palace. The higher they climbed, the further they could see. Beautiful meadows, forests and lakes stretched out all around them. Fluffy clouds floated above, and the girls glimpsed winged creatures darting in and out of them.

"I don't think those are ordinary birds," said Emily, staring up in wonder.

Aisha shook her head. "This place is amazing!"

When the girls reached the top of the hill, they saw that the palace was surrounded by a moat of crystal-clear water. A silver drawbridge swung down over the moat, chains clinking as it fell into place.

Then, trotting out over the bridge, came a unicorn.

Her mane and tail were shining gold, and her body was the colour of the dawn – pink one moment, then red the next … then orange, then gold … The colours seemed to come and go, like clouds

flitting across a sky. On the unicorn's
head was a delicate silver crown.

"I can't believe it! She looks just the
model in the attic!" said Emily.

The unicorn stopped at the end of the
drawbridge. She swished her tail, then
bowed her head at the girls. Her golden
horn sparkled in the sunshine.

"Hello, girls!" said the unicorn. Her voice was soft and gentle.

"You can speak!" gasped Emily.

The unicorn gave a laugh that sounded like sweet music, and tossed her mane. "I certainly can! My name is Queen Aurora. Welcome to Enchanted Valley!"

## Chapter Three
# Extravaganza!

For a moment the girls didn't know what to say. Then Aisha bowed low. "Hello, Your Majesty," she said. "I'm Aisha Khan."

"And I'm Emily Turner," said Emily, curtseying. "We love your palace!"

"Thank you!" said Queen Aurora.

"Why don't you come inside?" With a swish of her tail, she trotted back across the drawbridge.

"I don't understand. How did we get here?" whispered Aisha.

"I can think of only one explanation …" said Emily.

"Magic!" the girls said at the same time. With that, they held hands and followed Queen Aurora into the palace.

The unicorn led them through a gate and into a courtyard, where ivy-covered walls surrounded them. More unicorns trotted across a neat green lawn. In the middle of the grass, two silver unicorns were admiring a delicate paper chain hanging around a stone fountain that

was shaped like a leaping dolphin. Three
green-and-blue unicorns walked over
with little lanterns hovering beside them.
The lanterns settled in the branches of the
orange trees that grew around the edge of
the courtyard.

"What are they doing?" Emily asked.

"They're getting ready for a party," Queen Aurora said. "At the end of the week, we are holding our Nature Gala. We have it every summer! All our friends from Enchanted Valley are invited. The gnomes, the imps, the griffins … and the dragons, of course!"

"Dragons?" said Aisha, exchanging a wide-eyed look with Emily. "This place is amazing!"

Queen Aurora beamed with pride. "Come and see the kitchen. Our unicorn chefs are making party food!"

She trotted across the courtyard, and the girls followed. As they passed, each unicorn dipped its horn.

"That's how unicorns wave to each

other," explained Queen Aurora.

The girls dipped their heads to wave back.

Queen Aurora led them through a long, white stone corridor, down some steps and into a huge kitchen. It had a roaring fire and bronze pots and pans hanging from the ceiling. Several unicorns wearing chefs' hats were hard at work.

"Mmmm," sighed Emily and Aisha, breathing in the scents of vanilla, chocolate and cinnamon. The kitchen was full of the most delicious baking smells!

A pale blue unicorn wearing a chef's hat stood at an oven. He smiled at the girls before turning his gaze to a round

tin filled with cake mixture. He dipped his horn towards the tin, as if it were a magic wand, and sparkles surrounded it.

*Swooosh!* All at once, the mixture turned a pretty blue.

"More magic!" whispered Emily.

"Oh yes," said Queen Aurora. "Magic is what makes everything work in Enchanted Valley. Do you see what's hanging around his neck?"

The girls saw that the chef unicorn

wore a little crystal locket, hanging from a delicate golden chain.

"The lockets give us our magic," said Queen Aurora. "And we use them to look after Enchanted Valley. Each unicorn has a different kind of power." She lifted her head, and Emily and Aisha saw that she had a locket too.

"Mine is the Friendship Locket," Queen Aurora explained. "I protect all the friendships in Enchanted Valley."

Aisha carefully lifted up the locket for a closer look. Through the clear glass, she and Emily could see two tiny golden suns

floating around each other. They looked like a pair of friends playing.

"It's beautiful!" said Aisha.

Queen Aurora flicked her tail. "There are so many beautiful things in Enchanted Valley ... and in Enchanted Cottage, too!"

Emily gasped. "How do you know about the cottage?" she asked.

"Let me show you," said Queen Aurora. She led them out of the kitchen and down a grand corridor filled with vases of flowers. At the end was a wide staircase. Aisha and Emily followed Queen Aurora up the softly carpeted stairs and into a long white hall. Sun shone in through windows on one side, and on the other hung a row of large portraits. Some of the paintings were very old, with dusty golden frames. But there were newer ones too. Each one showed a pair of children in front of the palace.

The first was an oil painting of a girl and a boy wearing velvet tunics and frilly white collars. In another, a pair of boys were wearing smart jackets and ties. Aisha studied a painting of two girls in floor-length dresses.

"Who are all these children?" she asked.

"All the boys and girls in these portraits once lived in Enchanted Cottage," said Queen Aurora. "And they all found their way here, to Enchanted Valley. You see, there is a magical connection between the two places."

"Wow," sighed Emily. "We're so lucky!"

"I'm glad you think so," said Queen Aurora. "And we're lucky that you two came to visit!" She smiled, and her golden mane sparkled in the sunshine. "Now, let's meet the nature unicorns! They're in charge of the party."

Queen Aurora trotted under an arch at the end of the hall, into a sunny garden.

The girls came out after her and gasped. The garden was even prettier than the courtyard they'd first seen. It had lush green grass, colourful flowerbeds and a sparkling stream leading to a pool full of water lilies.

Four unicorns were gathered at a big,

round table with a white tablecloth. A
long scroll was laid out on top, and the
unicorns were looking at it and chatting
excitedly.

"That's their party plan," whispered
Queen Aurora. Then she called out,

"Hello, friends! Come and meet our visitors!"

The four unicorns looked around at Queen Aurora's call, then trotted over, swishing their tails happily.

As a red unicorn with a bright orange mane and deep brown eyes came closer, the girls saw tiny little fireworks exploding and glittering in her locket. "I'm Dawnblaze," she said. "I'm the fire unicorn! I keep Enchanted Valley lovely and warm."

"And I'm Shimmerbreeze, the air unicorn!" said a white unicorn. Her locket was full of miniature fluffy clouds. "I keep the air clean."

"I'm Glitterhoof, the earth unicorn,"

said a green unicorn, whose locket had a flower in it. "I make sure the flowers and plants can grow."

"And I'm Sparklesplash," said a deep blue unicorn, with a fountain in her locket.

"You must be the water unicorn!" said Emily.

"That's right!" said Sparklesplash. "I protect the water of Enchanted Valley."

Aisha grinned. "It's so lovely to meet you all!"

The unicorns grinned back, looking at Aisha and Emily in wonder. It was as if the girls seemed magical to them!

Just then, a cold wind swept through the garden. It ruffled the unicorns' manes and blew the scroll on to some bushes. The girls shivered. Dark clouds covered the sun and threw the garden into shadow.

Aisha felt a spot of rain on her head. Then another. Then down it came in a great shower.

The girls huddled together under one of the orange trees as the rain soaked their clothes.

"That came on fast!" said Emily.

Queen Aurora tossed her damp mane out of her eyes. "Oh dear," she said anxiously. "We should get inside, and—"

But before she could finish, lightning streaked through the sky. *Boooom!* Thunder rolled loudly, sounding like a whole herd of galloping horses.

With a flash of silver, another unicorn leaped over the palace wall. She landed on all four hooves in the garden. But this unicorn didn't seem like the others. Her silver body shone like the moon, and her mane and tail were twilight blue. She had purple eyes, and as she glared around, both girls felt a flutter of fear.

Emily gasped. "Who is that?"

# Chapter Four
# Selena's Big Moment

Queen Aurora's eyes were open wide, and her ears stood up with fright.

"It's Selena!"

The other four unicorns cowered behind their queen, frisking their tails anxiously.

"Surprise!" cackled the silver unicorn. She reared up, waving her hooves in the

air. Electricity
sparked over her
body. Then a
bolt of lightning
shot from her
horn. *Fffzzzappp!*
A nearby rose
bush burst into flames, frazzled by her
magic.

The girls ducked, holding on tightly to
each other.

"Look!" said Aisha suddenly. She
pointed at a glass locket hanging from
Selena's neck. Inside it was a little black
storm cloud, with a lightning flash inside.

"Uh-oh," said Emily. "She must have
made this storm with her magic!"

Just then, a furry
little black ball came
swooping down over the wall. It rolled
across the grass and sprang into the air,
fluttering a pair of silky wings.

"It's a bat!" cried Aisha.

"Here I am, Your Majesty!" said the bat,
bowing in mid-air to Selena. "Sorry I'm
late. I got really lost, and—"

"Silence, Flit!" roared Selena, stamping
her hoof. "You're spoiling my big
moment!"

She turned back to Queen Aurora. "So,
we meet again," she sneered. "Except
this time, I have a plan to take over the
Golden Palace, and rule over the whole
Valley!"

"Leave us alone, Selena!" cried
Dawnblaze.

"Aurora is our queen, not you," added
Sparklesplash.

"Not for long!" snapped Selena. "You
see, I'm going to steal the powers from
every unicorn and use them to take over
Enchanted Valley … starting with you
four!"

Selena whipped her horn from side to
side. Suddenly a great wind swept into
the garden, tearing rose petals from the
bushes and swirling them around in
circles.

Then the wind snatched up the four
lockets of the nature unicorns. *Clink!*
Four silver chains were lifted off the

unicorns' heads, and the
lockets went whirling
through the air. Queen
Aurora jumped up to
catch them, but with a
whoosh they zoomed
past her and landed
around Selena's neck.

"Oh no!" cried Emily.

"Give us back our lockets!" said
Shimmerbreeze, pawing at the ground.

Selena cackled. "Oh, I will," she
promised. "Just as soon as you make me
the queen of Enchanted Valley! Give
me the crown, or you'll never see your
precious lockets again!"

There was another flash of lightning

and a *BOOM* of thunder. Emily and Aisha clutched each other tightly. Then Selena flew off into the sky, her silver body shimmering in the rain.

"Wait for me!" puffed Flit. He went fluttering after her, and they disappeared among the dark clouds.

Dawnblaze hung her head in despair. "Oh no," she said. "This is our fault – we were so excited to meet you both, that we forgot to be on guard against Selena."

"What are we going to do?" Sparklesplash said. "We can't let Selena become queen! She'll turn Enchanted Valley into a horrible, scary place."

Emily and Aisha moved closer to Dawnblaze and stroked her mane, trying to cheer her up. Then, suddenly, the rain stopped. But just as the girls thought the sun might come out again, they felt the air getting colder. The tips of the grass went white with frost, and the pool turned to ice. A freezing wind blew through the garden.

"What's happening?" asked Aisha, shivering.

"It's because my magic is gone!" said Dawnblaze. "With my locket, I kept Enchanted Valley nice and warm. But now Selena has it, her magic will reverse the locket's power, and make the opposite happen. Instead of being warm, everything will freeze. It will be winter for ever!"

"I won't let that happen," said Queen Aurora. "I'll go and get the lockets back!"

"But you're the queen!" said Glitterhoof. "If you're not guarding the palace, Selena might try to take it over!"

"Then let us go," said Aisha, taking Emily's hand. "We'll find the lockets."

Emily gave Aisha's hand a squeeze and nodded. "Starting with Dawnblaze's," she added.

The unicorns all turned to look at them. Queen Aurora flicked her tail anxiously. "I'm not sure, girls," she said. "It's very kind of you … But Selena will try to stop you. It could be dangerous."

"We're not scared of her," said Aisha.

Aurora nodded. "Very well, then," she said. "But you must at least stay warm." Her horn glowed a deep orange, and the air sparkled with magic. When the girls looked down, they were astonished to see that over their summer clothes they were wearing cosy snowsuits, with furry hoods, thick gloves and boots.

"And I'll go with you," said Dawnblaze. "Just jump on my back."

"Thank you,

girls!" said the other unicorns together, as Dawnblaze kneeled down for the girls to clamber up on to her back.

"You are true friends," Queen Aurora added. "Good luck, and be safe!"

Aisha held on tight to Dawnblaze's fiery mane, and Emily sat behind her. Then the unicorn trotted forward. "Here we go!" she cried.

The girls gasped in shock as Dawnblaze galloped through the garden. Then – *whoosh!* – she leapt into the sky, flying up and over the palace wall.

## Chapter Five
# Firework Mountain

"You can fly!" cried Aisha.

"Of course!" laughed Dawnblaze. "All unicorns can!"

Emily glanced back and saw the Golden Palace getting smaller and smaller, until it looked no bigger than a toy castle. She felt a shiver of fear. "We're

very high up!" she murmured.

"Just hold on to my waist," said Aisha, gripping Dawnblaze's mane. "I won't let us fall."

Emily wrapped her arms around Aisha, and at once she felt calmer.

As they flew, the girls gazed around them in wonder. From up here they could see Enchanted Valley, laid out like a grassy green carpet beneath them.

A sparkling river ran near the Golden
Palace, and all around were thick, dark
forests, green meadows and castles.

Emily gasped as a flock of golden-
tailed creatures swept beneath them.
"Phoenixes!" she cried. "Those must
have been the creatures we saw flying in
the clouds!"

"Wow!" breathed Aisha. "They're just
like the statue in Enchanted Cottage!"

The wind roared in their ears and stung their eyes. Suddenly, they felt little cold pinpricks on their faces. "Snowflakes!" cried Emily. Sure enough, white flecks of snow were swirling and drifting around them.

"Oh dear," said Dawnblaze anxiously. "We must get my locket back soon – or it will never be summer again!" She shuddered. "If it gets much colder, the underwater creatures will be trapped under ice, and all the flowers will die … It will be terrible!"

"Where do you think Selena has taken the locket?" wondered Aisha.

Emily frowned. "Her magic makes your locket have the opposite effect, right?"

"That's right," said Dawnblaze.

Emily tried to think like a scientist. She peered all around, narrowing her eyes against the snow falling through the air. The cold seemed to be spreading out from a place in the far distance – a mountain. The top of it was white with snow, and ice lay on the slopes.

"See over there?" she said, pointing.

"That's Firework Mountain," said Dawnblaze. "It's a volcano. Usually it's lovely and warm there, but now it looks freezing!"

"It's where the cold's coming from," said Emily, "so I think it's where the locket must be. It must be what's made the volcano freeze."

"Nice one, Emily!" said Aisha. "Let's go!"

Dawnblaze whinnied with excitement and they soared towards the mountain.

As they flew, the wind howled louder, whirling the snowflakes in every direction. Aisha and Emily tightened their grip, clinging on for dear life.

When at last Dawnblaze swept over Firework Mountain, the girls looked down and saw a big crater at the top of it. Inside was a frozen pool of ice.

"I can't believe it!" said Dawnblaze. "Normally the volcano shoots out sprays of colourful sparks, like fireworks. But now everything is frozen! Even the dragons have gone. They're friends of mine, and we love to swim in hot pools on the mountain

slopes …" She looked
down below them.
"But those are all
frozen too!"

"Ooof!" gasped
Aisha. Something cold
and wet had hit her on
the back of the head. "What was that?"

"I think it was a snowball!" said Emily,
wiping snow off Aisha's hood.

"Oh no …" said Aisha, pointing to a
black spot in the sky. "It's Flit!"

The little bat flapped out from behind a
cloud, with two more snowballs clutched
in his claws. "Take that!" he squeaked,
and threw one at Emily.

Emily dodged it, but she leaned over

too far and lost her balance. "Woah!" she cried, slipping from Dawnblaze's back.

"No!" cried Aisha. She reached down to catch Emily's hand, but it was already too late – she was tumbling off the unicorn.

*Flumph!* Emily landed softly in a snowdrift beside the crater. She wiped snow from her face and sat up, smiling. "I'm all right!" she called. Then she spotted something glinting in the icy pool below. "Over here!" she cried.

Dawnblaze swooped down and landed gently in the snow at Emily's side.

Aisha climbed down off the unicorn's back, feeling a little dizzy. She wobbled and held on to some rocks at the edge of the pool.

Peering into the icy water, the girls saw something small, trapped in the ice and glowing with a hundred different colours.

"It's the locket!" cried Emily.

"And we only found it because of Flit!" said Aisha, grinning. "If he hadn't thrown snowballs, we would never have spotted it."

"I bet he was probably trying to keep us away from the locket," Emily said. "But his plan backfired big time!" She waved

at the bat, still fluttering above. "Thank you!"

"Oh, drat!" yelped Flit. He flapped his wings and darted off through the falling snow.

Dawnblaze frowned, swishing her tail. "But how can we get the locket out?"

"Leave it to me!" said Aisha. She picked up a big rock from the side of the pool and crouched down by the ice. She used the rock like a hammer … but it was no good. The ice didn't crack. She tried again and again, but the rock barely made a dent. At last Aisha put the rock down. "This isn't working," she sighed. "What now?"

Emily thought hard. "I know!" she said at last. "If we can't break the ice, we'll have to melt it! Then we can fish out the locket."

"That could work!" said Aisha. "But we'd need a lot of heat." She frowned, but then her eyes brightened with an idea. "Dawnblaze, do your dragon friends breathe fire?"

Dawnblaze tossed her mane with excitement. "They do! That's a great idea! I'll call them now." The unicorn stamped her hoof three times and gave a whinny that sounded like bells chiming.

A moment later, three huge, glittering

creatures came diving out of the clouds. The girls stared in wonder as the dragons looped the loop, their tails streaming behind them.

"I've never met a dragon before," said Emily, her eyes wide.

"Me neither!" said Aisha.

"They're very friendly," Dawnblaze promised.

The dragons landed all together and folded their big, shiny wings. Up close, Emily and Aisha saw that they were as big as buses, with kindly blue eyes. They were shivering in the cold. Frost lay across their backs, and snowflakes gathered on their eyelashes.

"Hello, dragons!" said Dawnblaze.

"These are my friends, Aisha and Emily."
She turned to the girls. "This is Sparky,"
she said, nodding at the first dragon,
which was gold. "And these are Smoky
and Coal." She nodded at the silver
dragon, then the bronze one.

"H-h-hello, Dawnblaze!" said Smoky,
his teeth chattering. "Have you come to

make it w-w-w-warm again?"

"We're trying!" said Dawnblaze. "But Selena has frozen my locket in there." She pointed to the crater with one hoof.

"That n-n-naughty Selena!" said Sparky. "Now our toasty home is f-f-frozen!"

"Will you help us stop her?" asked Aisha bravely.

The bronze dragon called Coal looked at Aisha. "Yes, little h-h-human. What can we do?"

"Can you melt the ice with your breath?" asked Emily.

"W-w-we'll certainly try," said Smoky. "W-w-won't we?"

The other two dragons nodded. They

stretched out their long necks like giraffes, until their heads were just above the icy pool. Then together, they breathed …

*Phut!*

Three little gusts of snowflakes blew out and settled on the ice.

"It's no good!" said Smoky sadly. "We're so cold, we don't have any f-f-fire left in us!"

The girls' hearts sank. Without fire, there was no way they could melt the ice.

"I have an idea," said Dawnblaze. "There is someone who could warm up the dragons. But I haven't seen him in a very long time. I'm not sure if he'll help us."

"Anything's worth a try," said Aisha.

"Can you take us to him?"

Dawnblaze stamped the snow with her hooves. "Hop on!" she said.

# Chapter Six
# Stinky Potion

"Who are we going to see?" asked Emily, as they flew down the mountainside through the falling snow.

"His name is Hob," said Dawnblaze. "He's very old and very wise. And he's a goblin! He lives near here."

"I hope he'll help us!" said Aisha.

Dawnblaze swooped down into a forest. Here and there, the tops of trees poked up through the snow. She looked around, stamping her hooves. "That's funny," she said. "I'm sure his home was around here somewhere …"

Just then, the girls heard something.

"What was that?" asked Aisha.

"It sounded like someone calling for help!" said Emily.

They looked around, puzzled. Then the cry came again.

"I think it's coming from under this snow!" said Aisha.

Quickly the girls climbed off the unicorn's back and began to dig. Dawnblaze helped, using her front hooves to shovel snow aside.

"Look!" cried Aisha, scraping away an armful of snow. Beneath it was the dark opening of a cave. The snow had completely covered it.

"Help!" cried the voice again, louder now.

A light shone from inside, then a funny little creature appeared, holding an old-fashioned lantern. He wore a long purple gown and a pointed hat with silver stars on, and his face was green and wrinkly. He wasn't much more than half as tall as Aisha and Emily.

"This is Hob!" said Dawnblaze.

"Oh dear me, thank you!" squeaked the
little creature. He pushed a pair of gold
spectacles up his nose. "I was worried I'd
never get out from under all that snow!"

"Don't mention it," said Emily. "Pleased
to meet you."

"I'm Aisha, and this is Emily," said
Aisha. "We've come to ask for your help!"

"Hmm," said Hob thoughtfully. "I don't

get many visitors … and you did dig me out. Very well – come in!"

Hob hurried off down a large, dark tunnel, humming to himself. Dawnblaze and the girls followed.

The tunnel led into a big cavern. Lanterns and crystals glittered from the ceiling. There were wonky wooden shelves propped up on the rocks, and every one of them was crammed with little pots and bottles full of strange ingredients.

Emily peered at the containers, but she didn't recognise anything from her science books. "What's Gossamer Glitter?" she asked.

"And what's Comet Dust?" wondered Aisha.

"Ingredients for my potions!" said Hob, rubbing his hands together.

"Actually, that's why we came," Dawnblaze said. "Could you help us make a potion?" She quickly explained what had happened.

"So you see, we need the dragons to melt the ice so we can get my locket back," Dawnblaze finished. "But they've become so cold, they're breathing snow instead of fire!"

"Dear me, what a pickle," said Hob, straightening his hat. "Let's warm up those dragons! I'll get my potion pot bubbling away. You two can fetch the ingredients."

Hob began calling out instructions as he placed a blackened pot over the fire. "Two pints of forest dew, please! And four ounces of spider silk!"

Aisha raced around, finding the ingredients, while Emily measured them out and put them in the pot.

"Very good!" said Hob, watching Emily mix in some silver dust.

"She's a natural!" said Aisha.

Emily blushed. "It's just like a science experiment," she said. But as she was

reaching for a bottle of
liquid rainbows, a black
shape darted from the
shadows and snatched it
away. "Oh!" she gasped.
"It's Flit again!" cried
Aisha.

Sure enough, Selena's bat flapped
around the cave, holding the bottle in his
claws. Aisha snatched at him, but he just
flew higher. "It's mine now!" he squeaked
in triumph. "You'll never finish your
stinky potion!"

"He must have sneaked in after us,"
said Emily. "What do we do now? We
can't reach him!"

Just then, the cave filled with a warm,

dazzling light. Turning, the girls saw that it came from Dawnblaze's horn. It was glowing like a torch.

"Gah!" squawked Flit. "Bright light!" He tried to cover his face with his wings, and he dropped the bottle. Down it fell, towards the rocky floor …

*Thump!* Just in time, Aisha dived and caught it. She curled up, holding the bottle tightly, like a goalkeeper with a football.

"What a save!" yelled Emily.

Hob snatched up a broom and jabbed it at Flit. "Out, you naughty creature!"

Squeaking crossly, Flit darted down the tunnel and disappeared.

"Whoa, that was close!" said Aisha.

"You did it, Dawnblaze!"

The unicorn stamped at the ground, looking pleased.

Hob quickly mixed the liquid rainbows into his potion pot. Then he took a glass flask from inside his robe and spooned the potion into it. It was thick and purple, and smelled very strange, like sour milk mixed with rotten bananas.

"It tastes better than you'd think," promised Hob, as he handed Aisha the flask. "Now, good luck, girls! All the creatures of Enchanted Valley are counting on you!"

## Chapter Seven
# Icy For Ever

Outside, the wind howled and the snow pelted down as Dawnblaze leaped into the air, Emily and Aisha holding tightly to her back. But the wind drove her down into the snow again. "Oh no!" puffed the unicorn. "I can't fly in this terrible weather."

"We'll just have to walk," called Aisha, over the roar of the wind. "We need to save Enchanted Valley!"

The girls and Dawnblaze started to struggle up the side of the mountain. The crater seemed a very long way off.

Emily stopped, panting. "I don't know if I'll make it," she said sadly.

"This won't do," said Dawnblaze. "But the dragons can carry you!"

"Not you?" Emily asked.

Dawnblaze shook

her head. "Unicorns don't mind being ridden, but we don't make very good riders! I know you girls will find a way to get the locket."

She stamped her hoof three times and whinnied. But no dragons came swooping through the snow.

"Where are they?" wondered Dawnblaze.

"I bet they didn't hear," said Emily. "This wind is too loud!"

"What if we all stamped together?" said Aisha.

"Good idea!" said Dawnblaze. "Are you ready? Now!"

The girls stamped their feet, and Dawnblaze stamped her hooves. Then

Dawnblaze whinnied and the girls
whistled as loudly as they possibly could.

They peered into the falling snow,
but there was nothing but whiteness all
around.

Dawnblaze hung her head. "I don't
think it worked."

But just then, three shining creatures
came swooping from behind a cloud.

"It's the dragons!" shouted Emily.

Sure enough, Sparky, Smoky and Coal
came gliding down towards them.

"Hello there!" boomed Smoky, as they
landed – *whumph!* – in the snow.

"Looks like you need our h-h-help," said
Sparky between his shivers. "C-c-c-climb
on. We'll get you back to the crater in

n-no time!"

Emily and Aisha looked nervously at
each other. But there wasn't a moment
to lose. Aisha climbed on to Smoky, and
Emily climbed on to Sparky. Their scales
were freezing cold, and not nearly as
comfortable to sit on as Dawnblaze's
soft, warm hair. But the girls clung on as
tightly as they could.

"I'll wait with Hob," said Dawnblaze.
"Good luck, girls!"

Then with a great whoosh, the dragons
soared up into the sky. Emily and Aisha
could feel the massive wings moving
beneath them as they flew closer and
closer to the mountaintop.

In a few moments they came gliding

down to land by the crater. Dawnblaze's locket was still there, buried deep in the ice.

The girls slid to the ground. Aisha brought out the flask, and Emily poured a few drops into each dragon's mouth.

"It tastes y-y-yummy!" said Coal.

"But did it work?" asked Aisha anxiously.

The girls held their breath, waiting. But the dragons looked just as cold and shivery as before.

Then all of a sudden, something strange began to happen. Woolly hats appeared on the dragons' heads, made of glowing golden light. Then came thick golden scarves, wrapping around their necks.

"I feel warm!" cried Smoky.

"Me too!" agreed Coal.

"This is much better!" said Sparky. "All together now. One ... two ... three!"

The dragons all breathed down on the crater.

*WHUMPH!* Three huge bursts of flame roared across the ice. Aisha and Emily gasped and stumbled back at the sudden heat. A great cloud of steam rose into the air. The girls saw chunks of ice breaking apart, and water bubbling beneath.

As the steam cleared, the girls peered anxiously into the pool. The locket was free! But now it was sinking fast through the water, out of reach and getting further and further away …

"Uh-oh!" gasped Aisha.

"If we don't get it back, summer will be lost for ever!" said Emily. "What are we going to do?"

"I'm going in!" yelled Aisha. She took off her magical snowsuit, boots, and gloves, so she was dressed in her leggings and vest again.

"Be careful!" Emily cried.

Aisha took a deep breath, ran and jumped.

*SPLASH!* She plunged deep into the water. The locket was below, the silver chain trailing as it sank …

Kicking her legs, she snatched hold of it. Then she swam upwards, holding her breath until she burst out into the air again.

Emily grabbed Aisha's arms and pulled her out. "You did it!" she cried. "Are you OK?"

Aisha nodded, shivering. "I'm f-f-freezing, though!"

Quickly, Sparky passed Emily her glowing scarf, and Emily draped it around Aisha's shoulders.

A warm glow spread through Aisha, and all the water vanished from her clothes. "Wow!" she gasped. "I'm dry!"

"Phew!" said Emily, helping Aisha put her snowsuit and boots back on. "You were so brave! Now we just need to get the locket back to Dawnblaze."

"Climb on," said Coal. "We'll have you there in no time!"

## Chapter Eight
## True Friends

They soon arrived at Hob's home. Emily
and Aisha hurried through the tunnel to
find Dawnblaze and Hob waiting by the
fire in the cavern.

"What happened?" asked Dawnblaze,
her eyes wide. "Did you manage to get
my locket back?"

Aisha grinned and held the locket up. Dawnblaze let out a whinny of excitement, and Aisha hung the locket back around the unicorn's neck.

At once, Dawnblaze's horn began to glow. A fiery redness spread across her mane and tail, and her eyes sparkled. She tossed her mane and rubbed her nose against Aisha and Emily's cheeks. "Thank you, girls!" cried the unicorn.

"You did it!" said Hob, dancing a little

jig. His glasses fell off, but he didn't seem to mind.

Back outside, the girls couldn't believe their eyes. The sun had come out again, and the ice and snow were melting. They could see grass and rocks appearing everywhere as the slush melted away.

"Summer is saved!" sighed Dawnblaze happily. Emily and Aisha grinned, shrugging off the winter clothes Queen Aurora had given them. The sunshine felt lovely on their skin.

"Look at Hob's home!" gasped Emily.

Aisha turned to look, and she saw that the entrance to the goblin's home wasn't a cave at all. It was a gap in the trunk of a huge old oak tree, which had been

completely
covered by
snow.

"And just you
wait, girls," said
Dawnblaze.
"Here comes
the best bit!"

*Whhhhhsshh!*
*Zzzzzzzipp!*
*Booooom!*

The girls spun round and stared in
amazement. Gigantic sparks were
shooting out of the top of Firework
Mountain. Reds, golds and yellows
shimmered in the sky, as though it was an
open box of firecrackers.

"It's amazing!" sighed Aisha.

The dragons flew up in the air, soaring and flicking their tails with delight. "Hurrah!" they cried. "Our home is warm again!"

But just then, someone came flying round the side of the mountain. The girls' hearts sank. *Selena!* And Flit was with her, flapping desperately to keep up.

"You human pests!" screeched the silver unicorn. She landed on a rock, stomping her hooves with fury. "You think you can stop me? I've still got three lockets, you know. The unicorns will make me queen!"

Flit landed beside Selena. "What did I miss?" he gasped.

Selena rolled her eyes. "Everything!" she snapped. Then she took off again, darting away across the sky. Puffing and panting, her little bat followed.

"She's right," said Dawnblaze. "She still has three lockets. We have to get them back."

"And we will!" said Aisha.

Emily nodded. "We promise."

Soon afterwards, Dawnblaze was gliding down towards the Golden Palace, with Aisha and Emily riding on her back. The girls grinned as they looked around at the valley, all green and summery once again beneath a clear blue sky.

As soon as Dawnblaze landed in the garden, Queen Aurora and the other Nature Unicorns galloped up to them.

"You did it!" said Aurora, beaming

as Dawnblaze's locket shimmered in the sunlight. "You're true friends of the unicorns! And now that summer is saved, it's time to celebrate."

Everyone cheered. The pale blue unicorn brought out the cake he had baked earlier. They all gathered around the table to eat it. The cake had chocolate icing and rainbow-coloured sprinkles. It was rich and fudgy, and the most delicious thing Emily and Aisha had ever tasted. It was almost like there was magic baked in …

"Selena can't stop us from enjoying ourselves," said Dawnblaze.

"The Gala must go ahead," said Queen Aurora. "No matter what!"

Aisha finished her slice of cake and sighed. "I wish we could stay here for ever."

"Uh-oh!" said Emily, her stomach dropping. "That reminds me … my parents! They've probably been looking everywhere for us!"

"Don't worry," said Aurora, shaking her head. "Whenever you are in Enchanted Valley, no time passes in your world. You will return exactly when you left. Even so, it's probably time I got you girls home. You've done so much today."

"But what about the other lockets?" asked Aisha.

"You'll know when it's time to come back to the Valley," said Aurora mysteriously. "For now, goodbye, girls. And thank you!"

Emily and Aisha threw their arms around Aurora's neck and hugged her tight. Her golden mane was soft against their skin.

Then Aurora's horn began to glow and sparkle. Sunshine spilled out of it, swirling around and around, until all Emily and Aisha could see was a bright golden light.

*Whhhhoooosh!*

*Thump!*

Emily and Aisha sat down heavily.
The Golden Palace was gone. They were
sitting on wooden floorboards, back in the
attic at Enchanted Cottage. Sunbeams
shone through the skylight.

Aisha checked her watch. "Aurora was right!" she said. "It's the exact same time as when we left."

"I just knew the cottage had some secrets!" said Emily. "But I never imagined anything like Enchanted Valley!" She smiled at Aisha. "And I never imagined I'd find such an amazing friend here."

Aisha hugged Emily tight – and caught sight of something floating up from the table by the sofa. It was the little crystal unicorn. "Look!" she gasped.

Right before their eyes, the unicorn turned gently in the air, glimmering with a thousand different colours. Then – *bang!* – it exploded in a shower of sparkles, just like the top of Firework Mountain.

Emily and Aisha blinked. When they
looked again, there were two tiny
unicorns floating in mid-air, each with a
shining silver keyring attached.

Silently, the girls reached out and each
took a unicorn.

"Do you remember what Aurora told
us?" asked Emily, as she attached her

unicorn to a belt loop.

"She said we'd know when it was time to come back," said Aisha. She tucked her keyring into her waistband. "I have a feeling that somehow, these little unicorns are going to tell us when."

"Then we'd better always wear them," said Emily.

The voice of Aisha's dad floated up to them from downstairs. "Aisha! Emily! Your tea's getting cold!"

"Should we tell your parents about Enchanted Valley?" asked Emily, as they climbed down the ladder from the attic.

Aisha laughed. "I don't think they'd believe us, even if we did! It can be our secret."

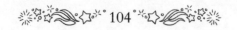

The girls grinned at each other.

"When do you think we'll go back?" Emily wondered.

"Really soon, I hope," said Aisha. "I can't wait to see some more unicorn magic!"

The End

Join Emily and Aisha
for another adventure in ...
# Shimmerbreeze and the Sky Spell
**Read on for a sneak peek!**

Aisha Khan pointed up at the sky. "Look!" she said with a grin. "There's an elephant!"

Aisha and her best friend, Emily Turner, were lying on the lawn of Enchanted Cottage, watching the fluffy clouds float past – and spotting the ones shaped like animals. Aisha and her parents had moved to Spellford Village just a few days ago, and the two girls were already close. Together they had explored Enchanted Cottage – and discovered that the old thatched house held a wonderful secret ...

"Aren't the clouds pretty?" said Emily. "Did you know that they're made of tiny droplets of water?" Emily loved science, just as much as Aisha loved sport.

"Cool!" said Aisha. Then she gasped. "Look at that one!" She pointed to where a large cloud was drifting over the top of the phoenix statue in the middle of the lawn. The cloud had a long tail and neck, and two great wings. It seemed to be pointing its tail down towards the outstretched wings of the magic bird below.

"Wow!" said Emily. "It's a dragon cloud!"

The girls shared an excited grin. On Aisha's first day in Spellford, they had found a beautiful crystal model of a unicorn in the attic of Enchanted Cottage. When a sunbeam had touched the glittering model, they'd been transported to Enchanted Valley, a wonderful kingdom ruled over by friendly flying unicorns, and full of other magical creatures, too – like goblins and dragons!

"I can't wait to visit the unicorns again," said Aisha with a sigh. She took out a crystal unicorn keyring from her shorts pocket. Queen Aurora, the unicorn ruler of the valley, had given matching keyrings to the girls and promised they'd return to Enchanted Valley very soon. Emily took her unicorn keyring out of her jeans pocket too.

Suddenly, the dragon cloud seemed to shimmer, then melted away – letting a beam of sunlight shine down on the girls. Their keyrings began to glow and sparkle like magical stars. "Is Queen Aurora calling us?"

Read
# Shimmerbreeze & the Sky Spell
to find out what adventures are in store
for Aisha and Emily!

# Also available

**Book One:**

**Book Two:**

**Book Three:**

**Book Four:**

# Unicorn Magic

## Look out for the next book!

Daisy Meadows

Unicorn Magic™

Three stories in one

Snowstar and the Big Freeze

From the author of RAINBOW MAGIC

If you like
Unicorn Magic,
you'll love ...

# Welcome to Animal Ark!

Animal-mad Amelia is sad
about moving house, until she
discovers Animal Ark, where vets look
after all kinds of animals in need.

Join Amelia and her friend Sam for a
brand-new series of animal adventures!

# Shimmerbreeze
# and the Sky Spell

## Daisy Meadows

ORCHARD

For Audrey Primrose Dawson
with love from Nanny Saran

Special thanks to Jan Burchett and
Sara Vogler

ORCHARD BOOKS

First published in Great Britain in 2019 by Hodder & Stoughton

3 5 7 9 10 8 6 4

Text copyright © 2019 Working Partners Limited
Illustrations © Orchard Books 2019
Series created by Working Partners Limited

A CIP catalogue record for this book is available from the British Library.

ISBN 978 1 40836 616 5

Printed and bound in Great Britain by Clays Ltd, Elcograf S.p.A.

The paper and board used in this book are made from wood from responsible sources.

Orchard Books
An imprint of Hachette Children's Group
Part of Hodder and Stoughton
Carmelite House
50 Victoria Embankment
London EC4Y 0DZ

An Hachette UK Company
www.hachette.co.uk
www.hachettechildrens.co.uk

# Contents

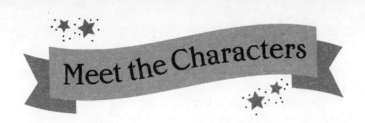

# Meet the Characters

Aisha and Emily are best friends from Spellford Village. Aisha loves sports, whilst Emily's favourite thing is science. But what both girls enjoy more than anything is visiting Enchanted Valley and helping their unicorn friends who live there.

Dawnblaze

Dawnblaze is the Fire Unicorn. She loves to swim in the hot springs on Firework Mountain with her dragon friends!

The Air Unicorn, Shimmerbreeze, is in charge of making sure the air in Enchanted Valley is fresh and clean. She likes to use her magic to create little breezes, so her friends can fly their kites.

Shimmerbreeze

Glitterhoof

Glitterhoof is the Earth Unicorn, who makes plants grow strong and beautiful. What she likes best is being part of a team – there's nothing she won't do for her friends!

Sparklesplash has so much fun playing in the rivers and lagoons of Enchanted Valley. This Water Unicorn wants everyone to love the water, just as much as she does.

Sparklesplash

Enchanted Cottage

Golden Palace

An Enchanted Valley lies a twinkle away,
Where beautiful unicorns live, laugh and play
You can visit the mermaids, or go for a ride,
So much fun to be had, but dangers can hide!

Your friends need your help - this is how you know:
A keyring lights up with a magical glow.
Whirled off like a dream, you won't want to leave.
Friendship forever, when you truly believe.

# Chapter One
# Trouble in Enchanted Valley

Aisha Khan pointed up at the sky. "Look!" she said with a grin. "There's an elephant!"

Aisha and her best friend, Emily Turner, were lying on the lawn of Enchanted Cottage, watching the fluffy clouds float past – and spotting the ones shaped

like animals! Aisha and her parents had
moved to Spellford Village just a few
days ago, and the two girls were already
close. Together they had explored Aisha's
new home, Enchanted Cottage – and
discovered that the old thatched house
held a wonderful secret …

"Aren't the clouds pretty?" said Emily.
"Did you know that they're made of tiny
droplets of water?" Emily loved science,
just as much as Aisha loved sport.

"Cool!" said Aisha. Then she gasped. "Look at that one!" She pointed to where a large cloud was drifting over the top of the phoenix statue in the middle of the lawn. The cloud had a long tail and neck, and two great wings. It seemed to be pointing its tail down towards the outstretched wings of the magic bird below.

"Wow!" said Emily. "It's a dragon cloud!"

The girls shared an excited grin. On Aisha's first day in Spellford, they had found a beautiful crystal model of a unicorn in the attic of Enchanted Cottage. When a sunbeam had touched the glittering model, they'd been transported to Enchanted Valley, a wonderful kingdom ruled over by friendly flying unicorns, and full of other magical creatures, too – like goblins and dragons!

"I can't wait to visit the unicorns again," said Aisha with a sigh. She took out a crystal unicorn keyring from her shorts pocket. Queen Aurora, the unicorn ruler of the valley, had given matching keyrings to the girls and promised they'd return to Enchanted Valley very soon. Emily took her keyring out of her jeans pocket too.

Suddenly, the dragon cloud seemed to shimmer, then melted away – letting a beam of sunlight shine down on the girls. Their keyrings began to glow and sparkle like magical stars.

Both girls leaped to their feet. "Is Queen Aurora calling us?" Aisha asked, excitement racing through her.

"I think so!" cried Emily. She could feel her keyring pulling towards Aisha's. "Whoa! They're like magnets!"

"Let's try putting them together," said Aisha.

The girls held the two tiny unicorns so that their horns touched. The keyrings glowed, with every colour of the rainbow swirling inside them. Then, suddenly, there was an explosion of light like dazzling fireworks. Emily and Aisha felt their feet lift off the grass.

In a whirl of sparkles, the garden and Enchanted Cottage vanished. Bright swirls of colour whizzed around them, and they were lifted up, up, up …

A few moments later, the girls drifted to the ground once more and the sparkles cleared. They found themselves at the foot of a hill, on which stood a dazzling gold palace.

"We're back in Enchanted Valley!" cried
Aisha, turning a cartwheel in delight.

Laughing, the girls held hands and
walked up the hill to the palace.

Sweet-scented flowers grew over the
palace walls, and twirling turrets, like
upside-down ice cream cones, rose in the
air. A river wound magically up from
the sea to fill the moat – when the girls

looked down over the valley, they could follow its path as it babbled through green meadows, forests and lakes.

"It's so amazing to be here again!" said Emily, with a sigh of happiness.

The palace's silver drawbridge lowered and a beautiful unicorn wearing a gleaming crown trotted out. Her coat

shone with all the shades of sunrise – from bright yellows to rich reds and fiery oranges. Her horn was long and elegant and gleamed in the sunshine.

"Queen Aurora!" The girls threw their arms around her soft neck in a tight hug.

Aurora laughed, the sound as beautiful as a flute's music. "Welcome, girls!" she said. "It's so lovely to see you." But then her eyes clouded with worry.

"What's the matter?" asked Emily.

"Come and see," said Aurora sadly.

She took them across the drawbridge and into a courtyard, past a fountain shaped like a leaping dolphin to where a pink-and-white stripy tent stood on a lawn. Beside it were the four Nature Unicorns!

"Hello!" cried the girls, hugging them each in turn.

"Hello, girls," said Dawnblaze the fire

unicorn, whose coat was red. "Oh, thank goodness you're here!"

"We need your help," said Sparklesplash the water unicorn, who was a shimmering blue. "Look!"

With her horn, Sparklesplash pointed at a heap of brightly coloured kites lying at the unicorns' hooves.

"We're hoping to have a kite-flying competition at the Nature Gala," said Glitterhoof the earth unicorn, who was a pretty shade

of leaf green.

"But the kites won't leave the ground," added Dawnblaze.

Shimmerbreeze the air unicorn gave a sad sigh. Her coat was as white as snow and her mane and tail were a glittery silver. Her pale blue eyes were wet with tears. "It's because my locket is missing," she said.

All the unicorns of Enchanted Valley wore crystal lockets around their necks that gave them magical powers.

Queen Aurora's locket contained two tiny
suns, dancing happily around each other
like friends playing – and she looked after
friendship in the valley. But out of the
four Nature Unicorns, only Dawnblaze
was wearing a locket now. The others had
been stolen by a wicked unicorn called
Selena, who would stop at nothing to rule
over Enchanted Valley.

Emily and Aisha had managed to get

Dawnblaze's locket back from Selena's horrible clutches, but it had been very difficult.

Queen Aurora turned to the girls. "This is why I've brought you to Enchanted Valley today," she said. Her eyes were wide and serious. "I'm worried that the kites are just the start of the trouble Selena will cause with Shimmerbreeze's locket. We need your help to get it back."

"We'd do anything to save the valley," said Aisha.

"Of course we will!" promised Emily.

Just then, the courtyard darkened, and they all looked up. A mysterious blanket of grey cloud was drifting over the palace, blocking out the sun. The air grew thick and dusty, making everyone cough and splutter.

"Yuck!" said Aisha. "The air's turned so dirty!"

"What's happening?" asked Emily, between coughs.

Then shrill laughter filled their ears – and the girls knew exactly who was behind the nasty, dirty fog. A silver unicorn with a twilight-blue mane burst from the filthy cloud, bolts of electricity flashing from her horn.

"Uh-oh," said Emily and Aisha. "It's Selena!"

## Chapter Two
# The Terrible Tornado

Selena landed in the courtyard in front of the horrified girls and unicorns. Her purple eyes blazed and her mane and tail bristled. She reared up, her hooves flashing. Inside her locket were tiny storm clouds, zigzags of jagged lightning crackling through them.

"So you snivelling girls are back,"
Selena sneered.

Swallowing down their fear, Emily and
Aisha stood their ground.

"That's right," said Aisha firmly. "The
unicorns are our friends, and friends help
each other."

"Two little squirts like you won't stop
me becoming queen of Enchanted
Valley," spat Selena, swishing her dark

blue tail menacingly.

A giggle came from the dirty cloud, and down flapped Flit, Selena's naughty bat servant. "Hee, hee!" laughed Flit. "They're little squirts and you're going to be queen! You tell them, Your Silver Greatness!"

"I just did, Flit!" screeched Selena. "Hand over the crown, Aurora!"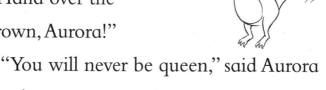

"You will never be queen," said Aurora firmly.

"We'll see about that!" Selena stamped her hooves. "The power of the air locket is mine now – and it's hidden where you'll never find it. If you don't make me queen, the air will get dirtier and dirtier, until

Enchanted Valley is covered in my
yucky-mucky fog!"

A bolt of lightning shot from her horn.
The filthy cloud began whirl around,
sucking up petals and leaves from the
garden.

"Oh no!" gasped Queen Aurora.
"Selena's creating a–a—"

"A tornado!" finished Emily.

The tornado spun faster and faster. It
pulled up the kites, then a whole rose

bush, like a gigantic vacuum cleaner.
Then the girls and the unicorns were
being tugged upwards – their hair, manes
and tails were standing on end. The
unicorns' hooves were still on the ground,
but the girls were smaller and lighter, and
the tornado pulled them up on to their
tiptoes. "Whoa!" they both cried, as they
were lifted off the ground.

Tumbling, whirling wind blasted around
them. Dust stung their eyes and they

felt horribly dizzy as they were swept higher and higher. Below, they saw Shimmerbreeze take off, but before she could get close enough to the girls to save them, she was sucked up into the tornado, too!

Soon, the palace and their unicorn friends had vanished from sight. Emily, Aisha and Shimmerbreeze were tossed helplessly about in the fierce wind as the tornado flew across Enchanted Valley. It hoovered up fir cones, twigs and stones, umbrellas and garden spades. Even a washing line full of tiny, flapping gnome clothes spun by in a swirling rush.

Emily shrieked as a flying sock whipped against her face.

A pebble hit Aisha on the arm. "Ow!" she yelped.

Then, as quickly as it had started, the tornado stopped spinning. The air became perfectly still. For a long moment, the girls, Shimmerbreeze and all the different objects floated high above the clouds. Then they began to plummet!

Terrified, the girls grabbed each other's hands. Down and down they fell, twisting and turning.

"Help!" screamed Emily.

Shimmerbreeze gave a whinny of alarm. "I'll save you!" she called.

She dived after the girls as they tumbled through the air, their hearts hammering with fright.

"Please hurry, Shimmerbreeze!" Aisha cried.

But Shimmerbreeze was fighting her way through the leaves and clothes and old umbrellas also falling to the ground.

"They're slowing her down!" shouted Emily. Then she spotted something else flying through the sky – a brilliant flash of red and gold, hurtling towards the girls like a rocket. When it got closer, they realised it was a beautiful giant bird.

The bird shot beneath the girls – and

they landed on her soft feathered back.

"Hold tight!" the bird squawked. She had a crest of orange feathers on her head and a long glossy tail that fanned out like flames. The girls clung on as they flew down towards a fluffy cloud. To their astonishment, the bird came to rest on top of it! She neatly folded her huge wings.

"We're safe!" breathed Aisha.

"Thank you for catching us!" said Emily.

"Don't mention it, my dears," chirruped

the kindly bird.

Shimmerbreeze landed next to them, shaking a pair of gnome trousers from her horn. "I'm so glad you're all right," she said, nuzzling their cheeks. "Thank you for your help," she said to the bird. Then she turned to the girls. "This is Ember. She's a phoenix."

Emily and Aisha grinned. They loved the phoenix statue in the garden of Enchanted Cottage. They'd never dreamed they'd meet one in real life!

"It's nice to meet you, Ember," said Aisha.

"Welcome to my cloud," the phoenix said. "Off you hop!"

The girls looked doubtfully at the cloud.

Shimmerbreeze and Ember might be able to stand on it, but they were magic! What if the girls fell straight through?

"It's quite safe," Shimmerbreeze assured them.

The girls climbed carefully off Ember's back. They felt their feet sink just a little into the fluffy surface. It was like stepping on to a soft cushion.

"This is amazing!" exclaimed Emily, looking at the wisps curling around her

Aisha jumped up and down, springing higher than Emily's head. "It's like a trampoline!" she cried, and turned a backflip.

Ember laughed in delight. "I do enjoy having visitors," she said, rustling the long feathers of her tail. "Especially today! My eggs have started to sing, which means it won't be long until they hatch!"

Emily and Aisha grinned at each other. Bouncy clouds and singing eggs! Enchanted Valley was full of amazing surprises!

Ember led them to a billowy white nest in the middle of the cloud. Six sparkling gold eggs lay snugly inside. And they were singing, in tiny, trilling voices!

Fluffy clouds that bob along
Listen to our happy song.
We're floating gently way up high
Warm and comfy in the sky.

"How sweet!" said Emily. "In Aisha's garden there's a—"

Her words were lost in a howling noise that filled the air. A whirling column raced above the clouds.

"The tornado's back!" cried Shimmerbreeze.

*Swoosh!* The girls watched in horror as the tornado whizzed through the sky above them. They clung tightly to Shimmerbreeze to keep from being swept up this time – but before anyone could reach it, the nest shot up into the sky.

"No!" yelled Aisha, and bounced up from the cloud. She tried to snatch the nest back, but it spiralled higher and higher in the spinning cone of wind.

With a whoosh, the tornado whisked
the precious eggs away!

## Chapter Three
# A Fluffy Surprise

"My chicks!" cried Ember, squawking with panic.

She took off and chased after the tornado, her flame-coloured wings flapping in a blur.

"We have to help her," said Emily.

"Jump on, girls," said Shimmerbreeze.

Aisha climbed on to her back, Emily behind her. Shimmerbreeze cantered across the cloud, wisps swirling around her hooves, then leaped into the air. Although they were on a rescue mission, the girls couldn't help feeling a rush of excitement – they were flying on a unicorn!

Shimmerbreeze sped through the sky, catching up with Ember. The phoenix's eyes were fixed on her precious nest, which was spinning around in the wind.

But the air was turning mucky and gloopy with dirt, slowing them down. The tornado was speeding away.

"It's just ... so hard ... to ... fly!" Shimmerbreeze panted. The tornado sped off into the distance until it was just a grubby dot on the horizon. Then it was gone.

"No!" cried Aisha.

"My chicks will be hatching any minute," wailed Ember. "They'll be all alone." She flopped on to a nearby cloud. "Oh, look at that!" She pointed a wing to the edge of the cloud, which the dirty air was turning a sludgy green. "And when they hatch, they'll be surrounded by this horrible dirt! The poor things!" She hid

her head in her
wings.

Shimmerbreeze
landed beside
her and the girls
jumped down.
They stroked
Ember's feathers
gently.

Emily shared
a glance with
Aisha. She knew her friend was thinking
the same thing – they needed to look
for Shimmerbreeze's locket to stop the
air getting even dirtier, but they couldn't
leave the poor phoenix. "We'll get your
eggs back," Emily told her.

"The tornado put us down earlier," said Aisha, "so maybe it's put the nest down too. Let's search the clouds for it."

"What a good idea," said Ember, wiping her eyes with a wingtip. "It's so kind of you to help."

"Follow me!" said Aisha. Using the cloud as a trampoline once more, she bounced on to the next one. Emily bounced after her, while Ember and Shimmerbreeze flew around, searching anxiously. They went from cloud to cloud, each now so tinged with dirt they looked more like puffs of smoke from a fire. The phoenix's nest was nowhere to be seen.

Ember coughed on the filthy air. "It's no good," she said sadly.

"Wait!" cried Shimmerbreeze. "Can you hear that?"

From somewhere nearby came a strange, sad whimpering sound.

"Is it the eggs singing?" asked Aisha.

Ember cocked her head to listen. "I don't think so," she said.

"It's someone crying," said Emily.

"Where's it coming from?" asked Aisha, puzzled.

"Oh, boo hoo! Boo hoo hoo!" went the crying sound. It was getting louder. The cloud the girls were standing on started to shake.

"Hang on tight!" squawked Ember. "It's another tornado!"

"Jump on my back!" cried

Shimmerbreeze.

Before the girls could move, the front of the cloud began to shift and grow, and suddenly became an enormous white furry head. It turned slowly towards them and blinked its big, wet eyes. The girls saw that it had two soft floppy ears, a round, shiny nose and wispy white whiskers. Emily and Aisha were open-mouthed in amazement. They weren't standing on a cloud – they were on a creature!

"He's a cloud puppy," whispered Shimmerbreeze.

"He's adorable!" breathed Emily.

"Hello," said the cloud puppy, sniffling softly. "My name is Fluffy."

"Hello, Fluffy," said Aisha. She leaned

forward and stroked his ears, giggling as
his whiskers tickled her face. "I'm Aisha
and this is Emily, and Shimmerbreeze, and
Ember …"

She stopped. Tears as big as footballs
were rolling down the puppy's face.

"Why are you sad, Fluffy?" asked Emily
anxiously.

"A horrid tornado stole my golden

ball," sniffed the cloud puppy. "It's my favourite one to play fetch with." He gave a mournful howl that made him tremble all over. The girls held hands so they wouldn't fall from his back.

"The tornado stole Ember's eggs, too," said Emily. "You haven't seen them, have you?"

"No!" wailed Fluffy, crying even harder.

"This is all because horrible Selena stole Shimmerbreeze's locket," explained Aisha. "It's why the air's so dirty. We're on a quest to find the locket, and we'll find your ball too."

Fluffy stopped crying. His tail wagged.

"Thank you," he said, and barked cheerfully. "Can I help too?"

"Of course you can," said Aisha.

Emily peered thoughtfully through the murky air. "Let's all fly higher," she said, "then we might spot where the tornado's gone."

"Hold on tight," said Fluffy, "and off we go!"

The girls rode on Fluffy's back while Shimmerbreeze and Ember soared beside them. Up they zoomed through the sky. Swirls of murky air billowed

around, making it hard to see. Below the clouds, the usually fresh green forests and sparkling lakes of Enchanted Valley had turned grey and sludgy.

"Everywhere is so miserable," said Emily sadly, gazing down at the horrible sight.

Fluffy gave a whine. "What's that down there?" he asked. "It looks horrible!"

Aisha followed his gaze – and saw a dark smudge skidding across one of the meadows. "It's the tornado!"

"Well spotted, Fluffy!" cried Shimmerbreeze.

"Chase it, Fluffy!" called Emily. "Hurry!"

## Chapter Four
# Hob Helps Out

Fluffy, Shimmerbreeze and Ember
swooped down after the twisting tornado.
Emily and Aisha clung on to Fluffy's fur
as they rushed towards the ground. The
tornado whirled over the fields towards
what looked like an enormous rubbish
heap. The tornado spun over the heap,

dropping all the things it had stolen. The whole mound was covered in grime, and blasts of filthy dust burst from its centre.

"The tornado's making a rubbish dump!" squawked Ember in horror.

A shudder rippled through Shimmerbreeze's coat. "I've never seen anything so filthy before!"

"It's the dirtiest place in Enchanted Valley," agreed Fluffy.

Emily frowned, thinking hard. Fluffy's words had given her an idea ... "We know from when we found Dawnblaze's locket that Selena's horrible magic comes from the locket," she said. "So wherever the locket is, it will be making everything around it dirty. Even dirtier than here ..."

"…So if the rubbish heap is the dirtiest place in Enchanted Valley," finished Aisha, "that must be where the locket is!"

They waited until the tornado had whirled away again, then landed beside the pile of rubbish. But as soon as they approached the dump, the dust made them all start coughing.

"This is no good," spluttered Aisha. "We can't go any closer."

"I know!" exclaimed Emily. "If I'm doing science experiments, I always wear a mask. It stops me breathing in anything bad." She frowned. "But where can we find masks in Enchanted Valley?"

Aisha's eyes lit up. "I know! Hob!"

Hob the little goblin was a very talented

potion maker. On their first adventure, the girls had helped him make a magic potion to warm up the dragons of Firework Mountain. "I bet he wears a mask when he's making his potions," Aisha said.

"His cave isn't far from here," said Shimmerbreeze eagerly.

"I'd love to take you," said Fluffy, "but I have to get away from here." He gave himself a shake and a shower of dirt fell from his coat. "Soon I'll be so grubby, I'll be too heavy to fly!"

"You've been really helpful already," said Aisha, stroking his soft head. "You spotted the tornado!"

"I'll carry the girls," Shimmerbreeze

told the cloud puppy.

"We won't forget your ball, Fluffy," Emily assured him.

She climbed on to Shimmerbreeze's silky back behind her friend.

"Goodbye," called Fluffy, waving a big, soft paw. "And good luck."

Shimmerbreeze took off, with Ember close behind. The air was growing thicker every minute, full of grit and flying objects – picnic baskets and tiny bicycles

swept past them towards the rubbish
heap. The girls covered their mouths and
ducked and darted to avoid getting hit,
but their throats were becoming sore.
As Shimmerbreeze battled through the
grimy mist they thought they could
hear awful coughing coming from every
corner of Enchanted Valley.

Finally, Shimmerbreeze dived towards a
forest at the foot of Firework Mountain.

As they dipped
below the trees,
they saw an old,
stooped goblin in a
long purple gown
and pointed hat. He
was trying to sweep
away the grime

piling up at the entrance to his cave.

"Poor Hob!" gasped Aisha. "This nasty
dust is spoiling his lovely home."

Hob dropped his broom as
Shimmerbreeze and the girls landed
nearby. Ember flapped down with a
friendly squawk.

"What a lovely surprise!" Hob
exclaimed, taking off his gold spectacles

to wipe them free of dust. "Come in, everyone, come in." Then a frown spread over his green, wrinkly face. "Mind where you walk. This horrible dust has made my garden very dirty. And just a few minutes ago, a terrible wind nearly swept me away! It pulled my best silver pruning scissors straight from my hands."

"It's not just here," Emily told him. "Selena is ruining the whole of Enchanted Valley." She and Aisha quickly explained what was happening.

"So we have to find Shimmerbreeze's locket," Aisha said. "But it's hard to breathe in this horrid air. Do you have any masks we could use?"

Hob nodded. They followed him inside,

down a dark, winding tunnel into a big
cavern, which glowed silver and gold from
the light of sparkling crystals and lanterns.
Wonky shelves had been wedged between
the rocks. They were full of thick books,
and colourful potions in old bottles. Each
bottle was labelled with neat writing –
*Thistle dewdrops*, *Wiggly woodbine*, *Midnight
rosebuds* and many more.

Hob pulled four white masks out from
a set of rickety
drawers.

"They look
just right!" said
Shimmerbreeze.

"They won't
be enough on

their own," said Hob, tapping his finger to his mouth. "This air is so filthy we need a fresh air potion." He scuttled round, peering at the shelves. "Would you help me, girls? You were such wonderful assistants last time you were here."

"Of course," chorused Emily and Aisha.

"Excellent!" The little goblin rubbed his gnarly hands together. "First I need a teaspoon of sweetmeadow water." He pointed up to the highest corner of the cavern.

In a flash, Aisha had climbed up a narrow ladder to a high shelf and pulled down a green jar. "Found it," she said, handing it down to Emily.

"Next it's ten moonflower petals," said

Hob, "then three sugar-apples and a sprig of windgrass."

When they'd fetched all the ingredients, Hob put each in turn into a blackened pot on the fire. He slowly stirred the mixture with a wooden spoon nearly as tall and gnarled as he was. Now and then, he sniffed at it.

Soon a wonderful smell of newly cut

grass wafted out of the pot. Hob gave
a final stir and a satisfied bob of his
head. "It's ready," he said with a smile.
He dipped each mask in the purply-
pink mixture. To the girls' surprise, when
the masks came out, they were already
dry. They put them on and helped
Shimmerbreeze and Ember to fasten
theirs. Aisha took a deep breath. The air
in her mask was fresh and cool, like a
dewy spring morning.

"Thank you so much, Hob," said Emily.

"Think nothing of it," said Hob. "I'm
glad to help beat that wicked Selena.
Good luck."

They waved goodbye and made their
way back through the dark passage and

out into the forest.

"How wonderful to be able to breathe properly again!" Aisha said, giggling through her mask. "I feel like I'm breathing the first air of the morning."

"Same here," said Emily.

"And here," said Shimmerbreeze and Ember together.

Shimmerbreeze knelt down so the girls could climb on her back. She sped into

a gallop and then took off towards the rubbish heap, Ember flying at her side.

"Now let's find that pendant!" said Aisha.

## Chapter Five
# Trapped

Even though they could all breathe easily now, a thick coat of grey dust clung to Shimmerbreeze's mane and Ember's feathers, and stuck to the girls' clothes.

"It's so hard to fly," panted Shimmerbreeze after a while.

"Maybe we should walk the rest of the

way," said Emily. "We must be nearly there by now!"

"Good idea, Emily," Ember squawked.

Shimmerbreeze and Ember battled through the murk to land by a stream that looked as though it were full of dirty treacle. The girls quickly jumped down, sending the dust on their clothes swirling.

The rubbish mound loomed up ahead like a horrible mountain.

"What an awful place," said Aisha. "But

it's not going to beat us. We're going to find Shimmerbreeze's locket."

"And your eggs, Ember," said Emily.

"Thank you, my dears," said Ember gratefully. "And we mustn't forget Fluffy's ball."

Aisha led the way as the group crunched over fallen tree branches and around scattered bits of furniture and clothing. It looked like everyone in Enchanted Valley must have lost

something to the tornado.

As they reached the heap, there was a loud flapping overhead.

They looked up through the clouds of dirt, but saw nothing.

Then Emily shrieked and Aisha pointed up, just as something dark and heavy fell on top of them.

"It's a net!" Aisha cried. "We're trapped!"

The four friends pulled at the rope net, but the more they struggled the more they became tangled up inside it. Something small and black was flying around them, making a familiar chittering sound.

"It's Flit!" gasped Emily.

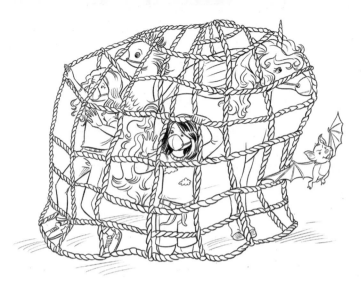

"I'm such a clever bat!" cackled Flit. "I've captured you, and now Selena will think I'm the best sidekick ever. I'll go and tell her, and she can decide what to do with you!" He flew away, screeching with laughter.

"What are we going to do?" squealed Ember. "We'll never get out. My poor eggs!"

"I'm sure there's a way," said Emily. "We've just got to think."

Shimmerbreeze took off her mask and tried to bite through the rope, while Aisha tugged at the net with all her strength.

"It's no good," she panted finally. "It's just getting tighter."

Emily caught sight of a glint of silver on the ground. She gently moved the dirt with her foot and uncovered a little pair of silver scissors.

Aisha gasped. "Hob said the tornado had stolen his scissors," she said. "Those must be his – they can help us escape!"

Emily wriggled in their rope cage until she managed to stretch down and hook her fingers round the scissors handles. She began to cut the net. It was thick and coarse, but Hob's scissors were sharp.

Finally she had cut a girl-sized hole.

"Well done, Emily!" said Shimmerbreeze.

Emily grinned and squeezed her way out. Aisha followed. Then they snipped away more of the net and helped Ember and Shimmerbreeze through the gap.

"What a relief!" said Ember, smoothing down her rumpled feathers.

Shimmerbreeze raised her head. "Can you hear that?" she asked.

Everyone listened. From the distance came a sweet song.

"That's my chicks, singing inside their eggs!" cried Ember.

"But where are they?" asked Aisha, peering through the murk. "I wish it wasn't so dark."

"I can help with that," said Ember. She curled her enormous tail all the way over her head. The tips of the long crimson feathers lit up and glowed like fairy lights.

"Wow!" gasped the girls.

"Follow me!" Ember squawked.

"Wait," said Emily. "We might get lost." She unravelled the net into a long rope and coiled it over her arm. "If we unwind it as we go, we'll be able to find our way back."

She slipped Hob's scissors into her pocket and they followed the phoenix over the rough ground. The wind howled round the rubbish heap as they climbed over piles of lanterns, dusters and garden

spades. Shimmerbreeze's hooves slipped
every now and then, and Aisha and Emily
clutched each other to keep from falling.

The song grew louder. The girls could
make out the words now:

> Fluffy clouds that bob along
> Listen to our happy song.
> Soon we chicks will hatch and fly
> Whizzing round the bright blue sky!

"We must be very close," said Shimmerbreeze.

Ember slowly turned so that the lights on her tail lit up the rubbish all around them.

Everyone looked closely at the grimy mess. There were heaps of books, stacks of teacups, a matching set of velvet armchairs and—

"Look!" exclaimed Aisha, pointing to a downy wisp of white just poking out from a pile of milk jugs. It was a nest made of cloud – with a clutch of golden eggs inside!

"My eggs!" exclaimed Ember, flapping her wings in excitement. Emily and Aisha moved the milk jugs out of the way, and

Ember folded her wings lovingly around her nest. She cooed softly to the chicks inside the gleaming shells.

"They're safe!" breathed Aisha. "You should take them home, Ember. Before they hatch!"

"Aisha's right," said Shimmerbreeze. "The girls and I will stay and find my locket."

The phoenix smiled at her friends, but planted her feet firmly on the ground and lifted her tail up even higher.

"I'm staying too," she said firmly. "You helped me, and now I'll help you defeat that dreadful Selena!"

## Chapter Six
# Into the Wind

"On with our search," said
Shimmerbreeze. "My locket must be
somewhere in this heap."

Ember picked up her precious nest and
sheltered it under one wing. Her bobbing
lights led them higher and higher up the
rubbish heap, Emily unravelling the rope

behind them as they went. The wind grew fiercer, tearing at the girls' clothes and whipping their hair around their faces.

As they reached the top of the heap, it began to tremble, and Emily gasped. Up ahead, a funnel of wind was spiralling quickly towards them.

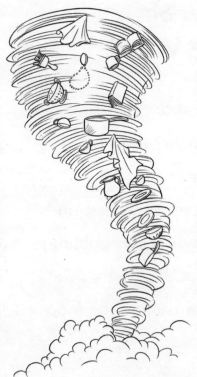

"It's that horrible tornado!" yelled Aisha over the wind. "Bringing more stuff!"

Emily could just make out something shiny tumbling round with all the rubbish in the tornado's winds. She squinted. It was a pendant on a silver chain!

"Look!" she cried.

Shimmerbreeze whinnied in delight –
but then her ears drooped. "How will we
get it back? The tornado will suck us in!"

Emily thought hard. She looked at the
rope she was carrying. It stretched out
behind her but there was plenty still coiled
around her hand. "One of us could go
into the tornado if they have the rope tied
around them, while someone holds the
other end," she said. "Then, when they've
grabbed the locket, we can pull them
back out."

"Sounds fun," said Aisha. "I volunteer
for tornado duty!"

Emily smiled gratefully at Aisha, who

fastened the rope round her waist. Emily
and Shimmerbreeze held the other end
tightly.

"Here I go," yelled Aisha. She leapt into
the rushing wind and felt herself being
lifted high off the ground. "Whoa!" she
shouted as she whizzed around. "I'm like
a human kite!"

All sorts of bits and pieces were flying
round her – forks and paintbrushes
and potted plants. As she dodged the

objects, Aisha could feel that her friends
were holding her firmly. The locket was
twirling in a dizzying circle, close by.
Aisha reached for it, but the locket spun
away. She felt the rope go slack and she
was pulled deeper into the roaring wind.

"What's happening?" she yelled.

"The rope's slipping through my hands,"
Emily yelled back. "I can't hold on for
much longer!" Aisha felt a flutter of panic.

"I'll help you, Emily!" came Ember's
voice.

Aisha could just see the phoenix below
her. The brightly coloured bird had
grasped the rope in her beak and dug her
talons into the ground. To Aisha's relief,
the rope went tight once more.

She peered anxiously through the spinning column of wind, looking for the locket. It flashed by just out of reach. It was going too fast! The next time it whirled towards Aisha, she made a desperate lunge. She felt her fingers close over the precious pendant.

"Got it!" she shouted in triumph.

Her three friends gave a great pull and towed her out of the wind.

Aisha looped the chain over Shimmerbreeze's head. Everyone took a deep breath and held it. Could the magic of the locket save Enchanted Valley?

Then, *whoosh!* A tablecloth rose from the rubbish heap and whizzed away. *Whizz!* Cups, saucers and plates followed. One by one, all the objects in the rubbish heap began to fly off. The girls felt themselves slowly sinking back to the ground as the heap shrank.

"What's happening?" asked Emily.

"I think everything's returning to its owners," Ember replied.

"Then Fluffy should have his ball back any minute!" said Emily. Just then, Hob's scissors wriggled out from her pocket and flew off, too.

"The air's cleared!" said Aisha taking off her mask. The others did the same, each taking in a deep breath of the clean, fresh breeze.

The rubbish heap had been hiding a lush green meadow. Dragonflies flittered between pink poppies and delicate yellow buttercups. A gentle wind rustled through the trees and the air was full of birdsong. Enchanted Valley was beautiful once more!

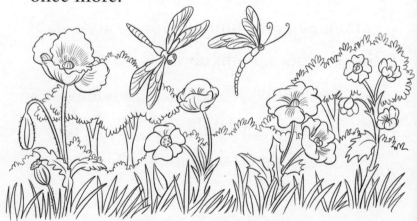

## Chapter Seven
# Phoenix Chicks

They all cheered in celebration. Aisha
turned somersaults over the grass while
Emily hugged Shimmerbreeze around
her soft neck. From above them came an
excited squawk. "My chicks are hatching,"
Ember called down. "Come to my cloud
and you can watch!"

"Hop on, girls," said Shimmerbreeze.

They didn't need telling twice.
Shimmerbreeze soared swiftly through
the fresh, sweet air towards Ember's cloud.
They could see Enchanted Valley spread
out below. Every speck of rubbish was
gone. Buttery sunbeams shone on its
lush mountains and crystal-clear streams
flowed down the hillsides. Unicorns were
galloping over the green slopes and little

dragons played happily in the water.

They rose higher and higher until
Shimmerbreeze landed on Ember's fluffy
white cloud. Ember perched next to
them and gently put down the nest. The
girls jumped off Shimmerbreeze's back
and knelt to watch the eggs. The singing
had stopped. Now a tapping sound was
coming from inside one of them. Emily
and Aisha held hands tightly and watched

a small crack appear in its shell. A tiny beak poked through. At last a little orange head popped out and gave a merry chirp.

"It's so cute," breathed Aisha.

Ember pulled the shell away with her claw and the baby phoenix waddled about, shaking its bright orange and red feathers. Another egg cracked, and another. Soon there were six adorable little chicks, squealing and hopping all over the cloud. Emily and Aisha stroked their downy heads.

"Thank you, girls," said Ember. "Thank you, Shimmerbreeze. You saved my babies."

"We're so glad we could help," replied Emily.

Then they heard a woof and turned to watch as Fluffy floated down beside them. "You've cleaned up the air," he barked happily. "Did you find my ball?"

Emily and Aisha exchanged a glance.

"Hasn't it flown back to you?" said Aisha, puzzled.

Fluffy's tail drooped and he shook his head sadly.

Just then, Emily spotted something caught in the down of Ember's nest.

"How many eggs did you have,

Ember?" she asked.

"Six, dear," said Ember. "And every one now hatched and happy."

Emily picked up the object from the nest. It was shiny and golden but it wasn't shaped like an egg. It was completely round. Emily smiled.

"I've found your ball, Fluffy!" she called.

The puppy gave a yip of delight and wagged his tail so hard that his whole body wiggled, sending wisps of cloud everywhere.

"Fetch, Fluffy!" Aisha took the ball and threw it high into the sky.

Fluffy gave a joyful bark and dashed off after his beloved toy as the others laughed with pleasure. All was right in Enchanted

Valley once again!

"We should be getting back to the palace," said Shimmerbreeze. "Hop on, girls, for one last ride!"

Emily and Aisha rushed round hugging Ember and kissing the chicks goodbye. Then they jumped on to Shimmerbreeze's back and they were off, soaring over Enchanted Valley while the sweet-smelling wind danced in their hair.

Soon the golden walls of Aurora's palace gleamed in the distance and the

spiral turrets sparkled in the sun's warm
rays. In the courtyard, unicorns were busy
decorating the walls and hedges with
streamers and bunting.

Dawnblaze, Sparklesplash and
Glitterhoof stood by the tent, blowing up
balloons all the colours of the rainbow.

Shimmerbreeze landed beside them.
Aurora galloped out from the tent, her
gold mane flying.

"We've been so anxious, girls," she said. "But when the air cleared we knew you'd found Shimmerbreeze's locket. Well done!"

Before the girls could reply, there was a distant rumbling. Emily, Aisha and the unicorns watched in horror as the sky darkened and a black cloud rolled towards them. The rumbling grew louder. The cloud boiled overhead, fizzing with daggers of electricity.

"Oh no!" cried Aisha. "Selena's back!"

# Chapter Eight
# Sky Dance

The black cloud suddenly burst and
Selena stood before them. Lightning bolts
shot from her horn, making the grass
sizzle where they hit. The locket around
her neck shook with the fierce storm
that raged inside. Flit flew above her,
chattering nervously.

Selena fixed Emily and Aisha with a furious glare.

"You think you're so clever," she snarled. "But you're foolish if you think you can beat me. One day soon, the kingdom will be mine, and everyone will bow down before Queen Selena."

"Not while we're here to stop you," Aisha declared.

"Stop me?" Selena's eyes blazed. "No one is going to stop me. Don't forget I've still got two of the precious lockets. I *will* be queen of Enchanted Valley!"

With a cackle and a final stamp of her hooves she launched herself into the air and flew off in a swirl of black cloud.

"You'd better watch out!" twittered Flit. "Selena always wins. She'll be back!"

"FLIT!" Selena screeched at him. Flit gave a yelp and swooped away.

When they had disappeared into the clouds, Aurora bent her beautiful head to Emily and Aisha. "Don't listen to her," she said. "She's just a bad loser. You've saved our kingdom again. I don't know what we'd have done without you. Now you must enjoy the rest of your visit here."

"Let's fly some kites!" suggested Shimmerbreeze.

Aisha chose a sky-blue kite decorated with silver moons. Emily's was star-shaped and had yellow ribbon streamers.

Emily frowned. "But these kites haven't got strings. How can we fly them?"

Shimmerbreeze gave her a wink, then looked at the kites. Her horn began to glow silver and the clouds inside her locket glimmered and twirled. At once, the two kites soared into the air. Shimmerbreeze waved her horn, and the kites bobbed round each other as they weaved back and forth in the sky.

"Now you try," said Shimmerbreeze.

The girls each moved a hand through the air, and the kites copied what they were doing.

Aisha made her kite fly in a figure of eight, while Emily made hers skim over the trees, sending the lanterns swinging.

"Wow!" cried both girls.

All of a sudden, a host of pink butterflies rose from the branches and joined in the merry sky dance. Aurora watched, her eyes twinkling with delight.

"Like you in the tornado!" said Emily.

"I don't think I was as graceful as those butterflies," Aisha laughed.

At last the sun began to dip below the faraway mountains, covering the valley in a warm glow like candlelight.

"Can you hear that?" asked Emily.

Aisha listened. A sweet song was drifting towards them on the evening breeze:

**Goodnight sun,**
**Hello moon,**
**Goodbye day,**
**See you soon.**

"Ember and her chicks are singing a lullaby together," said Aurora softly.

Emily and Aisha smiled at each other. The phoenixes sounded content – and very sleepy.

Aisha gave a great yawn.

"I think it's time for us to go home," said Emily. They ran to each of the unicorns, giving them a big hug goodbye.

Aurora gently touched her muzzle to their cheeks. "Enchanted Valley is sure to need your help again," she said. "After all, there are two more stolen lockets to find."

"You can count on us," said Aisha.

"We won't let Selena win," Emily added, nodding.

Queen Aurora swished her horn above their heads. A warm mist of golden sparkles surrounded them, and before they could blink they were back in the garden of Aisha's cottage. No time had passed while they were in the magical realm.

Aisha looked at the phoenix statue.

"It looks just like Ember," she said.

Emily nodded. "I bet she's having fun with her little chicks!" she said. "What an amazing adventure we had."

"Look, Emily," gasped Aisha.

A single cloud was moving lazily over the cottage.

"It has four legs!" said Emily.

"And a mane," said Aisha.

"And a spiral horn!" cried Emily. "It's a unicorn!" They hugged each other tightly.

"Maybe it's a sign," whispered Aisha. "A sign that we'll be seeing our friends again

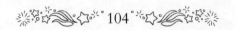

very soon."

"I hope so," said
Emily with a big
grin. "I can't wait
for another unicorn
adventure!"

The End

Join Emily and Aisha
for another adventure in …

# Glitterhoof's
# Secret Garden

Read on for a sneak peek!

Rain pattered hard against the windows of Enchanted Cottage.

"I don't think we'll be playing football today," said Aisha Khan with a sigh. She and her best friend, Emily Turner, were watching the rain from the warm kitchen. Drops fell from the flowers in the garden, and trickled over the wings of the phoenix statue in the middle of the lawn.

"Don't worry," Emily said with a grin. "I know what we can do instead!"

Aisha smiled back. "A science experiment?"

"How did you guess?" Emily laughed. She loved science as much as Aisha loved sport. "First we need some flowers …"

The two girls darted out of the back door into the wet garden. They hadn't known each other long, as Aisha and her parents had only recently moved into Enchanted Cottage. But already they did everything together – and they had even shared some magical adventures …

The girls picked a handful of flowers. Then they ran back indoors, shaking rain from their hair.

Soon Aisha's mum had helped the girls set up their experiment. On the kitchen table were several small bowls of water, with a few drops of food colouring in each one. The girls put the flowers in the coloured water.

"What happens now?" asked Aisha.

"Wait and see," said Emily with a smile. The two girls drank hot chocolate and chatted with Mrs Khan, who was stirring a saucepan of curry on the stove.

After a while, Mrs Khan pointed at the flowers. "Girls, look!"

Aisha gasped. The flowers were changing colour! The yellow petals were turning blue and the pink petals were turning green.

"They're drinking up the food colouring," Emily explained with a grin.

Aisha peered closely at some white petals, now edged with pink. "It's almost like magic," she whispered.

Emily knew they were both thinking about the same thing – Enchanted Valley, the magical realm they had visited, which was filled with unicorns and other amazing creatures!

Read
# Glitterhoof's Secret Garden
to find out what adventures are in store for Aisha and Emily!

# Also available

### Book One:

Daisy Meadows

**Unicorn Magic**

*Dawnblaze Saves Summer*

from the author of
RAINBOW
MAGIC

### Book Two:

Daisy Meadows

**Unicorn Magic**

*Shimmerbreeze & the Sky Spell*

from the author of
RAINBOW
MAGIC

### Book Three:

Daisy Meadows

**Unicorn Magic**

*Glitterhoof's Secret Garden*

from the author of
RAINBOW
MAGIC

### Book Four:

Daisy Meadows

**Unicorn Magic**

*Sparklesplash Meets the Mermaids*

from the author of
RAINBOW
MAGIC

# Look out for the next book!

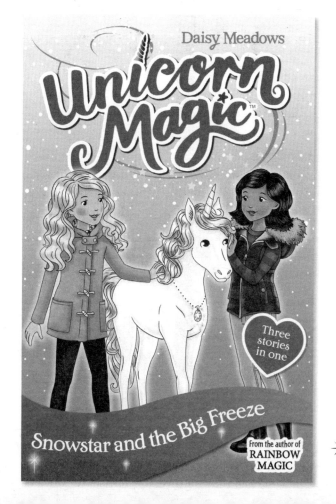

Daisy Meadows

Unicorn Magic™

Three stories in one

Snowstar and the Big Freeze

From the author of
RAINBOW MAGIC

If you like
Unicorn Magic,
you'll love …

## Welcome to Animal Ark!

Animal-mad Amelia is sad
about moving house, until she
discovers Animal Ark, where vets look
after all kinds of animals in need.

Join Amelia and her friend Sam for a
brand-new series of animal adventures!

# Glitterhoof's
# Secret Garden

## Daisy Meadows

ORCHARD

# Special thanks to Elizabeth Galloway

ORCHARD BOOKS

First published in Great Britain in 2019 by Hodder & Stoughton

3 5 7 9 10 8 6 4

Text copyright © 2019 Working Partners Limited.
Illustrations © Orchard Books 2019
Series created by Working Partners Limited

A CIP catalogue record for this book is available from the British Library.

ISBN 978 1 40836 617 2

Printed and bound in Great Britain by Clays Ltd, Elcograf S.p.A.

The paper and board used in this book are made from wood from responsible sources.

Orchard Books
An imprint of Hachette Children's Group
Part of Hodder and Stoughton
Carmelite House
50 Victoria Embankment
London EC4Y 0DZ

An Hachette UK Company
www.hachette.co.uk
www.hachettechildrens.co.uk

# Contents

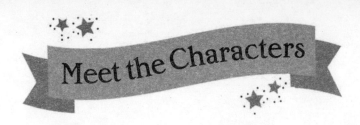

## Meet the Characters

Aisha and Emily are best friends from Spellford Village. Aisha loves sports, whilst Emily's favourite thing is science. But what both girls enjoy more than anything is visiting Enchanted Valley and helping their unicorn friends who live there.

Dawnblaze

Dawnblaze is the Fire Unicorn. She loves to swim in the hot springs on Firework Mountain with her dragon friends!

The Air Unicorn, Shimmerbreeze, is in charge of making sure the air in Enchanted Valley is fresh and clean. She likes to use her magic to create little breezes, so her friends can fly their kites.

Shimmerbreeze

Glitterhoof

Glitterhoof is the Earth Unicorn, who makes plants grow strong and beautiful. What she likes best is being part of a team - there's nothing she won't do for her friends!

Sparklesplash has so much fun playing in the rivers and lagoons of Enchanted Valley. This Water Unicorn wants everyone to love the water, just as much as she does.

Sparklesplash

Enchanted Cottage

Golden Palace

An Enchanted Valley lies a twinkle away,
Where beautiful unicorns live, laugh and play
You can visit the mermaids, or go for a ride,
So much fun to be had, but dangers can hide!

Your friends need your help ~ this is how you know:
A keyring lights up with a magical glow.
Whirled off like a dream, you won't want to leave.
Friendship forever, when you truly believe.

## Chapter One
# Rainy Day Magic

Rain pattered hard against the windows of Enchanted Cottage.

"I don't think we'll be playing football today," said Aisha Khan with a sigh. She and her best friend, Emily Turner, were watching the rain from the warm kitchen. Drops fell from the flowers in the garden, and trickled over the wings of the phoenix statue in the middle of the lawn.

"Don't worry," Emily said with a grin. "I know what we can do instead!"

Aisha smiled back. "A science experiment?"

"How did you guess?" Emily laughed. She loved science as much as Aisha loved sport. "First we need some flowers …"

The two girls darted out of the back door into the wet garden. They hadn't known each other long, as Aisha and her

parents had only recently moved into Enchanted Cottage. But already they did everything together – and they had even shared some magical adventures …

The girls picked a handful of flowers. Then they ran back indoors, shaking rain from their hair.

Soon Aisha's mum had helped the girls set up their experiment. On the kitchen table were several small bowls of water, with a few drops of food colouring in each one. The girls put the flowers in the coloured water.

"What happens now?" asked Aisha.

"Wait and see," said Emily with a smile. The two girls drank hot chocolate and chatted with Mrs Khan, who was stirring a saucepan of curry on the stove. After a while, Mrs Khan pointed at the flowers. "Girls, look!"

Aisha gasped. The flowers were changing colour! The yellow petals were turning blue and the pink petals were turning green.

"They're drinking up the food colouring," Emily explained with a grin.

Aisha peered closely at some white petals, now edged with pink. "It's almost like magic," she whispered.

Emily knew they were both thinking about the same thing – Enchanted Valley, the magical realm they had visited, which was filled with unicorns and other amazing creatures!

A glint of light caught Emily's eye, and she gasped – the unicorn keyring hanging from Aisha's belt loop was glowing! Aisha noticed the light as  well, and clasped her hand around the little unicorn. Emily pulled her matching keyring from the front pocket of her dungarees. It was glowing too.

Queen Aurora, a beautiful unicorn who ruled over Enchanted Valley, was calling them back!

"Er, Mum," said Aisha, "we're just going to get some more flowers …"

Mrs Khan was busy tasting the curry with a spoon. "Don't get too wet!" she said.

Aisha and Emily hurried back outside. Even though it was still raining, a shaft of sunlight shone through a break in the clouds, beaming on to the lawn beside the phoenix statue. The girls ran over to it. They touched the horns of their unicorn keyrings together and – *whooosh!* – rainbow-coloured sparkles shimmered around them.

"We're going to see the unicorns!" cried Emily. Excitement fizzed through them like fireworks. They held hands as the sparkles swirled faster and faster, and their feet left the ground. Clouds of the

whizzing sparkles surrounded them, red,
blue, purple and yellow, and the girls
could feel their hair being blown around
them as they were carried far away …

When the sparkles faded, the girls sank
gently back to the ground. They stood in
a beautiful meadow of soft grass under a
clear blue sky. Ahead of them was a green
hill topped with a golden palace. Flags

fluttered from its four turrets.

"It's so great to be here again," said Aisha. "But we'd better hurry – Queen Aurora might need our help!"

"I hope Selena hasn't come back," said Emily, with a frown.

The thought of the wicked unicorn made the girls shiver as they made their way up the hill towards the palace. They had already helped Queen Aurora by finding two of the unicorns' magical lockets, which Selena had stolen because she wanted to rule Enchanted Valley. But Selena still had two more lockets, and she was sure to cause trouble with them …

Even so, the girls couldn't help feeling a rush of happiness as they climbed higher

and saw Enchanted Valley spread out
all around. There were soft green fields,
glittering lakes and majestic forests, while
mysterious purple mountains stood on the
horizon.

Emily pointed up at a bird-like creature
fluttering over the forest, just like the
statue in the cottage garden. It was
followed by several little chicks. "That
must be Ember and her family!" she said
with a grin. The girls had helped the
phoenix on their last visit to Enchanted
Valley. "I wonder what creatures we'll
meet this time?"

At the top of the hill the palace stood
before them, its golden walls gleaming.
Silver flowers grew over it, and the

windows glittered like diamonds. A moat
of crystal-clear water ran around the
palace, with a drawbridge lying across
it. But the most magical sight of all was

the beautiful unicorn standing on the drawbridge. Her body shimmered with all the colours of the dawn – she was a dusky pink one moment, vivid orange the next, and then as golden as the palace itself. Her horn gleamed, and a silver crown sat on top of her head.

"Queen Aurora!" cried the girls.

"Welcome back, Emily and Aisha!" replied the unicorn, her voice lilting like beautiful music. "Thank goodness you're here … because we need your help again!"

## Chapter Two
# Sneezes and Stormclouds

Queen Aurora led the girls over the
drawbridge and through a grassy
courtyard. They followed her under an
arch of roses and into a pretty garden.
Cherry trees were dotted around, their
blossoms falling like confetti, and there
were rose bushes with sweet-scented

blooms. Gathered at a table in the centre of the garden were four unicorns the girls recognised – the Nature Unicorns! They looked up as the girls and Aurora approached.

"Hello, girls!" said a unicorn, with a bright orange mane.

"It's so nice to see you!" said the white unicorn.

"Hi, Dawnblaze! Hi, Shimmerbreeze!" said Emily and Aisha.

"It's wonderful to see you too," added Aisha, as both girls hugged them.

Around every unicorn's neck hung a glass locket which gave them the magic they needed to protect a part of Enchanted Valley. Dawnblaze's locket

contained tiny fireworks – she was the
fire unicorn, and kept the valley warm.
Shimmerbreeze the air unicorn kept the
air clean, and her locket contained tiny
fluffy clouds. Queen Aurora protected
friendship – inside her locket were two
tiny suns that spun around each other,
just like friends playing.

Emily and Aisha had got Dawnblaze's

and Shimmerbreeze's lockets back from
horrible Selena after she'd stolen them.
But the other two unicorns were still
missing theirs. The girls hugged them
too. "Hi, Glitterhoof!" they said. "Hi,
Sparklesplash!"

Dipping her horn, Glitterhoof the Earth
Unicorn picked up two flower garlands
from the pile heaped on the table. She
was leaf-green with a lilac mane and tail.
"We're making these to give to the guests
at the Nature Gala," she explained. The
Nature Gala was a party the unicorns
were throwing for all their Enchanted
Valley friends.

Sparklesplash, the blue Water Unicorn
who protected the lakes and rivers, flicked

her silver tail. "Try them on, girls!"

They lowered their heads and Glitterhoof placed the flower garlands over them. Emily's was made of yellow roses, while Aisha's had white daisies. But as soon as the garlands were hung around the girls' necks, their petals began to droop. The girls watched in dismay as, one by one, the flowers fell from the garlands on to the ground.

"Oh, not again!" said Glitterhoof. Her ears drooped too.

Queen Aurora sighed. "This is why I asked you to come today, girls," she said. "Glitterhoof's locket usually makes the soil rich and the plants beautiful, but without it, the plants are suffering. I'm worried that if we don't get it back soon, all the plants in Enchanted Valley will die."

Emily and Aisha both shook their heads in dismay. Looking around the garden, they realised that Aurora was right – the plants here were already wilting. The blossoms falling from the cherry trees were brown and the roses were limp.

"We can't let that happen," said Aisha fiercely. "We'll find your locket, Glitterhoof."

But just then, grey clouds rolled over the sky and turned it as dark as night. The air was suddenly chilly. Lightning crackled, making them all jump, and a burst of thunder like beating drums rumbled overhead.

In the darkness appeared a silver unicorn. She shone like the moon, and her mane and tail were deep blue. She landed in the garden, her purple eyes flashing as she looked around at the horrified girls and the unicorns. It was Selena!

"Oh n-n-n-no!" stammered Glitterhoof.

Her four legs quivered with fright.

Aisha and Emily were trembling too, but they huddled close to Glitterhoof. "We won't let Selena do anything mean to you," said Emily, putting her arms around the green unicorn's neck.

"It's n-n-n-not that," said Glitterhoof. "It's the d-d-d-dark that's so scary!"

"Quiet!" snapped Selena. She reared up on her hind legs

and the tiny storm inside her glass locket flashed. "So you girls are back, are you? Well, no matter. You can't stop me this time!"

"Yes, we can!" cried Aisha bravely.

Selena gave a cackle that echoed like the thunder. "You'll never get the Earth locket back!" She looked around, scowling. "Flit? Flit, get over here!"

"Aaaaah-choooo!" An enormous sneeze came from the other side of the palace wall. Then a little black bat shot over. It was Flit, Selena's naughty helper. He landed among the flower garlands and wiped his nose with his wing.

The girls gasped. Around Flit's neck hung Glitterhoof's locket, with its purple

flower growing inside!

"Aaaaah-choooo!" Flit's sneeze sent
him flying off the table. He landed in one
of the cherry trees. "Aaaaah-choooo!"
He fell on to the lawn and wiped his nose
again.

"Oh, stop that silly sneezing, Flit," said
Selena crossly, stamping a hoof.

"Sobby, Sebena," said Flit, sniffing
loudly. "All bees flowers are bunging

up by nose. I can't wait for bem to disappear."

"And you're going to make sure they do," said Selena. She sneered at the other unicorns. "Flit's going to hide the locket where you will never find it! The plants will die – and I will only bring them back if you make me the Queen of Enchanted Valley! Ha!"

She reared up again and slammed her hooves on the lawn. The girls and the unicorns cried out in alarm as the ground began to shake. The flower garlands fell off the table. Aisha and Emily had to hold tight to Glitterhoof to keep from falling.

Queen Aurora reared up too, her silver horn flashing. "You will never rule

Enchanted Valley, Selena!"

"We'll see about that!" cackled Selena.
She took off, spiralling up into the
air until she disappeared among the
thunderclouds.

Emily leaped back as her foot slipped
suddenly. "Look out!" she yelled. The
ground where Selena had slammed her

hooves was crumbling away to make a deep sinkhole. The hole quickly spread. The table and flower garlands fell into it, and then one of the cherry trees.

"Girls, climb on to Glitterhoof," cried Queen Aurora. "Hurry!"

The girls scrambled on to Glitterhoof's back, Aisha pulling up Emily behind her. All the unicorns took off just as the ground under their feet fell away completely. Nothing was left of the centre of the garden but an enormous hole.

Glitterhoof shook her head sadly. "It's all because I haven't got my locket," she said. "Instead of the earth being protected, it's being destroyed!"

"This is terrible," said Emily. "We must

stop Selena before things get worse."

Above them flapped Flit, his sneezes sending him zigzagging across the sky. Now that Selena had gone, the storm clouds drifted away. Glitterhoof gave a whinny of relief as the sunshine returned, allowing them a clear view as Flit disappeared over the palace wall, the stolen locket around his neck.

Aisha pointed after him. "Come on, Glitterhoof – let's follow that bat!"

## Chapter Three
# Caught!

"Good luck, girls!" called Queen Aurora. She was flying too, circling the ruined palace garden with the other unicorns. "Good luck, Glitterhoof!"

"Thank you!" the girls and Glitterhoof called back. Then they turned and soared after Flit. Aisha held tight to the unicorn's

mane, while Emily held on to Aisha's
waist. Glitterhoof's lilac tail fluttered in
the wind like streamers. From up high,
they could see more sinkholes appearing
among the forests and meadows, like an
outbreak of chickenpox spots.

Ahead, Flit began sneezing again.
"Aaaaah-choooo! Aaaaah-choooo!
Aaaaah-CHOOO!" The final sneeze sent
him plummeting down towards a patch
of trees. As he fell, the stolen locket glinted

in the sun.

"Hold on tight!" called Glitterhoof, and she dropped after him in a steep dive. The air whistled past Emily and Aisha's ears as they flew down, down, down and hurtled after Flit into the trees. Ahead, the little bat had recovered himself, and was flapping through the tree trunks.

Glitterhoof's hooves struck the ground with a jolt, and the girls clung on tight. The unicorn cantered after Flit. All around, the leaves from the trees were falling, and many branches were already bare.

"Sinkhole!" shouted Aisha.

It opened in front of them like a hungry mouth. Glitterhoof jumped into the air to clear it – but was suddenly yanked back down to the forest floor. Aisha and Emily screamed, and Glitterhoof whinnied, as they were thrown sprawling to the grond.

"What happened?" gasped Emily, sitting up and shaking leaves from her hair.

"Oh no, Glitterhoof!" Aisha scrambled over to the unicorn. She was sitting on her haunches, with a vine looped tightly around her front leg. "Are you all right?"

"I'm not hurt," Glitterhoof said. "But I

can't get this horrible thing off! It grew
out of the hole and grabbed me." The
vine began to writhe around like a snake,
dragging Glitterhoof towards the sinkhole.

Above them, Flit flew a loop-the-loop.
"Sibby unicorn!" he giggled. "Sibby girls!
Now you'll neber catch me! Aaaaah-
choooo!" He disappeared among the
trees, taking the locket with him.

Aisha yanked hard at the vine,
untangling the knot it had made around

Glitterhoof's leg. The girls grinned with relief as the vine slithered back into the sinkhole and Glitterhoof got to her hooves.

"Thank you!" the unicorn said. Then her ears twitched with worry. "But I'm afraid Flit was right – we've lost him."

They carried on through the forest, past more sinkholes and forest flowers that had lost their petals. But with no sign of Flit, they weren't sure what to do next. Soon, Glitterhoof's violet eyes filled with tears.

"There must be someone who can help us," said Emily.

Aisha suddenly sprinted ahead. "There is!" she cried. "Come on!"

Emily and Glitterhoof hurried after her.

Walking down a path at the edge of the forest was a familiar little creature. He wore a long purple gown and a pointed hat with silver stars, and he was pulling a wooden cart along with a rope.

"Hob!" cried Emily. The girls had met Hob the goblin on their previous visits to Enchanted Valley. He had made them magical potions, which had helped them get back the lockets of Dawnblaze and Shimmerbreeze.

Hob took off his gold spectacles and polished them with the sleeve of his gown. When

he put them back on, his wrinkly green face beamed at them. "Bless my stars!" he said. "If it isn't Aisha and Emily, and Glitterhoof too! What brings you here?"

Glitterhoof dipped her horn in greeting, while the girls stooped to give Hob a hug. He was only half as tall as they were.

Aisha quickly explained about Flit and the stolen locket. "But what are you doing here, Hob?" asked Aisha. The girls knew that their friend rarely left the cave where he created his magical potions.

Hob pointed to his cart, which was stacked high with empty jars and bottles. "None of my potion ingredients are working properly," he explained, "so I'm collecting some new ones." He took off his hat and scratched his bald green head. "Oh, it has been very tiresome! I heated up a cauldron of snugberries to make a magic hot water bottle, and do you know what happened?"

"What?" asked the girls and Glitterhoof.

"I popped the hot water bottle into my bed, but when I got under the blankets with my copy of *Peppers and Pickles for Perfect Potions*, it wasn't lovely and snug at all." He shuddered. "The snugberries had all gone hard and lumpy! And they weren't warm at all. It quite ruined my nap."

Aisha hid a smile. "That sounds horrible, Hob."

"It must have been because of my

missing locket," said Glitterhoof.

Hob nodded. "I bet that's it. I'm on my way to Flowerdew Garden to fetch some more ingredients," he said. "That's where all the magical plants in the valley come from. I just hope it's still all right."

"We'll come too," said Aisha. "Maybe we can find a magical plant that will help us get the locket back."

They all set off down the path, taking it in turns to pull Hob's cart. The jars and bottles jangled as they crossed a meadow

full of wilting grass, then a shallow
stream. "We're almost there," said Hob.
"But oh, piddleprickles – look at that!"

Ahead was a walled garden with a
wooden door and plants growing all
around it. But between the garden and
the four friends were sinkholes – lots of
them! There were so many holes that
there was barely any grass left. From each
hole writhed the same horrible vines that
had almost caught Glitterhoof.

"Why are there so many sinkholes

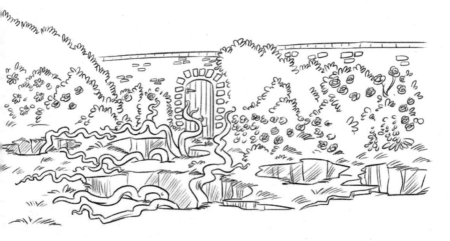

here?" asked Glitterhoof.

Emily and Aisha glanced at each other, eyes widening. "I think I know," said Emily. "Selena's horrible magic makes the lockets have the opposite effect they're supposed to. The closer you get to the locket, the worse the magic gets."

Aisha nodded. "These are definitely the worst sinkholes we've seen …"

"… which must mean Glitterhoof's locket is close by," Emily said, with a rush of excitement. "I bet it's inside the garden!"

Aisha grinned. "We'll soon have it back!"

## Chapter Four
# The Gnomes of Flowerdew Garden

Hob's pointed ears drooped in dismay. "That's all very well – but we can't get to Flowerdew Garden with all these sinkholes in the way."

"We can find a way if we work together," said Glitterhoof.

"Glitterhoof's right," said Aisha. "Hob,
you could push the cart while Glitterhoof
pulls it. Emily and I will keep back the
vines. We can do it!"

They got to work. The cart lurched
between the sinkholes, Glitterhoof gritting
her teeth with the effort as she heaved it
along. Hob pushed and caught any jars
and bottles that were jolted off, while
Emily and Aisha used large sticks to

whack the vines away. Soon everyone
was hot and sweaty, but they'd made it to
the other side.

"Bless my stars!" said Hob, mopping
his face with his hat. "I'm so glad we
bumped into each other."

There was a winding path up to the
garden door. As they walked along it,
Emily's eye was caught by a clump of
foxgloves with orange blooms. She gave
a gasp – the flowers
were shaped like tiny
fox heads! "Amazing!
I've never seen these
in any of my science
books!"

She and Aisha

leaned in for a closer look.

"Grrrrr!" The foxgloves were growling at them! The girls took a hasty step back.

"Careful, girls!" Hob said. "The plants here guard Flowerdew Garden from intruders – so don't touch anything! I'll lead the way."

They carried on, Hob in front, followed by the girls, then Glitterhoof pulling the cart. The little goblin hurried them past a plant with a candyfloss scent and green pods hanging from its stems. "It's a sweet-dream pea," he said. "Mind you don't sniff it too deeply, or you'll nod off into a magical sleep!" After the sweet-dream pea was a bush of red fruits that looked like raspberries, but were as sticky as chewing gum. "Glue gums," Hob explained. Emily used a leaf to carefully pull one out of Glitterhoof's tail.

The girls gasped as they came around the next curve in the path. In front of them was a plant as big as the cart. It looked like a huge, pink open mouth with pointed green teeth around the edges. In the centre of the mouth was something shiny.

"That looks scary," said Aisha, peering at the plant's teeth.

"Don't worry," said Emily, "it only eats flies! We've got them in our world, too – it's a Venus flytrap."

"Close, my dear," said Hob, "but this is actually a Venus spytrap. It spies thieves

who want to steal
things from the
garden. It uses sparkly
things to trap them,
you see."

They had almost
reached the door into
the walled garden. It
was painted green and
decorated with carvings of leaves. Aisha
pointed to a plant growing beside it with
tiny blue blossoms. "What does that one
do, Hob?"

He adjusted his spectacles. "Oh, this
one is perfectly safe!" Hob picked a sprig.
"It's just a very ordinary, utterly harmless,
forget-me-n ..." He trailed off. Blue

smoke suddenly swirled around him.

When it cleared, Hob peered at the girls and Glitterhoof, then he took his hat off and gave a little bow. "Good afternoon, dear strangers! Could you tell me where I am?"

Aisha and Emily stared at him in confusion.

"Oh no," said Glitterhoof. "That plant wasn't harmless – it's made him forget everything!"

The girls gave groans of dismay. "What are we going to do?" wondered Aisha.

"Flowerdew Garden doesn't just contain magical plants," said Glitterhoof thoughtfully. "It's also where the gnomes live. They have their own magic, and they

know about all the different plants in
Enchanted Valley. Perhaps they can help
Hob get his memory back ..."

She knocked on the garden door with
the tip of her horn.

For a moment, nothing happened. Then
a slot near the bottom of the door opened
to reveal the face of a very little person.

Her skin was the colour of rich earth, her eyes were blue and she had pointed ears. On her head was a bluebell hat.

The girls exchanged excited grins. They had never met a gnome before!

Glitterhoof bent down to speak to her. "Hello, Bluebell. These are my friends Aisha and Emily. Please could we come into your garden? We need your help."

Bluebell beamed. "Of course you can!" she said.

Immediately, the door to the garden swung open. Glitterhoof pulled the cart, while Emily and Aisha took Hob's hands, and they all went inside.

The girls gasped. The garden was beautiful, full of flowerbeds spilling over

with blooms. Flowers in every colour
grew up the walls, over wooden archways
and across the backs of little benches
dotted around the carpet of soft lawn.
The air was sweet with delicate scents,
and butterflies darted among the blooms.
Tending the flowers were busy gnomes,
each wearing a flower-shaped hat and
pushing their own little wheelbarrow.

"Welcome to Flowerdew Garden," said
Bluebell in a tinkling voice. Now they
could see that she was wearing overalls in
the same blue as her hat, and blue wellies.
Like all the other gnomes, she was tiny –
even smaller than Hob.

"This is Primrose, our head gardener,"
Bluebell said, as a gnome wearing a

yellow flower hat with matching overalls and wellies came over, pushing her wheelbarrow.

"Hello there," said Primrose. "How can we help?"

Quickly, the girls and Glitterhoof explained what had happened – from Selena stealing Glitterhoof's locket, right up to Hob losing his memory.

Primrose frowned, her face wrinkling like a little brown berry. "We heard that Selena had been up to no good again," she said. "Of course we'll help get the locket back. But first, let's fix poor Hob. He's always forgetting not to sniff the forget-mes …" She began rummaging inside her wheelbarrow.

Emily gazed around at the garden. "That's funny … The other plants in Enchanted Valley are suffering, but all the ones here seem fine!"

"It's the walls surrounding the garden," said Bluebell. "They're magical and keep everything inside them safe."

"That's good," said Aisha, then she gave a sigh. "But all the sinkholes outside made us think the locket must be here. I guess we were wrong."

Primrose was still searching through her wheelbarrow. She picked up a paper packet. "No, those are Speedy Seeds … Hmm, the Shrinking Can makes things smaller, and the Blooming Can makes them bigger, so those won't help …" She moved two watering cans aside, then picked up a spade. "The Flower Finder won't help either ... Aha!" She pulled out a pot with a blue flower growing inside.

Primrose showed the flower to Hob, who took a sniff. Blue sparkles began to swirl around him. Emily and Aisha held their breath, hoping it would work ...

As the sparkles faded, Hob took off his spectacles and rubbed his eyes. "Dancing dandelions," he murmured. "Hello there, Primrose! And hello, girls and Glitterhoof!"

"Hooray!" cheered Aisha.

"You remember us!" Emily added, as the girls hugged him.

"Of course I do," said Hob, putting his spectacles back on. "But what happened?"

"You picked a forget-me by mistake," said Emily. "We're still looking for Glitterhoof's locket, Hob. We don't know where ..." She trailed off as she noticed something strange. One of the butterflies fluttering on a rose bush was much larger than the others. Its antennae were made from two sticks. Orange paint was peeling from its wings, revealing black underneath ...

"Aaaaah-choooo!" sneezed the butterfly.

"That's not a butterfly at all," said Primrose. "In fact, it looks more like a bat …"

"Watch out," cried Emily. "It's Flit!"

## Chapter Five
# The Shrinking Can

"Aaaaah-choooo!" Flit sneezed again, and the twigs flew off his head. Around his neck he still wore Glitterhoof's locket. "Sebena will be pleased wib me! Now I can get bid of all the horrible magical plants in this garden!"

"I don't know how he got into the

garden!" cried Bluebell. "The magic walls should have stopped him!"

Flit zoomed in a circle, squeaking in delight. "Nobody saw me sneak in when der door opened! Cleber me! Aaaaah-aaaah-CHOOOO!"

The enormous sneeze sent him sprawling into a patch of daisies – and the locket flew from his neck!

Aisha sprang after it, her hands cupped together like she was catching a cricket ball. But the locket sailed through her fingers and landed on a square of grass. The garden trembled, making everyone stumble – then the ground crumbled. The soil fell away to create a sinkhole, and the locket tumbled inside!

All the gnomes stared at the hole, eyes wide with horror. "Our beautiful garden!" wailed a gnome in a daffodil hat.

The girls and Glitterhoof peered over the edge of the dark sinkhole. It was about as deep as the girls were tall. The locket glinted at the bottom.

"Don't worry, everyone!" said Aisha. "I can jump down and get it."

"You'll have to be quick, Aisha!"

said Glitterhoof, pointing her horn to where vines like octopus tentacles were springing up around the sinkhole.

Aisha crouched, ready to spring.

"Look, I bound der gnomes' Shrinking Can!" said Flit, from above. They looked up. In his claws was a watering can. "Bis will stop boo!"

"Run!" shouted Primrose.

The girls and Glitterhoof began to scramble away, but it was too late – Flit tipped the Shrinking Can over them.

"Urgh!" cried Emily, as the girls' hair and clothes were soaked through. The magical water made their skin feel tingly, and they stared down at themselves as they shrank smaller and smaller. They

were soon the
same height as
the gnomes, and
Glitterhoof was the size of a
cat. The flowers around them
seemed huge now – and the
sinkhole was enormous.

"There's no way
I can jump down
now," said Aisha
with a groan. "It's
deeper than a diving
pool!"

Glitterhoof's violet
eyes were wide.
"What are we going
to do?"

Primrose ran over. "Don't worry!" she said. "We can fix this! Hob," she called, "we need my Blooming Can! It'll make them grow again!"

Hob dashed to where Primrose had left her wheelbarrow. But Flit was faster – he snatched up the Blooming Can and sprinkled it over the vines growing around the sinkhole, sniffing and giggling gleefully.

The vines shot up. Within seconds, each was as thick as a tree trunk, circling the sinkhole in a twisting, writhing forest. On one side of the vines stood the girls, Glitterhoof and Primrose – and on the other side was everyone else.

"We're trapped!" cried Primrose.

Emily turned back to the yawning darkness of the sinkhole. She took a deep breath. "There's only one way to put everything right," she said. "We've got to climb down there and get the locket."

Aisha and Primrose nodded. Glitterhoof began to tremble. "I r-r-really want to help," she said, her violet eyes filling with tears. "B-b-but it's so dark!" Aisha put her arms around Glitterhoof's neck, while Emily stroked her silky lilac mane.

"We'll need a lookout in case Flit does anything else," said Aisha. "Could you do that instead?"

Glitterhoof nodded gratefully.

"I'll go first and find the safest way down," said Aisha. "It'll be just like the climbing wall at the gym!"

"Be careful!" said Emily.

Aisha lowered herself over the edge
of the sinkhole, feeling around with
her trainers for nooks to place her feet.
Emily went next, then Primrose, while
Glitterhoof stood guard at the edge.

Down they climbed into the darkness...

## Chapter Six
# Frightening Flowers

"Glitterhoof was right," said Emily with a shiver. "It is a bit scary in here."

The girls and Primrose were climbing down the sinkhole. Now that Emily and Aisha were gnome-sized, the roots and stones they used as handholds and footholds seemed huge. The further

down they
climbed, the
darker it
became,
until they could hardly see
at all.

Aisha called up instructions
as they went. "Watch out for this
bit!" she said, scrambling around a
thorny root that snagged on her shirt.
"And there's a sharp stone coming up on
your left!"

She stretched her right foot down,
searching the wall of the sinkhole for a
foothold. But here the earth was smooth.
She switched feet – but still had no luck.
"Weird," she muttered. She could feel that

below them, the wall had begun to slope like a giant slide. "We'll have to slide the rest of the way!" she called.

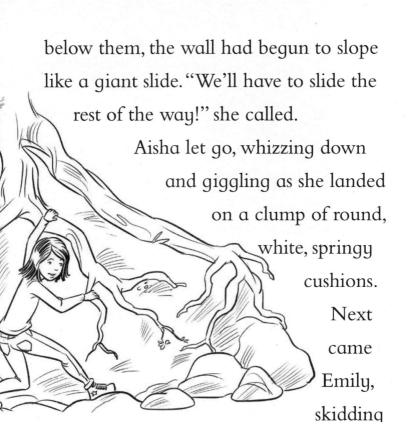

Aisha let go, whizzing down and giggling as she landed on a clump of round, white, springy cushions.

Next came Emily, skidding to a stop beside Aisha. Then Primrose landed next to them.

Aisha bounced up and down on the strange cushions. "These feel like marshmallows! All that climbing has made me hungry …" She broke a piece off.

"No, stop!" cried Primrose. "They're not marshmallows – they're mushrooms! Look here." She tapped the edge of one of them. Emily and Aisha peered through the gloom and saw clusters of pale grey spots. "This kind are called tummy troublers," Primrose explained. "If you eat them you'll be ill."

Aisha dropped the piece of mushroom.

Emily shuddered. "I don't like it down here," she said, glancing around at the shadowy darkness. "Let's hurry up and find the locket so we can leave."

The girls and Primrose searched the bottom of the sinkhole. It was covered with pebbles that seemed as large as melons, and they had to be careful not to trip. As their eyes adjusted to the darkness, Emily and Aisha noticed lots of other plants beside the mushrooms.

"There are some more forget-mes," said Emily, showing the others a patch of the tiny blue blooms. Beside them grew tall yellow flowers with scaly petals that snapped open and closed.

"Snapdragons," said Primrose. "Watch out – they've got a nasty bite."

"Where have all these horrible plants come from?" wondered Aisha. "When we first looked into the sinkhole, there wasn't anything inside it except the locket."

"Selena's wicked magic must have done

this," said Emily. "It's making all the dangerous plants grow, and really fast!"

They carefully searched through a clump of growling foxgloves and then a bush of glue gums.

"Look!" Aisha cried. "There's something there!"

Stuck in the centre of the glue gum bush was something shiny.

"It must be the locket!" cried Emily. "We just need to get it out!"

Excitement raced through both the girls. Primrose took off her yellow flower hat and carefully leaned into the bush. Using her hat as a scoop, she pulled the glinting object out.

Emily and Aisha's excitement deflated

like burst balloons. It wasn't the locket.

Aisha groaned. "It's just a little spade," she said.

But Primrose grinned at them. "It's no ordinary little spade," she said, "it's my Flower Finder! It will take you to whatever plant you need. One of the vines must have knocked it down here." She tucked it under her arm. "It might come in handy!"

They continued the search, peering under bushes covered in thorns and through patches of nettles. Primrose went to check another big

patch of forget-mes, while the girls made
their way to the centre of the sinkhole.
There they found a huge plant like a
gaping mouth, edged with sharp green
teeth.

"A Venus spytrap!" said both girls
together.

And gleaming in the centre of the
plant's deadly pink mouth was the locket.

"Yes!" cried Aisha.
She reached towards it.

"Be careful," said
Emily, her hands
clasped to her
mouth.

"I've got to try,"
said Aisha. She leaned

in, her arm muscles stretching. Her hand
was almost touching the locket. "Nearly
… got it …"

Aisha leaned in a little more. Her
fingers brushed the locket's chain … and
the spytrap lunged forwards, snapping
its enormous jaws shut. Emily gasped in
shock. Aisha was trapped inside!

# Chapter Seven
# Tickle-Me-Pink

"Let her out!" Emily shouted. She pulled at the spytrap's jaws, but they had clamped firmly shut.

Primrose ran up and pulled at them too – but it was no good. "Aisha won't be hurt in there," she told Emily, "but I don't know how we're going to get her out.

We usually use a potion to make flowers open, but I haven't got any down here …"

"Aisha, we'll rescue you!" Emily called. "Just hang on!"

She whirled around, scanning the dark bottom of the sinkhole. There had to be something here that would help …

On the ground lay Primrose's Flower Finder spade, where she had dropped it to try to open the jaws. Emily picked it up. "Maybe we can prise the spytrap open …"

But the spade suddenly glowed golden – then yanked Emily away from the spytrap.

"Hey!" she cried in surprise. The spade glowed again, and pulled her further

away. She clung on to the handle,
running to keep up. "Stop!" she cried. "I
need to open the spytrap!"

Primrose ran after Emily, holding on to
her yellow hat. "It's helping, Emily!" she
called. "Let it lead you – it's taking us to
the plant we need!"

The spade led them through the
darkness to a shaggy pink bush, with long,
feathery leaves. With a clang, the spade
dropped down in front of it.

Emily panted for breath. "This must be the one that will help us free Aisha!"

Primrose caught her arm. "Be careful," she warned. "It's a tickle-me-pink — it wraps people up in its leaves and tickles them silly!"

Moving very slowly and carefully, so the branches wouldn't brush her arm, Emily reached into the bush and plucked one of the feathery leaves. As she pulled it out, another leaf brushed her wrist, fluttering around it like tickling fingers.

"Hee!" Emily giggled. "It really does tickle!"

The tickle-me-pink leaves began waving about, like long arms trying to grab them. Emily and Primrose dodged them and hurried back to the spytrap.

Holding out the leaf, Emily brushed it against the closed green teeth. "Please work," she whispered.

But the spytrap stayed firmly closed. Emily bit her lip with disappointment.

"Try tickling it underneath," said Primrose. "I'm most ticklish on my tummy – maybe the spytrap is too!"

"Good idea!" said Emily. "Here goes …"

She stroked

the leaf against the bottom of the plant –
and it began to jiggle! It shook from side
to side, exactly like someone trying not
to laugh. Emily kept tickling. Then, with
a big *POP*, the spytrap's jaws burst open.
Out on to the ground tumbled Aisha.

"Hooray!" cheered Emily and Primrose.

Aisha got to her feet. "Phew, thanks! It
was pretty hot in there. But look!" She
held out her hand.

In her palm was Glitterhoof's locket! They all gazed at it in wonder. Because the girls had shrunk, the locket seemed the size of an orange. They could see every detail of the flower growing inside the glass – the purple petals speckled with white and yellow dots, the delicate leaves curling from the stem, and the roots as fine as cobwebs.

"Now we just need to get it back to Glitterhoof!" said Emily.

They hurried to the foot of the sinkhole wall. Aisha scanned it for handholds, but the smooth, sloping sides were impossible to grab on to. Aisha groaned. "What are we going to do? We can't slide back up ..."

Emily peered at the top of the sinkhole,
hoping to find some way out. But
just then, a shadow appeared over the
entrance – and swooped down towards
them! "Something's coming!" she cried.
"Hide!"

"This way!" yelled Primrose.

Aisha and Emily sprinted after her.
Primrose ducked beneath one of the
tummy-troubler mushrooms and the girls
scrambled under too. They held their
breaths.

*Thud! Thud, thud, thud!*

Whatever had flown into the sinkhole
had landed on the ground.

Her heart thumping, Aisha peeked out
from under the mushroom. She could see

four legs, and the swish of a lilac tail …

She turned to the others, grinning with relief. "It's Glitterhoof!"

## Chapter Eight
# Glitterhoof to the Rescue!

"Glitterhoof!" cried Emily. The girls and Primrose crawled out from under the mushrooms and ran to the unicorn. They threw their arms around her long neck. "You came!" said Emily. "But isn't it too dark down here for you?"

Glitterhoof nuzzled them with her silky

nose. "I had to see if you were all right,"
she explained. "I realised I was even more
worried about my friends than I was
about the dark!"

Primrose hugged her again. "That was
very brave of you."

"It certainly was," agreed Aisha. "And
Glitterhoof – look what we found!" She
held up the locket.

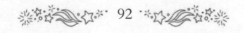

"We'll put it on you as soon as we're out of the sinkhole," said Emily. "We don't want it to close up while we're still down here!"

"Oh, thank you so much!" said Glitterhoof. Her violet eyes shone with happiness. "Now, who would like a lift?"

Moments later, the girls and Primrose were on the unicorn's back, holding on tight as she flew up and out of the sinkhole. As soon as they burst from darkness into bright sunshine, Aisha leaned forwards and fastened the locket around Glitterhoof's neck.

At once, the unicorn's horn glowed green and purple, and a shower of shimmering sparkles fell all around them.

The garden transformed – the vines shrank back into the ground, and the sinkhole closed over. The crowd of watching gnomes cheered and waved

their flower hats in the air. Hob linked arms with Bluebell and they danced a jig.

The girls and Primrose waved back at the gnomes as Glitterhoof circled the garden, weaving in and out of the flower beds. The blossoms seemed the size of footballs to the girls, and the butterflies fluttering around them were as big as blackbirds!

Glitterhoof landed on the grass where the sinkhole had been, in front of Hob and the gnomes. Bluebell was holding a Blooming Can. She sprinkled it over the girls and Glitterhoof. Emily and Aisha felt their skin fizzle all over once more, and soon they were back to their normal size.

"You saved Flowerdew Garden!" cried Bluebell, hugging them.

"My dears, you saved all the plants of Enchanted Valley!" said Hob, his eyes twinkling behind his spectacles. The gnomes cheered again.

Primrose found her wheelbarrow and pulled out two packets. "Speedy Seeds," she explained, giving the packets to Aisha and Emily, "to say thank you."

"Please come back to our garden whenever you like!" added Bluebell.

The girls hugged them both. They were just about to leave, when one of the rose bushes began to shake.

"Aaaaah-choooo!" Flit shot out from the flowers. His nose was very red and his eyes were watery. He sat on the lawn, rubbing his face with his wings. "Bese horrible flowers are still here!" He sniffed. "You girls – aaaaah-choooo – ruined

– aaaaah-choooo – ebberybing!" He flapped away over the garden wall.

"Poor Flit," said Emily, when the little bat was gone. "He's been really naughty, but I can't help feeling sorry for him."

"He looked so unhappy," agreed Aisha. "Maybe he would like the flowers if they didn't make him sneeze."

The girls grinned at each other as they both had the same idea.

"Hob," said Emily, "would you make a potion for us … ?"

Later that afternoon, the girls and Glitterhoof were back in the palace garden. The sinkhole had vanished – instead, cherry tree blossoms hung in fluffy pompoms and every leaf and flower was bright with colour. The four

Nature Unicorns, Queen Aurora and the
girls were gathered on the soft lawn. In
her dungarees pocket, Emily had a little
bottle Hob had prepared for them with
ingredients from Flowerdew Garden.

"I'm so proud of you, girls," Queen
Aurora said. "Thank you for finding the
third locket!"

"We couldn't have done it without
Glitterhoof," said Aisha.

"She was so brave," added Emily. "We'd never have got out of the sinkhole without her."

Glitterhoof's horn glowed purple with happiness – but then she looked up at the sky in alarm. The girls turned to see thunderclouds sweeping towards the palace ... followed by Selena!

The silver unicorn landed on the lawn, lightning crackling up and down her horn. She stamped her hooves and her purple eyes flashed. By her side hovered Flit.

"Go away, Selena," said Queen Aurora. "You've caused enough trouble!"

"Well, the trouble isn't over yet!" snapped Selena. "You girls may have found the Earth locket, but I've still got one more … and you'll never get it back! Isn't that right, Flit?"

"Aaaaah-choooo!" went Flit. "Aaaaah-choooo! Aaaaah-choooo! Aaaaah-CHOOO!"

Aisha and Emily glanced at each other. Now was their chance!

Emily took out the bottle Hob had given them from her pocket and sprinkled the pale blue mixture inside over Flit.

The little bat shook his wings. "What's that?" he said, sniffing the droplets suspiciously. "What have you put on me?"

The girls grinned at him. "Notice anything?" asked Aisha.

Flit's eyes widened. "I'm not sneezing!

You've cured
me!" He flapped
his wings in
excitement and
sniffed at a rose
bush. "Oooh! It's
actually quite
nice!"

Selena stamped her hooves again. "Stop
messing about with those nasty flowers,
Flit! We're going!" She leaped into the air
and flew over the palace wall. Flit flapped
after her with a cherry blossom tucked
behind one of his ears.

The thunderclouds cleared again,
leaving sunny blue skies. "We'll have to
get Sparklesplash's locket back soon," said

Queen Aurora, "but for now let's have some fun. Would you girls like to make flower crowns?"

"Yes, please!" said Emily and Aisha together.

They all gathered around the table. Glitterhoof used her horn to magically weave blossoms together, and explained to the girls how to make them into crowns. Aisha made a crown of pink cherry blossoms, while Emily used yellow tulips. Then the girls made crowns for each of the unicorns to wear around their horns. The garden rang with laughter.

Eventually, it was time to go. The girls hugged each of the unicorns in turn.

"Goodbye!" called Emily and Aisha.

"Goodbye!" called Glitterhoof. "And
thank you!"

"I'll summon you again very soon," said
Queen Aurora, "so you can help us find
the remaining stolen locket." Then her
horn glowed, sunshine spilling out of it
and around the girls. Colourful sparkles
shimmered all about them and Enchanted
Valley faded away …

When the light disappeared, the girls

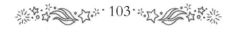

were standing in the rainy garden of Enchanted Cottage.

"What an amazing adventure," sighed Emily.

"Brilliant," agreed Aisha. She put her hand to her hair. Her flower crown had vanished, but then she remembered something else … She took her Speedy Seeds from her pocket. Emily smiled, and the two girls sprinkled their packets of seeds into one of the flowerbeds. As soon as rain fell on the seeds, flowers burst out from the soil. The girls watched in amazement as they formed a rainbow of blossoms, from red through to violet.

"What lovely flowers!" said Mrs Khan, who was coming out of the back door.

She opened an umbrella and walked across the lawn. "But I don't remember seeing them before. It's as if they've appeared by magic!"

As the two girls stood with her under the umbrella, they grinned at each other. If only she knew!

The End

Join Emily and Aisha
for another adventure in …
**Sparklesplash Meets
the Mermaids**
Read on for a sneak peek!

"Look, Mum!" exclaimed Aisha Khan.
"There they are!"

She pointed to three figures appearing
at the far end of the sunny little meadow.
Aisha took off, feeling the summer
dandelions tickling her shins. In a flash,
she was standing by the side of Emily
Turner, her best friend.

"My goodness," said Mrs Turner, who
stood next to Mr Turner, holding a picnic
basket on one arm. "You're a very fast
runner, Aisha!"

Emily laughed. "Aisha's good at all

sports, Mum!"

"Almost as good as Emily is at science,"
Aisha replied, smiling. "Come on. My
parents are setting up by the river. And
I have a special surprise!"

Emily and Aisha skipped through the
grass to where Mr and Mrs Khan waited
by a checked blanket laid out in a pool
of sunshine next to a sparkling river. Then
they watched nervously as the Khans
shook hands with the Turners. They
hoped their parents would get along as
well as they did!

"Pleasure to meet you both," said Mrs
Khan. "We love having Emily over at
Enchanted Cottage."

"We've heard wonderful things from

Emily," Mr Turner replied. "It sounds like an amazing place."

Emily and Aisha glanced at each other. Enchanted Cottage was where the Khans had moved when they arrived in Spellford Village only a few weeks ago. And it was an amazing place, from the phoenix statue that stood in the garden to the unicorn door-knocker. It was also a house with a wonderful secret …

"Look what I've brought!" Aisha said, picking up a piece of tupperware. She opened it to reveal a baker's dozen of brightly iced biscuits shaped like unicorns.

Emily gasped. "They're great, Aisha!"

"They match your keyring," said Mrs Turner. "You girls love your unicorns, don't you?"

Emily and Aisha giggled. If only Mrs Turner knew that the first time Emily had visited Enchanted Cottage, she and Aisha had found a crystal unicorn in the attic.

When sunlight had struck the little statue, they'd been whisked off to Enchanted Valley, a wonderful land of dragons, phoenixes and other fantastic creatures.

### Read
## Sparklesplash Meets the Mermaids
to find out what adventures are in store
for Aisha and Emily!

# Also available

**Book One:**

Dawnblaze Saves Summer

**Book Two:**

Shimmerbreeze & the Sky Spell

**Book Three:**

Glitterhoof's Secret Garden

**Book Four:**

Sparklesplash Meets the Mermaids

## Look out for the next book!

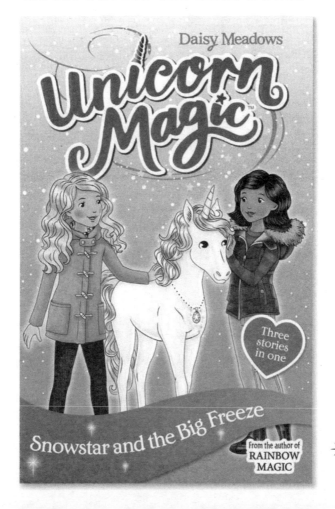

If you like
Unicorn Magic,
you'll love...

## Welcome to Animal Ark!

Animal-mad Amelia is sad
about moving house, until she
discovers Animal Ark, where vets look
after all kinds of animals in need.

Join Amelia and her friend Sam for a
brand-new series of animal adventures!

# Sparklesplash Meets the Mermaids

Daisy Meadows

ORCHARD

# Special thanks to Jan Burchett and Sara Vogler

ORCHARD BOOKS

First published in Great Britain in 2019 by Hodder & Stoughton

3 5 7 9 10 8 6 4

Text copyright © 2019 Working Partners Limited.
Illustrations © Orchard Books 2019
Series created by Working Partners Limited

A CIP catalogue record for this book is available from the British Library.

ISBN 978 1 40836 618 9

Printed and bound in Great Britain by Clays Ltd, Elcograf S.p.A.

The paper and board used in this book are made from wood from responsible sources.

Orchard Books
An imprint of Hachette Children's Group
Part of Hodder and Stoughton
Carmelite House
50 Victoria Embankment
London EC4Y 0DZ

An Hachette UK Company
www.hachette.co.uk
www.hachettechildrens.co.uk

# Contents

# Meet the Characters

Aisha and Emily are best friends from Spellford Village. Aisha loves sports, whilst Emily's favourite thing is science. But what both girls enjoy more than anything is visiting Enchanted Valley and helping their unicorn friends who live there.

Dawnblaze

Dawnblaze is the Fire Unicorn. She loves to swim in the hot springs on Firework Mountain with her dragon friends!

The Air Unicorn, Shimmerbreeze, is in charge of making sure the air in Enchanted Valley is fresh and clean. She likes to use her magic to create little breezes, so her friends can fly their kites.

Shimmerbreeze

Glitterhoof

Glitterhoof is the Earth Unicorn, who makes plants grow strong and beautiful. What she likes best is being part of a team - there's nothing she won't do for her friends!

Sparklesplash has so much fun playing in the rivers and lagoons of Enchanted Valley. This Water Unicorn wants everyone to love the water, just as much as she does.

Sparklesplash

Enchanted Cottage

Golden Palace

An Enchanted Valley lies a twinkle away,
Where beautiful unicorns live, laugh and play
You can visit the mermaids, or go for a ride,
So much fun to be had, but dangers can hide!

Your friends need your help - this is how you know:
A keyring lights up with a magical glow.
Whirled off like a dream, you won't want to leave.
Friendship forever, when you truly believe.

## Chapter One
# A Riverside Picnic

"Look, Mum!" exclaimed Aisha Khan.
"There they are!"

She pointed to three figures appearing
at the far end of the sunny little meadow.
Aisha took off, feeling the summer
dandelions tickling her shins. In a flash,
she was standing by the side of Emily

Turner, her best friend.

"My goodness," said Mrs Turner, who stood next to Mr Turner, holding a picnic basket on one arm. "You're a very fast runner, Aisha!"

Emily laughed. "Aisha's good at all sports, Mum!"

"Almost as good as Emily is at science," Aisha replied, smiling. "Come on. My parents are setting up by the river. And

I have a special surprise!"

Emily and Aisha skipped through the grass to where Mr and Mrs Khan waited by a checked blanket laid out in a pool of sunshine next to a sparkling river. Then they watched nervously as the Khans shook hands with the Turners. They hoped their parents would get along as well as they did!

"Pleasure to meet you both," said Mrs Khan. "We love having Emily over at Enchanted Cottage."

"We've heard wonderful things from Emily," Mr Turner replied. "It sounds like an amazing place."

Emily and Aisha glanced at each other. Enchanted Cottage was where the Khans had moved when they arrived in Spellford Village only a few weeks ago. And it *was* an amazing place, from the phoenix statue that stood in the garden to the unicorn door-knocker. It was also a house with a wonderful secret ...

"Look what I've brought!" Aisha said, picking up a piece of tupperware. She opened it to reveal a baker's dozen of brightly iced biscuits shaped like unicorns.

Emily gasped. "They're great, Aisha!"

"They match your keyring," said Mrs Turner. "You girls love your unicorns, don't you?"

Emily and Aisha giggled. If only Mrs Turner knew that the first time Emily had visited Enchanted Cottage, she and Aisha had found a crystal unicorn in the attic. When sunlight had struck the little statue, they'd been whisked off to Enchanted Valley, a wonderful land of dragons, phoenixes and other fantastic creatures who were looked after by a unicorn, Queen Aurora, and her unicorn friends. Queen Aurora had used her magic to create Emily and Aisha's unicorn keyrings out of the crystal one they had found.

The Khans and the Turners were chatting merrily now, and Aisha nodded to the river. "Let's leave them to it," she said, "and explore."

The girls jumped over stepping stones across the River Spell, to where a small waterfall spilled gracefully into a calm, blue pool. As they stared up at it, a sudden beam of sunlight fell around them, making the falling water sparkle like thousands of diamond strands. Emily and Aisha gasped, then looked at each other. At the same time, they reached into their pockets to draw out their unicorn keyrings. Queen Aurora had given them the keyrings so they could get back to Enchanted Valley whenever she called.

As the sunlight hit the crystal unicorns,
they lit up in a dazzling show of sparkles.

"You know what this means," whispered
Emily.

"Queen Aurora's calling us," Aisha
whispered back, excitement bubbling up
inside her. "Let's go!"

"We have to hide first," warned Emily.

Aisha turned back towards their parents
on the riverbank. "Mum," she called, "can

Emily and I go under the waterfall?"

Mrs Khan exchanged a glance with Mr and Mrs Turner, who nodded. "OK," she replied. "But just for a moment!"

Aisha grinned at Emily as she took her friend's hand and ducked under the waterfall. No time passed in their world while they were in Enchanted Valley. They'd be back before anyone missed them.

The girls found themselves in what felt like a tiny chamber with a cool stone wall opposite the waterfall and a floor made of smooth river rocks. Even through the water, the sunbeam made the rocks shine.

"Ready?" Emily asked.

"Ready!" said Aisha.

They held out their unicorn keyrings and gently touched the sparkling horns together. At once the crystal unicorns glowed even brighter, brilliant blues and reds and greens swirling inside them. Then … *WHOOSH!* Their hiding place suddenly disappeared as they were lifted off their feet, and a burst of light showered

the girls in twinkling stars. When the
stars faded away, the girls felt themselves
drifting down at the foot of a high,
grassy hill. On the hilltop they could see
Queen Aurora's golden palace. Its silver
drawbridge glinted in the sun and yellow
flowers as big as saucers climbed its walls.
Eight spiral turrets like unicorn horns
gleamed against the blue sky.

"We're in Enchanted Valley!" the girls
chorused in delight.

"Come on!" yelled Aisha, running up the hill. Emily pulled her hair back into its ponytail and followed, enjoying the feel of the soft, sun-dappled grass brushing against her ankles. Soon they were at the top, gazing breathlessly down at the great lush forests, green meadows dotted with blue forget-me-nots, and sparkling lakes that spread out below.

Emily turned towards the palace and spotted a beautiful unicorn standing on the drawbridge that ran over the palace's moat. Her coat shimmered with the pinks, oranges and golds of a perfect sunrise.

"Queen Aurora!" cried Emily happily. The girls flung their arms around the queen's neck and gave her a huge hug.

Atop her head was a silver crown, and
round her neck hung a locket that held
two dancing suns. Emily and Aisha knew
the locket was magic. Each unicorn had
one, and each locket protected something
in Enchanted Valley. As queen, Aurora was
in charge of peace and friendship, and
the suns in her locket looked like two best
friends playing.

"Thank you for coming!" said Aurora in
her soft, musical voice. "It's so wonderful

to see you!"

"You, too, Queen Aurora!" said Aisha. "But why did you call us? Is Selena making trouble again?"

Selena was another unicorn, and every bit as evil as Aurora was kind. And she wanted nothing more than to take the throne for herself. She had already stolen the four lockets belonging to the Nature unicorns, though the girls had managed to get three back.

Aurora nodded and her long golden mane drooped sadly. "We're supposed to be holding the Nature Gala today," she said, "but Selena's been spoiling things. Come and see."

Emily and Aisha exchanged a serious

look. The Nature Gala was a special party the unicorns held every year and all the creatures of Enchanted Valley were invited. The whole kingdom was looking forward to it, and so were Emily and Aisha. They couldn't let Selena ruin it for everyone.

The queen led them through the neat courtyard where small creamy butterflies weaved in and out of the grass, and out

into the lovely palace garden. It was decorated for a party, dotted with tables and tents hung with bunting. Emily and Aisha could tell that the Nature unicorns had been hard at work, using the magical lockets the girls had got back from Selena.

Everywhere was lit with golden sunrays, and from the palace kitchens came the smell of warm cinnamon cakes. The

girls knew that would be thanks to Dawnblaze, the fire unicorn.

Shimmerbreeze, the snowy-white air unicorn, stood by a line of beautifully patterned kites, and with a swish of her horn a gentle breeze swept them up into the air.

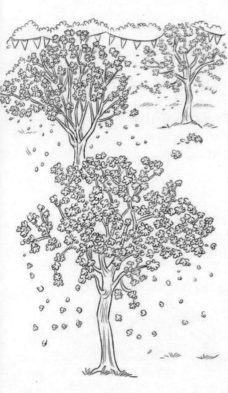

Pink petals fell from the rosy blossoms blooming on the cherry trees and floated on the breeze like confetti. The girls watched as Glitterhoof, the earth unicorn, flicked her horn at an empty flowerbed, and gasped as green stalks came shooting up and sprouted into bright daylilies.

Catching sight of the girls, the unicorns all whinnied and dipped their heads in greeting.

"I wonder what's wrong," Aisha whispered to Emily as they bowed their heads in reply. "Everything seems perfect."

Aurora brought them to a little pool with ivy climbing up its sides. Shining bubbles popped on the surface of its rainbow-tinted water. Sparklesplash, the water unicorn, was peering sadly into the pool, tears rolling down her velvety nose. Sparklesplash was the only Nature Unicorn still missing her locket.

The girls ran to her. "Sparklesplash, are you all right?" Emily asked gently.

"I'm so glad you're here," said Sparklesplash, looking up and nuzzling their cheeks. "I'm trying to make Fizzleberry Surprise for the party."

A big bubble burst beside the girls, showering them with glittery spray.

"It looks fantastic!" said Emily.

"But it tastes horrible," said Sparklesplash, hanging her head. "Try for yourselves."

The girls took two glasses from the side of the pool and had a sip. Yuck! The drink was very bitter.

"Well, it could be a bit better," said Aisha kindly, "but it's not your fault. This is Selena's doing!"

*Zzzappp!* A bolt of lightning shot from the sky, searing a black mark into the lush lawn. *Ker-rack!* Another hit the party tables. Glasses and plates scattered all over the ground. The unicorns reared in fright. Thunder crashed and a bright silver unicorn burst through a thundercloud above them, sparks flying from her

hooves. Flashes
of electricity
burst all over
her coat. Her
locket was full
of angry storm
clouds. Selena!

She cackled
as she came to land on the ground,
shrivelling the grass beneath her hooves.
Her purple eyes set on Emily and Aisha
and she gave an angry swish of her
twilight-blue mane. "There's no way
around it this time, silly girls," Selena said.
"Enchanted Valley will soon be mine!"

## Chapter Two
# Selena's Dreadful Plan

"You'll never rule over Enchanted Valley," cried Emily. "Not as long as Aisha and I are here to stop you!"

Before Selena could respond, Flit, her bat servant, flapped wildly into view. *Whumph!* He flew straight into a tree. "I'm sorry, Your Highness," he panted as

he struggled dizzily back into the air.
"I flew as fast as I could."

He suddenly spotted the beautiful
decorations. "Ooooh! Is this a party?
I love a party!"

"Silence!" shrieked Selena. "There's not
going to be a party." Her eyes were lit by
a wicked glow. "The Water locket is still
mine, and this time I'll be sending it to
the deepest depths of the lagoon. And I'll
be sending my best guard down with it!
You'll never see it again!"

"No!" cried Sparklesplash. "Give it back
to me!"

The rest of the Nature unicorns had
come to stand beside Sparklesplash.
They pawed the ground and neighed in

agreement.

"Oh, you'd like it back, would you?" asked Selena in a sugary-sweet voice. "Then all you have to do is crown me queen of Enchanted Valley."

"No way, Selena," declared Aisha. "Aurora is queen."

"And that's how it's going to stay!" added Emily.

"We'll see about that, you tiresome

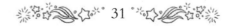

twosome," snorted
Selena. "Hold it up,
Flit!"

From behind his
back, Flit drew
Sparklesplash's stolen Water locket, its tiny
fountain tinkling inside.

*Gloop!* Thick smoke billowed from
Selena's horn. When it cleared the locket
was trapped in a floating green bubble.
Next, a lightning bolt shot from her horn,
sending the bubble flying.

"No!" yelled Aisha. She leaped for the
bubble like a goalie after a football, but it
spun out of reach and vanished into the
sky.

"Bad luck!" scoffed Selena, laughing as

Emily helped Aisha up from the ground.

"Excuse me, Your Great Wonderfulness," said Flit, tapping Selena with a polite claw. "Who exactly is your best guard?"

"You, of course!" said Selena.

Flit puffed himself up importantly, flapping his silky black wings. "What an honour—"

"Because you're my only guard," interrupted Selena.

Flit's ears drooped. "I've just had a teensy-weensy thought, Your Amazingness," he chittered anxiously. "If the locket's at the bottom of the lagoon, how can I guard it? I can't breathe underwater. I'm a bat!"

"You doubt my powers?" shrieked

Selena, stamping her hooves and sending electric jolts zigzagging along the ground. "My magic can do anything! Now come. I've had enough chat for one day!"

With that, she took to the air and zoomed away with a tremendous crash of thunder.

Flit didn't move.

"FLIT!" came an angry shout.

"Eek!" The little bat jumped in fright and flew off after his mistress.

"Oh no," said Sparklesplash. "Look at my Fizzleberry Surprise!"

The drink had turned sludgy-grey. It was bubbling out of the pool and oozing over the grass. The bitter liquid was making the cherry blossoms wilt.

"Look!" cried Aisha, pointing through an archway to the moat. Everyone turned to see the water in the moat churning as it rose steadily higher.

"It's going to overflow!" gasped Aurora, as unicorns leapt into action, trying to clear the party decorations from harm's way. "If we don't stop Selena's magic, the palace will be flooded."

Dawnblaze stared down into the valley.

"Not just the palace," she said quietly, nodding her horn towards a distant lagoon the girls hadn't noticed before. Even from here, they could see that the turquoise water was rising too.

"If the lagoon overflows," said Glitterhoof, her ears twitching with fright, "everyone who lives by it will lose their homes."

"We'll rescue your locket," said Aisha.

"We won't let anyone get hurt," added Emily.

"I knew we could count on you," said Queen Aurora gratefully.

"Hop on my back, girls," said Sparklesplash. "We'll fly to the lagoon right now."

Sparklesplash kneeled down and Emily climbed on behind Aisha. As they both held on tight, the Water unicorn galloped across the soggy grass and took off over the palace wall. The girls heard the unicorns below calling "Good luck!" as they swooped up into the air.

The wind ruffled their hair, and they soared through the crystal blue sky, almost as high as the craggy peak of Firework Mountain. They sailed over the great forest where their friend Hob the goblin lived in his hidden cave.

But as they left the forest behind, they saw Selena's horrid spell at work. In the meadows below, the lakes and streams were spilling over their banks. Worst of

all, water came from the vast lagoon and
swamped the nearby trees and meadows.
Emily and Aisha heard cries of fear as
frightened imps and gnomes ran from the
flood. Pixies and leprechauns clung to
the low branches of trees, but the water
lapped at their feet.

"They need help!" Emily cried. "We've
got to save them!"

## Chapter Three
# Flood!

Emily and Aisha gazed fearfully down at the swirling waves that were rolling through Enchanted Valley. The forest creatures were standing on the roofs of their houses, calling desperately for help.

"Let's go!" cried Sparklesplash. "We can fly them out."

"Wait," Emily said. "You're only one unicorn. You'd only be able to rescue a few at a time."

"But we've got to do something!" cried Aisha.

Emily thought about it as if it were a science problem to be solved. They needed someone who could fly, and who could carry lots of creatures at once. A memory popped into her head of an earlier adventure in Enchanted Valley – of flying through the clouds.

"Fluffy could do it!" she exclaimed.

Their friend Fluffy was an enormous cloud puppy who'd carried them on his back before and helped them save Shimmerbreeze's Air locket.

"Yes!" cried Aisha.

"That's a great idea," said Sparklesplash. "We'll find him. Hold on tight!" She whizzed up through the clouds.

The girls' keen eyes searched the soft, wispy billows.

"Fluffy!" they yelled. "Fluffy, where are you?"

"Look!" cried Emily. In the distance a giant cuddly cloud in the shape of a puppy was bounding about with a golden ball in his mouth.

Aisha gave a loud whistle. "Here, boy!"

The moment the cloud puppy spotted Sparklesplash and the girls, he sped towards them, a big smile on his soft white face. His huge tail wagged so hard

it sent puffs of cloud everywhere.

"Hello there!" he panted, dropping the golden ball on a cloud in front of them. "Would you like to play fetch?"

"We wish we could," said Emily. "But we need your help, Fluffy, and there's not much time." She quickly told him about the flood, and Selena taking Sparklesplash's locket.

"That nasty Selena," Fluffy growled. "We can't let her win. Don't worry, I'll help. And I'll ask some friends too."

"Thank you!" the girls said gratefully.

Fluffy threw back his head.
"Awooooooooo!" he howled. "Woof,
woof, awooooooo! That should do it," he
said.

"Wonderful. We'll meet you at the
lagoon," Sparklesplash told him. She
dived down through the clouds, sending
the wind whistling in the girls' ears. As
the sky cleared, the lagoon came back
into sight. The waters were higher than
ever, flooding the valley as far as the eye
could see.

"I hope Fluffy and his friends aren't far
be—" started Emily.

But just then they heard the sound

of flapping wings overhead. They all
turned to see what looked like a flock of
very large birds swooping down behind
them. As the flock came closer, the girls
made out the shapes of of dragons, cloud
puppies and phoenixes, their flame-
coloured tails streaming out behind them.
Fluffy was leading the charge.

"Great work, Fluffy!" Aisha shouted.
"We're sure to save everybody now!"

A beautiful orange-red phoenix waved
a wing at them, the plume on her head
wobbling with worry. Emily and Aisha
were delighted to see it was their friend
Ember. Near her flew six small chicks,
chirping to one another as they flapped.

"Hello, my dears," Ember squawked.

"Hello, Ember!" said Emily. "Your
chicks are flying!"

Ember smiled. "I'll never forget how you

saved them." The girls and Shimmerbreeze had found Ember's eggs when the nest had been whisked away by Selena's evil tornado. "Now we can all repay the favour."

The girls smiled. The adorable chicks were just big enough to carry a pixie each.

The flying rescue party was soon over the forest. Sparklesplash dived down to land among the trees, where the water covered her hooves. The dragons landed next to her, while the cloud puppies hovered in a nearby clearing so as not to wet their cloud-fur. The phoenixes skimmed over the forest, picking up poor stranded creatures from roofs and trees

and flying away with them.

Emily and Aisha slid off the unicorn's
back, splashing as their feet met the water,
and beckoned to the frightened creatures
who were running from the rising waves.
"This way," yelled Emily.

Imps, goblins, gnomes, leprechauns
and all sorts of forest animals swarmed
towards them. The girls hoisted a
family of dripping gnomes up on to

Sparklesplash's back.

"Can you take them to safety?" Emily asked her unicorn friend.

"Of course," Sparklesplash said, nodding. "I'll be back soon."

Sparklesplash took off. The girls raced over to help a group of elves climb aboard Fluffy's back. They sank, wet and shivering, into the puppy's fleecy coat.

"We're ready to go!" Fluffy announced to his passengers. He took off. "Good luck finding the locket, girls."

One by one, the dragons, phoenixes and cloud puppies rose through the trees. Finally, Emily and Aisha looked around to see that they were the only ones left in the water.

"Phew!" said Aisha. "Everyone's safe."

But something had caught Emily's eye. "Not everyone!" she said. She pointed at the water's edge. A girl was lying in the shallows!

Aisha's eyes widened. They'd never met another girl in Enchanted Valley before.

Ignoring the cold water that surged around them, they raced towards the stranded girl. She wore a crop top made of small white shells and her tangled hair fell in waves of purple, blue and pink around her shoulders. Her eyes were closed and she lay very still, half out of the water.

The water swirled away for a second and the girls gasped. Instead of legs, the

girl had a sleek fishtail that shimmered
with dazzling green scales!

"Wow!" breathed Aisha. "She's a
mermaid!"

## Chapter Four
# The New Mermaids

"Quick, let's get her deeper into the water," Emily said. Aisha took the mermaid's arms and Emily took her tail, and they gently lifted her up.

Just then, Sparklesplash landed among the trees. "Everyone is safe and dry on Firework Mountain," she called. She

gave a whinny of horror as she saw the
mermaid supported by Aisha and Emily.
"Oh, no! What happened to Pearl?"

"We aren't sure," Emily said. "It seems
like she got washed up here."

Sparklesplash watched nervously as the
girls carried the mermaid deeper into the
flood until she was covered in water.

But still she didn't move.

"What do we do now?" cried Emily,
tears pricking at her eyes.

All of a sudden Pearl shuddered. She took a great gulp of air, opened her eyes and sat up. She stared at Emily and Aisha in amazement. Then she noticed the trees sticking out of the water and her sea-green eyes opened even wider.

"What's going on?" she gasped. "Where am I?" Her voice was tinkling and sweet, like a trickling stream of water.

The girls and Sparklesplash explained what was happening, and how they had found her.

"Last thing I remember, I was practising my triple spin for our synchronised swimming routine," said Pearl.

"The mermaids are supposed to be performing at the Nature Gala,"

Sparklesplash told the girls.

"Thank you for coming to my rescue," Pearl added.

Aisha smiled. "Of course! I'm Aisha and this is Emily."

Pearl clapped in delight and gave a tinkling laugh. "I'm so pleased to meet you," she said. "You're famous in Enchanted Valley. You've saved us from Selena's nasty spells. I should have known you'd be here now that Selena's up to her tricks again."

"Can you help us get Sparklesplash's locket back?" Emily asked. "It's hidden in the deepest part of the lagoon."

Pearl shuddered. "The lagoon bed's much too deep for any human to dive to.

It can be dangerous too. Even mermaids don't go that far down alone."

"Then how will we get my locket back?" asked Sparklesplash, a hint of despair in her voice.

Pearl's forehead wrinkled in a frown. "I have an idea!" she said at last. "Wait just a minute." With a flick of her shimmering tail, she disappeared into the waves. No sooner had the girls begun to wonder where she'd gone than she surfaced again, holding out three pretty, shiny combs set with twinkling blue stones.

"These stones are sea sapphires," Pearl explained. "They'll help you swim and breathe underwater!"

Aisha and Emily helped fix a comb
in each other's hair and then placed
Sparklesplash's in her mane.

"But how do they work?" Emily said.

Pearl flashed a mischievous smile.
"You'll see. Come on!" Then she dived
back into the water, leaving hardly a
ripple behind her.

"On the count of three then," Aisha said.

"One …"

"Two …" said

Sparklesplash.

"Three!"

yelled Emily.

The girls and

Sparklesplash

plunged under

the surface. As they did, the water swirled around them, spinning them faster and faster. The girls felt a tingling start in their toes and climb up their legs. When the spinning stopped, they opened their eyes. Pearl was smiling at them.

"You look great!" she said.

Emily and Aisha looked down to see that their legs had turned into shimmering tails! Emily's was a pearly

pink, Aisha's a deep turquoise.

"We're mermaids!" they exclaimed together.

"And we can talk underwater," said Emily.

"Look at me!" cried Sparklesplash.

They turned to see their unicorn friend floating upright in the water, a new fin on her back and a spindly tail curled underneath her.

"You've turned into a giant seahorse!" said Aisha.

"A sea unicorn!" corrected Emily, pointing at Sparklesplash's horn.

Aisha flicked her tail, gliding through the sunbeams dancing in the water. "Wow! I can swim really well," she said.

"Imagine if your swimming class could see you now!" grinned Emily.

"They'd never believe it," said Aisha.

"I knew you'd like it," said Pearl happily. "Now let's go!"

## Chapter Five
# The Dark Lagoon

Pearl swam off and they sped after her through the strange underwater world. As they swam, they grew solemn – they were passing by tiny villages of flooded pixie houses, and all around them floated the pixies' broomsticks, boots and books. Forest primroses that were usually yellow

and bright wilted in the water. If they
didn't manage to find Sparklesplash's
locket, none of the creatures would ever
get their homes or things back.

Suddenly the ground dipped sharply
away, and the girls felt a strong current
like an underwater wind pushing against
them. Emily stared into the dark depths as
she and Aisha grabbed hands.

"Oh, no," Pearl breathed. "The lagoon
– it's so different. Usually there are
thousands of fish swimming around,
and everything's bright and cheery. The
water's always perfectly clear."

"Everyone is probably hiding," said
Sparklesplash. "The current is very
strong."

"But if you want that locket," said Pearl, "there's only one way to go, and that's straight down from here. Stay close to me."

Emily and Aisha took a deep breath. Then they flicked their tails and swam off into the deep.

Down and down they swam. Emily and Aisha held tightly to each other and swished their tails in rhythm to fight the powerful surges of water that were rising from below. *Swoosh!* A shoal of tabby catfish darted underneath them, meowing anxiously as they were tossed in the strong currents. Mermaids peered from the windows of little cottages built into the seabed below. Emily gasped as she caught sight of a brightly glowing starfish fighting to keep its grip on a nearby rock. She reached over and smoothed one of its swinging arms firmly down against the rock's surface. Everyone was struggling against Selena's horrible spell.

Sparklesplash tumbled sideways and used her spiralled tail to right herself. "The currents are growing stronger the deeper we go."

A giant ring of coral came into view below them. It glittered in breathtaking rosettes of green, yellow and pink. Blue bug-eyed frogs and silver sea snails gazed fearfully from every nook and cranny.

"It's beautiful!" breathed Emily. "I wish we had time to explore."

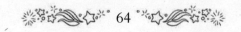 64

They reached the the coral and peered over it. Below, the water churned even more viciously.

"That's where we have to go to find the locket," said Pearl. "The deepest point in the lagoon." Her voice was wobbly with worry. A column of bubbling water suddenly shot up from the depths.

"What was that?" gasped Sparklesplash, shrinking back.

"That came from a geyser in the rock," said Pearl. "There are lots of them in the

coral ring. That's why even we mermaids don't go there."

"What's a geyser?" asked Aisha.

"It's a vent that shoots up jets of water and steam," Emily explained. "We have them in our world, too."

"Keep your eyes peeled, everyone," warned Pearl. "As soon as you see bubbles rising, get out of the way!"

Everyone took a deep breath and then set off into the coral ring.

But just as Aisha was diving down, she felt something brush against her. She whirled around in the water just in time to see a small, spindly creature shooting past her, squeaking hard as its floppy fins flapped wildly.

"What's that?" she exclaimed.

Pearl's eyes widened as she turned to look. "I've never seen a fish like that in the lagoon."

Catching sight of the fish, Emily saw that there was something very familiar about the creature. It swam almost like it was trying to fly …

"That's no fish," she gasped. "It's Flit! Selena's magicked him into a weird sea creature."

"How rude," called Flit, sticking out his tongue. "You're one to talk, with your scaly fishy tail. Anyway, Selena told me to guard the locket. I'm going to pick it up and hide it somewhere you'll never find it."

With that he flapped awkwardly and plunged into the dark depths.

"Quick!" cried Aisha urgently. "We've got to get the locket before Flit does!"

## Chapter Six
# The Brave Bat

Emily, Aisha and Sparklesplash followed
Pearl as she took off after Flit. The inside
of the coral ring was different to the rest
of the lagoon. The currents whirled them
this way and that through the darkness.
There were no mermaid homes here, or
creatures peeking out at them.

The four friends slowly battled their way down to the craggy lagoon bed, which was carpeted with broken shells and jagged rocks.

"Remember to watch out for the geysers," warned Pearl, "and if you see one starting to bubble, swim away as fast as you can!"

Emily and Aisha peered around the bottom of the lagoon, between sea

boulders and tangled patches of seaweed.
But there was no sign of Flit or the locket.
And it was hard to swim while they were
being thrown this way and that.

"Maybe Flit's already found the locket,"
said Sparklesplash anxiously.

Just then, the current threw Aisha
against a prickly sea cactus. Aisha tried
not to cry out as the thorns scratched
her hands. Then something moved – a

quivering
black shape,
hiding
behind a
sunken log. "Here he is!"
she exclaimed.

Flit squeaked and flapped
hurriedly away. Aisha saw
something clasped tightly in his claws. It
was a slimy green bubble, and the Water
locket was inside!

"He's got the locket!" cried Aisha,
setting off after him.

"Be careful, Aisha!" called Pearl.
"There's a geyser ahead."

Aisha spotted the bubbles rising just
ahead of her and swept her tail sideways

in the water, slowing herself down just in time.

"Phew," she breathed. "Thanks, Pearl. That was close!"

"Aisha!" Emily cried out. "Flit doesn't know about the geysers!"

Sure enough, Aisha turned to see Flit swimming straight into the upward stream of bubbles. With a flick of her tail she rushed forward.

Emily looked on in terror as Aisha grabbed Flit by the fin and pulled him out of the bubbles, just as a powerful jet of water came bursting up from the lagoon bed below.

But Flit had not been able to pull the green bubble clear of the geyser. Before anyone could reach it, the bubble was forced out of Flit's fins and catapulted high out of sight.

"Oh, no!" cried Sparklesplash. "The locket!"

"Oh dear," gulped Flit, round-eyed with fear as he looked up at Aisha. "Selena will be so angry with me! She already made me come here even though I was frightened. What will she do when she finds out I lost the locket?"

Aisha gave the little bat-fish a cuddle.

Emily joined them. "Stay with us, Flit," she said. "We'll protect you."

"But aren't you angry at me for losing the locket?" Flit asked, sniffling.

Sparklesplash nuzzled him with her

nose. "Don't worry," she said. "It's not really lost. As soon as the geyser dies away, the locket will come down again."

Emily suddenly caught sight of a slimy green object above them. "There it is now!" she cried.

Sparklesplash, who was closest, leapt to catch the falling Water locket in her teeth, but before she could, it was whipped away by the current and sank behind a patch of seaweed.

"I'll get it," said Aisha. She swam round the seaweed. "Oh no!" she groaned.

The others rushed over just as the bubble disappeared into a deep, narrow crevice in the rock.

"How can we reach it now?" asked Emily.

"We're far too big to go down after it," said Pearl in despair.

"I'm not!" said Flit. "I'll go."

"Would you do that for us, Flit?" asked Aisha.

"You've been so nice to me," said Flit eagerly. His eyes narrowed. "I thought Selena was nice at first – but she only pretended to be my friend so I'd help with her nasty plans."

"Real friends don't do that," said Emily. "We'll be your friends."

"I'll be yours!" exclaimed Flit, flapping his fins excitedly. He peered down into the dark crevice. "And friends help each other, don't they?"

Flit paused on the edge of the crevice for a moment more. With one of his fins, he saluted his new friends. Then he plunged out of sight.

## Chapter Seven
# Flit's Daring Swim

The girls, Sparklesplash and Pearl all peered down after Flit. The brave bat was swimming deeper and deeper, checking everywhere for the locket.

Then, suddenly, he disappeared.

"Flit, are you all right?" cried Emily in alarm.

There was no
sound from below.
"Do you think
he's stuck?" said
Aisha.

Then they heard a happy chittering. Flit
popped into view with something in his
claws. The bubble!

"Found it!" he called triumphantly.

"Well done, Flit!" cried the girls. Emily
helped him lift the bubble out of the
crevice while Aisha slapped his fin a high
five.

"Now let's get the locket out of this
bubble!" Emily said, pressing the green
bubble down on the tip of a sharp rock
nearby. But instead of bursting open, the

bubble sprang away like a rubber ball.

Aisha caught it and turned it in her hands. "How do you burst a magic bubble?" she pondered.

Sparklesplash gave an excited neigh. "My horn!" she said.

"That's it!" exclaimed Emily. "Your horn is magic, too. Maybe its magic will be stronger than Selena's."

Aisha held the bubble towards Sparklesplash.

The sea unicorn lowered her head and – *SPLAT!* – her horn burst the bubble into hundreds of slimy pieces.

The Water locket floated into Aisha's palm. With Sparklesplash's spiny head still lowered, Aisha quickly looped the locket's silver chain over Sparklesplash's neck. For a long moment, everyone held their breath.

"Did it work?" whispered Pearl.

Then, all at once, the waters became still and calm. The whirling currents were gone. Through the clear water, rays of sunlight filtered down, lighting up the lagoon.

"I think it did!" said Aisha.

"Which means the valley will be safe now," said Emily. "The water should all be drying up."

Sparklesplash nodded. "I think you're

right, girls. Thank you for your help!"

But Flit's nose quivered in fear. "Selena will be furious," he whimpered.

Aisha stroked his head. "We'll protect you," she promised. "Stay close to us."

They swam swiftly upwards. Without the terrible currents, the girls could see the underwater world clearly. The rocks gleamed with encrusted jewels, and rainbow seaweed forests fluttered on either side of them. A school of angelfish passed by, swimming in happy circles, flapping their lacy fins.

The mermaids were starting to come out of their little cottages now, each with a different coloured tail. They waved shyly at the girls as they passed, some of

them blowing kisses, which Aisha caught
with a wink.

The group was soon surrounded by all
sorts of wonderful creatures – roaring
lionfish, barking dogfish and groups of
clownfish juggling shells with their fins.
Everyone seemed to be coming out to
play now that the lagoon was safe again.
Then the girls sped upwards and popped
their heads out of the gently rippling

water. The flood had vanished from the forest, which was already looking green and dry again!

Aisha high-fived with Emily, sending warm spray high in the air.

"Everything is lovely again," whooped Pearl. "Thank you, Aisha, Emily and Sparklesplash. And Flit. You saved the day."

The little bat grinned shyly. "And I've

made four new friends!" he said.

"Come back to the palace with us," said Emily. "The Nature Gala will be starting soon."

"Yippee!" yelled Flit. "I love parties!"

"We'd better head for shore," said Aisha.

"Or," Pearl said, grinning mischievously, "I can show you a shortcut."

They swam after the mermaid to the mouth of a cave, its entrance hidden by a craggy rock covered in barnacles.

"This way," said Pearl. She dived through the entrance, and the girls found themselves not in a cave but in a secret, underground river! It twisted and turned and soon they saw light up ahead. The river opened up into a wide, sunny pool,

and waiting for them there was a crowd
of chattering mermaids! Their shiny scales
flashed blue, green and pink, and their
long hair billowed round their shoulders.

"Meet my synchronized swimming
team!" Pearl announced proudly. She
clapped her hands and the team dived. A
circle of bright tailfins appeared, waving
hello in perfect rhythm. Aisha joined in.
So did Flit, trying his best to wiggle his
legs just like the mermaids' tails.

"This will be the best party ever!" declared Emily, giggling at the little bat.

"It's probably time for us to get back on dry land," said Sparklesplash.

The girls, Sparklesplash and Flit followed Pearl up to the surface of the water. Blinking in the sunlight, they saw that she had brought them to the palace moat! Emily and Aisha propped themselves up on to the shore and handed Pearl the sea sapphire combs. *Whoosh!* In an instant they were dressed in their shorts and T-shirts and had legs again instead of tails.

Aisha felt a pang. Swimming had been fun as a mermaid. But it would be much easier getting around on land with two legs! Sparklesplash joined them, a unicorn once more.

The girls bent down to speak to Pearl. "Thank you for everything," they said.

"Happy to help!" answered Pearl, beaming.

"Welcome back!" came a soft, friendly voice. Queen Aurora and the Nature unicorns were hurrying towards them. The unicorns nuzzled them in greeting. Shimmerbreeze waved her horn over the girls' heads and at once they were completely dry.

"We're so proud of you," said Aurora. "You've saved Enchanted Valley once again!"

The girls looked around. Everything

had been set up for the party, but there was no one in the garden except the unicorns.

"Where is everyone else?" asked Emily anxiously. "Didn't they all make it to safety?"

Before Queen Aurora could answer, Aisha pointed up to the sky, where a giant flock of creatures was flying towards them, all waving paws, claws and wings as they came in to land. From their backs scrambled the gnomes, pixies, elves and imps. The girls were surrounded by creatures shaking their hands and thanking them for their help. Only one creature seemed to be missing.

"There's someone else who helped us,"

said Aisha. "A new friend. But where is he?"

"Check out the moat," laughed Emily.

A small black shape flashed by on its back. Flit was still practising his swimming!

"We can never have enough friends in Enchanted Valley," said Aurora, the suns in her locket shining extra brightly. "Let's hear it for our brave rescuers. Hip, hip …"

"… hooray," cried all the creatures. Emily and Aisha beamed. The wave of sound surrounded them like a warm hug.

"I must get ready for our display," said Pearl. She slid away under the water.

"And now let the Nature Gala begin!" announced Aurora.

## Chapter Eight
# The Nature Gala

Shimmerbreeze's horn glowed.

*WHOOSH!* Hundreds of balloons rose magically and danced in the air. Kites shot up and fluttered in the breeze. Glitterhoof gave the girls fragrant flower garlands to wear. Dawnblaze sent moonpetal muffins flying from the palace ovens while dragons barbecued fruit kebabs by breathing fire on them.

Sparklesplash led the girls to the fountain. "Try my Fizzleberry Surprise again," she said.

The little round pool gurgled gently. Aisha took a glass. The drink zinged on her tongue, filling her mouth with a glorious taste of sweetness and summer.

"It's delicious," she said.

"And so fizzy!" agreed Emily, giggling

as the bubbles went up her nose.

Emily and Aisha heard a happy chirp and were delighted to see Ember and her chicks flying overhead. The flame-coloured baby phoenixes were playing fetch with Fluffy. They darted around the cloud puppy, giggling all the time.

"Hello there!" said a familiar voice. Their friend Hob was standing there with Bluebell and Primrose. His wrinkled face was all smiles as he handed them each a pretty blue flower. "We're giving everyone a forget-me-not so they'll always

remember this splendid day."

"What a great idea," said Emily.

Just then, Aisha spotted something peeking over the garden wall. It was a unicorn, her cold black eyes narrowing as she watched the partygoers.

"Uh-oh!" Aisha whispered to Emily. "Selena's back."

Emily was puzzled. Selena didn't

 normally hide. She usually arrived with thunder and lightning. "Do you think she wants to join in, Aisha?" she

wondered out loud.

"Let's ask her," said Aisha. "She may have done nasty things, but it would be mean to leave her out. And she might realise that we can be her friends. It's like Queen Aurora said – we can never have too many friends."

"That's a brilliant idea," said Emily. But still, her heart pounded as she and Aisha marched towards the wall.

"Would you like to come to the party, Selena?" called Aisha.

Selena flew over the wall to land next to them. For a moment she gazed at the celebrations, her head on one side. Emily and Aisha looked at each other hopefully. Maybe Selena would say yes!

Then the unicorn's eyes narrowed and she stamped her hoof angrily. "I don't want to come to your silly party. I came to fetch my servant. Where are you, Flit?"

"Coo-ee!" Flit's head popped up from the moat. "I'm having the best time!" he squeaked – until he saw Selena, who gave a furious snort.

"Stop messing around in there!" she snapped.

A flash of lightning shot from her horn and surrounded Flit with smoke. When it cleared he was a bat again. For a moment, Flit's ears drooped as he flapped into the air. "Can I at least stay for cake?"

"No! You're coming home with me,"

Selena commanded in a steely voice.

Flit looked uncertain. Then he caught Emily's eye. She nodded at him and gave a thumbs-up.

"No thanks, Your Great Nastiness," said the little bat, puffing out his chest. "I've made new friends and I'm staying here with them."

Queen Aurora trotted over. "You could stay, too, Selena," she said. "If you

promised not to harm the valley again."

"Yes!" said Aisha. "Try some of Sparklesplash's Fizzleberry Surprise. You'll love it!"

"You think I'd give up so easily?" Selena roared. Sparks flashed around her. "Enjoy your silly party now, fools, because I'll be back, and there will be no stopping me then!"

There was a deafening crack of thunder as Selena turned and flew away.

Ember's chicks gave a little cry.

"Don't worry," Queen Aurora assured them. "We're all safe now."

Emily and Aisha glanced at each other. Queen Aurora was right, for now. But they knew that Selena would be back as she had promised. And when that time came, they would be right here, standing up for their friends.

"The mermaids have a surprise for us," announced Sparklesplash. "Everyone to the moat!"

Selena was soon forgotten as Pearl and her friends began their spectacular synchronised swimming routine. They swam in perfect formation, their arms making graceful movements. Sometimes just their tails showed, swishing intricate figures of eight in the crystal-clear water. At last they all sank under the surface.

"Have they finished?" squeaked Flit in disappointment.

Suddenly Pearl shot out of the water

in a spectacular triple spin. Everyone
clapped. The other mermaids appeared
and caught her, holding her up as if she
were the centre of a beautiful flower.

At that moment, there was a *whooosshh!*
*Whizz! Booooom!* and gigantic red, orange
and yellow sparks shot from the top of the
distant Firework Mountain. As the light
faded, the sky lit up again with exploding
gold and silver stars. There were *ooh*s and

*aah*s from every partygoer until the last dazzling rockets faded from the sky.

Emily and Aisha both gave a yawn as the sky went dark.

"That was a wonderful show, but it's time for us to go home," sighed Emily, turning to Aurora and the four Nature Unicorns.

"We have something to give you before you go," said Dawnblaze.

"It's a thank-you for getting our lockets back," added Shimmerbreeze.

Sparklesplash dipped her horn and – *pzzang!* – two crystal charms in the shape of rainbows appeared in the air, shining with every imaginable colour.

"They're to wear on your keyrings,"

explained
Dawnblaze.

"They're
beautiful," sighed
Aisha happily.
"Thank you."

"We thought they would remind you of
us," added Dawnblaze.

"They definitely will," said Emily,
stroking Dawnblaze's mane.

When they'd said goodbye to everyone,
Aurora took them into the palace.

"I have something for you," she said.

She led them to the hall of portraits that
the girls had seen before. Pictures of all
the children who'd ever found their way
to Enchanted Valley hung on the walls.

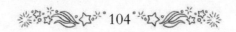

Aurora's horn glowed and a gilded frame
appeared and hovered in front of them.
It vanished and reappeared on the wall
between a boy and girl in frilly white
collars and two girls in long satin dresses.
Emily and Aisha gasped in delight at the
new portrait. It was an amazing painting
of them both.

"Now you're in our Hall of Honour,"
said Aurora. "And I'll be sure to call you

again when I need
your help."

The girls' hearts
were full. They
threw their arms
around the queen.

"Goodbye,

Aurora," said Emily.

"Thanks for everything," said Aisha.

Then Aurora waved her horn. A cloud
of golden sparkles surrounded them
and suddenly they were back under
the waterfall. The sun was still shining
through the water, and they could hear
the sound of their parents laughing over
the rush of the river. They checked their
keyrings. The little crystal charms were
still there beside the unicorns.

"What a brilliant party to end our
visit!" said Emily.

"I loved the synchronised swimming,"
added Aisha. Her eyes shone. "Let's ask
our parents if we can have a swim in
the river. I want to try out some of the

mermaids' moves."

Emily gave her a hug. "I'm so glad we found Enchanted Valley," she exclaimed. "I can't wait to go back again."

"Me neither," laughed Aisha, hugging her back. "We've made some wonderful new friends so far, haven't we?"

"Especially each other," grinned Emily.

Clasping hands, the girls ran to enjoy their afternoon by the river.

The End

Join Emily and Aisha
for another adventure in …
# Snowstar and the Big Freeze
**Read on for a sneak peek!**

Aisha Khan and her best friend, Emily Turner, stood in Aisha's garden, staring up at the grey sky.

"Come on, snow!" they wished together.

The air was freezing cold, and their breath puffed like dragon smoke. They shivered a little, even though they were bundled up in coats, hats and gloves. The grassy lawn behind Aisha's house, Enchanted Cottage, was white with frost, but the air was clear. "It's so cold, I wonder why there's no snow?" said Aisha.

"Perhaps the air is too dry," said Emily.

"It needs to be damp for the ice crystals to form and make snowflakes."

Aisha smiled. "Did you read that in one of your science books?"

"How did you guess?" laughed Emily.

Read
## Snowstar and the Big Freeze
to find out what adventures are in store
for Aisha and Emily!

# Also available

**Book One:**

**Book Two:**

**Book Three:**

**Book Four:**

# Look out for the next book!

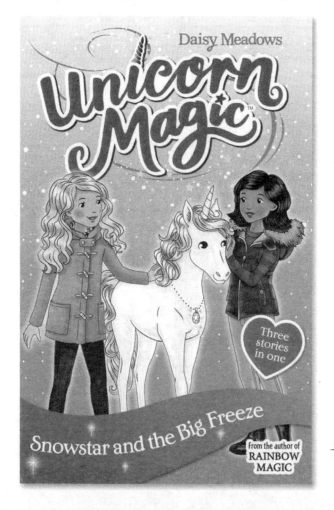

Daisy Meadows

Unicorn Magic™

Three stories in one

Snowstar and the Big Freeze

From the author of RAINBOW MAGIC

If you like
Unicorn Magic,
you'll love ...

## Welcome to Animal Ark!

Animal-mad Amelia is sad
about moving house, until she
discovers Animal Ark, where vets look
after all kinds of animals in need.

Join Amelia and her friend Sam for a
brand-new series of animal adventures!

# Silvermane
# Saves the Stars

Daisy Meadows

ORCHARD

# To Annabel Brady

# Special thanks to Conrad Mason

ORCHARD BOOKS

First published in Great Britain in 2020 by Hodder & Stoughton

3 5 7 9 10 8 6 4

Text copyright © 2020 Working Partners Limited
Illustrations © Orchard Books 2020
Series created by Working Partners Limited

A CIP catalogue record for this book is available from the British Library.

ISBN 978 1 40836 620 2

Printed and bound in Great Britain by Clays Ltd, Elcograf S.p.A.

The paper and board used in this book are made from wood from responsible sources.

Orchard Books
An imprint of Hachette Children's Group
Part of Hodder and Stoughton
Carmelite House
50 Victoria Embankment
London EC4Y 0DZ

An Hachette UK Company
www.hachette.co.uk
www.hachettechildrens.co.uk

Contents

# Meet the Characters

Aisha and Emily are best friends from Spellford Village. Aisha loves sports, whilst Emily's favourite thing is science. But what both girls enjoy more than anything is visiting Enchanted Valley and helping their unicorn friends, who live there.

Silvermane

Silvermane and the other Night Sparkle Unicorns make sure night-time is magical. Silvermane's locket helps her take care of the stars.

Dreamspell's magic brings sweet dreams to all the creatures of Enchanted Valley. Without her magical powers, everyone will have nightmares!

Dreamspell

Slumbertail

With the help of her magical friends and the power of her locket, Slumbertail makes sure everyone in Enchanted Valley has a peaceful night's sleep.

Kindly Brighteye is in charge of the moon. The magic of her locket helps its beautiful light to shine each night.

Brighteye

Enchanted Cottage

← Golden Palace

An Enchanted Valley lies a twinkle away,
Where beautiful unicorns live, laugh and play
You can visit the mermaids, or go for a ride,
So much fun to be had, but dangers can hide!

Your friends need your help ~ this is how you know:
A keyring lights up with a magical glow.
Whirled off like a dream, you won't want to leave.
Friendship forever, when you truly believe.

## Chapter One
# A Unicorn Made of Stars

Emily Turner gazed around in wonder. "Your garden looks even more magical at twilight!" she said.

Her best friend, Aisha Khan, grinned and spread a tartan blanket on the grass.

The moon shone like a new coin, and in the middle of the lawn, the stone statue of a phoenix gleamed against the deep blue sky. It looked as though it might take off at any moment.

"That's because of all this starlight!" said Aisha.

The girls lay next to each other on the blanket, staring upwards. The air was chilly, and they snuggled up to each other to stay warm. As their eyes got used to the dark, Emily and Aisha saw the stars glitter like silver pinpricks in a dark blue curtain.

"Wow …" breathed Emily.

"I'm so glad my parents let you stay over," said Aisha happily.

"And not just for one night," said Emily. "A whole week of sleepovers! It's going to be brilliant." She gasped. "Hey, I can see the Big Dipper!" Emily pointed to a small pattern of stars, shaped a bit like a wheelbarrow. "The stars always come out in patterns, which are called constellations. I've been reading about them. The Big Dipper is part of Ursa Major. Then there's Aquarius, Scorpio …"

"What about that one?" said Aisha. She pointed to a group of stars that suddenly began to shine brighter than all the others.

Emily frowned. "I don't know … It's not in my book. It looks almost like …"

"A unicorn!" said both girls, at the same time.

They sat up and looked at each other, eyes wide. They were thinking of Enchanted Valley, a secret land they had visited together, where unicorns lived with lots of other magical creatures.

Emily reached into her pocket and drew out the glass unicorn keyring that Aurora, Queen of Enchanted Valley, had given the girls so she could summon them back. To her delight, it was shimmering with multi-coloured lights. "Queen Aurora is calling us again!"

Aisha pulled out her own keyring. It was sparkling too, just like Emily's.

The girls knew what to do. They gently

touched the tips of the unicorn horns
against each other. At once there was a
whooshing sound and a burst of light,
like a firework going off. Colourful sparks
showered all around. Then the girls felt
themselves rising into the air. Their feet
left the blanket and they hovered.

"We're going back to Enchanted
Valley!" squealed Aisha. She and Emily
held hands tightly.

A haze of light glimmered all around.

Then slowly they began to drift down,
until they landed on a patch of grass.

They weren't in Emily's garden any
more. Instead they stood at the bottom of
a gentle hill. Up the slope was an elegant
golden palace with turrets shaped like
unicorn horns, silhouetted against the
purple sky.

"It's twilight in Enchanted Valley, too!"

said Aisha. "Wow!
Isn't it beautiful?"

"Let's go and see
Queen Aurora,"
said Emily. "I bet
she's waiting for us
at the palace!"

As the girls

climbed the hill, the sky turned a deeper purple, and shadows crept across the fields and woodland on every side.

They had nearly reached the moat that surrounded the palace, when the drawbridge began to swing downwards. Its silver chains rattled as it fell with a soft thump across the water. But to the girls' surprise, it wasn't Queen Aurora who came trotting out. Instead, four unicorns appeared, their hooves clip-clopping on the drawbridge. The first was the silvery colour of the stars, with a blue mane and tail with silver highlights. She was followed by a lilac unicorn wearing a silver saddlebag, then a very pale pink unicorn with a beautiful pink mane and

tail, and finally a pale blue one with a
gorgeous blue mane. Like all unicorns in
Enchanted Valley, every one of them wore
a delicate silver locket around their neck.

"Do you think they'll know where
Aurora is?" whispered Aisha.

Before Emily could reply, the four
unicorns formed a little circle on the

grass, then slowly lowered their heads until the tips of their horns touched.

A soft chime rang out, like the sound of a little bell. The four horns began to glow, and the girls saw that the unicorns' lockets were glowing too. *Magic!*

As the chime died away, night fell completely across Enchanted Valley. For a moment the glow from the unicorns was the only light in the darkness. Then Emily gasped and pointed up into the sky.

The stars were coming out, blinking into life like a sprinkling of magic dust. The whole valley glittered with a beautiful white light.

"It's incredible," gasped Aisha, gazing out over the fields and the forest.

Everything looked as though it had been made from silver.

"I'm so glad we get to visit at night-time," said Emily.

Just then, the silver unicorn turned and blinked at them. "Oh my," she said, flicking her tail. "You must be Emily and Aisha. Welcome!"

## Chapter Two
# Night Sparkle

"We've heard so much about you!" gushed the pink unicorn.

"You stood up to Selena when she stole the lockets from the Nature Unicorns!" added the lilac unicorn with the saddlebag. "Oh, it's so good to meet you!"

"We're the Night Sparkle Unicorns,"

said the blue unicorn, proudly lifting her
head. "We bring night-time to Enchanted
Valley."

"Hello!" said the girls.

"I'm Silvermane," said the last unicorn.
Sure enough, her mane and tail had
highlights as silver as her coat. "My locket
gives me the magic I need to take care of
the stars."

The girls peered closer at the little glass locket. Inside, they saw a golden gleam. It was a tiny shooting star, its tail sparkling behind it.

"It's beautiful," gasped Aisha.

"I'm Dreamspell," said the lilac unicorn. "I make sure everyone in the valley has nice dreams. Slumbertail here helps everyone sleep peacefully." The pink unicorn tossed her tail, looking bashful. "And Brighteye is in charge of the moon." The blue unicorn bowed her head.

"It's so nice to meet you all!" said Emily and Aisha together.

The girls admired the unicorns' lockets.
Slumbertail's had a tiny, fluffy white
pillow floating inside it. Brighteye's was a
little golden sliver – a crescent moon.

Dreamspell's locket was the strangest
of the four. As Emily and Aisha watched,
it changed from a little group of friends
having a picnic, to a sunny seaside scene,
and then to a birthday party.

"Oh, it's just like a lovely dream!" said

Emily with a happy sigh.

"Is Queen Aurora here, too?" asked Aisha. "We thought she summoned us."

"I hope Selena isn't causing trouble again," said Emily anxiously.

The girls exchanged a glance. Every time they had visited Enchanted Valley, the wicked unicorn Selena had been trying to force the other unicorns to make her queen by stealing their magical lockets.

Slumbertail gave a little shiver, her big eyes wide. "She's so mean and scary!"

"We haven't seen Selena since the last time you were here," said Silvermane. "But we know where Queen Aurora is."

"Actually, we were just about to go to

Shimmer Bay to meet her," explained
Brighteye. "When she left she said she'd
be back today. That must be why she
summoned you, because her ship is on its
way home."

"Her ship?" asked Aisha.

"A few days ago, we found a message
in a bottle, washed up on the beach,"
Dreamspell explained. "It was from
someone called Aneles, and it was asking
for help! So Queen Aurora went to find
this Aneles."

"We're bringing Aurora some hot
cocoa to welcome her home," said
Slumbertail. She nodded at the little
saddlebag that Dreamspell was wearing.
"And a warm, fluffy blanket. She'll be

tired when she gets back!"

The girls' hearts fizzed with excitement at the thought of seeing Queen Aurora's ship come sailing into Shimmer Bay. "Can we come too?" asked Aisha.

"Of course!" said Brighteye.

They all set off down the hillside. In the distance they could just see the ocean beyond the treetops. The waves sparkled like diamonds in the moonlight.

When they reached the bottom of the hill, the Night Sparkle Unicorns led the way through a shadowy forest. Their horns glowed softly, bobbing up and down like fireflies as they walked.

At last they emerged from the forest, and the girls saw a smooth, sandy beach

up ahead, curving in a shimmering
crescent around the bay.

"Wow!" gasped Emily. "It looks so
beautiful at night!"

On the beach, families of animals were
heading home after a day of playing. A
group of young rabbits shook out their
beach towels and rolled them up. A family
of pixies were packing up their buckets

and spades, their wings glinting in the
light of the stars. Overhead, bats wheeled,
squeaking happily to each other.

"The bats aren't going to bed. They're
nocturnal animals!" said Emily. "That
means they come out at night-time, and
sleep during the day."

"Hey," said Aisha, pointing at one of the
bats. "Isn't that Flit?"

Sure enough, the plump little bat flapped over to them, squawking cheerfully. "Hello, girls!"

"Hello, Flit!" called Emily and Aisha, waving. The bat had been Selena's servant, but after he realised how mean she was, he had helped Emily and Aisha to stop her horrible plans.

The girls' feet sank deep in the soft sand, as they followed the Night Sparkle Unicorns across the dunes. A breeze ruffled their clothes, and they could hear the waves lapping gently at the shore.

"We should have brought a bucket and spade!" said Emily with a grin.

Just then, the girls noticed a glittering golden creature swooping among the bats. It glided down and landed on the beach not far away, folding its wings neatly. It had a long, sweeping tail, shining black eyes and a silver beak. Every one of its feathers looked like it was made from pure gold.

"It's Lumi the Lightingale," said Slumbertail, as the bird hopped across the sand towards them.

Emily frowned. "Do you mean *nightingale*?"

Silvermane laughed delightedly. "No! Show them, Lumi."

Lumi spread his wings and closed his eyes. All at once, his golden feathers began to glow, as though they were on fire. They shone brighter and brighter, lighting up the whole beach until the girls had to look away.

"That's amazing, Lumi!" said Aisha.

Lumi's light faded, and he blinked several times. "Wow, that was really bright," he chirped, still squinting. "I mean ... thank you!"

The girls laughed. The lightingale seemed amazed by his own magic!

"Lumi is the keeper of the Starlight House," Silvermane explained. Using her horn, she pointed to a high, rugged cliff at the far end of the bay. The girls saw a tall white tower on top of it, surrounded by craggy rocks. A silvery beam shone from its topmost window.

"It's a special lamp," said Silvermane, "powered by starlight. Lumi uses it to show where the rocks are, so that ships can sail safely to the beach." She lowered her hoof, frowning. "But what are you doing here, Lumi? Queen Aurora's ship should be arriving any minute."

Lumi swished a wing impatiently. "Oh, don't worry about that. I've got something much more important to do." With a squawk he surged up into the air and began to fly in circles round and round the Night Sparkle Unicorns, furiously flapping his wings.

Emily and Aisha frowned at each other. They were both thinking the same thing. *Something's not right …*

"Look!" cried Emily suddenly. Purple smoke had swirled up from the sand, coiling round the unicorns. Silvermane and the others shuffled closer to each other, tossing their manes anxiously. Emily and Aisha couldn't help huddling

with them too.

"What's happening?" wailed Dreamspell.

"It's some sort of magic spell!" said Brighteye.

The smoke got thicker and thicker, until the girls couldn't see the unicorns at all. Then – *whoosh!* – the smoke evaporated. The unicorns looked around, puzzled.

Aisha gasped. "Your lockets! They're gone!"

Lumi was still flying in circles above their heads. But now the lightingale had four shining objects dangling on chains from his beak.

"And Lumi's stolen them!" cried Emily.

# Chapter Three
# Endless Night

One by one, the unicorns' horns stopped glowing. The stars winked out. A deep darkness fell across the beach, until the only light was the silvery beam from the Starlight House. Then, at last, that flickered and died too.

The animals all around squeaked and

squealed with dismay.

Emily and Aisha held hands. "I can hardly see a thing!" said Emily, peering at the shadowy shapes across the sand.

"Lumi, come back!" Aisha called into the darkness.

There was no reply.

"I can't believe Lumi stole our lockets!" cried Silvermane from nearby. "What's got into him?"

Emily and Aisha stared up into the sky, but they couldn't see the lightingale.

"Oh no!" said Aisha, clapping a hand over her mouth. "I've just realised … Without the Starlight House, Queen Aurora's ship won't be able to sail safely to the shore."

"She'll be stuck out at sea," said Emily. "Or worse — she'll hit a rock!"

The animals were still wailing with distress, and the girls heard scuffs and thumps as even the foxes and porcupines — who could normally see well at night — blundered into each other in the dark.

"We have to stick together," said Aisha, with determination. She squeezed Emily's hand tightly. "Hey, don't you think it's strange that Lumi stole the lockets just when Queen Aurora needs the light to get home from helping Aneles?"

Emily frowned. "Hang on a second. *Aneles* …" She quickly found a bit of driftwood. She traced out the letters of the name in the sand, kneeling down and squinting to see.

The girls both gasped at the same time.

"Uh-oh," breathed Aisha. "Aneles spelled backwards is … Selena!"

"She must have written the note to trick Aurora!" cried Silvermane.

"And it worked, of course!" said a triumphant voice.

Everyone looked around nervously. "Who was th-that?" stammered Dreamspell.

The whole bay suddenly lit up with a white flash of lightning. Then thunder rolled in the distance. *BOOM!* A silver unicorn came leaping from the sky, her purple mane and tail fluttering as she swooped down. Her hooves hit the beach with a thud, sending up a spray of sand.

The girls stared in horror. *Selena!*

Just then, a golden bird came fluttering from Selena's shoulders. It was Lumi, still clutching the lockets in his beak. The lightingale beat his wings. Then, with a *POP* and a puff of purple smoke, his tail grew shorter, his feathers turned brown

and his eyes became huge.

"He's not a lightingale at all!" gasped
Emily. "He's an owl!"

"And I fooled you all with my magical
disguise!" scoffed the little owl. "Ha ha!
I'm too clever for you!" He puffed his
chest out proudly.

"Quiet, Screech!" roared Selena. "It
was my plan, so I'm the clever one!" She
tossed her mane and drew herself up. "I'm
going to keep all your lockets, and this

horrible dark night is going to last for ever …"

"We won't let that happen," said Emily, stepping forward bravely.

"The only way to stop me is to make me Queen of Enchanted Valley!" Selena cried.

"No way!" said Aisha. "Aurora is the true queen!"

"You might just change your mind when you see how miserable Enchanted Valley will become," sneered Selena. "I hope you aren't scared of the dark!" She cackled, and Screech sniggered along. "Now if you'll excuse me," said Selena, "I'm off to hide the star locket in the darkest, most dangerous place in the whole valley! You'll never be able to get it back, and Aurora will never get back to shore safely!"

Still cackling, Selena rose into the air. Lightning flashed again, and thunder rolled in the distance as she soared through the sky with Screech flapping along behind her.

When the lightning faded, the wicked unicorn was gone, and the beach was left in darkness.

"Oh no," whispered Silvermane in a small voice. "What are we going to do? Without the lockets we can't look after night-time in Enchanted Valley."

"And the night will never end!" wailed Dreamspell.

"And Aurora will be in danger!" said Brighteye, bowing her head.

"Unless we make Selena queen," sniffed Slumbertail.

The girls held hands tighter than ever. They knew just what the other was thinking. *We can't let that happen!*

"Don't worry," said Emily firmly.

"We'll stop Selena."

"We're going to find those lockets," said Aisha. "And save Enchanted Valley!"

## Chapter Four
# Go Glow Potion

"First things first," said Emily. "We need to find the star locket, so that the stars will come out again, and the Starlight House will work properly. Then Queen Aurora can get home safely."

"And we have to find the real Lumi!" added Aisha. "I hope he's all right, wherever he is."

"I'll come with you," said Silvermane, tossing back her mane. "After all, it's my locket." Then she sighed heavily. "But how are we going to find the locket without any light?"

Aisha snapped her fingers. "I know! Let's ask Hob. He's always mixing up magical potions … I bet he could make some light for us."

"Great idea," said Emily. Their goblin friend had helped them out many times before. "And I think I know who can guide us to his cottage." She put two fingers in her mouth and blew a piercing whistle. "Flit! Where are you, Flit?"

There was a rustle of leathery wings.

Then a small, shadowy shape came gliding down to land beside them on the beach. "Is Selena still here?" said Flit, his voice trembling.

"Don't worry," said Aisha. "She's gone. But do you think you could help us find Silvermane's locket to end all this darkness?"

"Well, I actually love the dark," Flit mumbled. Then he shook his wings, rustling them again. "But that doesn't matter. Selena is trying to ruin Enchanted Valley for everyone! I'll help you stop her."

"Thank you, Flit!" said Emily, grinning. "I was hoping you could guide us to Hob's cottage. Since you're a bat and use sound instead of light to find your way around, you're the best person to get us there in the dark."

"I certainly am!" said Flit, his eyes gleaming with pride. "Follow my voice!"

"I'll carry you girls," said Silvermane, as the little bat flapped up in the air.

Aisha clung on to Silvermane's neck, while Emily held tightly on to Aisha.

"Ready?" called Silvermane. "Then off we go!"

Flit began to sing:

**"Some might say I'm a funny little bat**
**But that's OK, I'm fine with that."**

The girls giggled as they listened to Flit's silly song.

**"I've got my friends and that's all I need**
**Selena won't win, she'll never succeed."**

The girls could feel themselves soaring up into the night sky, circling high above the beach, but they could hardly see a thing in the darkness. Their eyes watered, and their hair tangled in the wind. The unicorn's mane fluttered as they flew, tickling Aisha's face.

"This way!" cried Flit, flying low over the forest. "Watch out – big tree on the left! Oops – flying squirrels on the right!"

Silvermane followed close behind.

The girls kept blinking and staring, hoping their eyes would get used to the dark ... but there was just blackness all around.

It felt as though they were flying for ages. But at long last, they heard Flit call out up ahead: "Time to land!" Then their stomachs lurched as Silvermane dipped downwards.

With a soft thump, the unicorn's hooves touched down. A short distance away they could just make out the familiar shape of a crooked old oak tree. They

heard the
creak of a door
opening, and
a little person
stepped out of
the tree trunk, a
glowing yellow
lantern dangling

from his hand. The girls felt a rush of
relief at being able to see light again.

"Hob!" cried Emily. The girls ran
forward and embraced the little goblin
tightly.

When they stepped away, Hob's
wrinkled green face had broken into a
huge smile. He adjusted his pointy hat
and pushed his spectacles back up his

nose. "My
goodness, it's
wonderful to
see you two!"
he squeaked.
"And dear old
Silvermane
too … and little
Flit! Come in,
all of you!"

Hob kept
chattering
away as he

led them into the tree trunk and down a set of winding wooden steps. "Don't tell me … This horrible darkness is Selena's doing, isn't it? What a wicked unicorn! Dear me …"

They reached the bottom and stepped at last into Hob's underground cavern home. It was large, bright and cosy, with candles and lanterns glimmering on ledges across the rocky walls. The light flickered on a thousand dusty old bottles and boxes. The girls knew that every one was full of magical ingredients.

"You're right, Hob. And we were hoping you might be able to help us," said Emily.

"We really need some light," added Aisha. "So we can find Silvermane's magical locket and put a stop to Selena's plans."

"Of course!" said Hob, rubbing his hands together. "Don't worry, I've got just the thing. Even better than my old lantern! We'll mix up one of my extra-special Go Glow potions. Now, quickly, girls … I need a pinch of Bright Blossoms, a cup of Sunshine Dew and plenty of Fire Moss!"

Hob began to stir his big black cauldron, while Emily and Aisha hurried to find the ingredients from the shelves.

Flit hung upside down from a coat hook to watch as Emily tipped in the shining pink Bright Blossoms and the glowing yellow Sunshine Dew. Then Aisha heaved in an armful of prickly orange Fire Moss.

The mixture bubbled and spat, as Hob stirred it with a huge wooden spoon.

"Is it ready?" asked Silvermane, staring into the cauldron with wide eyes.

"It is now!" said Hob, sprinkling in a final handful of silver dust. He unhooked a small lantern made of metal and glass from the rocky ceiling and ladled the potion into its container. The liquid was bright orange and glowed like lava.

"Time to test it," said Hob. "Shall we?"

They went outside and Aisha took the lantern from Hob. She opened its little metal door.

At once, the whole hillside was flooded with bright light. Emily and Aisha grinned. They could see every blade of grass, as clear as day.

"It's perfect!" cried Emily, giving Hob a hug. "Thank you!"

"Don't mention it," said Hob, blushing.

"Now we just need to find where Selena has hidden the locket!" said Aisha.

Emily frowned. "She said she was going to hide it in the darkest and most dangerous place in Enchanted Valley."

Hob scratched his head. "Well, that used to be the rocky cliffs around the cove. They were treacherous for ships, and steep and slippery to cross. But then the Starlight House was built, to make it light enough to see everything."

Emily gasped. "But the Starlight House isn't working any more."

"So the rocks around it are really dark again," said Silvermane. "And terribly dangerous for ships like Aurora's!"

"I bet that's where she's hidden the

locket!" said Aisha.

"You'd better find it, then," said Hob.
"Before it's too late for Aurora!"

## Chapter Five
# Lost in the Dark

Wind whipped against the girls' faces as Silvermane swept through the night sky. With the lantern they no longer needed Flit to lead them, and he'd gratefully gone back home to safety.

The ground below changed from grassy fields to rocks and sand. The wind began

to blow harder, and the smell of the sea
filled the air.

"We must be getting close to the cliffs,"
said Aisha.

Just then, they soared out over a ridge of
rocks, and below them was the silvery sea.
Aisha lifted the lantern, shining its light
all around. There was the Starlight House,
not far away – a tall white tower on a
ragged cliff.

Emily caught sight of something

beyond it, glimmering out in the distance on the sea. "Are those … sails?"

"It's Queen Aurora's ship!" gasped Silvermane. "Oh dear, we haven't a moment to lose. Without the light from the Starlight House, she'll sail straight on to the rocks!"

"Couldn't she fly to shore instead?" asked Aisha.

Silvermane shook her head. "She could, but there's a crew of sea sprites on board

her ship. Queen Aurora would never abandon them!"

"We could use Hob's lantern to signal to her," said Emily, thoughtfully.

"Great idea!" said Aisha.

Then a little voice came cheeping from the top of the dark cliffs. "Help! Oh please, won't someone help me?"

"Uh-oh!" said Emily. "Do you think someone's lost in the dark?"

"We'd better find out," said Silvermane.

They flew lower, until the unicorn's hooves touched down on the cliff edge.

Scrambling off Silvermane's back, Emily and Aisha listened out for the cries.

"Help! I'm so terribly lost and alone!" the voice wailed.

"Over here!" said Emily. Aisha rushed to her side and they followed the cries and sad sniffs to a scrubby bush that sprouted from among the rocks. They looked at each other.

"I can't see anything," said Aisha.

"Move the lantern closer," said Emily.

Aisha bent down and held the lantern closer to the bush.

There was a nasty little snort of laughter. Then – *whooosh!* – a feathered creature burst out from its hiding place. Wings flapping wildly, it tore the lantern from Aisha's hands. She made a grab for it, but the bird was already rising into the sky.

"It's Screech!" cried Emily.

The light swung wildly, as the lantern dangled from the naughty owl's talons. "Tricked you again!" crowed Screech. "Now I've got your lantern! What are you going to do about that?"

## Chapter Six
# Broken!

"Get him!" cried Aisha. She dived forward, grasping at Screech with both hands …
But at the same moment Screech flapped and rose higher, just out of reach.

"Missed me!" jeered Screech. "Ha ha!"

"Leave him to me!" said Silvermane. With a lurch she took off, flying straight at the little owl.

Screech's big eyes went even wider.
But he darted across the cliffside to a big
tree that grew right on the edge. With a
rustle of leaves, he disappeared among the
branches, taking the light with him.

Silvermane slowed down and hovered
beside the tree. She poked her horn

through the leaves,
then shook her
head sadly. "The
branches are too
close together! I
can't get in …"

"Woo hoooo!"
hooted Screech,
from his hiding

place in the tree. "Silly unicorn! Silly girls!"

Emily came panting to a stop beside Aisha. They both looked up at the tree. "What's he going to do with our lantern?" wondered Emily.

There was another rustle of leaves. Then Screech's head popped out of the very top of the tree. He lifted the lantern in a talon. "It's my lantern now!" he called.

"Oh no it's not!" Aisha ran to the tree trunk. Gripping the rough bark with her fingertips, she began to climb. She pulled herself on to the lowest branch as quietly as possible. It swayed a little, but Screech was too busy gloating to notice.

"I'm going to smash the lantern!" said

Screech. "Then you won't be able to see! What do you think of that?"

Holding her breath, Aisha pulled herself up to a higher branch … then another. She was almost at the top of the tree now. But as she stepped up on to the last branch, her foot slipped.

*Craaack!* A twig snapped.

*Twit twoooo!* Screech squawked in alarm. He turned his head right round, and spotted Aisha.

Aisha lunged for the lantern. Her hand closed over it, just as Screech tried to tug it away.

"Let go!" squealed Screech. He gave a yank with his talon, and the lantern flew through the air.

"No!" cried Emily.

Down fell the lantern, bumping and bouncing from branch to branch … then it dropped straight off the edge of the cliff. Aisha stared, pale with shock.

Leaning from Silvermane's back, Emily peered down the sheer cliff face. Far, far below, she saw a twisted bit of metal among the rocks. The bright orange liquid seeped out of it, then turned dull and disappeared.

"It's broken!" groaned Aisha.

Screech shot up into the sky in a flurry of feathers. "Let's see how you find that locket with no light!" he called back. Then he disappeared into the night, sniggering to himself.

"What should we do?" asked Aisha as she climbed back down through the branches. Emily, standing below, offered her a hand. Aisha took it, sliding carefully back to the ground. Now that darkness lay all around, she could hardly see a thing.

Silvermane landed beside the girls.

"There's only one thing we can do," said Silvermane. "We'll have to get the Starlight House working again.

Otherwise Queen Aurora's ship will hit the rocks! I really hope my locket is inside."

The unicorn was trembling, and Emily gently stroked her head. "Don't worry, Silvermane," she whispered. "We'll save Aurora … and we'll get your locket back too!"

## Chapter Seven
# The Starlight House

"I can almost see the Starlight House,"
said Aisha, peering into the darkness.
In the distance, the tall, pale shape of
the tower was visible. "I just can't see
anything else!"

Silvermane still looked worried, but she
stamped her hoof with determination.

"Hop on, girls," she said. "If we fly straight
towards it, we should be all right."

A moment later they were soaring
through the night. Emily and Aisha clung
on tighter than ever. Now they had no
stars to guide the way, no lantern and no
Flit either. They couldn't see a thing but
the ghostly tower up ahead … and below,
they could hear the waves crashing like
thunder.

"I just hope we don't fall off," whispered

Emily, wrapping her arms firmly round Aisha's waist.

Suddenly Silvermane reared up, jolting the girls. "Whoa!" yelped Emily, clinging on tighter.

"Sorry!" said Silvermane, coming to a stop in the air. "I nearly flew straight into the Starlight House!"

"Don't worry," said Emily. "You did an amazing job flying us in the darkness."

"And at least we've arrived!" Aisha reached out and laid a hand on the pale surface. "It's the wall of the Starlight House," she said. "Phew!"

The girls trailed their hands over the white stones as Silvermane glided gently down. At last, the unicorn's hooves crunched in pebbles at the base of the Starlight House. "There!" cried Silvermane. She gave a whinny of relief. "Now we need to find the door. Lumi lives on the ground floor."

The girls slid off Silvermane's back and set off on foot, feeling their way around the base of the Starlight House with their hands on the walls.

"Lumi!" called Silvermane. "Are you in there?"

There was no reply.

"I hope Selena hasn't hurt him," said Emily anxiously.

"Ooh!" cried Aisha. "I've found something."

Emily joined her, and together they felt

the outline of a little wooden door. But it was hanging wide open.

"Lumi always keeps this door closed," Silvermane told the girls.

Aisha shivered. "I think someone else must have come to pay Lumi a visit," she whispered. Together they stepped inside, where it was even darker than it had been outside. The girls couldn't see a single thing.

Then they heard a strange, muffled squawking sound. "What is that?" asked Aisha.

"It sounds like Lumi!" said Silvermane, from the doorway.

The girls stepped further into the Starlight House. They went slowly and carefully, holding their arms out as far as they could.

"Ouch!" cried Aisha, as she banged into the arm of a sofa.

"Oops!" yelped Emily, knocking her shoulder against what felt like a lampshade.

"Mmmmff!" said the strange, muffled voice.

"I think I'm getting close," said Emily. She took another step, and her fingers brushed against something soft. "I feel … feathers!"

"That must be Lumi!" cried Aisha. She stumbled over. Together the girls felt the shape of a bird. But it was sitting on a chair, with ropes tied tightly around its body and beak.

As fast as they could, the girls found the knots and untied them.

When they got the bird's beak free, he gasped and shook his head. "Oh, thank you, girls!" he murmured, in a soft voice. "I am Lumi, and you must be Aisha and Emily. Now step back, please!"

As the girls edged away, Lumi hopped up on the chair. With a ruffling of feathers, he spread his wings. His feathers began to glow with a dim but golden light, and at last the girls

could see the Starlight House all around them.

They were in a small, cosy living room with orange walls and comfortable-looking furniture all clustered around a fireplace. A wooden spiral staircase led to the floor above.

"What happened to you, Lumi?" asked Aisha.

"It was that wicked Selena!" the

lightingale explained. "She broke down my door, burst in and tied me up …" As he spoke, his light flickered and went out.

"I'm sorry," Lumi's voice came through the darkness. "I feel very weak now."

Silvermane stamped her hoof. "That wicked unicorn! How dare she?!"

Emily stroked Lumi's feathers. "Do you think Selena hid the locket in the Starlight House?"

"I don't think so," said Lumi, shaking his head. "She didn't stay for long."

Aisha groaned. "It's a dead end!" she said. Then she froze, staring out of the window. "Hang on … Do you see that?"

Out in the darkness, something was gleaming with a faint, silvery light.

Looking closer, Emily saw that the glow came from the jagged rocks at the edge of the cliff. "Do you think …" she breathed. "Could it be the locket? The edge of the cliff is probably the most dangerous place in the whole kingdom."

*Twit twooooo!* Beyond the window, a little creature came diving out of the night, heading straight for the glinting silver light.

*Screech!*

Hearts racing, Emily and Aisha dashed through the doorway. Silvermane was already galloping toward the cliff edge. "Go away, Screech!" cried the unicorn. "Shoo!"

"Shoo yourself!" squawked Screech.

He stretched out his wings as he soared
towards the rocks …

Then Lumi hopped up on the window
ledge. He lunged forward and made a
grab for Screech.

With a squeal of surprise, Screech jerked
away. "Urgh!" he yelped. "Where did you
come from? I thought we'd tied you up!"

Screech fell to the ground. Silvermane
reached forward and pinned Screech's
tail feathers under her hoof, just as Lumi's

light faded to a thin glow. The lightingale was panting from the effort.

"Hurry, girls!" Silvermane called. "You get the locket!"

Emily and Aisha ran to the jagged rocks where they'd seen the silver light. In the dim glow from Lumi's wings, they could finally see the locket clearly. It was dangling by its chain from a sharp bit of rock at the very edge of the cliff. Below, they could just make out the waves crashing against huge, jagged rocks on the shore. And beyond, Aurora's ship was coming, sailing straight into danger …

Holding hands, the girls stepped carefully across the rough and bumpy rocks, going as fast as they dared. As they came closer to the edge they crouched, staying low so they wouldn't fall.

"I think I can get it," said Aisha, her brow creased with concentration. "Just hold on to me …"

Emily knelt and held on to Aisha's top. Then Aisha crawled forward, reaching as far as she could with her right hand. Her fingers brushed at the locket.

She flinched, trying to ignore the terrifying drop just ahead of her, and the churning of the sea far below …

"Just a little further," Aisha muttered. She stretched as far as she could, until … *Yes!* She hooked a finger round the chain and flicked it free.

At once, Emily pulled Aisha back from

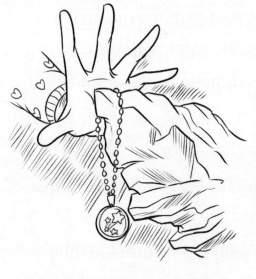

the edge.

Aisha
gripped the
locket tightly
in her hand, so
there was no
chance of it
slipping away.
"Come on!"

Emily gasped. "We have to save Aurora's
ship!" The silver-sailed vessel was leaping
over the waves … heading straight for the
rocks.

The girls scrambled back from the cliff
edge, towards the Starlight House. Screech
was still trying to pull his tail out from
under Silvermane's hoof.

Aisha broke into a sprint. As she reached Silvermane, the unicorn lowered her head, and Aisha draped the locket around her neck.

At once the locket shone, bright silver. A shimmer of sparkles ran across Silvermane's coat, and her horn glittered with a magical light. Silvermane let out a long, happy sigh and flicked her tail with joy. "Thank you, girls!"

"Noooo!" wailed Screech as he wriggled free.

Emily and Aisha gasped as they looked

up at the sky. The stars were coming out again, winking like fairy lights.

"You did it!" cried Lumi, dancing from talon to talon and shaking his golden feathers, which were bursting with bright golden light.

The girls looked at each other and grinned.

"Oops – I almost forgot … there's no time to lose!" cried Lumi. The lightingale swept up into the air, beating his golden wings and ducking through a window at the top of the Starlight House. A moment later, a white beam of light shone from the top of the Starlight House, making the ocean glint like a thousand diamonds.

"I can't see," said Silvermane, peering

towards the ocean. "Is the ship turning?"

Emily and Aisha looked at each other again. But this time, their faces were full of worry. *Oh no … did we make it in time to save Aurora?*

## Chapter Eight
# Aurora Returns

The girls held their breath.

They could see the waves crashing against the jagged black rocks now, far below, and Queen Aurora's ship was sailing straight towards them. The silver sails were smooth and full as the ship cut through the water …

"No!" gasped Emily.

Then Aisha gripped Emily's hand tight. The sails were turning. And the ship was too! It curved away, just missing the closest of the rocks, and steered towards Shimmer Bay.

"Phew!" The girls let out their breath in a sigh of relief.

"We did it!" cried Silvermane, rearing up joyfully.

"Curses!" howled Screech. The little owl twitched his wings and flapped furiously away. A moment later he had disappeared around the edge of the cliff.

Lumi came gliding down from the Starlight House to land beside the girls. He spread his wings around them. His feathers were warm and soft, and the girls hugged him tightly. "Thank you, Emily and Aisha!"

murmured Lumi. "You saved the stars! Now I can light the way for every ship that comes to visit Enchanted Valley."

"Thank you," said Aisha. "We couldn't have got the locket back without you."

"Or saved Queen Aurora's ship!" added Emily.

"Come on, let's go and welcome her back," said Silvermane.

Lumi waved with the tip of a golden

wing, as they climbed on to Silvermane's back once again. Then with a flick of her tail, Silvermane was swooping through the sky above the cliffside, towards Shimmer Bay. With the stars twinkling overhead, they could see the whole valley laid out below, like a beautiful map made of silver.

The girls couldn't stop grinning the whole way.

At one end of Shimmer Bay there was a long wooden pier, painted white. As Silvermane flew down low, the girls saw that Aurora's ship had just reached the pier. A gangplank was lowered on to it, like a drawbridge. Then a familiar unicorn came trotting off the ship. She

was glowing with a pinkish-red colour,
like a sunset, and her crown glittered gold.

*Queen Aurora!*

Silvermane landed with a gentle thunk
of her hooves on the wooden pier. The
girls slid off her back, then rushed to
Queen Aurora and buried their faces in
her soft coat.

"You came!" said Queen Aurora.

"And they saved Enchanted Valley

again!" Silvermane told her.

"You are clever girls," Queen Aurora said, nuzzling them.

"We weren't going to let Selena win," said Emily. "But we couldn't have done it alone."

"It's like Flit's song said," added Aisha. "*We've got our friends and that's all we need. Selena won't win, she'll never succeed.*"

Aurora whinnied in delight. "What a fabulous song!"

Behind her, the crew of sea sprites had begun tying up the ship and taking down the sails. They were little blue-green creatures with pointed ears and shaggy seaweed hair, and they scampered around

the deck like
monkeys.

"We're just glad
to see that you're
all right," said
Aisha. "We were
worried about you!"

Queen Aurora nodded gravely. "When
I got that message, I thought I'd find
someone in trouble. But instead, when
I got to the island there was just a big
black scorch mark in the sand … shaped
like a lightning bolt!"

"Selena!" said Emily.

"That's right." Queen Aurora sighed.
"I guessed she was up to something. And
that's when I summoned you girls."

"We're so glad you did," said Aisha.

"We'll always be ready to help the unicorns," added Emily.

Queen Aurora led them down the pier and on to the beach. All the little animals, pixies and elves had gathered around the three remaining Night Sparkle Unicorns. Huddled together, they all had their heads tipped back, as they stared at a sky bright with stars. Their eyes shone with wonder, and with happiness too.

Just then, the sky lit up with a burst of white light. *BOOOOM!* Thunder rolled in the distance.

The girls' hearts sank. *Uh-oh … Selena!*

Sure enough, the silver unicorn flew out from behind a cloud. She hovered in mid-

air, and Screech came flapping after her, scowling at the girls.

Selena snorted crossly. "I suppose you think you're clever?" she called. "Well, you might have got the Star Locket back … but I still have the other three! This night will go on for ever, until I'm queen. And I'll make sure it's the most miserable night ever!"

Selena threw back her head and cackled, and Screech hooted along with her. There was another flash of lightning, and a rumble of thunder. Then Selena and Screech surged up into the sky and vanished in the darkness.

"She really is wicked," said Dreamspell, hanging her head.

"She'll never give us our lockets back," added Slumbertail sadly.

Emily and Aisha ran across the sand and hugged each Night Sparkle Unicorn in turn.

"Don't worry," said Aisha when they'd finished. "We'll get your lockets back. We promise!"

"We'll stop Selena," said Emily. "Together!"

"Yes, we will," said Silvermane. "But first, how about some hot chocolate?"

"Yes, please," said Emily and Aisha together, giggling.

The girls opened Dreamspell's silver saddlebag, took out a fluffy white blanket and spread it on the sand. Then they passed round a purple thermos full of hot chocolate, as they settled down on the blanket. The drink was warm, sweet and delicious. Emily and Aisha lay back happily to gaze at the night sky, as Silvermane pointed out constellations with her glowing horn.

"There's the Pufflebunny," Silvermane was saying, as the girls looked at a pattern of stars shaped like rabbit ears.

"And there's the Teddy Bear!" She pointed at another little cluster of stars.

Queen Aurora yawned. "Speaking of teddy bears ... I'm exhausted after that journey! I think it's time for bed."

Emily and Aisha couldn't help yawning too.

"We'd better head home," said Aisha a little sadly. "But what about the other lockets?"

"We'll see you again very soon, and we'll find the lockets then," said Queen Aurora. "But you girls need your rest."

Emily and Aisha hugged Queen Aurora. Then they ran to Silvermane and threw their arms around the unicorn.

"Thank you, girls," whispered

Silvermane.

At last it was time to
go. Queen Aurora waved
her horn like a magic
wand, and a cloud
of golden sparkles
shimmered in the
air. They swirled
around the girls
like a gust of snowflakes, faster and faster,
brighter and brighter, until the girls could
see nothing but golden light. And slowly,
their feet lifted off the ground …

As the light faded, Emily and Aisha found
themselves standing in the dark garden at

Enchanted Cottage. The night was calm and silent, and their tartan blanket was still spread out on the grass. Everything was just as it had been when they left.

Emily glanced up and felt a rush of relief to see that the sky was studded with stars.

"It's just as beautiful as the night sky in Enchanted Valley," sighed Aisha. "Well … almost!"

Then both girls gasped. Something had swished across the sky. A streak of gold, trailing glitter behind it.

"Was that a shooting star?" breathed Emily.

"It looked more like Lumi the Lightingale!" said Aisha.

The girls turned to each other in amazement, and grinned.

"When do you think Queen Aurora will call us back?" wondered Aisha.

"I don't know," said Emily. "But I can't wait!"

The End

Join Emily and Aisha
for another adventure in …

# Dreamspell's
# Special Wish
**Read on for a sneak peek!**

In her cosy bedroom, Aisha Khan and
her best friend, Emily Turner, were getting
ready for bed. Bright moonlight shone
through the small window under the thick
thatched roof of Enchanted Cottage,
and faraway stars twinkled like magic
lanterns.

"Today was so fun," Aisha sighed
happily. "I still can't believe you get to
stay for the whole week!"

"Me neither!" said Emily. "School
holidays are the best. What shall we do
tomorrow?"

"Hmmm," Aisha said. "You showed me how to make that brilliant baking soda volcano today, so tomorrow, maybe I could teach you how to play badminton?"

"Sounds great!" laughed Emily.

Read
## Dreamspell's Special Wish
to find out what adventures are in store
for Aisha and Emily!

# Also available

**Book Five:**

*Silvermane Saves the Stars*

**Book Six:**

*Dreamspell's Special Wish*

**Book Seven:**

*Slumbertail & the Sleep Pixies*

**Book Eight:**

*Brighteye & the Blue Moon*

# Look out for the next book!

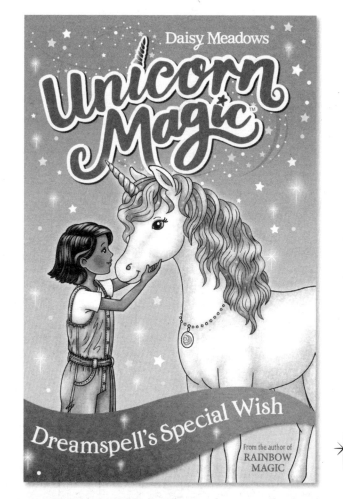

Daisy Meadows

Unicorn Magic™

Dreamspell's Special Wish

From the author of
RAINBOW
MAGIC

# Visit
# orchardseriesbooks.co.uk
## for

✳ fun activities ✳
✳ exclusive content ✳
✳ book extracts ✳

## There's something for everyone!

# Dreamspell's
# Special Wish

## Daisy Meadows

ORCHARD

# For Beatrice

# Special thanks to Adrian Bott

ORCHARD BOOKS

First published in Great Britain in 2020 by Hodder & Stoughton

3 5 7 9 10 8 6 4

Text copyright © 2020 Working Partners Limited
Illustrations © Orchard Books 2020
Series created by Working Partners Limited

A CIP catalogue record for this book is available from the British Library.

ISBN 978 1 40836 619 6

Printed and bound in Great Britain by Clays Ltd, Elcograf S.p.A.

The paper and board used in this book are made from wood from responsible sources.

Orchard Books
An imprint of Hachette Children's Group
Part of Hodder and Stoughton
Carmelite House
50 Victoria Embankment
London EC4Y 0DZ

An Hachette UK Company
www.hachette.co.uk
www.hachettechildrens.co.uk

# Contents

# Meet the Characters

Aisha and Emily are best friends from Spellford Village. Aisha loves sports, whilst Emily's favourite thing is science. But what both girls enjoy more than anything is visiting Enchanted Valley and helping their unicorn friends, who live there.

Silvermane

Silvermane and the other Night Sparkle Unicorns make sure night-time is magical. Silvermane's locket helps her take care of the stars.

Dreamspell's magic brings sweet dreams to all the creatures of Enchanted Valley. Without her magical powers, everyone will have nightmares!

Dreamspell

With the help of her magical friends and the power of her locket, Slumbertail makes sure everyone in Enchanted Valley has a peaceful night's sleep.

Slumbertail

Kindly Brighteye is in charge of the moon. The magic of her locket helps its beautiful light to shine each night.

Brighteye

Enchanted Cottage

Golden Palace

An Enchanted Valley lies a twinkle away,
Where beautiful unicorns live, laugh and play
You can visit the mermaids, or go for a ride,
So much fun to be had, but dangers can hide!

Your friends need your help – this is how you know:
A keyring lights up with a magical glow.
Whirled off like a dream, you won't want to leave.
Friendship forever, when you truly believe.

## Chapter One
# A Flight at Night

In her cosy bedroom, Aisha Khan and
her best friend, Emily Turner, were
getting ready for bed. Bright moonlight
shone through the small window under
the thick thatched roof of Enchanted
Cottage, and faraway stars twinkled like
magic lanterns.

"Today was so fun," Aisha sighed happily. "I still can't believe you get to stay for the whole week!"

"Me neither!" said Emily. "School holidays are the best. What shall we do tomorrow?"

"Hmmm," Aisha said. "You showed me how to make that brilliant baking soda volcano today, so tomorrow, maybe I could teach you how to play badminton?"

"Sounds great!" laughed Emily.

Their pyjamas were lovely and warm from the tumble dryer. Aisha closed the curtains and snuggled down in bed under her colourful patchwork quilt. Emily got into her blow-up bed on the floor.

Aisha's mum knocked and stuck her head in. "Teeth all brushed, you two?"

"Yes!" they said together.

"Faces washed?"

"Yes!"

"Good girls. Snuggle down, now. Goodnight! Sweet dreams!"

She switched off the light and closed the door.

A silver thread of moonlight shone in between the curtains.

"I hope we dream about Enchanted Valley," Emily whispered. Enchanted Valley was a secret magical world they were lucky enough to visit sometimes. Their unicorn friend Queen Aurora ruled kindly over all the creatures living there.

Aisha yawned. "Me too. Goodnight!"

"Goodnight."

A moment later, Emily sat up. "Aisha, where's that light coming from?"

Both girls looked around the room. Something on the bedside table was shining, making pretty, dancing shapes on the walls.

"It's our unicorn keyrings!" Aisha

whispered. Their treasured keyrings were little crystal unicorns, given to them by Queen Aurora.

"I bet Enchanted Valley needs our help!" Emily whispered back.

The girls knew all was not well in Enchanted Valley. The wicked unicorn Selena, who wanted to be queen, had

stolen four magical lockets from the
Night Sparkle Unicorns. Now Enchanted
Valley was stuck in an endless night!

Emily and Aisha had already helped
get the star unicorn Silvermane's locket
back, but there were still three more Night

Sparkle lockets to
find.

They both
scampered out of
bed and pulled on
their fuzzy animal
slippers – Aisha's
were bunnies, Emily's
pandas – and pressed
their keyrings
together.

*Whoosh!* Multicoloured sparkles swirled in the air as they were lifted gently off the ground, their hair floating around them.

As the sparkles faded away, their feet touched the ground again and they looked up in breathless excitement. Instead of Aisha's bedroom ceiling, the night sky of Enchanted Valley arched over them.

In front of them, Queen Aurora's golden palace glowed in the darkness, like a comforting light showing the way home. The eight turrets stood strong and proud, their spires reaching up to touch the blanket of stars.

Aisha and Emily walked towards the drawbridge over the bright blue moat

that surrounded the palace.

*Clip-clop* came the sound of hooves from up ahead. Queen Aurora came out to meet them, her glorious gold mane flowing behind her. Her body shimmered in all the changing colours of the dawn sun, and the silver crown shining on her brow was as delicate as morning dew. By her side walked the lilac unicorn, Dreamspell, who was in charge of sending lovely dreams to everyone.

"Queen Aurora! Dreamspell!" The girls gave them each a hug.

"Welcome back, girls!" Aurora bowed her head. "Thank you for coming so quickly."

"We always love coming here!" Emily

said. "But let me guess – Selena's been up to no good again?"

"I'm afraid so," Queen Aurora said. "She still has three of the lockets. It's very important that Dreamspell gets her locket back as soon as possible."

The girls remembered Dreamspell's special locket. It contained pictures of beautiful dreams. When they had first looked into it, they'd seen a birthday party, a sunny beach and a lovely picnic with friends.

"Oh dear, what's happened without the locket?" Emily asked.

Dreamspell said, "It might be easiest if I show you. Climb up on my back. I can fly you to where the trouble started."

She bent down, and Aisha and Emily climbed on. Aisha held on tightly to Dreamspell's shimmering lilac mane. Emily put her arms round Aisha's waist.

"Good luck," said Queen Aurora. "I shall stay and guard the palace, just in case Selena tries to take over."

Emily and Aisha waved goodbye as Dreamspell began to trot away.

"Hold on tight," Dreamspell said. "I'm a

fast flyer."

She galloped for a bit then leapt into the air as if she were jumping a gate. But instead of coming back down, she just kept going up and up!

They went flying like a comet over Enchanted Valley. Wind blew through the girls' hair. The girls could see the palace towers shining far below and the moat glistening blue like a sapphire necklace in

the starlight.

"Wow, you're the fastest unicorn we've ever ridden!" whooped Aisha.

"I LOVE flying," Dreamspell called back. "Hold on, let's do a loop-the-loop!"

The girls clung on tight as the lilac unicorn soared up and over. They were upside down for a moment, with the ground above their heads as they zoomed round the loop. The girls cheered.

"I wish I had time to show you more," said Dreamspell. "But we need to hurry."

Rolling green hills spread out in front of them like a rippling sea. Further on stood the towering trees of the forest, dark and mysterious. Once they reached the forest, Dreamspell began to glide back down to earth. She headed for a little grove among the trees, where a pink and white house stood. The walls bulged out like plump cushions and the roof sat on top like a funny little hat. A delicious smell like toasted buns came wafting up from a tiny chimney. Colourful windows shone with welcoming light.

"That house looks like it's made of marshmallows!" Emily said.

Dreamspell landed in front of the house. Aisha spotted a sign hanging beside the door, in the shape of a fluffy rabbit. "*The Pufflebunny Inn*," she read. "*The Cosiest Night's Sleep You'll Ever Have!*"

"Tonight was supposed to be Petey the Pufflebunny's grand opening," Dreamspell told them sadly as they slid off her back. "Everyone was looking forward to spending a lovely night here. And then ..."

Whimpering and sobbing sounds
floated out from inside the inn. From
time to time one of the lights in the
windows would go out, only to pop back
on again moments later.

From the sound of it, nobody was
getting any sleep at all!

"Oh dear," said Dreamspell. "It's getting
worse!"

## Chapter Two
# Blueberry Bursts

Inside the Pufflebunny Inn, a warm fire crackled in the hearth. Everywhere the girls looked, they saw soft, comfortable things. Mountains of pillows and cushions had been piled up invitingly in the corners. Fluffy blankets were draped everywhere, ready to snuggle under.

Delightful smells of roses, lavender and
hot chocolate wafted through the air.

Emily admired a velvety purple
armchair. "This is the cosiest place I've
ever seen!"

"Petey the Pufflebunny has the magical
power to make everything cosy and
comfortable," said Dreamspell.

Just then, a frightened squeak came
from upstairs.

"That guest doesn't sound very comfortable to me!" said Aisha.

She sprinted up the wide wooden stairs, with Emily and Dreamspell following close behind. They found themselves in a long corridor, full of worried guests milling about.

A little otter in pyjamas stood outside his room, crying.

Aisha knelt down next to him. "What's

the matter?" she asked gently.

"I want to go home," sobbed the otter. "I had a bad dream. A monster was chasing me!"

"It was only a dream," Aisha said soothingly, giving him a hug. "Everything's all right now."

Then Emily noticed that further down the corridor, there were more guests looking just as upset. She spotted a grumpy badger in a night mask, a family of pixies who were all shivering in fear, and a tiny dormouse in a pink nightie.

"What a horrid dream I just had!" the dormouse told Emily. "I dreamed it was raining day and night, and my house got washed away!"

"I dreamed I was all alone in a scary forest," said one of the pixies, quivering.

"Is everyone having bad dreams?" Emily asked.

"Indeed we are," the badger said gruffly. "Nobody's getting a wink of sleep."

Dreamspell hung her head sadly. "I'm supposed to keep bad dreams away," she said. "But I can't without my locket. Poor Petey's opening night is ruined. I feel so helpless."

"It's not your fault," Emily cried. "It's that nasty Selena!"

"We're going to get that locket back, right away!" Aisha said.

But just then, a big, fluffy pale brown bunny came scurrying around the corner.

He looked just like one of Aisha's bunny
slippers, except that he was wearing a
fluffy dressing gown and carrying a silver
tray.

"Time for some sweet treats before
bed. Help yourselves!" the bunny called.
"Plenty of nibbles to go around."

On the tray were heaps of treats: iced

pastries and gumdrops, cherry pies and chocolate buttons, marshmallow puffs and tiny, delicate cakes.

"Oho," said the bunny as he spotted Aisha. "You must be Aisha and Emily! My name is Petey. I'm so glad you've dropped by. Hello, Dreamspell! Please, sit down."

Aisha and Emily sat on two gigantic gold cushions so soft they sank into them.

"I'm sorry your grand opening isn't going well," Aisha said.

Petey looked confused. "Not going well? Everything's going exactly as planned!"

Emily looked at the miserable guests and whispered to Aisha, "It doesn't look like it to me."

"It's nice of you to come, but you needn't have," Petey went on. "A nice sweet treat will sort out all those bad dreams, I'm sure of it."

Aisha stood up. "Well I hope you're right, but in the meantime, we're going to do our best to find Dreamspell's locket!"

Petey hopped up and down, holding out his tray. "Oh, do have a snack before you go. Please? I worked so hard baking them."

Aisha and Emily weren't very hungry, but they didn't want to be rude to the poor pufflebunny. They each took a bright blue gumdrop in a little nest of spun sugar. Aisha gave one to Dreamspell as well.

Petey beamed. "Blueberry Bursts! Excellent choice."

The gumdrops were unbelievably delicious. First there was the crunch of the spun sugar, then the gumdrop burst in their mouths with a juicy pop that made their tongues all tingly.

A moment later, Emily felt a drowsy, dreamy feeling washing over her. She closed her eyes happily and sank back into her cushion. She yawned and stretched. "I think I'll just rest my eyes for a moment before we go."

Dreamspell curled up on a soft rug. "It's funny. Flying doesn't usually tire me out like this ..." Next moment, she started to snore.

Aisha's eyelids felt heavy. "No, wake up, guys," she mumbled. "Must … find … locket …"

It was no good. She curled up against Dreamspell's warm flank, laid her cheek against her smooth lilac coat, and fell fast asleep.

The girls woke up, shivering in the cold. The warm, cosy Pufflebunny Inn had vanished. Now they were in a dark stone room. There were rusty bars in the windows, covered with tangled, creeping vines. Murky moonlight shone in.

The wall they were leaning on was filthy with dust and old webs. Aisha tried to pull herself away, but iron chains held her fast.

Her heart sank even more when she saw Dreamspell chained to the opposite wall. Petey the Pufflebunny was sitting next to her.

"Where are we? What happened to the inn?" Emily cried out.

Petey blinked. "Hello! Who are you two? Dreamspell, what are you doing here?"

Aisha felt very confused. "It's us, Petey! We were all at your inn a moment ago, remember?"

"But how can that be?" Petey frowned. "I've been locked up here for three days."

"But that's impossible!" Emily protested.

"It's true," insisted Petey. "I was making the beds, getting ready for my first guests, when Hettie the Hedgehog offered me a Blueberry Burst. I must have fallen asleep, because the next thing I knew, I woke up here. That was three days ago."

"Where is here?" Dreamspell wondered. "Where are we?"

The girls looked around. Even though it was a horrible place, something about the dingy room looked familiar …

"We've been here before," Aisha said.

"Yes, I remember now! This is the tower

where Selena kept Wintertail locked up, isn't it?"

With a shiver, Emily remembered the time Selena had kidnapped the Winter Festival unicorn, Wintertail, and stolen all three of her lockets. Snowstar, Wintertail's foal, had helped them get the lockets back and rescue her mother.

Emily gasped. "But that means … we're

in Selena's castle! We must have been brought here in our sleep."

"We need to find a way out!" Aisha added.

Emily desperately looked around for some way out of the tower. But all she saw were dangling cobwebs drooping down, ready to drop into her lap, and spooky flickering candles on the wall. Outside, the wind howled like a lonely ghost.

She shuddered. Somehow, the tower had become even scarier than before!

Suddenly, thunder boomed above. Lightning flickered through the narrow tower windows. The door flew open and in came Selena!

Her silver body
gleamed in the
candlelight, and
her mane and tail
were the dim blue
of midnight mists.
On her head – to
Aisha and Emily's
horror – was

Queen Aurora's crown!

"Comfortable?" Selena laughed.

"Not really," Emily said, rattling her
chains.

Selena snorted. "Too bad. Get used to it!
You're my prisoners now. And I have my
trusty friend here to thank for it."

A big pale brown rabbit in a dressing

gown came hopping up to her side. Emily and Aisha stared. He looked exactly like Petey, who was sitting opposite them!

"Good heavens," Petey exclaimed. "It's like looking in a mirror."

"You didn't tell us you had a twin brother," Emily said.

Petey looked very confused. "I don't!"

Emily and Aisha looked at each other in total confusion. *What's going on?*

## Chapter Three
# Captured!

Aisha frowned at the new pufflebunny.
"Who are you?"

Selena's pufflebunny opened his mouth
and screeched. Aisha and Emily covered
their ears.

With a dark *whoooosh* of magic, the
bunny vanished. In its place appeared

Screech the
owl, flapping
his wings and
cackling!
Screech
was Selena's
latest servant. He had helped her steal the
Night Sparkle lockets in the first place.
He had the power to change shape to
look like anything he wanted.

"Now I understand! You used your
magic to look like Petey," Emily said. "We
thought we'd met the real pufflebunny,
but he was locked up here all along!"

Screech let out a hooty laugh. "Haha,
that's right! Those Blueberry Bursts I
worked so hard to make were really

Snoozy Chews!"

"No wonder we all fell asleep," Aisha groaned.

Selena pranced up and down. "Oh, clever, clever me. I've finally done it. I snatched the crown right off Aurora's silly head! Now you'll be trapped for ever while I rule over Enchanted Valley!"

"Aurora's the queen, not you!" Aisha shouted.

"Yeah!" Emily yelled. "And she always will be!"

"Those days are over!" Selena stamped her hoof on the floor. "I'm queen now. I've hidden Dreamspell's locket where nobody will ever find it. Aurora will never rule over this valley or see her precious

friends ever again. And there's nothing
you pesky little girls can do!"

Selena stomped out of the room. The
door slammed shut. They all heard the
clunk of a key turning.

"She's locked us in!" Petey wailed.

"It's going to be OK," Emily promised
him.

"We need to get out of here," Aisha said.
"But how?"

The room went quiet. The only sound
was the moaning of the wind outside.

"I wish we could change our shape,
like Screech," said Emily. "I'd turn into
a mouse and slip out of these horrible
chains."

"You poor girls look so uncomfortable

having to sit on the cold, hard floor!
I can't bear it," said Petey miserably.
"Would you like me to conjure up some
cushions for you?"

Aisha gasped. "Did you say conjure?"

"All pufflebunnies have the magical
power to make other people comfortable,"
Dreamspell reminded her.

"Magical, eh?" said Emily thoughtfully.
"I'm sure I'd be a lot more comfortable if
these chains were off. Do you think you
could fix them with your magic, Petey?"

"Oh, why didn't I think of that? Silly
old me!" cried Petey.

Petey puffed his cheeks and blew,
"Huffity puff!" like he was blowing a
dandelion clock. Sparkles of magic flew

from his mouth.

Aisha and Emily held up their hands. As the sparkles touched the chains, the chains changed into elastic hair scrunchies! The girls pulled them off easily.

The magic sparkles went on dancing around the room, changing whatever they touched. The rusty bars and tangly vines in the window disappeared and became pretty curtains, swaying in the breeze. The hard, stone floor was covered by a lovely patterned rug. The ragged cobwebs turned to fluttering butterflies, and the dangling chains were silky tassels.

"Hooray!" the girls cheered together. "We're free!"

Petey looked a little happier. "I'm afraid

we're not quite free yet. I can't unlock the door," he said.

"We'll just have to climb out of the window, then!" Aisha said.

They all gathered at the window and looked down. Far below the window lay jagged rocks and thorny bushes.

Emily gave a little gulp. "I forgot how high up we were."

Dreamspell laughed. "Have you forgotten how much I love to fly?"

Everyone excitedly climbed up on to Dreamspell's back. Petey sat in Aisha's lap.

Dreamspell stepped away from the window and took a deep breath. She rose a few centimetres off the ground … and sank right back down again. She took a deep breath then strained and tried again.

"Are you all right, Dreamspell?" Aisha asked.

"What's wrong?" said Emily.

"My worst nightmare's coming true," Dreamspell whispered. "I can't fly!"

## Chapter Four
# Comfy Jumps

Dreamspell's nostrils flared and her eyes were round with fright. "Why can't I fly?" she whimpered.

Aisha stroked Dreamspell's soft mane. "Don't worry," she said soothingly. "We'll figure it out."

"Yes, we will!" Emily said firmly. "But

right now we're going to have to think of another way out."

She slid off Dreamspell's back and peered down from the window. Then a brilliant idea popped into her head. "Hey, there are some great big thorny bramble bushes down there. They look really uncomfortable."

"Uncomfortable?" Petey squeaked. He hid his face in his paws. "Oh dear!"

"No, it's a good thing, Petey," Emily said. "Since they're so uncomfortable, perhaps you could turn those prickly bushes into big comfy pillows? Then we can jump down on to them!"

Petey's eyes grew wide. "Oh I see!" he cried. "In that case … huffity puff!"

And he blew!

More pufflebunny magic sparkles came shooting out, drifting down on to the bushes below like snowflakes. The bushes vanished, and a pile of plump white pillows popped up in their place.

"Well done!" The girls clapped.

They all gathered at the window. Aisha and Emily glanced nervously at each other.

"I'll go first," Aisha said, bravely.

She stepped up on to the window ledge and looked down. The pillows looked very small and far away.

"Here we go," she said nervously. "One, two, three …"

Aisha jumped. Wind whistled through

her hair as she fell. Then, with a *whoomph* like a duvet settling on a freshly made bed, she landed in the pillows.

"Phew," she gasped. "I'm fine, everyone! Come on!"

One by one, they all landed in the pillows and climbed out of the pile, laughing with relief.

The landscape was misty

and bleak, with withered grass all around, bare and crooked trees, twisty overgrown paths, and marshes bubbling in the distance.

Aisha and Emily looked up at the tower window high above their heads and grinned. "We did it!" cried Aisha.

"Now to find the locket!" Emily added.

Just then, something flew out of the window and zoomed down towards them. Something with big, angry, yellow eyes.

*Screech!*

"Get back in your cell, you miserable bunch!" he shouted.

"No!" said Petey, putting his paws on his hips and glaring.

"I'm telling Selena!" squawked Screech. "Then you'll be sorry!"

"No, we must stop him!" Emily yelled.

They all ran, galloped and hopped after Screech. He flapped away, hooting with laughter.

Aisha was a fast runner, but not fast enough. Every time she almost caught him, Screech darted out of the way. "Ha ha!" he teased. "Too slow!"

"I wish we had a net to throw over him," Aisha panted.

Petey took off his dressing gown and passed it to Aisha. "Will this do?"

"That's perfect!" Aisha said. "Thanks, Petey!"

The next time Screech swooped low,

she flung the robe over him. "Mmmf!"
he squeaked, trying to wriggle away,
but the robe was caught on some of the
remaining thorns. The more Screech tried
to break free, the more tangled up he got!

"Let me out!" hooted the struggling
lump.

Emily said, "Tell us where Dreamspell's
locket is and we'll let you go."

"Selena kept it with her," came the
muffled voice. "That means you'll never,
ever get it back. Queen Aurora will be a
prisoner at the Golden Palace for ever!"

Emily turned pale.

"Aurora is a prisoner?" Aisha gasped.

"That's right! Hoo hoo hoo!"

"My locket will have to wait," said

Dreamspell. "The queen is much more important. We must free her, right away!"

Petey bounded off across the withered grass. "This way to the palace. Follow me!"

They followed Petey up the slope of a hill. It was hard going. The grass was thick and tangled.

When they reached the top of the hill, they stopped and stared. Enchanted Valley stretched into the distance, lit by murky green starlight. But it was far from the happy place they knew. Everything had changed.

The orchards where apples had grown and birds had sung were now groves of silent, dead trees. The paths between the

meadows were overgrown and littered
with sharp stones. A few sad pixies tried
to gather wilted flowers in fields where
the ground was dry and patchy.

Aisha gasped. "Is this even Enchanted
Valley any more?"

"Cursed Valley is more like it!" Emily
said with a shiver.

"I can't understand any of this," Emily
frowned. "Selena must have done it, but
how?"

"She must be using Dreamspell's locket," Aisha replied.

"But my locket only has power over dreams, not the fields or the orchards," said Dreamspell.

"Maybe it's because she's made herself queen then?" said Emily in a small voice.

There was nothing for it but to keep going. The further they walked, the darker and more frightening their journey became. Twisted vines had grown over almost everything, and spindly-legged spiders with many shining eyes wove gloomy grey webs across their path. The friends picked their way through squelchy bogs and tangled thickets. Emily and Aisha held hands as they went.

Aisha groaned as her foot sank into yet another muddy patch. "This is going to take for ever!"

Just then, they smelled smoke, and a high-pitched shriek cut through the air. It was hard to see clearly in the darkness of the night, but they could just make out a row of lit-up windows moving steadily along.

A rickety old train was coming their way!

"It might be going to the palace," said Emily.

"If it will get us there quicker, we have to take it," said Aisha. "We must rescue Queen Aurora!"

# Chapter Five
# Out of Puff

"Look, there's a station over there," said Aisha, pointing. "Quick, let's run and catch the train!"

The four friends scrambled towards the run-down old train station. It was the most miserable thing they had ever seen in Enchanted Valley, after Selena's

castle. Half the tiles had fallen off the roof and long grass was growing up between the tracks. There was a cafe that might have been pretty once, but now it was all boarded up.

Two shabby little trains stood waiting at the station, billowing thick black smoke.

A crow in a scruffy, once official-looking blue cap wandered over.

He glanced warily at the friends. "Can

I help you?"

"We need to get
to the palace right
away," Emily said. "Can we
get there on one of these
trains?"

The crow chuckled.
"Either one will get you there," he said.
"One of the trains goes super-duper fast
but the other one goes very slowly."

"We'd like the fast one, please!" said
Aisha.

"Oh, you would, would you?" The
crow folded his wings. "We don't let just
anyone ride the fast train. You've got to
solve a riddle first – a tough one."

"I can do this," Emily whispered to

Aisha. Emily loved figuring out puzzles and riddles. After all, science was all about finding answers! She turned to the crow. "I'm ready."

"Right, then," said the crow. "A train leaves from Stinky Swamp, heading towards Tangle Town at one hundred kilometres per hour. Three hours later, a train leaves Tangle Town heading towards Stinky Swamp at two hundred kilometres per hour. If there are exactly two thousand kilometres between Stinky Swamp and Tangle Town, which train will be closer to Stinky Swamp when they meet?"

Emily frowned. Aisha could see her lips moving as she tried to figure it out.

"All the numbers are swirling around in my head," Emily moaned. "I can't work out the answer!"

Aisha squeezed her friend's hand. "You can do this, Emily. You're brilliant at puzzles."

"Not this one!" Emily sighed. "I'm sorry, Aisha. I can't even guess!"

"Don't feel bad," Aisha said. "I haven't got a clue either."

"Neither do I," said Dreamspell.

Petey's ears drooped. "Sorry," he said.

The crow let out a hoarse laugh.

"You fools! When the trains meet, they're at exactly the same place! So neither one is closer to Stinky Swamp!"

"Argh!" Emily put her head in her hands. "It's obvious. I feel so silly!"

"Me too," groaned Aisha. "It'll take ages to get to the palace now."

Dreamspell hung her head. "If only I could still fly."

They climbed on board the slow train. Petey conjured up some pillows and blankets to make the dingy seats more comfortable.

A whistle blew and the train lurched and puffed slowly along the track like an old, out-of-shape dragon going for a jog.

There was nothing to do but stare out

of the windows. The train trundled past empty houses with broken windows, where the wind made spooky noises as it howled over the chimney pots. It swayed its way past overgrown swamps, where hunched-over trees trailed vines in their path and clouds of smelly green gas hovered above bubbling mud.

Emily made a face. "This train may be slow, but I'm glad I don't have to walk through that!"

On and on chugged the lumbering train. Then, at long last, it came to a halt.

"Finally!" Aisha sprang to her feet. She threw open the door and bounded out on to the platform. The others followed.

"Oh no!" Dreamspell cried.

Aurora's lovely home looked like a crumbling old ruin. The golden rooftops were falling in, the walls were cracked and toppling and nasty green gunge was dribbling down the towers!

"We have to get inside and help Aurora," said Emily.

"But how?" Petey said. "Look. The drawbridge is up."

They all walked over to the stone ledge where the drawbridge usually lay. Now it was pulled upright by stout iron chains on the other side of the water. Normally, the moat was sparkling and crystal clear, but now it was muddy and murky.

"There's only one thing for it," Aisha said bravely. "I'll swim across the moat, climb up and lower the drawbridge for you all to cross."

Dreamspell nuzzled her. "Please be careful."

Aisha stroked Dreamspell's nose gently. "I'll be fine. I'm a strong swimmer."

She took off her bunny slippers and left them with Petey. Then she took a deep breath, swung her arms back and dived.

As soon as she hit the freezing cold
water, it started to churn and rush, like a
big river. Aisha kicked her legs and took
good strong strokes.

"Come on, Aisha!" Emily yelled
from the side. "You can do
it!"

Aisha swam as
hard as she
could,

but the current was growing stronger and stronger. The water buffeted her like a raging giant.

A wave washed over her head. Aisha spluttered, gasped and fought on. She had to keep going, but no matter how hard she kicked, she wasn't getting anywhere. She felt her arms and legs getting tired and before she knew it, she was being swept away! "Help!" she shouted.

## Chapter Six
# Friendship to the Rescue

Emily saw her friend being washed away
and cried out in horror. "We have to save
Aisha!"

Petey hopped to the edge of the moat
and stretched his little paw out as far as
he could reach. "It's no good, Emily. She's
too far away!"

"If only I could fly!" Dreamspell wailed.

"I'm going in after her," Emily said boldly.

She was just pulling off her panda slippers, ready to dive in, when she saw the flash of a sparkling green tail gliding through the dark water. "It's Pearl!" Emily exclaimed.

Their mermaid friend was by Aisha's side like a shot. "Don't worry, Aisha. I've got you!"

She wrapped her arms around Aisha and towed her through the churning water, over to the far side of the moat.

Emily, Dreamspell and Petey all burst out cheering!

Aisha gave Pearl a tight hug. "Thanks

for helping
me, Pearl.
I don't
understand
what happened to the moat. How could
still water become so choppy and wild?"

"It's whatever horrible magic has settled
in Enchanted Valley," Pearl said, shivering.

"Selena's behind it," Aisha said. "She's
taken Aurora prisoner."

Pearl gasped. "How did she do it?"

"We don't know," said Aisha. She
climbed out, dripping wet and shivering,
found the drawbridge lever and pulled
it. With a loud rattle and bang, the
drawbridge crashed down. Emily,
Dreamspell and Petey came running over.

Emily hugged Aisha. "I was so worried!"

"Uncomfortable, my dear? We can't have that!" said Petey. Quick as a *huffity puff*, Aisha's hair was dry and her pyjamas were soft and warm again. Petey gave her back her slippers.

"Thank you!" Aisha sighed, putting them on. "That's much better."

"Now we'll find Queen Aurora and set her free," said Emily. "Then she'll put everything right again."

"Please hurry," begged Pearl. "Even I can't swim in water as rough as this for much longer. Good luck!"

She waved from the moat as the four friends headed into the creepy palace.

Their
footsteps
echoed in the
huge, draughty
entrance hall.

"Where do
you think
Queen Aurora might be?" asked Emily,
peering around.

"I don't know," said Dreamspell, "but
Selena's all over the place. Look!"

She pointed to the wall with her horn.
From floor to ceiling, portraits of Selena
were on display. Selena sitting in a throne,
Selena lounging on a cushion, Selena
admiring herself in a mirror, portraits in
square frames, round frames, oval frames,

large and small … they went on and on
as far as the eye could see.

Aisha felt uneasy under the gaze of a
thousand painted Selenas. One of the
paintings showed Selena sticking out her
tongue, and Emily bravely stuck hers out
right back at it.

They crept on, making as little noise as

they could. Thankfully, the dust that had settled like a grey carpet muffled their footsteps.

"There're spiderwebs everywhere," Emily whispered and pointed at the ragged webs hanging down in every corner.

"It looks like nobody's cleaned this place in about a million years," muttered Petey.

"But these halls were gleaming like gold yesterday." Dreamspell sighed. "How did things go so wrong, so fast? It must be some truly powerful magic."

Aisha turned a corner and found her way was blocked by two tall glass doors, covered in dust. She tried to open them, but they were locked.

Through the misty glass she could make out the hallway beyond, where Queen Aurora kept all the paintings of the children who had visited Enchanted Valley over the years. The frames were still hanging there, but they were all empty.

And in the far corner sat Queen Aurora herself! But she was staring down at the floor, not moving at all. She looked lonely and sad, as if all hope had deserted her.

"Queen Aurora!" cried Aisha and Emily. They banged on the glass.

Aurora didn't move. It was as if she hadn't heard.

"Your friends are here to save you!" Aisha called as loud as she could.

Queen Aurora didn't even look up. "This is just another one of your cruel tricks, Selena," she said in a voice heavy with sorrow. "I have no friends."

"What?" Aisha gasped. "No friends? Why on earth would she say that?"

Emily pounded on the glass. "We're your friends!" she shouted.

"I don't believe you," Queen Aurora said sadly.

"We're going to have to get in there and prove it," Aisha said. "Can anyone see a key?"

It took only seconds of looking around before Petey shouted, "There!" He pointed to where the key was sitting. "Oh …" It was protected by a fat, furry spider.

"I'll get it," Emily said, bravely. "Selena must have thought spiders would scare us off, but they're actually really interesting, you know." She 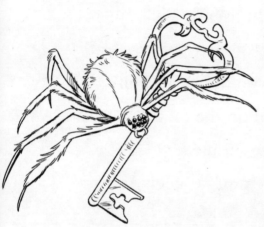 reached out and lifted the spider with one hand, grabbing the key with the other. The spider squirmed and Emily couldn't help shuddering a little as she put it down.

"Well done, Emily!" said Aisha. "Rather you than me."

She quickly slipped the key into the lock and turned it. Everyone breathed a sigh of relief as the door swung open.

Aisha and Emily charged down the hall towards Queen Aurora, who looked up in confusion. They threw their arms around Aurora's neck and hung on like they would never let go.

"It's going to be OK," Aisha said. "We're here now."

Aurora's eyes grew brighter. "Aisha? Emily? Is it really you?"

"Of course!" Emily laughed.

Aurora's whole face lit up. "Oh, it's so good to see you! Selena told me all my friends had gone away and left me. She said I'd be alone for ever and ever."

"We'd never leave you alone," Aisha promised.

"And we'll always come to help,

whenever you need us," Emily added.

Aurora closed her eyes and laid her head in Aisha's lap. "Thank you, girls," she murmured. "You're the best friends I could ask for."

## Chapter Seven
# What a Nightmare!

The girls were so relieved to see Queen Aurora looking happy again. Of all the horrible sights they'd seen in Enchanted Valley today, a lonely and heartbroken Aurora was the worst.

Dreamspell ran up to join them. "What happened to you, Queen Aurora?"

Aurora blinked in confusion. "Someone sent me a lovely package of Blueberry Bursts, so I ate some for a bedtime snack. Next thing I knew, I woke up here, and all my friends were gone. I couldn't even remember their faces. Can you imagine? A friendship unicorn with no friends!"

"Poor Aurora!" Aisha sighed.

"When I saw you, it was like waking from a terrible dream," Aurora said.

Aurora's words echoed in Emily's mind. *Like waking from a dream …*

"Of course!" Emily shouted. "The answer's been staring us in the face this whole time!"

"What do you mean?" Dreamspell said.

"Don't you see?" Emily began to pace

back and forth excitedly. "Everything that's happened since we woke up in that tower has been just like a bad dream! I'm brilliant at puzzles, but I couldn't figure out the train riddle."

"Yes! I love swimming, but I couldn't swim across the moat," Aisha said. "Aurora lost all her friends …"

"… and I couldn't fly!" cried Dreamspell. "You know how much I love flying."

"Everywhere I look I see uncomfortable things," Petey said with a shudder. "Sharp things, stony things … it's a pufflebunny's nightmare!"

"Exactly." Emily grinned. "A nightmare. We've all come face to face with our own

worst fears!
And all
the trouble
started
when we fell
asleep."

Aisha's mouth made an O. "But if we're all in a nightmare, that would mean …"

"We're all still asleep!" finished Emily.

"So none of this is real?" Aurora looked around her ruined palace. "I do hope that's the answer!"

Emily clapped her hands briskly. "OK, Aisha, let's put our theory to the test! How can we tell if this is all a dream?"

Aisha thought hard. "Maybe we could try to run away from something?" she

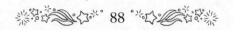

suggested. "Whenever something is chasing me in a bad dream and I try to run away, I can't get anywhere."

Emily nodded and bent down. "Petey, can you chase us, please?"

"I'm not very scary, but I'll do my best," Petey said. He held up his little paws, went "Rarr!" and chased after Aisha and Emily.

Both the girls tried to run away. Sure enough, it was like trying to run through thick glue. Their legs moved in slow motion.

"That answers that!" Emily said.

"Good thinking," said Aisha. "The only question now is, how are we all dreaming the same thing?"

"Hoo, hoo, hoo!" A laugh burst out from above them. They looked up to see Screech circling overhead. "You're so slow! You're all trapped in the same dream, of course!"

"But whose mind could be dreaming such horrible things?" asked Dreamspell.

"Selena's!" Emily burst out. "Why else would there be pictures and statues of Selena all over the place? This may be a bad dream for all of us, but for Selena it's the best dream ever!"

"That means Selena is asleep

somewhere too," Aisha added.

"With my locket!" said Dreamspell.

Petey rubbed his eyes. "This is all very confusing, I must say. If this is just a dream and we're all asleep, then where are we really?"

"It doesn't matter," Screech squawked. "Because you're never waking up!"

"We're in the same place we were when we fell asleep in the first place," Emily declared triumphantly, ignoring the owl. "The Pufflebunny Inn!"

It made Aisha smile to think they were really in that lovely, snuggly warm place and not in the crumbling palace. "Unless we get Dreamspell's locket back, the bad dreams will keep coming," she said. "So the first thing we need to do is wake up. Then we find Selena!"

"Let's pinch each other," Emily suggested. She saw the frightened look on Petey's face and added, "Not too hard, though. Just enough to wake us up."

"No, don't try that!" Screech yelled, swooping at them.

"Very well," Petey said, trying to sound brave. "Emily, Aisha, you pinch everyone, and then each other."

They all moved into their places.

"Stop it! Stop it!" Screech wailed.

"Will this work?" Petey asked nervously.

"Only one way to find out," Aisha said. "Here we go …"

## Chapter Eight
# Sweet Dreams

With a sudden start and a gasp, Aisha
woke up.

She sat bolt upright and looked around.
Thank goodness! They were back in the
cosy corridors of the Pufflebunny Inn.

Emily sat up next to her. Dreamspell
blinked sleepily and shook her tangled

mane out of her eyes. "What a relief,"
she sighed. "I never want to be stuck in a
dream that bad ever again."

Emily cupped her hand to her ear.
"Listen!"

From somewhere nearby came a dull
*thump thump thump*.

"Let's go and see what it is," said Emily.

They ran towards the sound. Soon
they found a little double door with a
sign reading BROOM CUPBOARD.
Someone had jammed a broom through
the door handles.

*Thump!* The doors shook.

Emily quickly pulled the broom out
and the doors burst open. There, gasping,
with messy fur and a mop bucket stuck

on his foot, was Petey the Pufflebunny!

Petey looked very upset. "After Selena and Screech put me to sleep, they must have stuffed me in here like an old rag!"

The girls helped Petey out, got the bucket off his foot and gave him a cuddle.

Just then, a strange sound came from upstairs. It was a sort of rattling, rumbling, gurgling sound, a bit like a cement mixer full of porridge.

Aisha froze. "What's that?"

"Let's find out," replied Emily.

Slowly, quietly, they climbed the twisting, turning stairs. The peculiar rumbling sound grew louder and louder the higher they climbed.

"It's coming from the master bedroom," Petey whispered. "The most comfortable room in my whole inn!"

Aisha gently pushed open the door.

There, tucked up in an enormous four-poster bed, was Selena. She was fast asleep, and snoring – that's what the noise was! Screech sat on the end of the bed, wearing a long white nightcap with a bobble on it. He was asleep too, muttering and moving his wings restlessly.

Selena rolled over. Her pyjamas had spiders on them, with big, happy smiles. She was holding on tightly to an old, scruffy, custard-coloured teddy bear with one button eye. Something was twinkling from around its neck.

Aisha moved closer to get a better look.

The teddy bear was wearing Dreamspell's locket! Aisha could make out a crescent moon shining inside it. As

she watched, the
moon changed to
a huge bowl of
ice cream, then to
a toy shop, then
a patterned rug
covered in sleepy kittens.

"We've got to get that locket!" Aisha
whispered.

"We can't just grab it," said Emily.
"She'll wake up."

Aisha tried gently pulling the teddy
away, but Selena mumbled in her sleep
and wrapped her front legs around it even
more tightly.

"Perhaps I could take the bear's place,"
suggested Petey.

"Are you sure?" Aisha said. "I think it might be pretty … uncomfortable."

Petey looked determined and nodded, his ears flapping. "We have to get the locket back, whatever it takes!"

"Good luck!" Aisha whispered.

Petey hopped up on to the bed. He slowly nuzzled his way up beside Selena, pushing the bear out of the way. She mumbled again and squeezed him tight. Petey gave the girls a helpless look.

Aisha quickly snatched up the bear. She took off the locket and slipped it over Dreamspell's neck.

"Hurrah!" Petey squeaked.

"Mmm?" Selena stirred.

She looked dozily at the pufflebunny

cowering beside her and her eyes flew wide open. "What? You're not my teddy! Where's Mr Snuggy-Wugs?!"

At the sound of her shrieks, Screech suddenly woke up. The cap flew off his head. "Hoo! Hoo!" he yelled, beating his wings wildly. "Alarm! Intruders! Wake up, Selena!"

"Oh, be quiet, you useless bag of feathers," Selena snapped. "You're too late!"

She leapt out of bed and snarled at the girls. "How dare you take that locket from me? I was queen! How dare you ruin my lovely dream!"

"And that's all it'll ever be," Aisha said. "A dream."

"So long as we're around, it'll never come true," added Emily.

"I wouldn't be too sure about that," Selena said. "Don't forget, I still have two of the Night Sparkle lockets left. I'll be back, you meddlesome pests! Unpleasant dreams!"

She let out a wild laugh. Lightning

crackled through the air and a boom of thunder shook the inn to its rafters. The window blew open, and Selena and Screech flew out into the night.

The friends all walked back downstairs to find all the frightened little creatures back out in the corridor.

"Good news, everyone," Emily called. "Dreamspell has her locket back!"

All the creatures burst out cheering.

The girls turned to Petey.

"What do you say we restart your opening night?" Aisha asked him.

Petey hopped up and down with excitement. "What an excellent idea! Hot chocolates all round!"

"And then you will all have the sweetest

dreams you've ever had," Dreamspell
promised.

Everyone cheered again.

The girls stayed long enough to enjoy
a hot chocolate with their friends. Then,
as all the guests started to drift towards
their comfy bedrooms, they said goodbye

to Petey. Dreamspell flew them back to Queen Aurora's palace.

Queen Aurora came out to meet them. "It was so nice to wake up back in my lovely palace, with all my good friends still here," she said. "Thank you for helping us once more!"

Dreamspell smiled. "I can't wait to conjure up sweet dreams for everyone."

"You girls were very brave to stand up to Selena like that," added Queen Aurora.

"It wasn't just us," Aisha said. "We couldn't have done it without Pearl, Petey, and Dreamspell's help."

Emily agreed. "That's what makes dreams come true. Friends working together as a team."

Aisha yawned, and Emily did too.

Queen Aurora laughed. "Perhaps the two of you need some proper sleep."

"Good idea!" Emily said.

"I'm ready to go home and go to bed," Aisha agreed.

They walked to the top of a grassy green hill. "We'll be back to find the other Night Sparkle lockets!" Aisha called. "We promise!'

They hugged Aurora goodbye.

Aurora's horn began to glow bright as a lantern. Shining sparkles

appeared, swirling around Aisha and Emily. They rose even higher into the air than they had flown on Dreamspell's back.

Then, quick as a candle flicker, they felt themselves come back down into Aisha's room. All the familiar things of Enchanted Cottage were around them once more.

Aisha looked at her clock. No time at all had passed while they had been away.

She yawned and stretched. "I'm worn out after all those adventures!"

"Me too," Emily said. Then she added with a giggle, "But it's not the Snoozy Chews this time!"

They snuggled down under their covers and closed their eyes, each of

them hoping they would dream about
Enchanted Valley and all their wonderful
friends.

The End

Join Emily and Aisha
for another adventure in ...

# Slumbertail and the
# Sleep Pixies
Read on for a sneak peek!

"Aisha?" whispered Emily Turner. "Are
you awake?"

The duvet on the bed next to Emily's
shifted, and her best friend Aisha Khan's
face appeared. By the moonlight shining
faintly through the curtains, Emily could
see her grin.

"I've been trying to keep my eyes
closed," Aisha whispered back. "But then
I start thinking about unicorns, and I'm
wide awake again!"

Emily giggled. "Me too!" The two girls
were having a week-long sleepover at

Enchanted Cottage, where Aisha lived with her parents. They were in Aisha's bedroom, each snuggled under a cosy duvet.

"I tried counting sheep, but that didn't work," Emily said. "So then I tried counting unicorns. But that just made me wonder what Queen Aurora was doing!"

Read
# Slumbertail and the Sleep Pixies
### to find out what adventures are in store for Aisha and Emily!

# Also available

**Book Five:**

Silvermane Saves the Stars

**Book Six:**

Dreamspell's Special Wish

**Book Seven:**

Slumbertail & the Sleep Pixies

**Book Eight:**

Brighteye & the Blue Moon

## Look out for the next book!

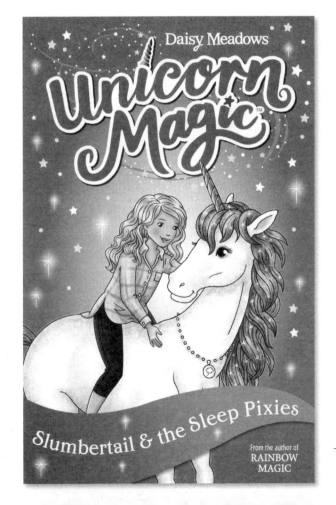

Daisy Meadows

Unicorn Magic™

Slumbertail & the Sleep Pixies

From the author of
RAINBOW
MAGIC

# Visit
# orchardseriesbooks.co.uk
## for

✳ fun activities ✳
✳ exclusive content ✳
✳ book extracts ✳

# There's something for everyone!

# Slumbertail
# and the Sleep Pixies

### Daisy Meadows

ORCHARD

# For lovely Lily Banks

# Special thanks to Elizabeth Galloway

ORCHARD BOOKS

First published in Great Britain in 2020 by Hodder & Stoughton

3 5 7 9 10 8 6 4 2

Text copyright © 2020 Working Partners Limited
Illustrations © Orchard Books 2020
Series created by Working Partners Limited

A CIP catalogue record for this book is available from the British Library.

ISBN 978 1 40836 622 6

Printed and bound in Great Britain by Clays Ltd, Elcograf S.p.A.

The paper and board used in this book are made from wood from responsible sources.

Orchard Books
An imprint of Hachette Children's Group
Part of Hodder and Stoughton
Carmelite House
50 Victoria Embankment
London EC4Y 0DZ

An Hachette UK Company
www.hachette.co.uk
www.hachettechildrens.co.uk

Contents

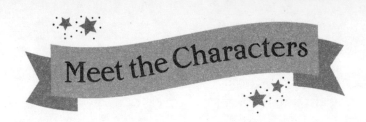

Aisha and Emily are best friends from Spellford Village. Aisha loves sports, whilst Emily's favourite thing is science. But what both girls enjoy more than anything is visiting Enchanted Valley and helping their unicorn friends, who live there.

Silvermane

Silvermane and the other Night Sparkle Unicorns make sure night-time is magical. Silvermane's locket helps her take care of the stars.

Dreamspell's magic brings sweet dreams to all the creatures of Enchanted Valley. Without her magical powers, everyone will have nightmares!

Dreamspell

With the help of her magical friends and the power of her locket, Slumbertail makes sure everyone in Enchanted Valley has a peaceful night's sleep.

Slumbertail

Kindly Brighteye is in charge of the moon. The magic of her locket helps its beautiful light to shine each night.

Brighteye

Enchanted Cottage

Golden Palace

An Enchanted Valley lies a twinkle away,
Where beautiful unicorns live, laugh and play
You can visit the mermaids, or go for a ride,
So much fun to be had, but dangers can hide!

Your friends need your help – this is how you know:
A keyring lights up with a magical glow.
Whirled off like a dream, you won't want to leave.
Friendship forever, when you truly believe.

## Chapter One
# A Sleepless Night

"Aisha?" whispered Emily Turner. "Are you awake?"

The duvet on the bed next to Emily's shifted, and her best friend Aisha Khan's face appeared. By the moonlight shining faintly through the curtains, Emily could see her grin.

"I've been
trying to keep
my eyes closed,"
Aisha whispered
back. "But then
I start thinking
about unicorns,
and I'm wide awake again!"

Emily giggled. "Me too!" The two girls
were having a week-long sleepover at
Enchanted Cottage, where Aisha lived
with her parents. They were in Aisha's
bedroom, each snuggled under a cosy
duvet.

"I tried counting sheep, but that didn't
work," Emily said. "So then I tried
counting unicorns. But that just made me

wonder what Queen Aurora was doing!"

Queen Aurora was the unicorn who ruled over Enchanted Valley, a magical world of wonderful creatures – and the girls' special secret. They had been to Enchanted Valley for lots of adventures, and helped save their unicorn friends from a wicked unicorn called Selena. She wanted to rule over the whole land and would do anything to make that happen.

"We're both too awake to sleep now," Aisha said. "I know! Let's have some milk and cookies instead."

The girls got up and put on their fluffy slippers and dressing gowns. Emily went over to the chest of drawers to fetch their matching unicorn keyrings, which were hanging from one of Aisha's athletics trophies. The magical keyrings were gifts from Queen Aurora, so she could call them back to Enchanted Valley. The girls took them everywhere.

Slipping the keyrings into their dressing-gown pockets, they padded quietly down the stairs, careful not to wake Mr and Mrs Khan. In the kitchen, Aisha filled two glasses with ice-cold milk while Emily took a box of hazelnut cookies out from one of the cupboards.

They sat down at the kitchen table. The curtains were open, and the girls gazed out at the velvety black night sky, sprinkled with stars. The moon was a curl of silver. "It's called a waxing crescent

when it's like that," Emily explained. "In about three weeks it'll be a full moon."

Aisha was impressed – but not surprised. Emily was a science whiz! "I wonder if—" she started. Then she gasped. "Emily, look!"

Emily glanced down to where Aisha was pointing – at her dressing-gown pocket. Light shone through the fabric.

Her heart racing, Emily took out her keyring. Aisha pulled out hers too. The crystal unicorns were glowing!

"You know what this means," said Aisha, grinning.

Emily grinned back. "We're going to Enchanted Valley!"

The girls held the keyrings together so the unicorn horns were touching.

Immediately, the kitchen seemed to melt away. A dazzling rainbow of sparkles whooshed around them. They held hands tightly as they were lifted up, up, up …

When their slippers touched the ground again, the girls were no longer in the Khans' kitchen. They were standing on grass, under a night sky. Ahead of them they could just make out a hill where there stood a palace, gleaming faintly gold through the dark.

They were back in Enchanted Valley!

The two girls hurried up the hill. "It looks like Selena's horrible magic hasn't gone away," said Aisha, her slippers rustling through the grass. Selena wanted the throne of Enchanted Valley for herself.

She was responsible for this darkness, and had threatened she would never end it unless the unicorns made her their queen.

They reached the palace. Roses grew up the golden walls, filling the air with their sweet scent. A drawbridge lay across a moat of water, and standing on it was a beautiful unicorn. She glimmered with soft shades of orange, gold and red – all the colours of a beautiful sunrise. She dipped her long, elegant horn in greeting.

"Welcome back, girls," the unicorn said. Her voice was low and sweet, like a cello.

"Queen Aurora!" Emily and Aisha cried together. Aisha threw her arms around Aurora's neck and hugged her. Aurora laughed.

Queen
Aurora was
followed
by another
unicorn, who
was candyfloss
pink with a
deep pink
mane and
tail. Her horn
was pink and
sparkling. The girls had met her before
– she was Slumbertail, one of the four
Night Sparkle Unicorns who looked after
night-time in Enchanted Valley.

"It's lovely to see you!" said Slumbertail,
and the girls hugged her too.

When she pulled away, Emily glanced at Slumbertail's neck. All the unicorns wore a locket that gave them the magic they needed to do their job in Enchanted Valley. Queen Aurora was in charge of friendship, and her locket contained twin suns playing together. But Slumbertail's neck was bare.

"Selena's still got your locket," said Emily in dismay.

Slumbertail nodded sadly. Selena had stolen the Night Sparkle Unicorns' lockets, and was using them to make life horrible in Enchanted Valley. Aisha and Emily had rescued two of the lockets, but they knew the endless night wouldn't be broken until all four were safely back with their owners.

"We'll do our best to find it," Aisha promised Slumbertail.

"We know you will," said Queen Aurora. "But in the meantime, I have decided we must make the best of this darkness." Her eyes shone. "Girls, how would you like to come to a unicorn sleepover?"

Both Emily and Aisha grinned. "We'd love to!"

## Chapter Two
# The Unicorn Sleepover

Aisha and Emily followed Queen Aurora and Slumbertail over the drawbridge and into the golden palace. They walked through a courtyard dotted with lilac trees. It was still and quiet, and there were no lights at the windows.

"I love sleepovers," said Slumbertail, as

they passed a fountain. "Lots of fun with friends, and then I use my magic to send everyone into a beautiful, restful sleep. I can't wait!"

The girls exchanged puzzled glances.

"But Slumbertail, you're the sleep unicorn," said Emily. "If your locket is missing, doesn't that mean you haven't got your magic any more?" She frowned. "How can anyone in Enchanted Valley sleep until we get it back?"

"No sleep!" said Aisha. "That would be horrible."

Slumbertail gave the girls a wink. "Just wait and see!"

They stepped through an archway, crossed another courtyard, then went

through a big pair of wooden doors into
a huge hall. Unlike the rest of the palace,
the hall was brightly lit – and filled with
unicorns!

Soft pillows and blankets covered the
floor. Some of the unicorns were snuggled
up on them, chatting together. One

corner of the hall had been set up as a
little salon with tables and mirrors. There,
a unicorn with ribbons plaited into her
tail nodded her horn, transforming a
little unicorn's straight mane into a spiky,
punky style. Another group of unicorns
were playing board games, and in the
centre of the hall was a table covered
with snacks – crisps, sweets, chocolates,

and popcorn. All the unicorns had cosy
dressing gowns draped over their backs
and some wore fuzzy slippers.

Aisha's eyes were wide. "This is the best
sleepover ever!" she declared.

"Definitely!" agreed Emily, smiling.

Three familiar unicorns got up from
watching a film and came to join them.
Along with Slumbertail, they were the

Night Sparkle Unicorns. "Hi, Emily! Hi, Aisha!" cried Silvermane. The girls had already retrieved Silvermane's locket, which held a tiny shooting star and gave her the magic she needed to look after the stars in Enchanted Valley. Beside her were Dreamspell, who looked after dreams, and Brighteye, who took care of the moon. Emily and Aisha had also found Dreamspell's locket, which contained a dreamy image of friends having fun – but, like Slumbertail, Brighteye was still missing hers.

Aisha and Emily gave them each a hug.

"We're about to do our hair," said Brighteye. "Come and join us!"

"Would you like some snacks?" asked

Dreamspell.

"Yes, please!" said the girls.

It really was the best sleepover ever. The girls piled their plates high with chewy star gummies, creamy chocolates and crunchy crisps.

Then Fancymane, the hairstylist unicorn, gave them both new hairdos.

"I hope you like them," she said, as Emily examined her pink highlights and Aisha admired her new curls. Fancymane tried to stifle a yawn. "Goodness! It must be getting late."

Just then, Slumbertail appeared next to them. "Hey, girls, I've got something special to show you!"

Emily and Aisha exchanged excited glances, and followed the pink unicorn across the hall to a large window. Through the darkness they could just see a tall golden tower at the edge of the palace, with a clock face at the top. Instead of numbers, the clock had two pictures – a sun where the number twelve would usually be, and a moon where ordinary clocks had the number six. It had one hand, which was pointing at the sun.

Emily stared at it curiously. "I've never seen a clock like that before," she said.

"It tells us when it's bedtime," said
Slumbertail. "Even in this endless night,
it knows when bedtime ought to be …
which is any moment now!"

The girls watched the clock for a few
seconds. Then, suddenly, its hand swung
from the sun to the moon. Instantly,
tinkling chimes rang out and a door
beneath the clock face swung open. Out
flew several tiny creatures. At first the

girls thought they must be butterflies, but when the creatures flew closer to the window they saw that they were pixies! Each had silvery wings and lavender-coloured skin, and wore a bright pair of pyjamas and matching nightcap. Their pointy ears poked out from under their caps. The girls gasped with amazement.

"Wow!" said Aisha. "Who are they?"

"My helpers," said Slumbertail proudly. "The sleep pixies!"

The tiny creatures whizzed past the window. They were carrying miniature pillowcases, and when one of the sleep pixies almost dropped his, a shimmering powder spilled out.

"What's that?" wondered Emily.

"Sleepy dust," explained Slumbertail. "I use the magic from my locket to make it. Every night, when the clock says bedtime, the sleep pixies fly across Enchanted Valley and sprinkle the dust over everyone to help them fall asleep."

"We've never noticed the sleep pixies before!" said Aisha.

"They stay high up when they sprinkle their dust," explained Slumbertail.

"Usually everyone drifts off into a peaceful sleep without even noticing the sleep pixies have visited."

"Thank goodness Slumbertail had made a big batch of sleepy dust before Selena stole her locket!" said Queen Aurora, appearing behind them.

All of the sleep pixies flew off in different directions, clutching their pillowcases – except one. She landed on the window frame, and tapped the glass. Her purple eyes were large, and curly purple hair spilled out from under her nightcap. Emily hurried to open the window, and the sleep pixie flew into the room, her wings fluttering as fast as a hummingbird's. "Sweet snoozes to you!"

she said in a voice
as soft as a lullaby.
She stuck out her
tiny hand. "My
name's Trixie!"

## Chapter Three
# Sleepy Dust

Aisha and Emily both offered Trixie
a finger to shake, and introduced
themselves.

"It's lovely to meet you," Trixie said.
"I've heard all about your adventures in
the valley. Now, watch this!" She scooped
some sleepy dust from her pillowcase and

tossed it high into the air. For a moment
it hung there, like a glittering golden
cloud. Trixie sang very sweetly:

**"The moon is bright**
**So say good night,**
**And now sleep tight**
**Till morning's light."**

Both girls sighed happily – Trixie's
singing was so soft and lovely. "I just
hope the lullaby comes true and it's light
in Enchanted Valley again soon," Emily
murmured to Aisha.

The dust floated down over the
unicorns who were playing board games.
One of them, a little black foal, sneezed
when some of it landed on his nose.

Trixie carried on sprinkling the

sleepy dust until it had landed on all the
unicorns and the girls. There was even
some sparkling in Queen Aurora's mane.

"In a few minutes, everyone should fall
asleep," said Slumbertail.

Trixie perched on Emily's shoulder
to wait. "Are you feeling sleepy?" she
whispered.

Emily and Aisha shared a look. Neither
of them felt very sleepy.

"Maybe a little?" said Emily, not

wanting to upset the pixie.

The girls watched the unicorns. But no one was closing their eyes.

"Everyone should be nodding off by now," Slumbertail said, with a worried toss of her horn.

Trixie anxiously clutched her empty pillowcase. Queen Aurora's brow was furrowed.

*Tap, tap, tap* …
Aisha turned around to see another sleep pixie at the window, knocking to be let in. She hurried to

open it, and he fluttered inside. He was
carrying an empty pillowcase and his
little lavender face was scrunched up with
worry.

"What is it, Dixie?" Slumbertail asked
him.

"The sleepy dust isn't working!" Dixie
cried. "All the other sleep pixies are saying
the same thing. We've sprinkled all our
dust, but everyone in Enchanted Valley is
still wide awake!"

Slumbertail gave a whinny of dismay.

"Oh, goodness. No one is falling asleep
here, either," said Aurora.

Emily and Aisha glanced around the
room of tired-looking unicorns. "But
why isn't it working?" wondered Emily.

"Maybe—"

She stopped with a gasp as, outside the window, a fork of lightning cut through the inky black night. There was a rumble of thunder, and the hall filled with shouts of alarm.

"Look out!" cried Trixie.

At the window appeared a silver unicorn. Her mane and tail were twilight blue, and her horn was very long and sharp. She gave an evil grin.

"It's Selena!" cried Aisha and Emily at once.

Selena thrust her horn forwards, and the window shattered with a crash. The unicorns whinnied in alarm. Trixie and Dixie the sleep pixies flew, trembling, to

hide behind the girls.

"Get back, everyone!" cried Queen
Aurora.

Selena flew through the broken
window and landed before them. Flashes
of lightning rippled up and down her
horn, and she stomped the floor with her
hooves. A brown owl swooped in after
her and gave a mocking hoot – it was

Screech, Selena's horrible helper.

Queen Aurora drew herself up. "You are forbidden from the palace, Selena!" she said sternly. "You and your evil magic are not welcome here."

Selena smirked. "I thought you were supposed to be the friendship unicorn. That wasn't very friendly, was it?" Her gaze flickered around the hall. "But it doesn't matter. This palace will soon be mine. Then *you* won't be welcome!"

Screech hooted with laughter. "Good one, your

nastiness!"

Aisha clenched her fists. "Get lost,

Selena!" she said bravely.

Selena turned her attention to the girls.
"I might have known you two would
be here," she said. "I'm sick of your
interfering ways! But you won't stop me
this time."

"We will," said Emily, hoping she
sounded more certain than she felt. "Give
back Slumbertail's locket!"

Selena tossed her head and cackled.
"The locket is mine, and you won't get it
back – not unless you agree to make me
queen!"

"That will never happen," said Aurora.

"Then say goodbye to the locket for
ever," Selena said. She narrowed her eyes.
"You meddlesome girls stole the last

locket from me while I was asleep, so this time I will be staying wide awake. And so will everyone else!"

Slumbertail gasped. "So that's why no one's falling asleep — you've stopped the sleepy dust from working!"

"That's right," said Selena. "I've twisted the magic of the locket so no one in Enchanted Valley will ever sleep again, no matter how much of that silly dust you throw around. You'll be too exhausted to stop me from becoming queen!"

She cackled and flew back through the shattered window. Another rumble of thunder made the hall shake.

"Night, everyone!" Screech taunted them. "Sleep well! Oh, wait — no you won't! Ha!" He flapped away after his mistress.

"Oh no!" cried Slumbertail. She dipped her horn low in despair.

Trixie and Dixie emerged from behind the girls. "No more sleep," said Trixie in a horrified voice. "No more snuggling on soft blankets and nodding off!"

Panic spread around the hall. "We'll be too tired to do anything!" cried the unicorn with the spiky mane.

"We won't be able to make food, or tend the flowers, or look after any of the other creatures in the valley!" a red unicorn cried.

The little black foal gave a sob. He still had sleepy dust on his nose. "But I'm so tired already," he said, his eyes brimming with tears. "I wish I could go to sleep!"

Queen Aurora turned to Emily and Aisha. "Girls, this is terrible." Her tail twitched with worry. "Without sleep, we won't just be too tired to stop Selena – Enchanted Valley will fall apart!"

Emily glanced at Aisha. They knew what they had to do.

"We'll stop Selena," Aisha said. "And we'll get the locket back. We promise!"

## Chapter Four
# Hob's Potion

"The other pixies will be wondering what's going on," said Dixie, adjusting his nightcap. "I'd better go and tell them." He zoomed away through the broken window.

Emily rested her chin on her clasped hands, thinking hard. "Do you remember when Selena gave Wintertail the Winter Unicorn a potion to make her sleep?" she asked. "Maybe we could make one. That way everyone can have a nap, at least."

"Oh, yes!" cried Slumbertail. "If the unicorns are rested, they'll be able to take care of Enchanted Valley while we search for my locket."

Aisha's eyes shone. "Nice idea, Emily! I bet Hob could help us." Hob was a very old, very clever goblin, who knew how to make all kinds of potions. "Let's go and ask him."

Everyone agreed this was a good plan.

"I'm coming with you," insisted Slumbertail.

"And me," said Trixie. She put her hands

on her tiny hips. "We must turn this nasty nightmare into a nice nap!"

Queen Aurora needed to stay at the palace, to guard it in case Selena returned. "Be careful," she said. "Selena and Screech will try to stop you. And good luck!"

As soon as the girls were sitting on her back, Slumbertail took off and flew through the broken window, Trixie fluttering beside her. They soared up into the night sky. A thrill fizzed through the girls. Even though they'd had many rides on their unicorn friends, shooting through

the air was still as exciting as the first
time they'd done it. They couldn't help
beaming with delight as they looked
down to see the palace already shrinking
into the distance.

Slumbertail flew lower than usual, using
the light glowing from cottage windows
below to guide her way. Looking
down, the girls saw that even though
it was dark, lots of creatures were out.

Flowerdew Garden was bustling with gnomes.

"I'm going to dig and dig and dig until it sends me to sleep," they heard a gnome wearing a dandelion cap say.

A gnome in a poppy cap rubbed her eyes. "I'm so tired I can't think straight," she said with a groan. "Was I going to mow the roses or prune the grass?"

Slumbertail flew on. They passed nests

of birds
trying to sing
themselves
to sleep, and
when they
went over one
of the rivers
that wound
through the valley, they saw mermaids
having swimming races.

"Everyone's trying to wear themselves
out," said Slumbertail in dismay. "But it
won't do any good – until we find the
locket, no one will be able to sleep no
matter how tired they are."

In the distance were three large shapes,
flying in circles.

"They don't look like unicorns,"
said Trixie. She gave a squeal. "Biting
bedbugs! They're not Selena's helpers too,
are they?"

Aisha peered at the flying creatures.
They were moving so slowly it was
obvious they were exhausted too. She
could make out jagged wings, pointed
tails and snouts with smoke coming out
of them. "Don't worry, Trixie," she said.
"It's just the dragons from Firework
Mountain." The girls had met the

dragons on their first ever adventure to Enchanted Valley and knew that they were very friendly.

Slumbertail landed in front of the cave where Hob the goblin lived. The girls climbed down on to the mossy ground, and Emily knocked on the stone door. They could hear shuffling noises inside, and then it swung open.

In the doorway stood a little creature with wrinkly green skin. He was half as tall as the girls, and wore a dressing gown decorated with moons and suns. He was cleaning his spectacles on one sleeve.

"*Yaaaaaaaaaawwwn!* Oh, excuse me, so tired …" He put his glasses back on. "Bless my stars, it's Emily and Aisha! And

Slumbertail! And you must be one of the sleep pixies."

"Hi, Hob!" said the girls, hugging him. "This is Trixie."

"You all look very worried, my dears," Hob said, gazing around at them. "Why don't you come in and tell me about it, and I'll do my best to help."

They followed him through the cave and into a long tunnel that led to several spacious rooms. Aisha caught Emily's

eye and grinned – they always enjoyed
visiting Hob's house. In his cosy kitchen,
the girls sank into armchairs, while
Slumbertail settled on the rug and Trixie
perched on a bookcase. As Hob heated
a saucepan of hot chocolate over the
fire, they quickly explained what had
happened – about Selena and the stolen
locket, the sleepy dust that wouldn't
work, and their idea about a potion.

Hob poured the hot chocolate into
a bowl for Slumbertail, mugs for the
girls and a thimble for Trixie. "A –
*yaaaaaaaaaawwwn!* – commotion?"
said Hob.

"Oh, no, a potion," said Emily.

"And Selena has stolen the sleepy

dust?" asked Hob in confusion.

Aisha shook her head. "She's stolen Slumbertail's locket."

Hob took off his glasses and rubbed his eyes. "Ah, of course. I'm sorry, my dears, I'm so tired I can't concentrate properly."

"It's not your fault," said Aisha.

Trixie put down her thimble. "You can still make us a sleepy potion, though, can't you?" she asked in a worried voice.

"I shall certainly try," said Hob. "Anything to stop Selena!" He shuffled out of the kitchen. The girls could hear clinking, clanking and several enormous yawns, and then Hob returned with his arms filled with bottles and jars. He set them on the table and gathered bowls, spoons and a pestle and mortar.

They all clustered around the table to help. Hob asked Emily to grind up some yellow Dreamweed Seeds with the pestle and mortar, while Aisha stirred Lullaby Liquid with Dozy Drops to make a thick orange syrup. Slumbertail cracked Night Nuts on the floor with her hooves, and Trixie retrieved the kernels and dropped them into a bowl of green Snooze Jelly. Finally, Hob used his magical wooden spoon to mix everything together into a bright blue potion. He poured it into a glass bottle.

"Ta-dah!" he said. "Who would –
*yaaaaaaaaawwwn!* – like to try it?"

"I will," said Trixie eagerly, fetching the
thimble.

Emily filled it with potion. As the little
pixie took a sip, the girls held their breath.
Would it work?

## Chapter Five
# Dragon Crash!

"Do you feel sleepy, Trixie?" asked Slumbertail. They were all watching her closely.

Trixie shook her head. She gave a puzzled frown. "But I do feel strange …" Suddenly, she bounced up into the air like a spring. She landed on a pile of pots

and pans, and immediately bounced up
again. "Eeek!" she squealed, and landed

on Slumbertail's
nose. Then she slid
down, into Aisha's
waiting hand.

"Oh, crumpets!"
Hob cried. He
picked up the
ingredients. "This
isn't Lullaby Liquid – it's Jumping Juice!
And these are Bouncing Beans, not
Dreamweed Seeds …" He groaned in
dismay. "I didn't make a sleepy potion – I
made a *leapy* potion! If only I wasn't so
tired … I'm very sorry, Trixie!"

Trixie shook out her wings. "Don't

worry, it was fun!"

Hob slumped in his rocking chair. "I'm so sorry," he said sadly. "I don't think I can – *yaaaaaaaaawwwn!* – help you after all."

"Please don't feel bad, Hob," said Aisha. "We'll just—" She broke off, as the floor began to tremble. Suddenly, everything was shaking. Books fell from shelves. Hob's mug of hot chocolate fell on the rug, and the potion ingredients rained down on to the floor.

"What's happening?" cried Slumbertail.

Emily grabbed hold of a chair to steady herself. "It feels like an earthquake!"

"An earthquake?" cried Slumbertail. Her hooves skittered on the trembling floor. "In Enchanted Valley? But there's never been one before!"

Trixie flew around the kitchen in panicky loops. "Dancing duvets!" she squealed. "This is terrible!"

Aisha caught the two bottles of potion before they could fall off the table, and tucked them in her dressing-gown pockets. "There's only one way to find out what's happening," she said. "Let's go outside!"

The friends hurried out of the kitchen and along the tunnel, bumping into the shaking walls. They rushed out of the cave door into the endless night – and gasped. In the branches of the tree that grew above Hob's cave were the dragons!

One was gold, one silver and one bronze.
All three were blinking sleepily.

"Stinging nettles!" cried Hob. "What
are you three doing up there?" He was so
shocked, he wasn't yawning any more.

"We're so sorry," rumbled the silver
dragon, who was called Smoky.

The gold dragon, whose name was
Sparky, nodded his big scaly head. "But
we were so tired …"

"… we couldn't fly straight," finished Coal, the bronze dragon, "and we crashed into Hob's tree!"

The branches creaked and groaned under their weight.

"No wonder we thought there was an earthquake," said Aisha. "You'd better come down before the tree topples over!"

The dragons flew down to the ground. "If only we could sleep," grumbled Coal. He yawned, blowing out a big puff of smoke.

"I'm afraid none of us will sleep until we find my locket," said Slumbertail.

The dragons looked at each other. "Oh, yes! That's why we were flying here!" said Smoky.

"We saw Selena!" said Sparky.

"She's so mean!" Smoky added.

"She stole our pillows!" said Coal.

Trixie tilted her head. "But what would horrible Selena want with slumbery soft pillows?" she wondered. "She probably likes to sleep on slabs of cold stone."

"They weren't just any pillows," said Sparky, covering a yawn with his gold tail. "They were filled with Feather Flowers!"

Trixie gasped. "Those are the softest, sleepiest pillows in all of Enchanted Valley!" she cried. "No wonder you're cross!"

"We are," agreed Coal. "Or we would be, if we weren't so tired."

"Where did you see Selena?" asked Emily.

"In the mountains," said Sparky. "Are you going to find her? She's so scary!"

Aisha tightened the belt of her dressing gown. "We're going to try," she said. "We'd do anything to save Enchanted Valley. Right, Emily?"

"Right," said Emily.

"Right," Slumbertail said.

"Right," said Trixie. "Stealing lockets *and* Feather Flower pillows? We can't let Selena get away with it!"

Hob gave them each a hug. "In that case, good – *yaaaaaaaaawwwn!* – luck, my dears!"

## Chapter Six
# The Pillow Fort

The air above the mountains was chilly. Aisha and Emily huddled together on Slumbertail's back, pulling their dressing gowns tight around themselves. In the dark it was hard to see much at all, except the jagged peaks jutting into the sky.

Aisha scanned the steep, empty slopes.

"Nothing," she said with a sigh.

"Maybe the dragons made a mistake, and Selena wasn't here," said Emily.

Slumbertail flew over more rocks and boulders. "I can't see anything either," she said. "I'm afraid this is hopeless, girls. Let's turn back. But where's Trixie?"

Aisha and Emily looked around. "Trixie!" they both called. "Trixie, where are you?"

"Down here!" Trixie's lullaby voice floated up to them. Slumbertail followed it down to a heap of dull grey boulders. Fluttering above them was Trixie, her lavender face lit up in a grin. "Look what I've found!"

The girls' gazes followed Trixie's tiny,

pointing finger. Lying between two
boulders was a glittering silver flower,
with long, soft petals shaped like feathers.

Emily gasped. "Is that a Feather
Flower?" she asked. "From the dragons'
pillows?"

Trixie whizzed around in excitement. "It
is!"

"Selena might have been here after all!"
cried Aisha.

Hope fluttered inside the girls as Slumbertail skimmed over the mountains.

"There's another one!" called Emily, pointing to a shimmery pink Feather Flower lying on the stony ground.

"There's one here, too!" Slumbertail said, flying past a pale blue Feather Flower caught in a scrubby bush.

The trail of Feather Flowers led them up to the top of a mountain peak, where a lilac flower shimmered in the snow, and down the other side. The dark mountains stretched out before them, but closer by something huge and white loomed on the steep slope.

"That's odd," said Aisha. "It looks like a cloud."

But when they flew nearer, they saw it
wasn't a cloud at all. It was a big white
castle!

"Do you see what it's made of?" asked
Emily.

"Pillows!" cried Aisha.

She was right. The walls of the castle
were built from stacks of fluffy pillows.
Little pillows made up the battlements.

Trixie's eyes were huge with amazement. "It's the biggest pillow fort I've ever seen!" she said.

"The dragons' pillows must be part of the fort," said Slumbertail.

Aisha nodded. "And if Selena stole the pillows …"

"… this fort has to be hers," finished Emily. "She might be here now, with the locket!"

Slumbertail landed on the stony ground, and the girls jumped down from her back. Moving from boulder to boulder, careful to stay out of sight, they all crept closer to the pillow fort. There was an archway that led into the fort, made from several pillows as large as Slumbertail. Standing

outside it were
two big trolls.
They had
warty orange
skin and messy
tufts of hair.
One of them
was wearing
pyjamas and
the other was

in a nightdress. The girls, Slumbertail and
Trixie ducked behind a large rock to
watch.

The troll wearing a nightdress scratched
her armpit. "This isn't fair, Stinker," she
grumbled. "We've been on guard for ages
now. All I want is a nice mug of cocoa

and a sleep. Is that too much to ask?"

Stinker yawned, showing rows of rotten teeth. "Quite right, Surly," he agreed. "This isn't what we signed up for." He waved a hand at the fort. "All these pillows, and she won't let us sleep! Not even one wink!"

"What's all this complaining I can hear?" a voice boomed from inside the pillow fort.

Emily and Aisha shared a glance. They'd know that cruel voice anywhere...

Sure enough, out of the archway strode Selena. Lightning flashed around her horn and her eyes were narrowed with annoyance. Flying at her shoulder was

Screech the owl.

Surly and Stinker immediately saluted her.

"Talking about me, were you?" Selena asked the trolls icily.

"No, your nastiness," said Surly. "Well, yes, maybe a bit. We were just wondering if we could have a rest now."

"We've been working really hard," added Stinker. "Honest."

Selena stamped a hoof. "How many times must I explain?" she shouted. "You two guard the pillow fort, while

Screech and I guard the locket. If I hear
any more complaining, you will have
no more yucky cocoa, no more silly
bedtime stories, and no more sleep! Ever!
Understand?"

"Y-yes, your horribleness," stammered
the trolls.

Selena marched back inside.

"Have a nice night!" sniggered Screech,
and swooped inside after her.

Crouching behind
the rock, the four
friends leaned close
together to work
out what to do.

"I feel a bit sorry
for those trolls,"

whispered Emily. "But we need to get past them somehow."

Aisha nodded. "If we could just distract their attention from the archway …" she said.

Trixie grinned. "I've got an idea!"

Keeping away from Surly and Stinker, she whizzed up to the top of the battlements and grabbed one of the small pillows. Then she floated down, holding on to the pillow, until she was right above the trolls. Surly was yawning while Stinker picked his nose. Suddenly, Trixie darted down and – *whumph!* – bumped Stinker on the back of his head with the pillow.

"Oi!" cried Stinker, turning to Surly.

"What did you do that for?"

"Do what for?" asked Surly.

"Someone hit me!" Stinker grumbled.

Both trolls looked around, scratching their tufty heads. Trixie zoomed down again, and this time hit Surly with the pillow. *Whumph!*

"Hey!" Surly whirled around. "Someone's playing a prank on us, Stinker!"

The trolls began searching the area

around the pillow fort, peering through the darkness to check behind rocks and under the prickly bushes.

Trixie raced back over to rejoin Slumbertail and the girls.

"That was brilliant, Trixie!" whispered Aisha. "Come on, before they see us!"

While Surly and Stinker were bent over, searching a knobbly tree, the friends crouched low and ran through the darkness, towards the archway that led into the pillow fort. The girls' hearts were racing. Would they make it in time? The fort was getting closer … and closer …

"Nearly there," panted Emily.

But Stinker gave a shriek. "Intruders!" he yelled. "I've found them, Surly!"

Emily and Aisha looked back in horror.
The trolls were pounding towards them!

## Chapter Seven
# A Big Leap

Slumbertail galloped in front of the girls and halted, her hooves skidding on the rocky ground. "You go on ahead, girls," she told them, picking up a pillow. "I'll hold off Stinker and Surly!"

"Oh, thank you!" cried the girls.

"I'll help!" added Trixie. She hovered

next to Slumbertail, her tiny hands on her hips. "I'm not scared of any troll!"

Aisha grabbed Emily's hand and used her extra speed to pull her along, sprinting for the archway. They burst into the pillow fort, panting for breath.

It was like being inside a cloud. Everything was soft and white — the walls, the ceiling, even the floor. The girls caught their breath and listened. An excited, high-pitched squawk was coming from somewhere within the fort.

"Screech," whispered Emily, and Aisha nodded.

Still holding hands, the girls made their way towards him. Doing their best not to stumble on the pillow floor, they tiptoed down a corridor made of pillows, hurried through a pillow hallway, and peeked around a corner into a pillow room.

Screech was swooping from one end to the other, then back again. "Night-time is the best time!" he yelled. "No horrible sunshine! Just lovely darkness! Don't you agree, Selena?"

Selena was sitting in a corner, her legs tucked underneath her, scowling. "Will you be quiet, Screech?" she snapped. "I'm actually getting bored with this endless night, but it's necessary to make sure those girls are too tired to find the locket."

Screech fluttered in front of her. "But the dark is fun, Selena—"

"I SAID BE QUIET!" Selena shouted, then yawned loudly.

Emily caught Aisha's eye. Selena was obviously as exhausted as everyone else in Enchanted Valley.

Screech dropped down on to the pillow floor. He put a wing over his beak. "Won't say another word," he said. "Promise!"

Something glinted against his feathery chest. Aisha stifled a gasp and gave Emily a nudge. Hanging from Screech's neck was a pendant containing a tiny pillow spinning round and round. Slumbertail's locket!

Selena yawned again. "It's a good thing

*you're* not tired, Screech," she said. "It means you can guard the locket. Otherwise I'd put you on guard duty with Surly and Stinker …" Selena's pointed ears pricked up. "Hang on! What's that?"

Emily and Aisha listened too. They could hear faint shouts coming from outside the pillow fort. Slumbertail and Trixie must be fighting the trolls! "I hope they're OK," murmured Aisha in Emily's ear.

Screech made muffled noises through his closed beak.

Selena rolled her eyes. "You may speak, silly owl!"

"Thank you, your nastiness," said Screech. "Shall I go and see what Stinker and Surly are doing?"

"No," snapped Selena. "You must stay here with the locket. I'll go." She stood up and huffed. "It's impossible to find reliable minions these days ..."

The girls pressed themselves into the soft walls as Selena stomped past them, kicking pillows out of her way.

"Now's our chance!" whispered Aisha.

The girls peeked into the room again. But Screech wasn't on the floor any more. After a moment, Emily spotted him. She pointed to where he was perched high up in the wall, nestled between two pillows. The locket still hung from his neck.

"Oh no!" mouthed Aisha. "How are we going to get up there?" She frowned. "The pillow walls will just fall down if we try to climb them. And it's too high to jump …"

Emily gasped. "I know!" she whispered. "Have you still got Hob's potion?"

Aisha's eyes went wide. "The leapy potion! I think I have it somewhere … but where did I put it?" She stuck a hand into her dressing-gown pocket and pulled out the bottle of bright blue potion with a grin. Emily grinned back, and the girls each swallowed a few drops. The potion fizzled on their tongues, filling their mouths with the taste of blueberries and lemons. Then they stepped into the pillow room.

Screech gave a startled squawk. "Not you two again!"

"Hi, Screech," said Aisha. Then she jumped. And she soared up into the air.

*This must be how the unicorns feel when they fly!* thought Aisha.

She jumped almost as high as Screech, before she fell back down and landed on the soft pillow floor.

"Get lost!" Screech yelled. "Interfering girls!" He flapped to the opposite wall and crammed himself on to a pillow right by the ceiling.

Emily jumped next. She sprang up as if she were on a trampoline, stretching her

arms up towards
the owl.

"Selena!" shrieked
Screech. "Selena,
come back!"

He took off again,
just swooping
through Emily's
hands.

While he was still
flying, Aisha leaped
up again. She
twisted in the air,
aiming just ahead
of Screech, her
hands cupped as if
she were catching

a cricket ball. Screech flew right into her path. He flapped desperately, trying to swerve, but Aisha's fingers closed around the locket. *Click!* The clasp came undone and she pulled it free from Screech's neck.

"No!" yelled Screech. He landed on the pillowed floor in a feathery heap.

Aisha's jump was so big, she carried on soaring, the locket in her hand, and hit the soft ceiling.

The pillows began to wobble. As Aisha landed beside Emily, a pillow fell down. *Ffflump!* Then another fell, and another. *Ffflump! Ffflump!*

"Watch out! The whole fort's collapsing!" cried Emily.

## Chapter Eight
# Feather Flower Pillow Fight

Screech flapped to avoid being buried
in pillows, as an entire wall of the fort
toppled around them. Aisha and Emily
tried to bounce aside, but the leapy
potion had worn off. Batting away the
falling pillows with their hands, they
scrambled through the collapsing fort and

out on to the mountain.

Slumbertail, Trixie and the trolls were fighting – but with pillows, and they were clearly having fun! Surly giggled with delight as a pillow wielded by Slumbertail hit her bottom and burst open, sending up a cloud of Feather Flowers.

"Me next! Hit me!" Stinker cried, hopping about with excitement. Trixie bopped a pillow on his head and he doubled over with laughter.

Selena stamped her hooves beside them, her face as angry as one of her thunderclaps. "Stinker! Surly! Stop that at once!" she ordered them furiously. "Or I'll fire you!"

"We don't care," Surly said gleefully. "This is much more fun than being your guards!"

Just as Selena opened her mouth to reply, Screech shot out of the collapsing fort. "Your nastiness," he yelled. "Emergency! It's the girls – they've got the locket!"

Selena whirled around.

Her eyes flashed as she took in the girls, the locket clutched in Aisha's hand, and the fort collapsing behind them. Lightning crackled from her horn. "How dare you interfere with my plans again!" she snarled. "That locket belongs to me!"

She marched towards them. Aisha and Emily took a wary step back.

"Actually," retorted Slumbertail, "that locket belongs to *me*!"

Before Selena could reach the girls, Slumbertail galloped up to them in a blur of pink. Emily and Aisha scrambled on to her back and Slumbertail sprang up into the night sky, Trixie whizzing along with them. Selena gave a furious whinny, rearing up and kicking her hooves.

"Curses!" Selena shrieked. "You may have won this time, but I've still got one more locket. I *will* be queen of Enchanted Valley!"

"Not while we're around to stop you!" yelled Aisha.

Selena's horn blazed with lightning. Beside her, Surly and Stinker were playing in the collapsed pillow fort, throwing up

armfuls of Feather Flowers and giggling.
But all three of them were all already
fading from the girls' view, as Slumbertail
carried them high into the night sky.

Aisha leaned forwards and fastened
the locket back round Slumbertail's neck,
where it belonged.

"Sweet sleeps!" cheered Trixie. "Now
everyone in Enchanted Valley can have a
nice long nap. I can't wait!"

The girls, Slumbertail and Trixie burst
into the hall where the unicorns were
holding their sleepover. Everyone looked
towards them, their faces filled with hope.

Queen Aurora beamed. "Slumbertail is wearing her locket!" she called. "We can all sleep again!"

Cheers rang through the hall. "Hooray for Emily and Aisha!" the unicorns cried. "Thank you, Slumbertail! Well done, Trixie!"

The three Night Sparkle Unicorns cantered up to nuzzle each of them in

turn. "Now we just need to find *my* locket," said Brighteye, a little sadly, "and night-time will be safe from Selena at last."

"We promise we'll help," Emily told her, wrapping her arms around Brighteye's soft neck.

The other sleep pixies, led by Dixie, flew in a fluttering cloud through the window Selena had broken.

"You're just in time!" Slumbertail told them with a smile. She waved her horn. Golden light swirled around it, and her locket glowed. Then all the pixies cheered – their pillowcases were now brimming over with sleepy dust!

Dixie led the pixies away to sprinkle

the dust over Enchanted Valley. Only
Trixie stayed in the hall, and she held her
pillowcase out towards the girls. "Would
you like to be my helpers?" she asked.

Emily and Aisha grinned. "Definitely!"
Emily said.

Trixie poured sleepy dust into their
palms, and Slumbertail flew the girls
around the hall. The unicorns looked up
in delight as Emily and Aisha sprinkled

shimmering dust over them, singing the lullaby they had learned from Trixie:

**"The moon is bright**
**So say good night,**
**And now sleep tight**
**Till morning's light."**

As the dust settled over the unicorns, they began to yawn and snuggle down among the pillows and blankets. The little black foal was already snoring softly.

"It's bedtime in Enchanted Valley at last," said Slumbertail, landing beside Queen Aurora. "Thanks to you, girls!"

"We're so glad—" began Emily, and then she yawned too, and so did Aisha.

"It's bedtime for everyone, I think," said Aurora with a smile.

Trixie gave each of the girls a tiny kiss on the cheek. "Sweet dreams, sweet friends," she said. "I'll make sure the dragons get  some new Feather Flower pillows."

"Thank you, Trixie!" said Emily.

"And please tell Hob that his leapy potion saved the day after all!" added Aisha.

Slumbertail nuzzled them both. "Thank you for everything," she said. "And sleep well!"

"I think we will," said Aisha, then gave another big yawn.

Queen Aurora's horn glowed, and a swirl of rainbow sparkles surrounded the girls. They felt themselves drift up, as light as sleepy dust, and Enchanted Valley melted away. When the sparkles cleared, they were in the Khans' kitchen once more, sitting at the table with their milk and cookies.

"Wow," said Emily. "That was amazing. We'll need to fix our hairdos, though, or your mum might wonder where I got my pink highlights and you got your curls."

"Let's do it first thing in the morning," said Aisha with a laugh. "Right now I'm so—" But she couldn't finish speaking – she was yawning too hard.

The girls put their glasses and plates in the dishwasher, then padded back up the stairs. They snuggled drowsily under their duvets.

"Sleep tight, Emily," Aisha murmured. Her eyes had already drifted closed.

"Sleep tight, Aisha," said Emily softly. "I hope we dream about unicorns ..."

The End

Join Emily and Aisha
for another adventure in …

# Brighteye and the Blue Moon
Read on for a sneak peek!

It was bedtime, but Aisha and her best friend, Emily Turner, weren't ready to go to sleep just yet. They were sitting on the floor of Aisha's cosy bedroom in Enchanted Cottage, playing another game of cards. Emily had spent the entire week with Aisha, sleeping over every night and having a great time.

"Come on, girls," Aisha's mum called from downstairs. "Time for lights out."

The girls sighed as they abandoned their game for the night, but climbed into their beds.

After ten minutes Aisha still felt wide awake. So did Emily. Although the light was off, a golden glow shone even brighter than the silver moon. The girls both gasped with delight. "Our keyrings!" they said together.

Their little crystal keyrings, in the shape of unicorns, were presents from Queen Aurora. She was the wise and friendly unicorn who ruled over Enchanted Valley, a secret magical world where Aisha and Emily had had many adventures together.

When the keyrings glowed like this, it meant Queen Aurora was calling them.

Aisha quietly scrambled out of bed. "Time to go back to Enchanted Valley!"

"I can't wait!" Emily said with glee.

They snatched up their keyrings and pressed them together. A swirling fountain of rainbow sparkles whirled around them, lifting them up off the floor.

Quick as a shooting star, the sparkles began to fade away and their feet settled back down on to lush green grass.

Emily looked around and saw they had landed on the slope of a hill they knew well. Queen Aurora's palace stood before them, a beautiful golden building with eight tall turrets that spiralled like unicorn horns.

Aisha looked up into the dark sky with a sigh. "It's still night in Enchanted Valley! It's been night here for ages now."

"We've got to put a stop to it," Emily sighed. "Once and for all!"

### Read

# Brighteye and the Blue Moon

to find out what adventures are in store
for Aisha and Emily!

# Also available

**Book Five:**

**Book Six:**

**Book Seven:**

**Book Eight:**

## Look out for the next book!

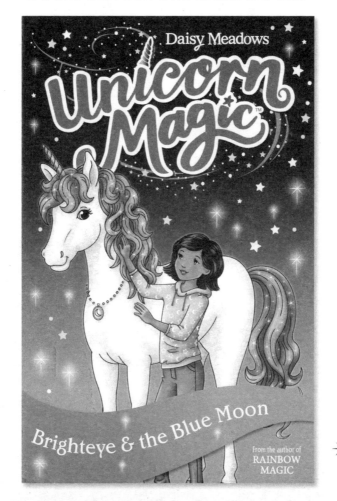

Daisy Meadows

Unicorn Magic™

Brighteye & the Blue Moon

From the author of
RAINBOW
MAGIC

If you like
Unicorn Magic,
you'll love …

# Welcome to Animal Ark!

Animal-mad Amelia is sad
about moving house, until she
discovers Animal Ark, where vets look
after all kinds of animals in need.

Join Amelia and her friend Sam for a
brand-new series of animal adventures!

# Brighteye and the Blue Moon

## Daisy Meadows

ORCHARD

# For Isla and Evelyn Blyth

## Special thanks to Adrian Bott

ORCHARD BOOKS

First published in Great Britain in 2020 by Hodder & Stoughton

3 5 7 9 10 8 6 4 2

Text copyright © 2020 Working Partners Limited
Illustrations © Orchard Books 2020
Series created by Working Partners Limited

A CIP catalogue record for this book is available from the British Library.

ISBN 978 1 40836 621 9

Printed and bound in Great Britain by Clays Ltd, Elcograf S.p.A.

The paper and board used in this book are made from wood from responsible sources.

Orchard Books
An imprint of Hachette Children's Group
Part of Hodder and Stoughton
Carmelite House
50 Victoria Embankment
London EC4Y 0DZ

An Hachette UK Company

www.hachette.co.uk
www.hachettechildrens.co.uk

Contents

# Meet the Characters

Aisha and Emily are best friends from Spellford Village. Aisha loves sports, whilst Emily's favourite thing is science. But what both girls enjoy more than anything is visiting Enchanted Valley and helping their unicorn friends, who live there.

Silvermane

Silvermane and the other Night Sparkle Unicorns make sure night-time is magical. Silvermane's locket helps her take care of the stars.

Dreamspell's magic brings sweet dreams to all the creatures of Enchanted Valley. Without her magical powers, everyone will have nightmares!

Dreamspell

With the help of her magical friends and the power of her locket, Slumbertail makes sure everyone in Enchanted Valley has a peaceful night's sleep.

Slumbertail

Kindly Brighteye is in charge of the moon. The magic of her locket helps its beautiful light to shine each night.

Brighteye

Enchanted Cottage

← Golden Palace

An Enchanted Valley lies a twinkle away,
Where beautiful unicorns live, laugh and play
You can visit the mermaids, or go for a ride,
So much fun to be had, but dangers can hide!

Your friends need your help ~ this is how you know:
A keyring lights up with a magical glow.
Whirled off like a dream, you won't want to leave.
Friendship forever, when you truly believe.

## Chapter One
# Midnight Howl

It was bedtime, but Aisha and her best
friend, Emily Turner, weren't ready to
go to sleep just yet. They were sitting
on the floor of Aisha's cosy bedroom in
Enchanted Cottage, playing another
game of cards. Emily had spent the entire
week with Aisha, sleeping over every

night and having a great time.

"Come on, girls," Aisha's mum called from downstairs. "Time for lights out."

The girls sighed as they abandoned their game for the night, but climbed into their beds.

After ten minutes Aisha still felt wide awake. So did Emily. Although the light was off, a golden glow shone even brighter than the silver moon. The girls both gasped with delight. "Our keyrings!" they said together.

Their little crystal keyrings, in the shape of unicorns, were presents from Queen Aurora. She was the wise and friendly unicorn who ruled over Enchanted Valley, a secret magical world where Aisha and

Emily had had many adventures together.

When the keyrings glowed like this, it meant Queen Aurora was calling them.

Aisha quietly scrambled out of bed. "Time to go back to Enchanted Valley!"

"I can't wait!" Emily said with glee.

They snatched up their keyrings and pressed them together. A swirling fountain of rainbow sparkles whirled around them, lifting them up off the floor.

Quick as a shooting star, the sparkles began to fade away and their feet settled back down on to lush green grass.

Emily looked around and saw they had landed on the slope of a hill they knew well. Queen Aurora's palace stood before them, a beautiful golden building with eight tall turrets that spiralled like unicorn horns.

Aisha looked up into the dark sky with a sigh. "It's still night in Enchanted Valley! It's been night here for ages now."

"We've got to put a stop to it," Emily sighed. "Once and for all!"

Every evening in Enchanted Valley, the four Night Sparkle Unicorns would combine the power of their magical lockets to bring the night. Then they did the same thing at dawn, to bring back the

day. But ever since the wicked unicorn Selena had stolen their lockets, Enchanted Valley had been trapped in an unending night.

Aisha took big strides up the hill and saw the full moon above the palace towers, shining like a silver coin. With a loud rattle of chains, the drawbridge dropped. There, standing on the other side, was Queen Aurora! Even at night-time, they could see the way her coat rippled with all the colours of a dawn sky, and they could make out the glitter of the little crown she wore on her head. The girls ran up to her and threw their arms around her neck.

"Welcome back!" Queen Aurora

laughed. "I've
missed you both."

"We've missed
you too," answered
Emily.

"But is there
anything wrong?

Has Selena been causing trouble?" Aisha
asked.

"I didn't call you because of a problem
this time," Aurora explained with a smile.
"It's more of a fun reason. You see … even
though this is the longest night we've ever
had, there is one good thing about it."

"What's that?" Emily asked eagerly.

"The full moon is here already!" said
Queen Aurora. "So we can have our

monthly campfire party. I thought maybe you both might like to come."

Emily and Aisha glanced at each other and grinned. "Yes, please!" both girls chorused.

"Wonderful! Follow me," Queen Aurora said. She trotted in front of them, leading the way down the hill. Aisha and Emily bubbled over with excitement.

They soon found themselves deep in thick woods full of the lovely scents of pine needles and moist night air. Although there were dark shadows everywhere and strange noises all around, the girls knew they had nothing to fear while they were with Queen Aurora.

"Look!" Emily cried. Up ahead, firelight

flickered between the tree trunks and they
could hear many happy voices chatting
and singing together. Aurora led them
into an open glade bathed in moonlight.
In the centre was a large pit containing a
roaring campfire, and glimmering firefly
lanterns hung from the low branches of
the surrounding trees.

The party was already in full swing.
Unicorns, phoenixes and even a family
of tiny gnomes all sat on logs around the

campfire, singing songs and sipping hot
chocolate. Hob, the little green goblin
who had often made the girls potions to
help them on their quests, was playing
a lively jig on his fiddle. Marshmallows
floated above the campfires, suspended
there by some unseen magic.

Aisha clapped her hands. "It's lovely!"

"Off you go! Have fun." Aurora
beamed.

"Look over there," Emily told Aisha.
"Isn't that Dreamspell?"

"Yes!" Aisha exclaimed. "And the rest of
the Night Sparkle Unicorns, too. Come
on!"

As they ran towards their friends, Emily
could see that Dreamspell, Silvermane
and Slumbertail were all wearing the
lockets the girls had helped to rescue
from Selena. Only Brighteye, the moon

unicorn, was still missing hers. They needed all four magical lockets to make daytime come again.

Aisha was just about to say hello when something made her freeze in her tracks – a long, mournful, eerie howl. She felt goose pimples rise all over her body. Emily shot Aisha a frightened look and reached for her hand.

"Was that ... a wolf?" Aisha whispered.

Emily glanced into the dark shadows between the trees, expecting glowing eyes to appear there.

"It definitely sounded like one," she said, her voice quaking with fear. "And who do you think wolves would work for?"

Aisha shuddered. "Selena!"

## Chapter Two
# Lights Out, Moonwolf

Aisha and Emily huddled anxiously together by the fire until Brighteye stepped forward. "Don't worry," she said soothingly. "That howl is just our friend Milo the Moonwolf. He's on his way."

"Moonwolf?" said Aisha.

"Yes! He lives on the moon," said

Brighteye. "Milo is very important. During the day, Aurora guards the valley from Selena. But at night, Milo the Moonwolf comes here from his den to keep watch over us all."

Brighteye pointed to the sky with her horn. Emily could just make out a faint moonbeam shining down over the trees, like a shaft of silver mist.

As she watched, something appeared in the distance, giving off a strange glow — a four-legged shape, with a huge head and a great hairy tail! It was galloping down the moonbeam. As the shape came closer, it grew larger and larger.

Emily and Aisha squeezed each other's hands. "I didn't know wolves could be so big!" said Emily, still a little scared.

They watched as Milo the Moonwolf leapt off the moonbeam and landed in the middle of the glade with a tremendous thump. He turned his shaggy head from side to side, looking at all the creatures who were gathered there, waving. "Hello, Milo!" they called. "Welcome back!"

Some of the creatures ran up to give him a snuggle or pat his head.

He gave them all a wide grin. His long tongue lolled out of his mouth happily, and the girls giggled. Suddenly he looked more like a big friendly dog than a scary wolf!

"He seems nice," Aisha whispered.

"And so pretty," said Emily. Milo's fur wasn't just glowing, it was as bright as the full moon. His whole body seemed to be made from moonlight.

Milo took another step towards the Night Sparkle Unicorns, which wasn't easy, because so many of the party guests were still crowded around him. Some of the little animals had even climbed up on to his back.

Brighteye bowed her horn in greeting.

"Milo," she said, "this is Aisha and Emily, the wonderful girls we told you about!"

Milo leaned his enormous head in for a closer look. Aisha gave a little gasp at the sight of his luminous eyes.

"How lovely to meet you both at last!" Milo said in a deep, rumbling voice. "Thank you for coming to my party."

"*Your* party?" asked Aisha.

"Is it your birthday?" asked Emily.

The moonwolf chuckled and shook his head.

"No," Queen Aurora explained. "We have a campfire party in Milo's honour every full moon – because he is such a brave and loyal moonwolf."

"So it's a thank-you party!" Aisha said.

No wonder everyone was making such a fuss over Milo.

The moonwolf sighed happily, and his misty breath was like a lovely cool night breeze that tickled the girls' cheeks. "It's so good to see all my friends! It can be lonely, patrolling the fields and the forests at night while everyone else is fast asleep."

"But it's obviously such an important

job," Emily said.

"I bet even Selena would think twice before starting any trouble, with you around," Aisha agreed.

But just at that moment, a crash of thunder ripped through the trees. The girls felt the ground shake under their feet. A bright blue-and-white scribble of lightning zigzagged down through the sky and suddenly Selena appeared!

She gave a wicked whinny as she shook her twilight-blue mane over her shining

silver coat. Her eyes flashed dangerously, and all the party guests squealed and ran for cover. Selena's little owl servant, Screech, came flapping along by her side, holding a wooden box in his talons.

"Having fun, are we?" Selena crowed. "Well, fun's over now! I still have the Moon Locket, and you're never getting it back. Screech, open the box!"

Screech didn't seem to have heard

her. He looked around and blinked his big yellow eyes. "Are you all having a party?" he asked.

"I said *open the box*, you overstuffed cushion!" shrieked Selena.

Stuck in the box's keyhole was a little silver key on a long chain. Grumpily, Screech turned the key with his beak and flipped the lid open with his claw.

Light poured out from the box. Inside, lying on the velvet lining, was a small round object that looked just like the full moon.

Brighteye gasped. "My locket! Give it back!"

"Not a chance," gloated Selena. "This box is off to a secret hiding place. You'll never, ever find it. And even if you did, you'd never get it open. Because I'll have the key!"

Screech grabbed the key, flew up and hung the chain around Selena's neck.

"If you don't make me queen, the locket will stay shut away. Then the moon will disappear for ever," Selena said. "You know what that means? No moon, no moon*wolf*! Your overgrown lapdog will vanish quick as ... as ... this marshmallow!" And with that, she snatched a marshmallow from a nearby fox cub and gobbled it up.

Milo snarled, baring his teeth. He began to lope towards Selena.

"Get away, you mangy mutt!" she exclaimed.

Aisha saw a glimmer of fear in Selena's eyes.

"Hurry up, Screech. We are leaving!" said Selena.

The pair of them flew off, vanishing into the depths of the forest and taking the box containing the locket with them.

Suddenly, everything seemed much darker. The stars were still shining overhead, but only a few hints of light showed through the tree branches. The fire

was down to its embers. It wasn't nearly enough to light the clearing.

Everyone in the glade huddled closer around the campfire and cast fearful glances into the shadows.

"Look!" Emily pointed up into the sky. "The moon's gone!"

Where the moon had hung a moment ago, silver and bright, now there was nothing but darkness. Screams and gasps rang out.

Luckily, the girls were standing right next to Milo, whose coat shone like a lantern. They squeezed closer to him.

"Don't worry, everyone!" Milo's powerful voice boomed out. "I'm here to protect you. There's nothing to be afraid of."

"Thank goodness for you, Milo," Emily said.

But then Aisha gasped and pointed. "Emily, look!"

Milo's light, which had been so clear and strong, was flickering.

"Milo!" they cried together.

Then Milo's light went out completely. Just like the moon.

## Chapter Three
# The Dark Forest Monster

As quickly as it had vanished, Milo's light came back on. But it was definitely dimmer than before.

Brighteye paced back and forth. "I was afraid this would happen," she said. "Milo is made out of moonlight. If we can't bring the moon back ..."

"… then I'll just keep fading and fading until there's nothing left of me," Milo finished. His tail drooped and his ears sagged.

Emily and Aisha looked at each other with concern.

"Milo disappearing is awful enough by itself," whispered Emily, "but Queen Aurora can't protect Enchanted Valley at night like he does. What'll happen to the kingdom if he's not here?"

"I don't want to find out," Aisha whispered. "We've got to save him."

Emily gave Milo a cuddle while Aisha went and stroked Brighteye's mane reassuringly. "Don't worry," she said. "We'll help you get your locket back.

Then Milo will be just fine."

Silvermane stepped forward. "It looked to me like they were heading for the Dark Forest," she said.

There were little squeaks of fright from the creatures in the clearing. Even the unicorns looked scared.

"What's so bad about the Dark Forest?" asked Emily.

Silvermane took a deep breath. "A monster lives there!"

"A monster?" Aisha asked, shivering. "So there really are monsters, even here in Enchanted Valley?"

Slumbertail nodded and whispered, "I've heard it has a hundred eyes!" She glanced around as if she feared the monster was watching her right then. "It wouldn't dare leave its lair while Milo is here," she said. "But now that his light's starting to fade, who knows what it might do?"

"We're still going," Emily said bravely.

"Of course we are," agreed Aisha. "If there are monsters around, it's even more important that we get the locket back, and fast!"

"Wait!" Brighteye said. "I'll go with you. It's my locket, after all."

"I'll come too," rumbled Milo. "To light your way." He turned aside, closed his eyes and murmured, "… while I still can."

Brighteye knelt down so the girls could climb on to her back. Then the party guests, along with Queen Aurora, all

wished them good luck.
Leaving the flickering
lights of the campfires
behind, they headed
through the trees and
into the darkness of the
waiting forest.

Soon, the sounds of the gathering died away. Nothing broke the silence but the clip-clop of Brighteye's hooves, and Milo's paws crunching on the bracken.

Milo trotted beside Brighteye, looking keenly into the dark. Suddenly he stopped. "I can smell musty feathers," he said. "I think … yes, it's Screech! He came this way. I have his scent!"

"Hooray!" cheered Emily. "Well done,

Milo!"

With the moonwolf leading the way, they rode on into the forest. They had to squeeze between huge trees that loomed overhead like great swooping ghosts. Chattering, buzzing, squeaking noises filled the night air as they travelled deeper and deeper into the woods. Sometimes they heard a distant hoot, or a soft rustling nearby, but they could see no one

else through the darkness.

Aisha huddled up to Brighteye and shivered. "What if Silvermane and Slumbertail were right?" she whispered to Emily. "What if there really is a monster?"

Emily hugged Aisha tighter around the waist. "Milo's here," she reminded her. "He won't let anything happen to us."

But just then, Milo's whole body blinked out again, from his nose to his

tail. It reminded Emily of the light in her parents' kitchen, which sometimes flickered before it turned on properly.

When it returned, Milo's light was even dimmer than before. They could only make out the closest trees now. He gave a little whimper so Emily ruffled his fur.

"What's that, up ahead?" Brighteye said.

Bobbing along in the air, weaving through the trees, was a little white shape.

"It's not the monster, is it?" Aisha said warily.

"I think it's Screech!" exclaimed Emily.

Milo sniffed the air. "It's him all right."

"Can't catch me, you silly old wolf!" mocked Screech, and flapped away.

Milo growled.
"You three wait
here. I'll grab that pesky
owl and bring him back
in two beats of a moth's
wing!"

Before any of them could say another
word, Milo had gone bounding off after
Screech. His huge, dimly glowing body
vanished into the distance.

Aisha, Emily and Brighteye were left all
alone in the darkness, right in the middle
of the forest.

For a few moments, nobody said
anything. They just huddled together,
their hearts beating fast, while the spooky
night-time sounds rustled and hissed all

around them.

"I hope he's OK out there," Aisha said.
"Milo? Milo! Can you hear me?"

No answer came back.

"I wish I could fly us out of here,"
Brighteye said, "but we can't leave Milo
behind. And besides, it's too dark to see
where I'm going."

Nearby, a swaying branch creaked with
a sound like an old door slowly opening.

Emily squeezed Aisha's hand nervously.
Then she gasped as she saw a glow of
light.

"Oh, thank goodness!" Aisha burst out.
"Milo's coming back."

To both the girls' relief, they could
soon see that it really was the moonwolf

trotting back towards them. But something wasn't quite right. He was walking in a weird, stiff way, as if he had a leg cramp.

"Are you OK?" Aisha asked him.

Milo blinked. "Me? Oh! Yes, I'm fine. I just, er, tripped. That's it. I was chasing after that owl, and I tripped over a tree root. He can fly very fast, you know."

Aisha and Emily exchanged a look. Once Milo's back was turned, Emily whispered, "I'm not sure he *is* fine."

"He's acting strangely," Aisha agreed.

"Where's Screech?" Brighteye asked.

"I'm afraid he got away. He's very clever," Milo said. "But I did hear him say something about a cave nearby. That must be where Selena hid the locket."

"A cave?" Aisha said anxiously, wondering what might be lurking inside.

"Yes, and I think I know where it is. Come on!"

They followed Milo through the Dark Forest to a spot where the ground rose up to form a rocky wall. Sure enough, there was an arched cave mouth with tree roots dangling down above it. Inside, it was pitch black.

"In you go," Milo said.

"Can't you go ahead and light the way?" Aisha suggested.

"I'll be right behind you, shining my light from there," Milo promised.

The cave's ceiling was low so Aisha and Emily climbed off Brighteye's back. Hand in hand, they took their first steps in. Water dripped nearby, *plip-plop*. A root touched the back of Emily's neck and made her yelp.

Step by nervous step, they made their way deeper and deeper into the cave. Milo's light, shining behind them, seemed dimmer than ever.

Then, from the pitch blackness up ahead, they heard a sound. Something was stirring. Something huge, that rustled and flapped and scratched.

Suddenly, eyes were peering at them out of the darkness. Big, round, yellow eyes. Dozens and dozens of them.

"A hundred eyes!" cried Emily.

Aisha fought hard not to scream. "The monster! It's real!"

## Chapter Four
# Scaredy-Wolf

Milo yelped in alarm. He turned around and ran out of the cave.

"Milo, come back!" Aisha yelled. "We need you to protect us!"

"I thought he was supposed to be b-brave," Brighteye stammered.

The girls stroked Brighteye's neck.

"Well, we'll just have to be brave ourselves," Emily whispered.

"The locket might be here," said Aisha. "And if we've got to face the monster, at least we'll do it together."

"OK," Brighteye whispered, her voice wavering.

As they listened to the sound of Milo crashing clumsily through the undergrowth, they stood side by side, ready for anything.

Suddenly two of the eyes broke free from the rest as something fluttered forwards. Aisha squinted, trying to see what it was. She made out beating wings, little hooked feet, a curved beak, feathery tufts like ears …

"It's an owl!" she cried. "That's all. Just an owl. No bigger than Screech."

More pairs of eyes came towards them, and the girls saw they didn't belong to a monster at all. They belonged to more owls – dozens and dozens of them!

"Hello!" the girls said together.

The owl in front gave a sweeping bow. "Hello to you too-hoo-hoo! My name is Blink," he said. "I'm so happy to meet you! Finally, a

visitor to our humble cave."

Aisha and Emily looked at one another
and giggled. Even Brighteye joined in.
How had they been so scared of these
nice owls?

"We thought you were a monster!"
Aisha told Blink.

"A monster?" Blink tipped his feathery
head. "Is that why nobody ever wants to

come and visit us?"

A few of the owls
behind him hooted
sadly, their feathers
drooping.

"Yes!" said
Brighteye. "We all
thought a monster

lived here."

"But now we know it's you, you'll make loads of new friends!" said Emily.

"In fact," said Aisha, "there's a party in the clearing in the woods right now. Go and introduce yourselves!"

The owls all began to bob up and down and ruffle their feathers excitedly. "Thank you so much," Blink hooted. "We can't wait to meet some new friends!"

"We'd take you to the party but we have to find Selena and Screech, and Brighteye's locket," said Emily. "Goodbye! See you all soon!"

"Goodbye!" came the chorus of hooting voices.

Aisha, Emily and Brighteye made their

way out of the cave, feeling a lot less scared than they had been when they entered.

"We should have known there was nothing to be scared of," Emily said. "Just like we had nothing to be afraid of when we met Milo."

"Poor Milo. *He* must have been really frightened, to run away like that," Aisha said.

"Yes," said Brighteye, cocking her head in thought. "It's so unlike him. I've never seen him get frightened like that."

"Well, it *was* pretty scary in the cave," Emily said.

"But Milo's been in dark caves before, lots of times," Brighteye said firmly.

"If I didn't know better, I'd say it wasn't Milo at all."

Aisha and Emily looked at each other. They both had the same thought at the exact same moment. Screech had a secret power to change into the shapes of other creatures.

"Oh no," they said together. "Not again!"

Just then, they spotted Milo bounding back towards them. When he saw the girls he came to a sudden stop and stared, open-mouthed.

"What are you doing here?" he asked. "Didn't the monster get you? I mean ... thank goodness the monster didn't get you."

"Drop the act, Screech," Emily said. "We know it's you."

In a puff of magic, Milo disappeared and Screech was suddenly there in his place.

"Took you long enough to work it out!" he taunted.

Brighteye stamped her hoof. "Where's the real Milo? What have you done with him?"

Instead of answering, Screech just flew away, hooting with laughter.

From somewhere in the forest, a sad howl rang out.

"Milo!" Aisha yelled.

"Climb on my back, quickly!" said Brighteye.

Aisha and Emily held on tight and Brighteye took them through the forest. It was hard to see, so she couldn't go very fast. All they could do was follow the howls. Soon, Emily spotted a silvery glow shining up from the ground.

Brighteye headed for the light and stopped. They were right at the edge of a deep pit!

And there on the floor of the pit, looking miserable, was Milo the

Moonwolf.

"Milo! Thank goodness we've found you!" Aisha called out.

"What happened?" Emily shouted.

"Screech and Selena set a trap!" Milo growled. "I fell for it. Or rather *into* it."

Aisha looked down. "Can you climb out?" she called.

"I tried," Milo answered. "The walls are too steep."

Emily had an idea. "Brighteye, can you fly him out?"

"I don't think so," Brighteye said sadly. "He's too big for me to lift."

"Maybe there's something in the forest that can help us," Aisha said. "Let's have a look."

Although it was nearly pitch dark, with only the light from the stars to see by, Aisha and Emily headed into the forest.

"Oof!" Aisha said as she tripped over something half-hidden in the ferny undergrowth. "What was that?"

Emily looked down. "It's a log!"

"Perfect!" said Aisha. "Milo can use this to climb out of the pit! Brighteye, can you help us push this log over there?"

Together the three of them shoved the log over to the pit.

Brighteye gave it a good hard kick with her hind hooves. It tilted over and slid down.

Milo pressed on the log with his paw, testing its strength. "Perfect!" he said. "Just like a moonbeam to run along."

He scrambled up the log and burst out triumphantly in a shower of dry leaves. Aisha and Emily gave a cheer, then hugged him.

"Thank goodness you're safe," Aisha said.

But as they stepped back, they saw Milo's light had faded. A lot! And not only had his glow dimmed, but the edges of his fur were almost invisible now. They could see the trees through his body!

Aisha and Emily shared a worried glance. They were running out of time to save Milo.

## Chapter Five
# The Watery Hiding Place

Milo sniffed the air. "I've got Screech's scent again," he said.

Brighteye laughed. "He can change his shape, but he can't change how he smells!"

"He won't get away this time," Milo growled.

Brighteye and the girls followed Milo
through the Dark Forest once more.
Soon they heard the gurgle and splash
of running water nearby. Moments later,
they emerged through a gap in the trees
and found they were on the bank of a
stream. Even without the moon overhead,
the water glittered in the light from the

stars, as if it were full of a million silver fishes.

"This is where the scent trail ends," Milo said. He leapt across the stream, sniffed, shook his head and leapt back over again. "It doesn't carry on from the other side, either. I can't tell where Screech went from here."

"Maybe he flew up into the sky and hid the locket in a tall tree?" guessed Brighteye.

"Or maybe he followed the stream through the forest?" suggested Emily.

But Aisha noticed something the others hadn't. She pointed the other way, where the stream flowed down a rock face in a little waterfall, creating clouds of mist.

"Remember when Selena said she had a secret hiding place for the locket?" Aisha said. "What if it's behind that waterfall? That would be a great hiding place!"

"It's got to be worth a look!" Emily said. "Let's go!"

The waterfall was like a fine,

shimmering curtain. Aisha cautiously reached through with one arm. Sure enough, there was a hollow behind the waterfall!

She took a deep breath, bent her knees and jumped through the cold water.

Emily and Brighteye followed her through, shivering as the water splashed them.

Milo jumped through the waterfall last and squeezed in to join them, but they could tell right away that something was wrong. Instead of a shining, pearly moonwolf, he was a dark, shadowy, wolf-shaped smudge. They could hardly see him at all any more.

"We've got to find that box fast, and get Milo his light back!" Aisha whispered to Emily.

"Yes, but how?" Emily replied. "It's so dark in here. I can't even see my hand in front of my face!"

Just then, another voice spoke from the back of the cave – a familiar, grumpy, hooting voice. "Gah!" it squawked. "You found my hiding place!"

"Screech?" gasped Aisha.

"Well, that's it," Screech groaned. "Selena's going to be so cross with me. She'll get a new helper, and I'll have to go back to spending every single night all by myself without any friends."

"Is that why you were helping her?" Emily asked gently. "Because you didn't want to be alone?"

Screech sighed. "Yes. I know Selena isn't very nice, but everyone else goes to sleep at night. I just get so bored with nobody to talk to or play games with."

"I understand," came Milo's faint voice. "I get lonely during the long nights, too."

Aisha suddenly felt an idea lighting up her mind like a brilliant spark. "Hey, Screech? If we promised to take you to meet a lot of new friends, would you help us instead of Selena?"

The whole cave echoed with flapping noises as Screech beat his wings in excitement. "Of course I would! It's a deal!"

"Thank you, Screech!" Emily cheered. "The first thing we need to do is to find that box. Can you tell us where it is?"

"Hmmm," said Screech. "Hoo. I definitely hid it in here somewhere. But it's so dark, I don't know how I can find it again."

"We need some light!" Aisha said.

"I'm sorry," whispered Milo. "My light is all gone."

"Let me try," Brighteye said. She was quiet for a second, then her horn lit up with a very faint light. The girls could see Brighteye's face for just a moment, before being plunged into darkness again.

"It's no good," Brighteye gasped. "Without my locket, I can't make it last."

"Wait!" Aisha said. "Screech, can you change into Milo, the way he looked before Selena made the moon disappear?"

"Of course!" Screech said proudly.
"I can change into anything!"

Instantly, the whole cave lit up as
Screech shifted into Milo's form. The light
that shone from his body was as bright as
the full moon had been.

"Well done, Screech!" yelled Aisha.

Then Emily gasped. She'd spotted the
box under the very
rock ledge that Screech
had been sitting on
moments before! She
quickly scooped it up,
cradling the box in
her hands.

"Got it!" she said.

"Now we just have to open it."

Aisha glanced at Milo, who was nothing but a shadow now, and said, "We need to do it fast, or Milo might vanish completely!"

# Chapter Six
# Party Crashers

"There's only one problem," said Emily. "Selena has the key, and we don't know where she is!"

"And we don't have time to go searching for her!" cried Aisha.

Emily held up the box and peered closely at it. "Maybe we can get it open without the key," she said. "I know! Hob has all sorts of magical potions and things. He might know something we can do."

"Good thinking!" Aisha said. "We saw him at the party, playing his fiddle, remember? Let's go back there and ask him to help."

Brighteye bent down. "You girls get on my back. Screech, if you stay in Milo's form and light the way, we can see where we're going and gallop back through the forest."

"Happy to!" Screech said.

"Thanks, Screech," Emily said, patting him on the head. He blinked in surprise, then smiled.

They burst through
the waterfall and
thundered off through
the trees. Brighteye's
hooves pounded the
mossy ground and

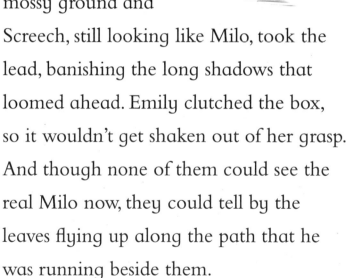

Screech, still looking like Milo, took the
lead, banishing the long shadows that
loomed ahead. Emily clutched the box,
so it wouldn't get shaken out of her grasp.
And though none of them could see the
real Milo now, they could tell by the
leaves flying up along the path that he
was running beside them.

It was a wild, breathless ride. The
girls held on to Brighteye's neck as she
galloped. The forest was so huge and so

dark that the girls sometimes felt sure they would get lost, but Brighteye never stopped or paused for even a second. She directed Screech confidently as they raced along.

"Don't worry," she gasped. "Trust me. I know the way."

Sure enough, they soon saw the distant glimmer of firelight. They were back at the party!

But as they drew closer to the wide clearing, strange sounds reached their ears. There was no more music and no laughter. Instead, they could hear squeals and cries of fear, and the hasty footsteps of several creatures running away at once.

"Our friends are in trouble!" Aisha cried.

"Let's go and help," said Emily.

But Brighteye stopped in her tracks. "Wait. We should be careful. Let's see what's happening before we go charging in."

Moving as quietly as they could, they hid behind a tree so they could watch without being seen.

Emily gasped as she finally saw Selena in the middle of the forest clearing, stamping her hooves and bucking her head! All the party guests were cowering in terror.

"What a lovely party!" Selena mocked. "Shame there's no moonwolf to enjoy it!" She pranced around in a circle, a huge smirk on her face. "Who's going to protect you now he's all faded away? Nobody, that's who! The kingdom is as good as mine! You silly creatures may as well bow down to me now. I'm your new queen!"

In the darkness nearby, Milo gave a whisper of a growl … fainter than a fading dream.

"He's almost out of time," Aisha warned.

Brighteye said, "Look, Selena's still got the key round her neck! This is our chance to get it. But how?"

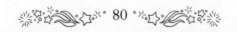

Aisha thought hard. "I've got an idea," she said. "Remember when Selena first saw Milo, and he growled at her? She was scared silly of him."

"That's right!" said Emily.

"So why don't we get Screech to keep on pretending to be Milo and chase her right past where we're hiding? We can fly up as she goes by, and grab the locket!"

"OK," said Screech, readying himself.

"I hope this works, just to see the look on her face!"

As Brighteye hid behind the tree, Screech went bounding into the clearing. He charged right up to Selena, bared his teeth and let out a growl so loud it made her mane flutter.

Selena stared. Her eyes went as wide as pufflebunny tails.

"Whaaaaat? This can't be!" she howled. "You're meant to be all fizzled out! Argh! Get away from me, you mangy mutt!"

She reared up, flailing her hooves wildly. All the party guests cheered as Screech barked and growled at her.

Suddenly, Selena leapt from the ground and took flight, soaring over the party guests' heads.

But Brighteye, Aisha and Emily were prepared. As Selena came flying in their direction, Brighteye rushed up through the air at her. "Now, Aisha!" she called.

Aisha held on to Brighteye's mane with one hand and reached out for the key with the other. As Selena passed by, she grabbed at the key. Her fingers brushed the metal but closed on empty air. She had missed!

Selena flew up higher, cackling at the top of her voice. "Nice try, silly girl!" she shouted. "You'll never get the key from …"

A high-pitched whistle sounded from down below, startling everyone – even Selena.

Emily could hear an uncanny rustling as the trees began to shake.

"Something's coming from the Dark Forest!" she shouted.

"I don't know what it is," Aisha added, "but it sounds big!"

The creatures at the party cried out together, "Monster!"

## Chapter Seven
# In a Flap

The treetops quivered. The branches shook.

Suddenly, with a great whirring of wings, dozens and dozens of owls rose up from the forest. They swept and soared through the sky above Selena, their wide wings spread out like the sails of a whole fleet of ships.

"It's Blink and the owls from the cave!" shouted Aisha.

"They must have come to the party, just like we said," added Emily.

There were so many owls filling the sky over the clearing that Selena couldn't push through them. They were trapping her in like the lid on a sandwich box. She had to fly lower, her hooves almost brushing the highest trees.

"Out of my way, you feathery rats!" Selena yelled. "Don't you know royalty when you see it?"

"Get ready for another go at that key, Aisha!" said Brighteye.

"Ready," Aisha said firmly.

Brighteye rushed through the sky, heading straight for Selena.

This time, Selena didn't see them coming. She was too busy trying to force her way through the barrier of beating owl wings. "I said *move*!" she howled.

"Now!" yelled Brighteye.

As Brighteye flew past Selena, Aisha

 reached for the key, closed her fingers tightly around it and tugged the chain right off Selena's neck.

"I've got it!" she whooped.

Emily shoved the box under her arm and reached out. "Quick, pass it to me!"

Aisha's heart was pounding. Careful not to drop the key, she pressed it into Emily's hand. Emily slid it into the lock and twisted. With a click, the box flew open.

The Moon Locket sat inside on a little velvet pillow. Bright moonlight poured out from it, misty and magical.

Emily took it from the box and quickly hung it around Brighteye's neck.

A beautiful sight filled the sky as the moon suddenly blazed with light once

more, flooding the clearing and shining on the upturned faces of the girls and creatures. The circling owls hooted happily. Their gliding bodies and beating wings made dancing moon-shadows on the ground below.

Selena let out a furious shriek. "Gah! You meddling girls! Think you've won just because you found the Moon Locket, do you? Well, I'm just getting started!" She snorted crossly. "Screech and I will be back, you mark my words!" She looked around. "Where is that blasted bird, anyway?"

But there was no reply.

"Screech?" Selena bellowed. "I can't find you among all these owls! Where

have you gone?"

Screech changed back into his owl form and fluttered up towards Selena.

"I'm right here," he said. "But I'm not going anywhere. Not with you."

"Oh yes you are," Selena said, "if I have to drag you out myself!"

She flew down towards Screech, who trembled at the sight of her.

Suddenly, a powerful voice roared out from among the party guests. "He said he didn't want to go with you, Selena. Leave him alone!"

Milo strode out from the crowds, his body glowing with bright moonlight.

Selena let out a little high-pitched noise, as if she were a mouse instead of a unicorn.

"In fact, you'd better leave all of us alone," Milo growled. "Or ELSE!"

Emily and Aisha cheered. "Milo's back!" they shouted.

Selena cringed. Turning toward the girls she sneered, "You think that overgrown dog can protect you from me?"

"Actually … yes," grinned Aisha.

"Ha! Well, dog or no dog, you haven't seen the last of me!"

With a crash of thunder, Selena flew
away over the trees and into the sky.
They all watched as she grew smaller
and smaller, until she was no more than a
tiny dot.

## Chapter Eight
# Campfire Funtimes

"Whoopee!" cried Hob, tucking his fiddle under his arm and throwing his hat into the air. "Hooray! She's gone!"

Laughter, cheering and applause broke out all around.

Brighteye flew down into the clearing, carrying Aisha and Emily on her back.

The girls climbed off into the middle of the delighted crowd. Everyone wanted to hug them and say thank you.

Then the crowds parted to let Milo through. The girls ran up to him and gave him a great big cuddle, burying their faces in his thick, glowing fur.

"I'm so glad you're OK!" Aisha said.

"We were scared you'd be gone for

ever," said Emily.

"I'm fine now, thanks to you," Milo said. His huge tail wagged happily.

Queen Aurora stepped forward, with a delighted smile on her face. Behind her came Dreamspell, Slumbertail and Silvermane, each with their lockets glittering proudly on their chests. Brighteye went to join them.

"Well done, girls," Aurora said. "You've saved Enchanted Valley once again!"

"We couldn't have done it without our friends, Brighteye and Milo," said Emily.

"Or our new friend, Screech!" Aisha added.

Queen Aurora looked up to the trees. All the owls from the Dark Forest had perched in the branches. They sat in shy, feathery rows, watching the festivities.

"It looks to me like you made quite a

few new friends!" Queen Aurora said.

"Yes, we did!" Emily said proudly. "Can
I have everyone's attention, please?"

The party guests turned towards Emily
and Aisha, quietly waiting to hear what
Emily had to say.

"We'd like to introduce you all to the
owls of the Dark Forest!" Emily said, with
a grand flourish. "Everyone thought the
hundred eyes belonged to a monster, but

it was really these lovely owls."

"And they'd really like to get to know you!" Aisha added.

The owls bowed and all the party guests clapped or cheered, as relieved laughter spread through the crowd.

"I can't believe it," said Silvermane. "The monster wasn't even real!"

Blink flew down and landed on Aisha's shoulder. "If any of you would like to

come and visit us in our cave, we would love to see you-hoo-hoo. Everyone's welcome."

"I already know someone who'd like to visit," said Aisha. "Screech!"

Screech flapped forwards and perched on her shoulder. "Hello," he said eagerly. "I had no idea there were other owls in Enchanted Valley! I'm a screech owl. What kind of owls are you?"

"We're all night owls," explained Blink. "We've never met a screech owl before! You can come and stay in our cave any time you like."

"Can I? Oh, thank you!" Screech fluttered up and down joyfully. "I can't wait. This is going to be such fun!"

Nobody could remember a better full moon campfire party than this one. The owls of the Dark Forest mingled with all the other creatures and were soon chatting away, making friends and telling stories. Aisha and Emily toasted marshmallows over the golden flames and joined in with the traditional unicorn campfire songs. But of all the people and creatures at the party, no one had more fun than Screech.

"He's a changed owl," Aisha whispered to Emily.

"It's funny, really," Emily whispered back. "All this time, he's been pretending to be other creatures. But now that he's being himself, he's having the time of his life!"

As the embers of the campfires began to die down, the four Night Sparkle Unicorns gathered in the middle of the glade and touched their horns together. A deep chime rang out.

At long last, the first rays of dawn began to shine in the east. A beautiful melody echoed through the forest. Queen Aurora was singing.

"What's that gorgeous song?" Emily

asked Brighteye.

"It's the song of welcome to the sun,"
Brighteye said. "Queen Aurora sings it
every morning."

Fresh cheering broke out across the
camp. The night was finally coming to
an end, and it would soon be daytime in
Enchanted Valley once again!

"I suppose that means you have to go
home now," Aisha said to Milo.

Milo yawned very wide. "That's right. I've loved meeting the two of you, but it's been a very long night, and I ought to get back to the moon. I'm ready for a good day's sleep!"

Brighteye smiled. "Let's get you home, then." Her locket glimmered with light. The next moment, a strong moonbeam streamed down from the sky.

Everyone waved goodbye to Milo as he trotted up the moonbeam.

Aurora turned to the girls. "You must both be tired, too, after all your adventures!"

Emily and Aisha nodded sleepily.

"It's definitely past our bedtime." Aisha gave a great yawn. "I've never stayed up until dawn before!"

"But we'd love to come back again soon," Emily said. "Just call us if Selena gives you any more trouble, OK?"

"I will," Aurora promised. "But for now, I have a special gift for you both, to say thank you for all your help!"

She gave them each a crystal charm in the shape of a glittering star. Emily and Aisha gasped.

"Thank you!" Emily said.

"They're beautiful!" Aisha added.

The girls added the stars to their

keyrings, where they hung next to the other charms Aurora had given them. Every time they looked at the shining stars, they would remember the Night Sparkle Unicorns and all the adventures they had had together.

The girls said a drowsy goodbye to everyone at the party.

"Sleep well," said Aurora. "See you very soon!"

Aurora bowed her horn. Shimmering sparkles whirled up and around the two girls. Before they even had time to blink, they were back in Aisha's bedroom.

It was still night-time in the ordinary world as not a moment had passed since they left. The full moon shone brightly through the curtains, and their new star charms twinkled in its friendly light.

Emily sighed happily as she climbed into bed. "That was so much fun!"

"It really was," Aisha said. "And do you know what the best part is?"

"Hmm?" said Emily, who was already almost asleep.

"I'm finally sleepy!"

Emily laughed and closed her eyes. Even though she was tired out, she couldn't wait for their next adventure in Enchanted Valley to begin.

The End

Join Emily and Aisha
for more fun in ...
# Sparklebeam's
# Holiday Adventure
Read on for a sneak peek!

"Get ready, Emily – here comes a big wave!" cried Aisha Khan. She was lying face-down on her surfboard, gripping the edge. As the wave came towards her, Aisha leaped to her feet. She crouched, ready to ride the wave as it lifted up her surfboard.

Emily Turner, Aisha's best friend, grinned up at her. She was lying on her surfboard too, but the girls weren't really in the sea – they were in the living room of Enchanted Cottage, where Aisha lived with her parents. Both girls were giddy with excitement, because their families were going on holiday together! Outside, their parents were packing the Khans' car. Soon they would set off for the coast, to stay in a seaside cabin. But it was pouring with rain, and their parents were wearing anoraks over their summer clothes.

### Read
# Sparklebeam's Holiday Adventure
### to find out what's in store
### for Aisha and Emily!

# Also available

**Book Five:**

Daisy Meadows

Unicorn Magic

*Silvermane Saves the Stars*

From the author of RAINBOW MAGIC

**Book Six:**

Daisy Meadows

Unicorn Magic

*Dreamspell's Special Wish*

From the author of RAINBOW MAGIC

**Book Seven:**

Daisy Meadows

Unicorn Magic

*Slumbertail & the Sleep Pixies*

From the author of RAINBOW MAGIC

**Book Eight:**

Daisy Meadows

Unicorn Magic

*Brighteye & the Blue Moon*

From the author of RAINBOW MAGIC

# Look out for the next book!

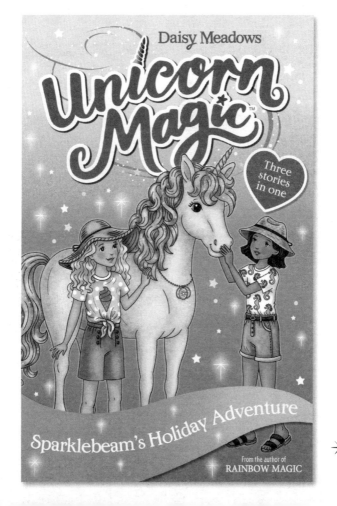

Daisy Meadows

Unicorn Magic™

Three stories in one

Sparklebeam's Holiday Adventure

From the author of
RAINBOW MAGIC

If you like
Unicorn Magic,
you'll love …

Welcome to Animal Ark!
Animal-mad Amelia is sad
about moving house, until she
discovers Animal Ark, where vets look
after all kinds of animals in need.

Join Amelia and her friend Sam for a
brand-new series of animal adventures!

# Quickhoof and the Golden Cup

## Daisy Meadows

ORCHARD

# For Kirsten Fox

# Special thanks to Val Wilding

ORCHARD BOOKS

First published in Great Britain in 2020 by Hodder & Stoughton

3 5 7 9 10 8 6 4 2

Text copyright © 2020 Working Partners Limited
Illustrations © Orchard Books 2020
Series created by Working Partners Limited

A CIP catalogue record for this book is available from the British Library.

ISBN 978 1 40836 623 3

Printed and bound in Great Britain by Clays Ltd, Elcograf S.p.A.

The paper and board used in this book are made from wood from responsible sources.

Orchard Books
An imprint of Hachette Children's Group
Part of Hodder and Stoughton
Carmelite House
50 Victoria Embankment
London EC4Y 0DZ

An Hachette UK Company

www.hachette.co.uk
www.hachettechildrens.co.uk

Contents

# Meet the Characters

Aisha and Emily are best friends from Spellford Village. Aisha loves sports, whilst Emily's favourite thing is science. But what both girls enjoy more than anything is visiting Enchanted Valley and helping their unicorn friends, who live there.

Quickhoof

The four Sports and Games Unicorns help to make games and competitions fun for everyone. Quickhoof uses her magic locket to help players work well as a team.

Feeling confident in your skills and abilities is so important for sporting success. Brightblaze's magic helps to make sure everyone believes in themselves!

Brightblaze

Games are no fun when players cheat or don't follow the rules. Fairtail's magic locket reminds everyone to play fair!

Fairtail

When things get difficult, Spiritmane's perseverance locket gives sportspeople the strength to face their challenges and succeed.

Spiritmane

Enchanted Cottage

Golden Palace

An Enchanted Valley lies a twinkle away,
Where beautiful unicorns live, laugh and play
You can visit the mermaids, or go for a ride,
So much fun to be had, but dangers can hide!

Your friends need your help ~ this is how you know:
A keyring lights up with a magical glow.
Whirled off like a dream, you won't want to leave.
Friendship forever, when you truly believe.

## Chapter One
# A Silvery Surprise

Emily Turner and Aisha Khan skipped joyfully ahead of their parents. It was a gloriously sunny day and they couldn't wait to watch the football match! The Spellford Seals were playing their rivals, the Greenlea Gazelles.

The Khans lived in a pretty thatched

house in Spellford called Enchanted Cottage. Aisha and Emily had met on the day Aisha's family moved in and the girls had been best friends ever since.

Emily touched the blue and gold striped scarf she wore. "Thanks for lending me a Seals scarf," she said. "I look like a real football fan."

"You soon will be," said Aisha excitedly. "The Seals' best players are Sasha Fry – she's their top striker – and Dena Walton. You should see Dena race down the wing!"

Emily grinned. "I haven't a clue what strikers and wings are, but I'm looking forward to the match," she said. "Who's your favourite player?"

"Bella Bates, the goalkeeper," said Aisha. "I'd love to be able to save goals like she does, but I'm better at passing and scoring."

"I'm no good at any of those things!" Emily sighed. "I can tell a battery clip from a crocodile clip in science, but I'll struggle with football."

"Well, I struggle in science," Aisha laughed. "We could help each other!"

Emily grinned. "Teamwork!"

"Exactly," said Aisha. "It's the team that matters, you don't need to know individual players. The Seals are the best team ever!" She laughed again. "In my opinion, that is."

Mrs Khan handed out tickets as they joined the queue for the turnstile. Emily peered past the line and saw a grandstand on each side of the pitch. As she looked

down at her ticket to see where their seats were, a glow of light caught her eye. She drew a sharp breath, and nudged Aisha. "Your keyring," she whispered.

Aisha glanced

down at the crystal unicorn keyring that dangled from her belt. It was glowing!

Emily pulled a keyring from her pocket. "Mine's glowing, too!"

The girls knew what this meant. Queen Aurora was calling them back to Enchanted Valley!

Aisha and Emily had discovered an amazing secret in the attic of Enchanted Cottage – a crystal statuette of a unicorn. When a sunbeam shone on it, the girls were magically carried off to Enchanted Valley, a beautiful land of unicorns and other magical creatures. Aurora, the unicorn queen, had used a spell to create the crystal keyrings after their first adventure together.

The girls' eyes shone with excitement.

"Do you think this means Selena's causing trouble again?" Emily asked.

Selena was a mean unicorn who wanted to take Queen Aurora's crown and rule Enchanted Valley herself.

"If she is," Aisha said grimly, "we'll stop her. We've done it before. Come on!"

They knew that no time would pass while they were in Enchanted Valley. They wouldn't miss the match, and no one would miss them!

The girls ducked behind an ice cream kiosk and held up their keyrings. The crystal unicorns glimmered in the sunshine.

"Ready?" said Emily.

"Ready!"

They felt the
keyrings pulling
towards each other.

When the horns touched, dazzling
sparkles swirled around Aisha and Emily
– blue, pink, indigo and green. Faster and
faster the sparkles whirled, lifting the girls
right off the ground! They laughed with
excitement as Emily's long hair whipped
around her head.

As they touched down and the sparkles
started to fade, the girls knew that in a
moment they would see Queen Aurora's
glittering golden palace sitting on a
lush green hilltop, overlooking peaceful
meadows and gently bubbling streams.

"Oops, look out!" An imp wearing running shoes leaped to one side to avoid crashing into Emily.

"Coming through!" cried a little bunny, turning a series of flips.

The girls looked around them. Although they were in front of the palace, the usually peaceful grassy slopes were crowded with unicorns and magical creatures, all running, jumping, skipping or doing gymnastics. The air was filled

with excited squeals and laughter.
Unicorns trotted in and out of the palace,
carrying baskets of bunting, banners and
balloons.

On the hillside beyond was a huge
stadium of gleaming silver.

Emily's mouth dropped open. "That
wasn't here last time," she said.

The stadium's delicate walls looked as if
they'd been woven from strands of silvery
candy floss. Flags of every colour fluttered

high above on tall silver poles.

"Cool!" Aisha gasped. "I think something sporty's happening!"

Emily grinned. "Definitely!" She pointed to the sky, where their friend Fluffy the cloud puppy was playing a game. It looked like rugby, except that his ball was a small grey raincloud. Other cloud creatures chased him, until a cloud bunny caught him and grabbed the fleecy ball. Fluffy rolled on his back and lay giggling in the air.

The cloud bunny flicked the ball with her puff of a tail. It floated down towards an elderly pixie on the ground below. The cloud bounced once, gently, on his head, then began raining on him. His eyes widened in surprise.

Aisha giggled. "It's a cloudburst!"

They headed for the palace, passing
a team of gnomes in swimming
trunks marching towards the moat.

Chuckling pixies practising broomstick racing whizzed overhead, and a great beating of wings made the girls look up. They waved to a tumble of dragons, who were having an upside-down flying race.

Near the palace, the girls spotted their mermaid friends shrieking with laughter as they played water polo in the crystal-clear moat. The mermaids waved.

"Everyone's gone sport mad!" said
Aisha, waving back.

A unicorn came out of the palace and
trotted lightly over the silver drawbridge.
Her mane and tail were glossy gold and
her coat shimmered with the pearly

colours of a summer
dawn: pink, orange,
yellow and red.

"Aurora!" cried Emily.

The unicorn queen
wore a silver crown, and
her horn gleamed gold.
Around her neck hung
a locket with two tiny
golden suns dancing
around each other.

All the unicorns in Enchanted Valley wore magical lockets. Aurora's was the Friendship locket. While she wore it, her magic made sure that Enchanted Valley remained peaceful and friendly.

"Welcome, girls!" Queen Aurora said in her soft, lilting voice. "I'm so happy you came. We're getting ready for the Enchanted Valley Games!"

"It looks exciting!" said Emily.

"What's going to happen?" asked Aisha.

Aurora's golden mane sparkled. "Once every four years we get together to enjoy lots of different sports and fun games," she said. "This evening, at sunset, we're having a grand opening ceremony. I thought you'd like to join us."

"We'd love to!" Emily said. "It looks like the sports here are a bit different from the ones we play at home."

Aurora smiled. "Some are, but there'll also be lots you know."

Hoofbeats pounded, and four unicorns cantered over the hillside towards them.

"Here are the Sports and Games Unicorns," said Aurora. "They'll be judges and referees, and they'll make sure everything goes well."

Aurora introduced them. "Quickhoof takes care of Teamwork," she said.

A unicorn with a buttercup-yellow coat dipped her horn to say hello. Her chestnut mane and tail matched her soft brown eyes. Her locket contained a twinkling golden cup.

"Hello, Quickhoof," said the girls.

"Brightblaze is in charge of Confidence," Aurora continued, as a pearly-coloured unicorn with a scarlet mane and tail dipped her horn in greeting. Her locket had a shining medal inside.

"Fairtail sees to Sportsmanship." A sea-green unicorn lowered her horn, and as she got up they could see her locket – a beautiful rosette.

"And Spiritmane looks after Perseverance."

A lavender unicorn with a creamy mane and tail greeted the girls. Her locket held a scroll tied with red ribbon. She was smiling but then her smile suddenly dropped and she stared over Emily's shoulder.

The girls turned to see a

small greeny-brown whirlwind moving swiftly across the meadow. The leaves twisted as it swirled along.

The whirlwind was heading straight towards them!

## Chapter Two
# Emily Tries

"Oh no!" cried Aisha. "Is that Selena?"

She clutched Emily's hand as the whirlwind began to slow down. Selena was the last person they wanted to see. She'd be sure to ruin the Enchanted Valley Games.

"It can't be her," Emily said, frowning.

"That whirlwind looks too small and green to be her!"

As the whirlwind came to a stop, several small creatures somersaulted to the ground. They were half as tall as the girls, with brownish-green skin which was rough and knobbly, like tree bark. Their hair seemed to be made of twigs and leaves, with little patches of bright green moss dotted here and there. Each wore a necklace of hazelnut shells, and they huddled together, holding hands.

Quickhoof and the other unicorns dipped their horns to the creatures.

"These are our friends, the wood nymphs," Aurora explained. "One of the best football teams in Enchanted Valley!"

The girls smiled and giggled in relief. "Hello!"

"*Lo*," squeaked the biggest nymph.

"*Lo*," the others echoed.

"Aisha and Emily," said Aurora, "would you like to watch the nymphs practise?"

"Yes please!" they said.

Aurora's horn glowed deep orange, sending a swish of magical stars flashing over the meadow below the hill. They cleared, leaving a flat, grassy football pitch with line markings and goals.

Tucked into one of the nets were four footballs, as white as snowberries.

The nymphs pulled strands of ivy from their pockets, and used them to tie up their twiggy hair. One nymph had trouble with a knot, so Emily stepped forward to help.

The nymph looked startled, but smiled a thank you and joined her teammates, jogging on to the pitch.

"Wood nymphs are shy," Aurora said. "They rely on each other for confidence."

Quickhoof nodded. "Confidence and trust makes them a great team."

After some warm-up exercises, the nymphs began kicking balls to each other. One nymph would call a name and pass the ball to that person.

Aisha saw how accurate their passes were. The ball always landed almost at the little wooden boot of the nymph whose name was called … then on to the next.

"They're good!" Emily said. "Even I can see that."

Suddenly, the nymphs huddled together.

"What's going on?" Emily wondered.

Aisha shrugged. "Maybe they're planning a set piece." To her surprise, the nymph who Emily had helped left the huddle and ran towards the girls.

"We wonder … would you like to join our training session?" she asked shyly.

Aisha was thrilled. "Yes, please!" She fetched a ball that had rolled off the pitch and did a few keepy-uppies. Then she dribbled it towards the nymphs.

Emily hung back. Aisha called her, but Emily gave a tiny shake of her head. "I can't," she mouthed.

Aisha ran to her.

"I've never played football," Emily said.

"I'll ruin it."

"You won't," Aisha said. "Everyone starts somewhere. It's taking part that counts! You'll soon get the hang of it."

Emily looked at the length of the pitch. "I couldn't kick a ball that far by myself," she said.

"You don't have to," said Aisha. "You're part of a team. Everyone helps everyone else. That's why we practise all that passing. Just look for someone in a space." She ran backwards, calling, "Pass to me!"

Emily took a deep breath, then kicked the ball and jumped in delight when it almost reached Aisha.

They joined the wood nymphs, who were taking turns shooting for goal.

Everyone cheered when Emily scored.

After a while, Emily noticed that the
nymph she'd helped was behaving a little
oddly. She was jumping around all by
herself at the other end of the pitch.

"Look, Aisha," she murmured. "What
on earth is she doing?"

"Sapling's the goalkeeper," Quickhoof
explained. "She trains alone, because her
job is different."

"I get it," said Aisha. "She doesn't need

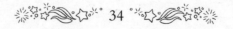

to practise kicking goals, because she never does that in a match."

"It's a shame," said Emily. "She looks a bit left out."

*Boomp! Boomp! Boomp!*

Thumping and pounding shook the ground. Everyone looked puzzled. It was hard to tell where the noise came from.

Something crashed through the trees at the far side of the pitch, and out burst a huge figure.

Aisha and Emily clutched hands.

"Pitch invader!" the nymphs squealed.

A huge, hulking figure lumbered across the grass. He had a bumpy, lumpy face and flabby, outsize ears. Tufts of bristles sprouted from his head and chin, and he grunted with every step. "Gurr! Gurr! Gurr!"

"Who is that?" Aisha cried.

Quickhoof tossed her head. "An ogre!" She gave a worried glance in Aurora's direction. "What's an ogre doing here?"

## Chapter Three
# Popped Balls

The ogre thumped across the pitch.

The nymphs crouched behind the goal as the ogre picked up a sparkling white ball in his grimy hands. He clutched it to his chest.

"That's *my* ball!" he said in a rumbly, grumbly voice.

"It's not yours!" Aisha yelled.

"You can play with it, but you must share," Quickhoof added.

The ogre grinned, showing three large grey-green teeth. He hugged the ball tighter and giggled.

Some of the creatures ran on to the pitch and surrounded Grubb, trying to stop him from escaping with the ball.

The ogre jumped up and down crossly, but then the sky darkened.

*Crash!* Thunder roared, making everyone jump.

*Crack!* Lightning speared through dark clouds, and a unicorn flew towards the pitch. Her body gleamed silver against the grey sky, and her deep blue mane and tail flew wildly in the wind. Fluffy and his cloud friends were sent rolling and tumbling out of the way, and the racing dragons scattered, squealing.

"Selena!" Aisha gasped.

The mean unicorn flew over to Brightblaze, swooped down and shook her horn from side to side, creating a sharp breeze that whipped Brightblaze's locket from her neck. It flew to Selena and looped itself around her neck. Her hooves spat sparks as she swooped over Spiritmane and Fairtail.

"Don't, Selena!" cried Quickhoof.

One whisk of Selena's horn sent Fairtail's locket flying into the air. The same thing happened to Spiritmane's. Now Selena had three lockets draped around her neck.

She turned her purple eyes towards Quickhoof.

"Don't let her get yours as well!" Emily yelled. "Run!"

Quickhoof galloped away, but then she glanced back over her shoulder, and almost ran into the goalmouth. She

swerved, and stumbled.

Selena reared, and crackling sparks shot towards Quickhoof. In a second all four lockets were hanging beside Selena's own one, which was filled with angry black thunderclouds.

"Oh no, she got them!" Aisha cried, as Selena flew down beside the ogre. He was tossing the stolen ball into the air.

"Well, Aurora," said Selena. "That'll

stop your silly Enchanted Valley Games."

Aurora stood between her friends and the mean unicorn. "Give those lockets back."

"Ha ha!" cackled Selena. "Declare me queen and you can all have your lockets and your stupid games."

"No!" said Aurora. "If you were queen, there'd be no more games. There'd be no happiness or fun in the kingdom ever again."

"We'll never let you become queen," said Emily.

"And we'll get those lockets back," added Aisha.

Selena gave a flick of her horn. "You pesky girls?" she sneered as Quickhoof's locket flew from her own neck and dropped around the neck of the surprised ogre. "I don't think so! Grubb?"

"Yes?" he grunted.

"Leave that ball," Selena ordered, "and keep the locket well away from these fools."

Slowly, the ogre put the ball down. Then he jumped on it, bursting it with a loud *POP!* He stuck out his tongue and blew a raspberry at the girls.

"Hey!" cried Emily.

As Grubb shambled towards the forest, he jumped on the footballs, one by one.

*POP! POP! POP!* One of the nymphs gave a loud sob.

Selena's shriek of laughter was followed by a *crack!* as lightning zapped across the sky. She vanished.

The girls and Aurora comforted the nymphs, who were shaking with fright.

"Don't be scared," said Emily.

"Selena's gone," Aisha added.

"How can the games go on without our lockets?" asked Fairtail. All the Sports and Games Unicorns looked bewildered.

Spiritmane lifted her lavender head. "We have to try," she said. "We'll never get anywhere if we don't."

Aisha stroked her neck. "You're right, Spiritmane. We mustn't give up." She smiled at the nymphs. "Come on," she said.

"We can't play without a ball," said Willow.

"I can fix that," said Aurora kindly. She pointed her horn at the grass. A stream of silver twinkles formed themselves into a globe. When they faded, they left behind a gleaming white ball.

The nymphs cheered up and started a kickabout. Seconds later, two of them ran for the ball at the same time and bumped into each other.

"That was mine, Leaf!" said one.

"Conifer! I got there first!" said the other.

"Didn't!"

"Did so!"

They kicked at the ball with their little wooden boots. When it rolled away, Leaf snapped, "Fetch it, Twiggy!"

"No, you kicked it."

Aisha looked at Emily and the unicorns. "Now the Teamwork locket's gone, they can't work together."

"We must sort this out," Queen Aurora said anxiously, "or soon nobody will be able to work in a team. But I daren't leave the palace unguarded while Selena's around."

"We'll go after Grubb," said Emily.

Aisha shot a worried look at Emily. "Maybe even best friends won't be able to work together soon."

Aurora thought for a moment. "You have my keyrings of friendship," she said. "I'll cast a little spell to help your friendship bond keep the effects of Quickhoof's stolen locket at bay. First, you must hold hands."

The queen's horn glowed deep orange, and the air fizzed with magic. A swirl of pastel sparkles drifted towards the girls. They clasped hands as a ribbon of pink, blue and lilac twisted and knotted itself around them. A magical tingle ran through their fingers.

As it faded, Aisha and Emily hugged. Their friendship felt stronger than ever.

"Now you can share the magic," Aurora told them. "If you touch someone, they will feel the bond, too. It won't last for ever, but it will help for a while."

The girls touched Quickhoof's neck, under her chestnut mane. "This is brilliant," said the unicorn. "We'll be the best team ever!"

Queen Aurora was deep in thought. "Grubb's in the forest," she said, "so it would be helpful if one of the wood nymphs went with you. They know the forest better than anyone."

"Not me!" said one of the nymphs. "That ogre is scary!"

"Me neither," declared another.

"Well, if *you* won't go, *I* won't go!" said a small nymph, crossing her arms.

Aisha frowned at Emily. It was the effect of the missing locket, for sure. "What shall we do?"

Emily thought for a moment. "I've got an idea. You can draw straws," she said. "Well, twigs, anyway." She ran to the foot of a tree and picked up a dozen thin twigs. One was shorter than the rest. She held them in her hands so only the tips showed. "Whoever picks the shortest twig comes with us," she said.

Conifer pulled out a long one, then Leaf did the same. Then it was Sapling's turn. She pulled out the short twig. The others breathed sighs of relief, but Sapling just shrugged. "I never feel like part of the team anyway," she whispered to the girls. "So – fine. Might as well go."

"Hold our hands. It will make you feel better," Aisha said.

Sapling reached up and slipped each of her hands into the girls'. "Ooh, I do feel better!" she cried. "I feel like we

can do anything together!"

Aisha and Emily shared a smile. Aurora's magic was working!

Aisha grinned. "Now, let's go and get that Teamwork locket!"

## Chapter Four
# Jump, Scramble, Wobble

As the friends headed for the forest, Emily kept a hand on Quickhoof's neck whilst Aisha held Sapling's hand.

"Aurora's magic will keep our friendship strong," said Emily, "but we must keep touching."

"It might get difficult at times," said

Aisha, "but we can do it."

They passed two gnomes standing on ladders, trying to hang bunting for the opening ceremony.

"Curly, your end is too high!" snapped one gnome.

"No, Hickory, your end is too low," huffed Curly, who was holding the other end of the string. He yanked the bunting upwards, sending Hickory tumbling down to the ground.

"Oof! You silly gnome!" Hickory scolded. "I should have done this by myself."

"When the locket's back, they'll work as a team again," said Emily, as they entered the forest. It was easy to see which way

Grubb had gone. He'd left a trail of fallen trees and broken branches.

"This forest is our home," Sapling said tearfully. "That nasty ogre's ruining it. He's smashing young trees and crushing ferns. What will happen to the birds and mice who live here?"

Emily hugged her. "We'll stop him," she promised. She had no idea how, but they wouldn't give up until they did.

They followed Grubb's trail, scrambling over fallen branches and slipping on squashed toadstools. All the time, they kept touching, to keep their friendship strong.

Then suddenly, *crack!* A lightning flash made them clutch each other in fright.

They looked up. Selena hovered overhead, grinning down at them.

Sapling pressed close to Emily, who shouted, "What now, Selena?"

The evil unicorn clapped her front hooves together, sending a shower of burning sparks to the ground. Emily and Quickhoof stamped on them.

"That's dangerous!" Aisha yelled. "You could set the forest on fire!"

"Ha! That would stop you following Grubb," laughed Selena. "But I've something better than that. If you all think you're so great at sports, try tackling my obstacle course!" Her laughter echoed through the treetops as she flew away.

"What obstacle course?" Sapling asked nervously.

But as they followed the narrow path around a bend, the answer was in front of them: a twisted tangle of spiky tree branches. Beneath them was a net of thick knotted vines! Fat yellow berries grew among the vines, and each one had a sharp, curved thorn on top.

"Clawberries!" said Sapling. "They

grow on Selena's mountain. They'll rip your clothes if they get half a chance."

"It looks like we have to crawl under that net," said Emily. "Be careful, everyone."

They gripped on to one another tightly and scrambled under the net.

"Ouch!" said Quickhoof as a clawberry snagged her mane.

"Eek, this is hard," Sapling moaned as a clawberry scratched her arm.

"Let's take turns holding the net up for each other with our spare hands," Emily suggested.

"Good idea," said Aisha.

"I'll use my horn," said Quickhoof.

They took turns, first holding the net

up, then scrambling through. They had to keep touching each other and, at the same time, keep away from the berries' sharp claws.

At last they made it.

A little way ahead lay a half-fallen tree, with thick thorny weeds growing around it. Aisha went to push past it, through the weeds.

"No!" cried Sapling, pulling her back. "Those weeds are itchy-scratchies. If you touch them the itching will drive you wild."

"This must be the next obstacle, then," Emily said. "We'll have to walk along the trunk without touching the itchy-scratchies, then jump off." She peered through the trees. It looked like the trunk sloped upwards. "It could be quite a drop at the far end." She looked at Quickhoof. "Maybe you … ?"

The unicorn shook her head. "I can't fly you over. Look, the tree branches are quite low, and the itchy-scratchies have grown up into them."

"Why don't we go in pairs?" Aisha suggested. "Sapling, you go with Emily and then Quickhoof and I will follow."

Emily held Sapling's hand and clambered on to the tree trunk. "Whoooa!" she cried. "It's wobbling." She slipped, dropping Sapling's hand.

Aisha reached up and grasped Sapling's hand. "Oh dear, it looks like we need to

use our arms to balance. We'll have to go one at a time."

"What about our friendship bond?" asked Quickhoof.

"Aurora's spell is protecting Emily and me," said Aisha, "so we'll be all right. Quickhoof and Sapling, you'll just have to be fast. I'll go first and test it out."

Aisha stepped up on to the trunk, holding her arms out wide. She moved carefully, as if she was on a balance beam in gymnastics class, putting one foot directly in front of the other. She reached the end and leaped down, landing with a thud.

"Bend your knees when you land," she called back to the others. "The ground's rock-hard."

Quickhoof went next. As soon as Emily took her hand off the unicorn's neck, she started grumbling. "I'd get along much better on my own," she said as her hooves clip-clopped along the trunk. "The rest of you are holding me back."

As soon as the unicorn jumped down, Aisha stroked her neck.

"Oh no! Sorry I was rude," said

Quickhoof. "It's because the magic left me when I let go …"

"We know," Aisha said gently.

Emily lifted Sapling on to the tree trunk, and as soon as she let go Sapling began to moan. "Don't see why I should do this. Why couldn't someone else go? Why me?"

She ran lightly along the trunk, but stopped at the end. "I'm not jumping.

That drop is way too high!"

"I'll catch you," Aisha promised.

Sapling scowled. "You'd drop me. Anyway, I don't need help from you!"

Emily climbed up and ran along the trunk, up behind Sapling. She tried to catch Sapling's hand, but the nymph snatched it away and leaped off the tree, away from Aisha. She stumbled as she landed.

"Ow! My ankle!" she cried.

Aisha lifted her up. As soon as they touched, Sapling burst into tears. "I'm sorry I was horrible. I didn't mean it!"

"We know," said Emily. "It's the magic's fault."

Sapling took a step and yelped. "It

hurts! I can't walk!"

"Poor Sapling," said Aisha. She put an arm around the nymph to support her.

Emily did the same, then she looked at Aisha over Sapling's head and said quietly, "Now what do we do?"

# Chapter Five
# A Wild Ride

Quickhoof nuzzled Sapling's forehead.
"You can ride on my back," she said.

Emily and Aisha boosted Sapling up.
Emily kept her hand on Quickhoof's neck
whilst Aisha held on to Sapling's good
ankle.

"Great!" said Emily. "We'll soon catch

Grubb and get the locket back. It should be easier going now."

But they had only walked a short way when Quickhoof stopped suddenly. Her ears twitched. "Listen."

A rushing sound came from just over a rise ahead.

"What's that?" Aisha said with a worried frown.

They scrambled over the rise and saw a fast-flowing river.

"Wow! That's three times as wide as the palace moat," said Quickhoof.

There were rapids, too, where the water surged and pounded over hidden rocks.

Emily spotted a movement way downriver. It was the lumbering, hulking

figure of the ogre on a little raft. "After him!" she cried.

"How?" asked Quickhoof.

Aisha gave a delighted shout and pointed to the water's edge. A raft with four paddles bobbed on the river. A rope of vines tied it to a tree.

"Come on!" she cried. "We can use that raft to catch up with Grubb. But be sure to keep touching each other, so we work

as a team."

They climbed aboard the raft. Emily sat with Sapling behind her, and Quickhoof sat behind Aisha.

Emily leaned over and pulled the vine free. Everyone tumbled backwards as the raft shot out into the middle of the river.

"Keep the raft balanced," Emily cried, "otherwise we'll tip over."

Aisha and Emily paddled, while Sapling and Quickhoof held on to them. But the raft seemed to have a mind of its own. The girls weren't strong enough to control it.

"We need more paddle power!" cried Aisha as the raft bounced off a rock and wobbled dangerously. "It'll mean letting go of each other, but let's risk it."

Sapling picked up an oar and Quickhoof took the last one in her mouth.

"Paddle hard!" cried Aisha, as they hurtled downriver. "Grubb's heading back towards the bank."

"Padda iss ay!" Quickhoof shouted to Sapling.

"Can't understand you with your mouth full," yelled Sapling. "Paddle this way!"

The raft crashed sideways into a huge rock, and Quickhoof's paddle was knocked out of her mouth. She tried paddling with her hooves but they were too dainty. Sapling, meanwhile, was paddling backwards, making the raft go around in circles.

"That's the wrong way, Sapling!" Emily shouted.

"No, *you're* all going the wrong way," Sapling yelled.

"It's out of control!" cried Aisha.

"Hold tight, everyone!" Emily yelled, as the raft tipped dangerously. They gripped the sides, but Quickhoof couldn't hold

on and rolled towards Sapling. The raft overbalanced and, with a huge *SPLASH*, they were in the water.

Aisha and Emily plunged deep into the river. Luckily both were good swimmers and when they bobbed up, they saw Sapling and Quickhoof already scrambling out on to the bank, soaking wet. The raft had whirled away downriver, far out of reach.

Quickhoof groaned.

"Are you hurt?" Emily called as she crawled up the bank and turned to help Aisha.

"No," said the unicorn. "As I swam ashore, I saw Grubb. On the other bank of the river."

The girls could see that she was right. The ogre's trail of destruction continued on the far side.

Behind them Sapling grumbled, "It's Quickhoof's fault!"

The unicorn stamped. "I'm fed up with this!" she said. "I don't need you lot. I'll fly over the river on my own, and I'll get the locket back myself!"

"No!" cried Emily, leaping forward.

"You'll need our help!"

"Touch her!" Aisha yelled.

But Quickhoof took off and flew swiftly across the river.

Emily hugged Sapling as Aisha stared after the unicorn.

"This is bad," Aisha said. "Quickhoof won't manage to deal with Selena and Grubb on her own."

Quickhoof landed on the bank and disappeared into the trees ... along with any hope of getting back the locket.

## Chapter Six
# Not Another Challenge!

Emily, Aisha and Sapling sat on the
riverbank, holding hands.

"How can we cross the river?" Aisha
wondered gloomily. "I wish we could fly."

"Hmm …" Emily said. She sat up.
"Maybe we can! Sapling, how do you
do that whirlwind thing? You know, like

when you arrived at football practice?"

Sapling shrugged. "We hold on tightly to each other, then we run round and round as fast as we can and then we say the magic words to make a whirlwind and take off. We shout out where we want to go and we usually tumble over when we land."

Aisha felt a twinge of hope. "Could your whirlwind carry us?"

"Maybe," Sapling said, "but I can't run with my hurt ankle."

Emily's eyes sparkled with excitement. "If you put your arms across our shoulders," she said, "we'll support you. We do the running, you do the magic! How about it?"

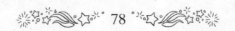

78

Sapling grinned. "Let's give it a go!"

The girls held her up, with Sapling's arms gripping their shoulders and her little legs dangling between them. Then Aisha took a deep breath. "When I say go, Emily, we must run in a circle as fast as we can. One … two … three … GO!"

They ran around and around.

"Keep going!" cried Sapling.

Everything became a blur.

"Faster!" the nymph cried.

*Swoooosh!*

The girls felt their feet leave

the ground. "Wooo!" Emily yelled in excitement. It was weird running in mid-air.

They heard Sapling shout, "Whirly wind and windy whirl, over the river – twirl, twirl, twirl!" Then she said, "Nearly there, girls, slower … slower … careful …"

They somersaulted to the ground in a dizzy, giggling heap.

"That was amazing!" said Aisha. She tried to stand. "Ooh, I'm woozy!"

Emily blew her hair out of her eyes. "My head's spinning!"

Once the dizziness had cleared, the friends hurried off through the forest. The girls carried Sapling between them, her arms around their shoulders.

They skirted a
thicket of purple
tangleweed and
emerged into
a clearing. On
the far side was
Quickhoof. She
was pawing
the ground and

tossing her head crossly. The girls could
see why. Selena and Grubb were standing
on a rock shaped like a platform, looking
down on Quickhoof and teasing her.

"Want your locket, do you?" Selena
sneered.

"It's *my* locket now," the ogre taunted.

"It's not yours!" Emily shouted.

Quickhoof turned. She glared at the friends and snorted grumpily. "Go away! I can handle this on my own!"

"You can't!" Aisha yelled.

"Let us help you!" Emily added.

Lifting Sapling between them, the girls ran to Quickhoof and put their hands on her neck.

Quickhoof's head drooped right away. "I'm sorry," she said, with a sob in her voice. "I didn't mean to be horrible. It's because I've lost my locket."

Grubb laughed. "I told you, it's *my* locket!"

Selena shoved him off the rock. "You lot got through my obstacle course," she said with a sly look in her purple eyes, "but I have another game for you."

The girls sighed. "Why would we play against you?" Aisha said, hands on hips.

"Because if you win, you get the locket back," Selena said. "But if my team wins, you get Aurora to step down and make me queen. Deal?"

Emily looked at Aisha. "We've no choice."

"Deal," Aisha told Selena. "What game?"

In reply, Selena reared up and electric sparks ran over her silver body. Then – *fffzzzaaaappp!* – a bolt of lightning shot across the clearing, and – *pow!* – a football pitch appeared. But it was nothing like the rich green one Aurora

had conjured up. There was no grass, just
stinky, swampy black mud.

Selena jumped off the rock and touched
her horn to the hairy spot between
Grubb's eyes. Four bright flashes shot out
from it and hit the ground. *Zzzap!* Four

more ogres appeared, identical to Grubb.

They giggled together, flapping their ears. Only the Teamwork locket around Grubb's neck showed which one he was.

"Five-a-side football," said Selena.

"Fine," said Aisha. At least it was a game she knew.

"There's only three of us!" Emily whispered urgently.

"Four," said Sapling. "I'll be in goal. At least I won't have to run on my ankle."

"We'll still beat the Grubbs," Aisha insisted. "Right, team?"

Sapling and Quickhoof both said a shaky, "Right."

"But if we let go of each other," Emily said, "we won't work as a team."

Aisha looked into Emily's eyes. "We. Can. Do. This."

"But …" Emily wasn't so sure.

Sapling pulled at Aisha's sleeve. "There's no referee," she said. "Those Grubbs will cheat."

"Oh, you've got a referee," Selena cackled. "Me!" She tossed her head and a whistle appeared, hovering in front of her mouth.

Emily groaned. "This will be *impossible!*"

## Chapter Seven
# Friends v Grubbs

The game was a struggle from the first whistle blast, when an ogre shoved Emily over and banged the ball into the net. 1–0.

Emily picked herself up from the mud and saw Aisha haring down the pitch, dodging the lumbering ogres.

"Shoot!" yelled Sapling, who was leaning on her goal post, resting her ankle.

*Wham!* Aisha slammed the ball into the ogres' goal. 1–1!

Selena blew her whistle. "Free kick to Team Grubb!"

"Why?" Aisha demanded.

Selena raised an eyebrow and grinned. "Because I say so."

Grubb took the kick and scored. 2–1

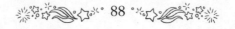

to the ogres. They kicked off again, but
Aisha slipped between a Grubb's legs,
whipped the ball away, raced down the
wing and scored! As the ball hit the net,
Selena blew the whistle.

*Phweee!*

"Goal disallowed!" she screeched. "You
didn't bow to me before you kicked."

Quickhoof flew over. "Selena, you're
making up rules as you go along!"

Selena blew a whistle blast. "So?"

"You can't do that," Emily yelled.

"Yellow card for answering back," Selena snapped.

The ogres had got the ball and were thundering down towards the friends' goal. Aisha ran out, tackled and got possession of the ball. She passed to Emily, who passed to Quickhoof. The unicorn dribbled past Grubb, heading for the goal.

*Phweee!*

"Foul!" bellowed Selena. "Free kick to the Grubbs!"

Sapling hopped up and down crossly. "Unfair!" she shouted.

Selena trotted over. "Yellow card for being rude to the ref," she said, holding it right up against Sapling's nose.

The game got harder still when Selena used magic to make the friends' goal bigger and the Grubbs' goal smaller. Sapling was too little to save many goals, and the Grubb goalie practically filled his net.

Luckily, whenever Aisha did manage to get the ball, she took a shot at goal.

The score was 9–8 to the Grubbs, when Selena shouted, "I'm fed up with this." She took a deep breath to blow her whistle, but just before she did, Aisha kicked the ball away from a Grubb and booted it between the goalie's legs into the net.

Goal!

"You must allow that one, Selena," said Emily. "It's a draw!"

Selena scowled. "Fine! Each team gets one penalty kick. Whoever scores, wins."

"Great," said Aisha. "I'm good at penalties."

"Grubbs first," Selena said spitefully. "It'll save you bothering."

Sapling stood in goal, looking very tiny.

The real Grubb shambled halfway up the pitch, turned and began his run-up, grunting at each step. "Get ready!" He swung his foot at the ball and booted it with all his might straight for the top corner of the goal.

Sapling was ready. She leaped, stretched out her arms and grabbed the ball safely with both hands. She landed, clutched her ankle and gave a yelp.

"Poor Sapling," said Aisha. "Are you going to be OK?"

Sapling just pouted and hobbled to the sidelines.

"We should help her," said Emily, "but we have to get the locket first. This is our final chance. Aisha, you're up."

Aisha ran to the penalty spot. As she did, the Grubb nearest her took a dive.

"Ow!" he roared. "She stamped on my little toe. Ow!"

Selena shoved a red card in Aisha's face, pointed to the side of the pitch and

snapped, "Off!"

"Off! Off! Off!" chanted the Grubbs.

It meant Aisha couldn't take the shot.

"Cheats!" Emily said.

Aisha looked at Emily, eyes wide. "Sapling can't kick with her bad ankle," she said. "Quickhoof won't find it easy with hooves. It must be you!"

Emily gulped.

"You can do it!" Aisha insisted. "You think you can't, but you can."

"Let's hope so," muttered Sapling.

Aisha ignored her and put the ball on the spot. "All you have to do, Emily," she said, "is think positively. Believe in yourself and boot it!"

Emily took a deep breath and eyed

the ball. She ran – and kicked. It flew through the air and curved down, down towards the net. The ogre dived to the right, and the ball slammed deep into the left corner of the net.

"Goooaaalll!" Aisha screamed. "We won! Well done, Emily!"

The girls went straight up to the real Grubb and Emily held out her hand. "The locket, please."

The ogre's face fell. "I never wanted it anyway," he snapped, and took it off.

Selena screeched angrily. "Don't give it to her," she said. "I've changed my mind."

Emily gasped. "You can't do that!"

"Oh yes I can," Selena said. "And I'll be able to do whatever I like when I'm queen."

"We'll see about that!" Aisha fumed. She booted the ball straight at Grubb's hand. The locket flew out of his hand and over their heads.

Everyone turned to see a little green and brown figure leap up and snatch the locket out of the air.

The girls clapped and cheered. "Well saved, Sapling!"

## Chapter Eight
# Friendship For Ever!

Quickhoof flicked her horn, sending showers of sparkles towards the golden cup locket in Sapling's hand. It rose up, drifted towards Quickhoof and draped itself around her neck.

Selena shrieked in fury. Her deep blue mane sent out flashes of green light.

Emily and Aisha held out their arms
to Sapling and Quickhoof. The unicorn
bent to rub her velvety cheek against the
girls' faces, and Sapling hobbled over. The
magic was back.

"Team hug!" Emily yelled.

"Sorry I was awkward," said
Quickhoof.

"And sorry I was moody," said Sapling.

"No, I'm sorry," said Aisha.

Emily laughed. "We're all sorry! And

we're all friends again."

They jumped up and down in delight, but stopped when Sapling winced. "Silly ankle," she said.

Quickhoof offered her a ride until they could find someone to look at her poor foot.

"Thanks. That's kind," said Sapling.

"It's what friends are for," said Quickhoof, "to help and support each other."

The girls lifted Sapling up, and she buried her hands in Quickhoof's chestnut mane.

Selena galloped over and slid to a stop. "Fine! You've got your stupid Teamwork locket, but just remember, I've still got the other three. Ha! You'll never get those."

She stamped her front hooves, then leaped into the air amid crashing thunder and flashing, crackling lightning.

"Our friendship's too strong for you!" Emily yelled.

Quickhoof said to the girls, "Jump up behind Sapling."

The girls shivered with excitement. They never got used to the thrill of flying! As Quickhoof soared into the sky, they held each other tightly.

"Friendship for ever!" cried Aisha.

The others echoed her, their words whipping away on the wind. "… for ever!"

As Quickhoof swooped down, they saw

that the silver stadium and the grounds around the palace were as busy as before.

"Everyone's working together!" Emily shouted happily.

As they landed, Aurora came to meet them. "Congratulations!" she cried. "We knew Quickhoof had her locket back because everyone suddenly started being friendly and working as a team again. Thank you!"

Aisha and Emily jumped off Quickhoof's back and helped the little nymph down.

"We couldn't have done it without Sapling," said Aisha. "She saved the locket!"

Emily patted the nymph on her twiggy

head. "She saved the day!"

"And the goal!" said Quickhoof.

A crowd gathered to congratulate the friends, and Sapling's teammates hugged their goalie. She looked surprised, but

pleased, too!

Emily whispered to Aisha, "I don't think she's ever had attention like this before."

The nymphs' team captain heard and said, "Everyone, please listen!" She turned to Sapling. "It's easy for us to forget how important our goalie is. But we always appreciate you, Sapling. We'll make sure you take part in all our practices. You don't *need* to practise shooting, but it's good for the team to be together. You'll help us bond. That's the important thing."

Everyone clapped, and Aisha shouted, "Three cheers for Sapling, the nymph of the match! She's saved the Enchanted Valley Games. Hip hip!"

"Hooray!"

Cheers echoed around Enchanted Valley as Aurora stepped forward. Her golden horn sent a stream of deep red sparkles straight into Aisha's hand.

The sparkles cleared to reveal a scarlet pouch, tied with a fine golden thread.

"There's something in there that will help Sapling's hurt ankle," Aurora explained.

Aisha opened the pouch, and Emily took out a strip of glistening, gold-tipped lichen. She wrapped it around Sapling's ankle.

The little nymph wiggled her foot. She stood on it. She jumped on it. "It's better!" she cried. "Thank you, Queen

Aurora. And thank you, Aisha, Emily and Quickhoof. You've helped me make so many friends." She looked around at the crowd, who cheered again.

Aurora said to the girls, "The sun's nearly set."

Emily nodded. "It's time for us to go," she said. "We're sorry to miss the opening ceremony."

Aurora's eyes twinkled. "You won't," she said. "The Enchanted Valley Games can't go ahead until we have all the stolen lockets back. Will you come again and help us find them?"

The girls hugged her. "Of course we will," they said.

"I know I can count on you," said

Aurora. "I'll call you soon. Goodbye."
Her horn glowed deep orange, spilling
sunshine sparkles that swept around the
girls, bathing them in golden light. As
they felt their feet leave the ground, they
shouted, "Bye!!"

Moments later, the sparkles faded. The
girls felt firm ground beneath their feet
again, and heard football fans chanting
"Spellford Seals for ever!" Emily and
Aisha ran out from behind the ice cream
kiosk and hurried to take their seats with
their parents.

Ten minutes after the match began, the
Greenlea Gazelles' striker shot for goal.
The ball headed straight for the crossbar,
but Bella Bates, the Seals' goalkeeper,

leaped high in the air and punched it backwards over the goal net.

Aisha and Emily cheered.

"Spectacular!" said Mrs Khan, as the whole team hugged Bella.

Mr Turner said it was the finest save he'd ever seen. "She'll be player of the match, I'll bet," he said.

Emily and Aisha both spoke at once. "The team's the most important thing!"

Mrs Khan laughed. "You two seem to be quite a team," she said.

The girls shared a smile. They were part of a much bigger team – the friends of Enchanted Valley.

The End

Join Emily and Aisha
for more fun in …

# Brightblaze Makes a Splash

Read on for a sneak peek!

Aisha Khan stood outside her classroom door with her best friend Emily Turner, wishing she was anywhere else in the world.

"I don't know if I can do this," she whispered.

Emily squeezed her hand comfortingly and said, "It's only a book report."

Aisha fiddled with the bookmark in her copy of *Black Beauty*.

The two friends both loved the book. They must have read it a hundred times. But while Emily felt confident in the classroom, Aisha was more at home outside on the sports fields. This book report was giving her butterflies in her tummy.

She groaned and leaned against the wall. "I wish Black Beauty would come so I could ride away!"

### Read
# Brightblaze Makes a Splash
#### to find out what's in store for Aisha and Emily!

# Also available

**Book Nine:**

**Book Ten:**

**Book Eleven:**

**Book Twelve:**

## Look out for the next book!

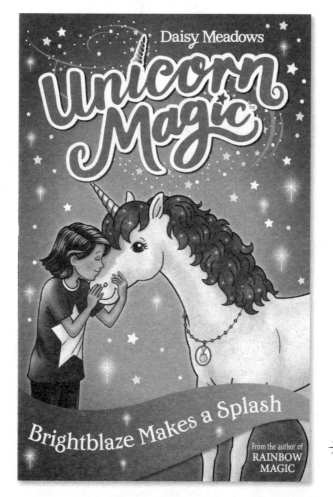

Daisy Meadows

Unicorn Magic™

Brightblaze Makes a Splash

From the author of RAINBOW MAGIC

Visit

# orchardseriesbooks.co.uk

for

✳ fun activities ✳

✳ exclusive content ✳

✳ book extracts ✳

There's something for everyone!

# Brightblaze
# Makes a Splash

## Daisy Meadows

ORCHARD

# Special thanks to Adrian Bott

# For Ruby and Eliza, both very good
# friends of the unicorns

ORCHARD BOOKS

First published in Great Britain in 2020 by Hodder & Stoughton

3 5 7 9 10 8 6 4 2

Text copyright © 2020 Working Partners Limited
Illustrations © Orchard Books 2020
Series created by Working Partners Limited

A CIP catalogue record for this book is available from the British Library.

ISBN 978 1 40836 625 7

Printed and bound in Great Britain by Clays Ltd, Elcograf S.p.A.

The paper and board used in this book are made from wood from responsible sources.

Orchard Books
An imprint of Hachette Children's Group
Part of Hodder and Stoughton
Carmelite House
50 Victoria Embankment
London EC4Y 0DZ

An Hachette UK Company

www.hachette.co.uk
www.hachettechildrens.co.uk

Contents

Aisha and Emily are best friends from Spellford Village. Aisha loves sports, whilst Emily's favourite thing is science. But what both girls enjoy more than anything is visiting Enchanted Valley and helping their unicorn friends, who live there.

Quickhoof

The four Sports and Games Unicorns help to make games and competitions fun for everyone. Quickhoof uses her magic locket to help players work well as a team.

Feeling confident in your skills and abilities is so important for sporting success. Brightblaze's magic helps to make sure everyone believes in themselves!

Brightblaze

Fairtail

Games are no fun when players cheat or don't follow the rules. Fairtail's magic locket reminds everyone to play fair!

When things get difficult, Spiritmane's perseverance locket gives sportspeople the strength to face their challenges and succeed.

Spiritmane

Spellford

Enchanted Valley

Enchanted Cottage

Golden Palace

An Enchanted Valley lies a twinkle away,
Where beautiful unicorns live, laugh and play
You can visit the mermaids, or go for a ride,
So much fun to be had, but dangers can hide!

Your friends need your help – this is how you know:
A keyring lights up with a magical glow.
Whirled off like a dream, you won't want to leave.
Friendship forever, when you truly believe.

## Chapter One
# Schoolroom Nerves

Aisha Khan stood outside her classroom door with her best friend Emily Turner, wishing she was anywhere else in the world.

"I don't know if I can do this," she whispered.

Emily squeezed her hand comfortingly

and said, "It's only a book report."

Aisha fiddled with the bookmark in her copy of *Black Beauty*.

The two friends both loved the book. They must have read it a hundred times. But while Emily felt confident in the classroom, Aisha was more at home outside on the sports fields. This book report was giving her butterflies in her tummy.

She groaned and leaned against the wall. "I wish Black Beauty would come so I could ride away!"

Emily put her hand on Aisha's shoulder. "There's a special trick you can do if nothing else is working. Shall I tell you?"

"OK," Aisha whispered.

Emily said, "When you're feeling nervous, just imagine something funny!"

"Like what?"

"How about Miss Mayhew dressed as a clown? You'll feel much better, I promise."

Aisha frowned. "I'm not sure that'll work. But I'll try."

Just then a bright twinkling caught Emily's eye. There was a light shining out of Aisha's pocket. Aisha was so anxious she hadn't even noticed!

"Aisha, your keyring's glowing!" Emily pulled her own keyring out. "And so is mine!"

A big, relieved grin spread across Aisha's face.

"This is even better than Black Beauty

coming to rescue me," she said. "We're off to Enchanted Valley for another adventure!"

When their unicorn-shaped crystal keyrings glowed, it meant the girls' unicorn friend, Queen Aurora, was calling them to come and visit. Aurora ruled over Enchanted Valley, a magical kingdom

filled with unicorns and all kinds of other wonderful creatures. Emily and Aisha had travelled there many times.

Neither of them was worried about missing their presentation because no time passed in the real world while the girls were in Enchanted Valley. But they couldn't just disappear in the middle of a school corridor – someone might see.

Round the corner there was a big bookcase, full of picture books for the youngest children. Emily and Aisha quickly ducked behind it. They touched their keyrings together.

Instantly, rainbow-coloured sparkles rushed up and whirled around them. Aisha and Emily rose up off the floor as the magical sparkles swirled and glittered, dancing in the air.

A moment later, they sank gently back down to the ground. When the sparkles faded, the school corridor had vanished. Now they were standing on the lush green grass of Enchanted Valley!

They looked around and saw they were outside Queen Aurora's beautiful castle. Its towers, twisty and golden like unicorn horns, rose up into a clear blue sky. On the hill beyond the castle stood the huge silver stadium where the Enchanted Valley Games would soon be held. It was a special event in which the creatures of the valley would compete in every sport and game imaginable!

Queen Aurora came trotting over the
palace drawbridge to meet them. Her
coat shimmered with all the warm and
radiant colours of the dawn. Around her
neck hung her magical Friendship locket,
and a little crown sat on her head. Emily

and Aisha both gave her a big hug.

"Hello, Emily and Aisha! It's lovely to see you again!" Aurora said, whisking her golden tail with happiness.

"It's lovely to see you too," said Aisha, pressing her cheek against Aurora's. She felt so much better now she was here with her unicorn friend.

Emily asked, "Is everything OK? Has Selena caused more trouble?"

The wicked unicorn, Selena, who wanted to take Aurora's place as queen, was always causing problems. Last time Emily and Aisha visited Enchanted Valley, Selena had stolen the magical lockets from the Sports and Games Unicorns. The girls had helped Quickhoof get her

Teamwork locket back, but they still needed to find Brightblaze's Confidence locket, Fairtail's Sportsmanship locket and Spiritmane's Perseverance locket.

"Selena is refusing to give the lockets back unless we make her the new queen," Queen Aurora said. "Don't worry. We will never let that happen. But Selena's timing is especially bad just now."

Emily looked across to the stadium, where colourful flags were fluttering in the wind. "Of course. The Enchanted Valley Games are about to start!"

Aisha had a terrible thought. "You're not cancelling the Games because of the stolen lockets, are you?"

"I bet Selena would love it if that

happened," Emily scowled.

"Indeed she would," Aurora said. "We're not cancelling, but we are postponing the Games until we get the lockets back."

Aisha and Emily both frowned. "That's such a shame," said Emily.

"Don't be downhearted," Aurora said with a secretive smile. "We're still sports mad here. In fact, practice is about to start for one very special event."

The girls brightened.

"I called you both to Enchanted Valley because I thought you might like to watch the kelpies racing," said Aurora.

"What's a kelpie?" both girls asked at the same time.

"You'll see!" laughed Aurora. "Climb on

my back, and we'll be there in a flash!"

The girls didn't wait to be asked twice. Eagerly, they jumped on to Aurora's back.

The majestic unicorn gave two graceful bounds, and flew up into the air. They went soaring high above the hills and forests. Moments later, Emily and Aisha saw an astonishing sight. In the middle of a green meadow was a gigantic building shaped like a blue whale! A jet of water was shooting up from its blowhole and running down its sides.

As Aurora flew them closer, they saw the whale was actually see-through. Emily soon realised what it was.

"I can see swimming pools inside the whale!" she cried. "Loads of them. And they're really big ones!"

"Welcome to the Swimsplash Arena!"
Aurora announced.

## Chapter Two
# The Swimsplash Arena

"It's the finest swimming playpark in all of Enchanted Valley," Queen Aurora said, as the girls clung tightly to her mane. "This is where we're going to hold the swimming events when the Games begin."

They landed at the front, just by the whale's huge smiling mouth. Goblins, animals and many magical creatures were all hurrying inside through the mouth, holding their rolled-up towels and swimming costumes.

"In we go!" said Aurora.

The girls jumped off Aurora's back and walked hand in hand into the Swimsplash Arena. They looked around in wonder. This was better than any water park in the real world, by miles!

There were swimming pools, of course – deep ones and shallow ones – but that wasn't all. At the back, near the whale's tail, was an extra-deep pool with a diving board where an otter in swimming goggles was getting ready to jump. To one side was a special fun zone, where twisty slides and tubes led into the water. Lots of creatures were having a noisy, splashy time there. A group of young pixies were soaking one another and laughing, while nearby a family of penguins lined up to dive in one by one. On the other side was a peaceful zone, with wave pools where several creatures were relaxing as the water washed back and forth over them. Two pufflebunnies waved from rubber tyres as they floated past down a lazy river.

Even the little baby creatures were included. They had a bubble garden, safely behind a barrier, where they could crawl about and play with Bubble Blasters – water pistols that fired streams

of bubbles instead of water. There were gentle little waterfalls and fountain jets, as well as toys for them to play with.

"There's a café too," said Emily, pointing. "'The Babbling Brook'. Imagine playing in the pools all day and then going for a milkshake afterwards!"

"Or a hot chocolate," said Aisha. "This place is wonderful!"

Aurora smiled. "Glad you like it! Look, our friends are here already."

In a pool decorated with seashells, Pearl the mermaid was swimming. She waved across at Aisha and Emily, who waved back. A group of other mermaids popped their heads up out of the water and waved too.

"I'm not surprised to see Pearl here," Emily said. "All this water. She must love it!"

"And there's Prism the Rainbow Parrot," added Aisha. "Hi, Prism!"

Prism came swooping down in a flurry of shining colours. He wrapped his wings around Aisha and Emily in a big friendly hug. "Hello, you two! Great to see you again."

"Are you here to swim?" Emily asked. She wasn't sure if parrots liked swimming.

"Oh, I'm here because of the slide races," said Prism proudly. "They'll be part of the Enchanted Valley Games."

"*Slide* races?" exclaimed Aisha.

"First one into the water wins!"

explained Prism.

"Slide races sound so cool," said Emily.

"And I'm in charge of making the slides," Prism said. "Watch this!'

He spread his wings wide. A rainbow shone out, created by Prism's own special magic. The girls looked on in amazement as the rainbow trail went up and along, then curled in a gentle spiral down into the water.

Aurora waved her horn, and a glimmer of magic sparkled through the air. Prism closed his wings, but the rainbow didn't vanish like it usually did. Aurora's magic made it stay!

Prism bowed, sweeping his wings. "Hey presto! One magical rainbow water slide.

And because they're magic, you can slide up them as well as down!"

Aisha and Emily looked at each other in delight and clapped their hands.

"Why don't we go and find Brightblaze?" Queen Aurora suggested. "She's trying to give everyone confidence before the races, but she's finding it hard without her locket. I think she'd be glad to have some help."

Emily, Aisha and Aurora found Brightblaze the Confidence unicorn by the racing pool. Her body was a gorgeous pearly colour, and her mane and tail were scarlet. She was bending her head down, talking to a group of bluish-green horses who were neck-deep in the water.

"Wow!" Aisha said. "I didn't think horses could swim."

"They can, actually," Emily said. "Swimming is a brilliant way for a horse to get exercise, especially when it's recovering from an injury."

Aurora chuckled. "That's right, Emily. Just one thing, though. Those aren't horses."

"Really?" Emily exclaimed.

"They're the kelpies I've brought you to meet!" Aurora said.

As the girls came closer, they saw the creatures they'd thought were horses had two forelegs with hooves, but fish tails instead of hind legs. Their manes were made of trailing seaweed, not slimy but fine, like green silk.

"How cool!" Aisha said in awe.

The kelpies lined up at one end of the pool, each one in a lane. Brightblaze gave them the signal to start. They thrashed their tails and galloped with their front hooves. Waves washed out and foam flew up as the creatures powered through the water. They seemed completely at home there, moving as fast underwater as normal horses could on land. It was a thrilling sight!

Aurora and the girls said hello to Brightblaze, who seemed nervous.

"It's good to see you," she said. "I just wish I had my locket back! The Games are due to start very soon, you know.

How am I supposed to give everyone confidence when I haven't even got my locket?"

The girls and the unicorns were showered with water as one of the kelpies suddenly popped his head up. "Hellooo,

you two!" he bellowed. "Oops, sorry about that. Call me Eddie. Kelpie team captain!"

"Hi, Eddie!" the girls said.

"Now, don't you fret about that locket, Brightblaze," Eddie said. "I can give my team a rousing pep talk, and they'll be all fired up with confidence. You'll see."

"I hope he's right," Aisha whispered to Emily. "Poor Brightblaze does look nervous."

Eddie turned to Aisha and Emily. "Now, you two. I've got a very important question to ask you."

"Go on," said Aisha.

In a serious voice, Eddie asked, "Do you like swimming?"

Both the girls laughed. "Of course," they said. "We love it."

Eddie gave them a truly enormous grin. "Well, what are you waiting for? Jump on in!"

Emily and Aisha looked at one another, both thinking the same thing. They were still dressed in school uniform! They couldn't jump into a swimming pool like this!

But just then Aurora waggled her horn. Sparkling twinkles danced in the air and next moment, Aisha and Emily found they were wearing shiny purple swimsuits.

"That's better," Aurora said with a smile.

Emily and Aisha got ready to jump in. But then—

*Kaboom!*

A crash of thunder echoed across the arena. The girls turned to see where it had come from. A bright flash of lightning lit up all the pools. Then came a high whinnying laugh that the girls knew only too well. A silvery unicorn appeared on the high diving board, prancing and gloating. Creatures ran in fright at the sight of her.

Emily shuddered. "Oh, no! It's Selena!"

## Chapter Three
# Selena Shows Her Face

Selena stood at the top of the high diving platform. She sneered down at the creatures who were scattering out of the way. Next to her was a lumpy-looking creature with big arms, pointy ears and greyish skin. He was wearing a baggy, stripy swimming suit.

"It's Grubb!" said Aisha. The ogre was
Selena's latest henchman.

"And look what he's got round his
neck," Emily said. "It's Brightblaze's
locket!"

Grubb stomped to the end of the diving

board. Even though he was really high up, he didn't seem scared at all. "Hello down there!" he bellowed.

Down below, the creatures went into a panic. Mermaids, pixies, goblins and even otters all crowded to the edges of the pool. Some of them scrambled out of the water as fast as they could. Others just huddled there, quivering in fear.

Selena laughed out loud to see the uproar. "Well, now! You two silly little girls may have got the better of me last time by winning back the Teamwork locket, but guess what? I've still got the other three lockets!" She tilted her head and smiled as sweetly as she could. "I'm willing to give them back, of course, on one teeny-weeny little condition ..."

"You want to be queen," said Emily.

"That's right!" trilled Selena. "Come on, Aurora. Give me your crown, bow down to me, and your Games can go ahead!"

"Never!" shouted Aurora.

Aisha folded her arms and glared. "Aurora's the queen of Enchanted Valley and she always will be!"

"Oh, is that so?" Selena smirked. "Look! I've given Grubb the Confidence locket. You'll never be able to take it from him. You haven't got the nerve!"

Grubb the ogre jumped up and down on the diving board, which went *wubba-wubba-wubba* like a ruler twanged on the edge of a school desk. He shouted,

"CANNON
BAAAALLLLL!"
And he jumped.

All the creatures
around the diving
pool squealed and
cowered away.

Grubb curled
up into a ball as
he plummeted
through the air.

Next second:
*splathoooooom!*
He plunged into
the diving pool like
a boulder.

A massive spray

of water shot up and out. Almost the entire diving pool emptied itself over the Swimsplash Arena – and everyone inside it!

The spectators up in the stands howled as water crashed over them. Queen Aurora caught a gush of water in the face and blinked. Even the baby creatures crawling around in the bubble garden got splashed. From one end of the arena to the other, creatures were soaked to the skin. A few of them tried to duck behind tables or behind signs, but they got drenched all the same.

The water steadily began to flood back into the diving pool. Dripping creatures began to look around for dry towels and

wring out their sodden clothes.

"Selena's disappeared!" Aisha exclaimed, peering up at where the silver unicorn had been moments ago.

Emily scanned the arena. "You're right, there's no sign of her."

Grubb was still there, however. He was running around the arena in his baggy swimsuit, calling out to all the frightened creatures and making faces at them.

"Grubb, be careful!" Queen Aurora called out. "You mustn't run by the pool. You'll slip and hurt yourself!"

Grubb stuck out his tongue and blew a raspberry. "Me, fall over? Ha! That'll never happen!" And away he went, running even faster than before.

Just then, they heard a cry. "We want to get out! Help! We're scared to swim!"

In the racing pool three goblin children were floating, holding on to a big inflatable toadstool. The massive wave from Grubb's cannonball had washed them right into the middle of the pool, and now they couldn't reach the side.

"Hold on!" called Emily.

"We're coming!" Aisha added.

They sat on the side and slid down into the water. As soon as they were in, a shiver struck Emily, even though the water wasn't cold. "It looks very deep," she said, nervously.

Beside her, Aisha held on tightly to the edge of the pool.

"I'm scared to let go," she said.

"Me too!" said Emily. "What's going on? We usually love swimming."

"Oh dear, girls. I think you've lost your confidence," Aurora said sadly.

"And Grubb has way too much," said Emily. "Look at him!"

She pointed to Grubb, who was pounding his chest like a gorilla.

"Help us!" wailed the three little goblins together.

But the girls were just too nervous to leave the side.

"Let's ask the kelpies for help," Aisha suggested.

The girls climbed out of the water and shuffled over to where the kelpies had been practising. But when they reached the kelpies, they found them clinging on to the sides. Their eyes were all big and wide and their teeth were chattering.

"Those goblins are stuck. Can you help?" Aisha asked, pointing towards the three scared little goblins.

"I'm sorry," said a kelpie, shaking her head. "I swim every day, but I just *can't* face swimming now."

"Oh dear, Grubb's stolen *everyone's* confidence!" Aisha said to Emily.

"Not quite everyone!" said a familiar voice.

It was Eddie!

With a huge flick of his tail, the brave kelpie rocketed towards the helpless goblins. He swam up to the inflatable toadstool that they were all clinging to. Using his nose, he pushed it through the water and kept swimming until it was safely at the pool's edge.

Brightblaze, Aurora and the girls helped the very relieved goblin children out of

the pool. "Let's take them to the Babbling
Brook Café," Aurora said. "They need to
get warm and dry!"

They hurried over to the café. A purple
flamingo wearing a tall white chef's hat
opened the door for them. "Welcome! I'm
Lofty," he said. He looked down at the

little goblins. "In you come, quickly now!"

Soon everyone was sitting together in a comfy corner, with plenty of soft cushions to rest on. Lofty went to get some magical air-blowers that looked like spinning paper windmills on straws. The air they blew out was wonderfully warm and dried everyone off in no time.

"Now how about some hot chocolate?" Lofty said.

"Yes please!" they all said.

Moments later they were sipping on big mugs of frothy hot chocolate with marshmallows in it. It warmed them up from the inside like a radiator, and Emily and Aisha soon felt much better.

Lots of other creatures had taken refuge

inside the café, to hide away from Grubb.
Lofty did what he could to cheer them up
with warm towels and hot drinks. It was
getting quite crowded!

"OK," said Brightblaze, when she
finished her drink. "Let's go and get my
locket back from Grubb. This has gone on
long enough!"

Queen Aurora stood up to leave, but
all the little creatures huddled up to her,
whimpering with fear. "Don't go!" they
begged. "What if scary Selena comes
back?"

"You'd better stay here in the café and
look after everyone," Emily told Queen
Aurora.

"And we'll help Brightblaze find her

locket!" added Aisha.

The three of them headed back to the pool. Grubb put his hands up to his ears and waggled them. "You'll never catch me!" he yelled, and off he went, running around the pool.

The girls started to chase after Grubb, but the poolside was still awash with water from his divebomb. It was so slippery, they had to walk slowly just to stay safe. Meanwhile, Grubb had run all the way round to the far side of the pool.

"We'll never catch him like this," Aisha groaned. "Brightblaze, can you fly after him?"

"I would," Brightblaze said, "but … I'm not feeling very confident about flying right now. What if I hit the ceiling? What if you fall off?"

Brightblaze's confidence had gone, too.

And without it, they'd never get her locket back, and Selena would win!

## Chapter Four
# Bubble Trouble

Emily looked around to see if there was anything nearby that could help them.

Next to the café was the Bubble Garden. All the little creatures who had been playing there had dropped their toys and run inside the café to hide. There were brightly coloured toys like water pistols lying around.

"What are those?" Emily asked Brightblaze.

"Bubble Blasters," the unicorn explained.

Emily rubbed her chin thoughtfully. "Hmm. What if we baffled Grubb with some bubbles?"

"Let's try it!" Aisha said. She went and grabbed a Bubble Blaster and passed one to Emily.

The three of them crouched down behind a tall plastic plant with lots of green fronds hanging down.

Grubb was doing another lap of the pool. He was coming in their direction.

Brightblaze shook with nerves as he

stomped towards them. "Get ready to babble Grubb with the buffles!" she said through chattering teeth.

Aisha and Emily turned the power dials on their Bubble Blasters all the way up to eleven.

"Now!" Emily yelled.

The girls jumped out from their hiding

place, aimed their Bubble Blasters at Grubb — and fired.

An amazing stream of bubbles shot out. In seconds they were as thick as a snowstorm. The girls could hardly see their hands in front of their faces for all the bubbles in the air. It was like being dunked in a gigantic glass of lemonade!

Grubb flapped his arms about, trying to clear the bubbles away. "I can't see!" he bellowed. "What's all this?" A bubble flew up his nose and he sneezed.

"Quick, grab the locket!" Aisha called to Emily.

Emily looked around, and saw nothing but swirling bubbles. "I can't see it," she said. "I can't even see Grubb!"

They heard him blundering about for
a few moments, then there was a sudden,
heavy splash.

"He's fallen in!" Aisha said.

As one by one the bubbles popped
and the girls slowly became able to see
again, they saw Grubb bobbing about in

the pool. He looked quite pleased with himself.

"We ought to jump in and catch him!" said Emily.

"Come on, then," Aisha said.

The girls looked at one another nervously, then reached to hold each other's hands. This wasn't how swimming usually went for them at all. Normally they couldn't wait to get into the water. But now, the pool looked deep, cold and frightening.

"Don't worry, girls!" Eddie called over from the racing pool. "I'll get the scallywag. I'll teach him to scare *my* friends!"

Eddie began to swim towards the pool's

edge, going very fast. Then, like a leaping salmon, he launched himself out of the water. He flew through the air, turned a full somersault, and splashed down in the big pool next to a very surprised Grubb.

"Hooray for Eddie!" cheered the girls and Brightblaze.

Grubb doggy-paddled away as fast as

he could, while Eddie churned up the water swimming after him.

"Eddie was so confident to begin with that it looks like the missing locket hasn't affected him!" said Brightblaze.

As they watched Eddie chase Grubb in the pool, they suddenly heard a voice calling, "Emily! Aisha! Over here!"

They looked over to see their mermaid friend Pearl waving at them. Pearl and the other mermaids were all swimming in the Glitter Grotto, a special pool decorated with sparkly coral and shiny stones. The girls and Brightblaze went hurrying over.

"We've had an idea," Pearl said. "We think we can help!"

"How?" Emily asked.

"Mermaid magic!" Pearl grinned. She took a beautiful coral comb out of her hair.

Emily's eyes went wide as she remembered. "Of course. If a human wears a mermaid comb, they can breathe underwater and swim like a fish!"

"Yes!" Aisha agreed. "Maybe swimming won't seem so scary if we can breathe underwater, just like mermaids do."

They took a comb each and ran back to the pool, where Eddie was still chasing Grubb around.

"Time to get that locket back!" Emily said. Aisha nodded firmly.

They reached up to slide the combs into their hair. Soon they'd have mermaid powers, and they'd teach that ogre a lesson …

But as he swam past, Grubb reached up and slapped Emily's comb out of her hand!

"Whoops-a-daisy!" he sneered. "Butterfingers!"

The comb flew through the air and landed with a *PLOP* – right in the middle of the deep pool.

"Oh, no!" Aisha cried. "Your comb!"

Emily couldn't go into the pool without the comb, but she couldn't get the comb without going into the pool!

Emily groaned. "What on earth am I going to do now?"

# Chapter Five
# Mermaid Magic

Aisha took a deep breath. "I'm still feeling nervous about going anywhere near the water," she said. "But I've still got *my* mermaid comb. So I think … maybe … I can get your comb back."

Emily gave Aisha a tight hug. "I *know* you can!" she said.

Aisha gulped. "OK. Here we go," she said. "Wish me luck!"

She quickly slid the comb into her hair. Before she had time to worry about it, she threw herself into the water.

Emily cheered, "Go on, Aisha!"

Aisha gasped and spluttered. The water began to swirl around her in a mini whirlpool. It carried her with it, spinning her in a circle, faster and faster like a skater on the ice.

A strange feeling was starting to creep into her toes and up through her feet. It was a sort of tingling, like when you come indoors after walking through the snow.

Her legs had disappeared completely.

Aisha had a mermaid tail!

Emily clapped delightedly. "It worked! Now you can swim! I believe in you!"

"Go, Aisha!" said Brightblaze, stamping her hooves.

"I'll do my best," Aisha promised.

The funny thing was, even with her new mermaid tail, she *still* didn't feel confident. Her mind was buzzing with all the things that could go wrong. What if the comb fell out? What if Grubb blocked her way?

Aisha made up her mind. She might be scared, but Emily was counting on her, and so were Queen Aurora and the whole kingdom. With a determined flick of her tail, she duck-dived down under the surface.

To her surprise, she could see underwater, just as if she was wearing swimming goggles. Her eyes weren't stinging at all. There were Grubb's legs kicking away, and there was Eddie chasing him. And there was Emily's comb, gleaming on the bottom of the pool.

Aisha swam for all she was worth. The
water got cooler and darker the deeper
she swam, and she started to feel scared.

Just as she was about to lose her nerve, she got to the bottom.

She reached down and grabbed Emily's comb. Holding it tightly, she flipped over and swam back the other way.

Emily and Brightblaze watched nervously from the side of the pool. Emily crossed her fingers for luck. Next moment, Aisha suddenly burst out of the water, waving the comb triumphantly in her hand.

"Well done, Aisha!" Emily cheered. "You did it!"

Aisha passed the comb up to Emily. "Come on in, and let's help Eddie catch Grubb."

Emily popped the comb into her hair.

She was about to jump into the pool, but before she could, Grubb jumped *out*!

"Get back here, you ruffian!" shouted Eddie from the water.

"Nah," said Grubb. "I've had enough. Bored now!"

And off he ran, whooping and skidding in the puddles.

Emily sighed in frustration. She took Aisha's outstretched hand and helped her to wriggle out of the pool. They both took the mermaid combs out of their hair, and, with a swirl of magic, Aisha's tail turned back into legs.

Eddie laid his long head on the poolside and stuck his bottom lip out. "Oh, barnacles and bladderwrack," he grumbled. "I wish I could come out of the water and help you!"

"I wish you could too, Eddie," said Aisha. "You're the only one of us who has any confidence left."

Emily peered over to the back of the Swimsplash Arena. "What's that rotten ogre up to now?"

Grubb was back at the diving pool.

Emily shuddered. "He's not going to do another cannonball, is he?"

Grubb climbed up the ladder to the very top, where the diving board was. The moment he reached it, the whole diving tower grew. It became taller and taller, rising like a magic beanstalk until it was right up to the ceiling!

"That's more like it!" Grubb laughed. "Nice and high! But not too high for me." He held the locket up. "I thought you wanted this?" he taunted the friends. "Come and get it!"

Emily and Aisha looked on in horror. The diving board had been frighteningly high up before. The thought of going

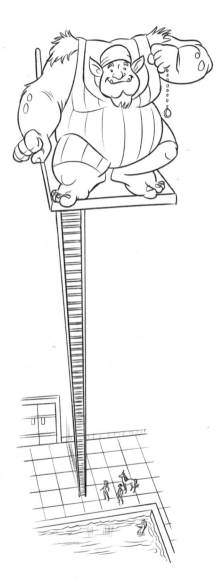

up there now made them go weak at the knees.

Brightblaze was shivering with fear. Aisha gave her a hug. "What's wrong?" she asked.

"I can't climb the ladder because of my hooves," Brightblaze said. "And I can't fly you up. All my confidence is gone. I'm too nervous to fly."

Emily and Aisha gripped one another's hands and squeezed tightly.

"We've got to try," Aisha said.

"I know," Emily agreed. "We've got no choice. We can't let Selena win. We just can't."

They walked to the bottom of the ladder and looked up. It stretched

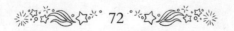

dizzyingly high above them.

"One step at a time," said Aisha.

"And whatever you do, don't look down," Emily added.

Aisha took the lead, Emily followed, and they began to climb. Grubb's mocking voice echoed in their ears, but they did their best to ignore him.

Rung by rung, they climbed up. Aisha's foot skidded on a wet rung and she stopped, clinging tight to the ladder and breathing hard, until she felt ready to go on again. Emily reassured her friend. "Almost there," she said. "Just keep going, nice and easy."

It was like being in an endless dream, climbing up a ladder but never seeming to reach the top. But finally, they pulled themselves on to the very highest platform. They clung to the safety rail for dear life. The tower was so high it seemed to wobble beneath them. They could have reached out to touch the glass ceiling!

Grubb was there waiting for them. He

folded his arms and said, "What a couple of babies. Fancy being scared of a little diving tower like this!"

He strode over to the ladder and gave it a kick. The ladder snapped clean off, and fell with a clattering crash to the ground far below!

Aisha gasped. "Grubb, *no!*"

Grubb laughed. "Only one way down now, girls. Cheerio!"

With that, he ran to the end of the diving board and dived right off. The girls watched him plummet through the air and splash in the pool below.

The diving pool seemed impossibly far down, like a blue flag fluttering on a distant white hill. They could just see

Grubb climb out of the pool and give a triumphant dance before racing off to cause more havoc.

"We're higher than a house up here," whispered Aisha.

"And the ladder's gone!" Emily whispered back.

"And we have to stop Grubb!" Aisha cried.

But unless they jumped, the girls were stuck.

## Chapter Six
# The Biggest Leap

"Hello up there!" called a voice from below.

Aisha and Emily looked down and saw Eddie, who was swimming in circles down in the diving pool, his hooves galloping ahead of him while his tail swished behind. "Gosh, look at you both," he said.

"You made it all the way to the top! You're doing brilliantly!"

"It doesn't feel like it," Aisha called down.

"You'll be amazed at what you can do if you believe in yourselves," Eddie said, and grinned. "Shall I tell you a big secret about confidence?"

The girls nodded.

"It's always easier to feel confident if you're part of a team," Eddie said.

Aisha and Emily looked at each other.

"We *are* a team," Aisha said.

"Best friends," Emily agreed. She looked down. "I … I think maybe I *can* do it. But only if you're there with me."

"I was going to say the same thing!"

exclaimed Aisha.

"I'll be down here in the water when you land," Eddie said. "There's nothing to fear. I promise you that."

The girls held hands and walked to the end of the diving board. They took deep breaths.

"On three. OK?" Aisha said.

Emily nodded, holding Aisha's hand very tight. "One, two ... *three!*"

At the exact same moment, they jumped.

As Emily fell, she thought, *This isn't so bad!*

And as Aisha plunged into the water, she thought, *Is it over already?*

The girls swam up to the surface. They

trod water, gasping for air. Eddie quickly
swam up to them and they held on to his
mane. That felt a lot better.

"Well done, girls!" he said. "See? You
were scared, but you did it!"

Emily and Aisha hugged one another.
"Thank you, Eddie!" they said together.

"We couldn't have done it without you cheering us on."

Meanwhile, Grubb was on the move again. The girls watched as he ran over to one of the twisty rainbow slides that Prism had made earlier. He stood at the bottom of the slide and paused.

"Selena told me I had to hide this locket," he said. "I'm brilliant at hiding things. Aha! This slide looks like a good place! They'll never find it in here."

The girls laughed. Aisha called out, "Silly Grubb! You're a bit too confident for your own good."

"Yeah," said Emily. "We love waterslides. We'll get that locket back easily!"

Grubb chuckled. "Oh? We'll see about

that." He waggled his fingers, calling on his ogre magic. The rainbow slide began to change.

It curled up on itself until it was a narrow pipe instead of a slide. Then it went twisting and curling all around the arena! It zoomed up and down in scary zigzags and finished with a long drop right into the middle of the pool.

Aisha and Emily stared at it. It hung in the air like a giant, crazy straw, defying gravity.

Grubb bellowed with laughter. "Now *that's* what I call a waterslide!"

He jumped into it, waving the locket as he vanished.

Brightblaze came over to the diving

pool. "Do you think you can get my locket back?" she asked anxiously.

Aisha and Emily gulped. Emily said, "I mean, we *normally* love waterslides ..."

"... but this one looks a bit too much!" Aisha finished.

Eddie gave each of them a boost out of the water with his nose. "I know you can do it," he said warmly. "All you have to do is believe in yourselves. Believe in each other!"

Aisha stroked his soft green seaweed mane. "Oh, Eddie, I wish you could come with us! You always know what to say."

Eddie looked back at his fish tail. "It's a pity I can't climb up to the waterslides. I'd just flollop about. Very funny to see, but not much use."

Emily thought about that for a moment. "I wonder ..."

She took out the coral comb that Pearl had given her before.

"Eddie," she said, "the comb turned Aisha's legs into a fish tail. Maybe with you it'll work the other way around."

Eddie beamed. "Let's give it a go!"

Emily tucked the comb into Eddie's mane. Water began to swirl around him, just like it had around Aisha before. In a flurry of foam and bubbles, Eddie's tail disappeared and two strong-looking horse legs took its place.

Brightblaze, Aisha and Emily helped Eddie scramble up and out of the pool.

He stood there on four legs, dripping, with a big smile on his face.

"Hooray!" they all cheered.

"This feels amazing!" Eddie roared happily. "It worked! Good thinking, Emily. Now for the locket!"

## Chapter Seven
# Waterslide Ride

Eddie tried to walk over to the slide, but his brand-new legs wobbled about under him. "Whoops!" he muttered, and tried again. He reminded Aisha of a newborn foal learning how to walk.

"Are you OK?" Brightblaze asked him.

"Takes a bit of getting used to, this," he

said. He slipped on a patch of wet floor
and his four legs skidded out in different
directions. "Whoa!"

Emily and Aisha helped him to stand up
again. "Just do your best," Emily said.

"That's the spirit," Eddie said, sounding

more cheerful. But Aisha noticed he was shivering all over.

Together, the four of them headed to the slide's entrance. There was a stack of double ring floats for people to ride in, and magical water was gushing inside.

Emily looked in. She had expected the slide to glow with bright, jolly colours, but Grubb's magic had changed all that. It was pitch black.

"Oh dear," Aisha said. "It's even scarier than I expected."

At least they had Eddie with them. Emily turned to ask him what they should do, but to her surprise, he had stopped in his tracks. It was like he'd been frozen in place.

"Can't do it," he said.

"Eddie!" Emily cried. "What's wrong?"

"I just can't face going on that slide," Eddie said. "These legs feel funny! I'm not used to them yet."

"We'll take the comb back out," Aisha suggested.

"You'll turn right back into a kelpie with a tail," said Emily, "and you can go down the slide that way."

Eddie hesitated. He looked down into the dark opening, and shook his seaweedy mane. "Sorry, girls. It's too much. I still can't do it."

Aisha knew she had to do something, or the locket would be lost for ever. She suddenly remembered Emily's advice from when they were outside the classroom back in their world.

"We should just pretend the slide is something funny!" she said.

Emily said, "I know. Let's pretend we're going down a pipe in a sweet factory, and we're going to land in a big pile of marshmallows!"

"That *would* be funny." Aisha giggled.

Eddie looked a little happier.

"And we could pretend the floats are jelly rings," Brightblaze suggested.

"Ooh, yes, and the water is toffee sauce and we're little gummy bears! Yum!" said Emily.

Eddie smiled. "That does sound funny! You know … I think I'll do it after all."

"Hooray!" the girls cheered.

Eddie took a deep breath and a step forward. "Righto, then. Into the sweetie tube we go, for Aurora and for Enchanted Valley."

Brightblaze wiggled her horn and it lit up, shining bright light all around. "Now the slide won't be so dark," she said.

They climbed into double ring floats, ready to slide. Aisha and Brightblaze went first, and Emily and Eddie followed on behind. Aisha gave one brave push, the float started to move up the magical slide, and they were off!

Brightblaze made little frightened noises as they went whooshing up the pipe. Aisha was nervous too, but reached

over and hugged her. They thundered
upwards, as fast as an underground
train, then without warning they were
rocketing down. Next moment they were
zooming up again! Aisha's tummy felt

very strange, like when the car went over
a speed bump back home.

They whooshed around a long curve.

Aisha tilted over in her seat. Then the pipe swung back the other way, and she nearly fell out.

"Remember, it's a sweetie factory!" she yelled. "There's going to be a lovely pile of marshmallows at the end."

Up ahead, something twinkled in the dark. Brightblaze's locket! It was dangling from the roof of the tunnel.

"I see the locket!" Aisha yelled. "Hold on!" As they rushed by, she reached up, grabbed for it … and missed! "No!"

"Don't worry, I'll try!" Emily yelled from behind. She stretched her arm up as high as she could. Her fingers knocked the locket off its hook, but she couldn't hold on to it.

The locket fell through the air and tumbled behind the float, out of Emily's reach.

Eddie quickly flipped his head back and caught the locket in his mouth!

"Yay!" they all cheered as they burst out of the tube and splashed down into the pool. Everyone laughed with relief. Eddie neighed with triumph and shook his long green mane.

"That was fun!" Brightblaze said.

"It was, wasn't it?" grinned Aisha.

And Emily joked, "Who wants to go again?"

## Chapter Eight
# Pool Party

Aisha took the locket out of Eddie's
mouth and hung it around Brightblaze's
neck.

Instantly she felt her confidence coming
back. What on earth had she been so
worried about? It was only a swimming
pool – and she loved swimming!

"Come on, everyone!" Emily called to the creatures in the Babbling Brook Café. "You can get back in the water now."

"Let's have a pool party!" Aisha shouted.

With squeals of joy, all the creatures who had been hiding in the café came flooding back out.

The first ones ran up to the pool and just dived straight in. Others climbed up the rainbow slides and went scooting down into the water. The three little goblins jumped on to their inflatable toadstool and drifted across the pool with cries of "Wheee!"

Baby creatures splashed and giggled in the fountains and danced in streams of bubbles. Eddie's team of kelpies went racing up and down their lanes again, full of winning spirit. The whole Swimsplash Arena echoed to the sound of everyone having fun!

But suddenly thunder boomed and lightning flashed. There stood Selena, up on the diving platform again.

"What are you lot all doing back in the water?" she demanded.

Emily and Aisha looked around anxiously. They expected the creatures in the pool to scatter and hide, like they had before.

But strangely, none of them did. They all looked confidently up at Selena.

"Why aren't you scared, you pathetic fools?" Selena screeched.

But nobody so much as twitched. Not even the little goblins or the babies in the bubble garden looked scared.

Pearl the mermaid said, "We don't need to be scared of you with Aisha and Emily around. They'll never let you win, and we all know it!"

Selena stamped her hoof and glared at the girls. "You horrible, meddling little pests! And as for you, Grubb, you miserable failure … Grubb? Grubb! Wherever you're hiding, come out at ONCE!"

The girls spotted Grubb in the Bubble Garden, hiding in one of the plastic plants.

Selena shouted "GRUBB! Stop pretending to be a bush! I can see you!"

Grubb squeaked in fear, jumped up from behind the plant and ran away. He sprinted through the entrance of the Swimsplash Arena and vanished from sight.

Emily and Aisha giggled. "Looks like we've found something Grubb is scared of after all," Emily said.

"That's right," said Aisha. "Selena!"

"I'll be back," Selena scowled. "And I'll get my revenge on you all. Just you wait and see!" She vanished with another thunderous crash.

"Good riddance!" Eddie called and everyone cheered.

The pool party was the best Aisha and Emily had ever been to! They had swimming races, splashing competitions and slide races. They played pool volleyball, and the kelpies taught everyone how to play water polo.

Eventually, the girls started to feel tired – and their fingers and toes had gone all wrinkly from being in the water for so long!

They climbed out of the pool and headed to the Babbling Brook Café, where Lofty the flamingo chef was waiting with hot chocolate and Queen Aurora had the hot air blowers ready.

In moments they were dry and toasty warm. Queen Aurora's horn twinkled with magic, and the girls found themselves back in their school uniforms again.

They couldn't leave without saying goodbye to their new friend Eddie, so they sat to watch the kelpies practise racing. The kelpies zoomed through the water as fast as dolphins, launched themselves up and over the hurdles in their path, then splashed gracefully back down.

"Look at them go!" Aisha said. "They're swimming even faster than before, and they're jumping so high!"

"That's the magic of confidence," Queen Aurora said.

"Wow, if the practice is this exciting, I can't wait to watch the actual Games!" said Emily.

"Please call us when they start," Aisha pleaded Aurora.

"Of course I will," said Aurora. "But I fear we might need your help again before then. Selena still has two of the lockets and we can't hold the Games without them."

"We will always help, whenever you need us," Emily promised.

They hugged Eddie, Brightblaze and Queen Aurora. "See you soon!"

Queen Aurora waggled her horn. Multi-coloured magical sparkles whooshed around the girls, and once again they felt themselves rushing through the air.

They landed exactly where they had started, behind the bookcase in the school corridor.

"Well, we've still got to do our book report," Aisha said with a sigh.

"You're not going to let standing in front of the class scare you, surely?" said Emily. "Not after everything we've been through!"

Aisha thought about it. "I'm still nervous," she said. "But I don't have to feel totally confident, do I? It's just like on the diving board. I can still do this. I just need to have my best friend by my side."

Emily smiled. "And you have."

They held hands and walked into the classroom, knowing that when best friends were together they could do anything.

The End

Join Emily and Aisha
for more fun in …
**Fairtail and
the Perfect Puzzle**
Read on for a sneak peek!

Aisha Khan looked at the board game boxes spread over the sitting-room floor. She sat with her best friend, Emily Turner.

"Which shall we play?" she asked.

Emily laughed. "I want to play them all!"

They had planned to practise skateboarding together after lunch, but it was pouring with rain, so Emily had raced over to Aisha's house – Enchanted Cottage – with her jacket over her head. Now they were trying to choose a game.

"What about Greedy Goat?" said Aisha,

holding up a farm-themed board game. "That was really fun last time!"

But Emily wasn't listening. She was pointing to the crystal unicorn keyring that was clipped to Aisha's belt.

"It's glowing!" said Emily.

Read
# Fairtail and the Perfect Puzzle
to find out what's in store
for Aisha and Emily!

# Also available

**Book Nine:**

**Book Ten:**

**Book Eleven:**

**Book Twelve:**

## Look out for the next book!

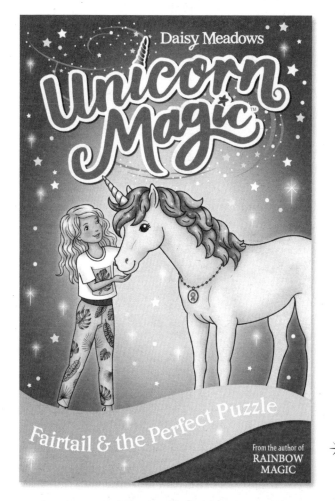

# Visit
# orchardseriesbooks.co.uk
for

✳ fun activities ✳

✳ exclusive content ✳

✳ book extracts ✳

There's something for everyone!

# Fairtail and the Perfect Puzzle

### Daisy Meadows

ORCHARD

# For Romilly Deal

# Special thanks to Valerie Wilding

ORCHARD BOOKS

First published in Great Britain in 2021 by Hodder & Stoughton

3 5 7 9 10 8 6 4 2

Text copyright © 2021 Working Partners Limited
Illustrations © Orchard Books 2021
Series created by Working Partners Limited

A CIP catalogue record for this book is available from the British Library.

ISBN 978 1 40836 626 4

Printed and bound in Great Britain by Clays Ltd, Elcograf S.p.A.

The paper and board used in this book are made from wood from responsible sources.

Orchard Books
An imprint of Hachette Children's Group
Part of Hodder and Stoughton
Carmelite House
50 Victoria Embankment
London EC4Y 0DZ

An Hachette UK Company

www.hachette.co.uk
www.hachettechildrens.co.uk

Contents

# Meet the Characters

Aisha and Emily are best friends from Spellford Village. Aisha loves sports, whilst Emily's favourite thing is science. But what both girls enjoy more than anything is visiting Enchanted Valley and helping their unicorn friends, who live there.

Quickhoof

The four Sports and Games Unicorns help to make games and competitions fun for everyone. Quickhoof uses her magic locket to help players work well as a team.

Feeling confident in your skills and abilities is so important for sporting success. Brightblaze's magic helps to make sure everyone believes in themselves!

Brightblaze

Fairtail

Games are no fun when players cheat or don't follow the rules. Fairtail's magic locket reminds everyone to play fair!

When things get difficult, Spiritmane's perseverance locket gives sportspeople the strength to face their challenges and succeed.

Spiritmane

Enchanted Cottage

Golden Palace

An Enchanted Valley lies a twinkle away,
Where beautiful unicorns live, laugh and play
You can visit the mermaids, or go for a ride,
So much fun to be had, but dangers can hide!

Your friends need your help – this is how you know:
A keyring lights up with a magical glow.
Whirled off like a dream, you won't want to leave.
Friendship forever, when you truly believe.

## Chapter One
# Bawling Billy and Weeping Whiskerina

Aisha Khan looked at the board game
boxes spread over the sitting-room floor.
She sat with her best friend Emily Turner.

"Which shall we play?" she asked.

Emily laughed. "It's too hard to decide. I
want to play them all!"

They had planned to practise skateboarding together after lunch, but it was pouring with rain, so Emily had raced over to Aisha's house – Enchanted Cottage – with her jacket over her head. Now they were trying to choose a game.

"What about Greedy Goat?" said Aisha, holding up a farm-themed board game. "That was really fun last time!"

But Emily wasn't listening. She was pointing to the crystal unicorn keyring that was clipped to Aisha's belt.

"It's glowing!" said Emily. She pulled a matching keyring from her pocket. "Mine's glowing, too!"

Aisha's eyes sparkled. "Hooray! Queen Aurora's calling us! We'll see all our friends again."

Soon after the Khans had moved to Enchanted Cottage, Aisha and Emily found themselves transported to Enchanted Valley. This was a wonderful land of unicorns and other fantastic creatures, ruled by the kind and gentle unicorn, Queen Aurora. After their first adventure, they were given two magical keyrings. These keyrings were what they used to get back to the valley.

Emily grinned. "A magical adventure would be just the thing to brighten up a wet day!" she said.

The girls held out their keyrings and felt them being pulled together, as if by a strong magnet. When the unicorns' horns touched, a flurry of dazzling colours surrounded Emily and Aisha. Blue, indigo, pink and green sparkles whirled around them, faster and faster. The girls felt their feet lift right off the carpet as they were swept into the magical swirl.

Excitement fizzed through them. They were off to Enchanted Valley!

Moments later, the sparkles began to fade. Aisha and Emily felt their feet touch the ground once more. When the sparkles cleared they found themselves standing on rich green grass at the foot of a familiar hill. At the top was Queen Aurora's glittering golden palace, topped with twisting turrets shaped like unicorn horns.

Nearby was the stunning silver sports

stadium the girls had seen on their recent adventures. Sunlight glinted off its silvery walls, and brilliantly coloured flags fluttered high above from tall, twisty poles.

Aisha and Emily knew that the Enchanted Valley Games were due to be held there soon. They hugged each other.

"Isn't it great to be back?" said Emily.

Aisha pointed to the palace. A beautiful unicorn was trotting over the silver drawbridge. "Here comes Queen Aurora!" she said.

The unicorn's golden mane and tail glittered and sparkled, and her coat shimmered like a summer dawn: pink, yellow, soft red and orange. She wore a silver crown and her golden horn gleamed brightly in the sunshine.

Four other unicorns followed the
queen. The girls recognised them as their
friends, the Sports and Games Unicorns.

Emily and Aisha smiled. "Hello, Queen
Aurora! Hello, everyone!"

"Welcome back," Aurora said in her soft,
musical voice.

Quickhoof, the buttercup-yellow Teamwork unicorn, and Brightblaze, the scarlet-maned Confidence unicorn, dipped their horns in greeting and said, "Hello!"

"It's lovely to see you again," said Emily.

Aisha stroked Spiritmane's soft lavender neck. "I see you haven't got your locket back yet," she said.

All the Enchanted Valley unicorns wore a magical locket that protected something important to everyone who lived there. Spiritmane took care of Perseverance, which meant never giving up.

Spiritmane shook her head. "I haven't. Nor has Fairtail," she said, glancing over at the sea-green unicorn, who looked after Sportsmanship.

Queen Aurora said sadly, "I'm afraid Selena still has them."

Selena was an evil unicorn. She'd stolen the lockets from all the Sports and Games Unicorns. Aisha and Emily, with help from their friends, had managed to get two lockets back, but Selena still had the others. She was refusing to give them up unless she was made queen of Enchanted Valley.

There was no way Aisha and Emily were going to let that happen. Selena didn't care about peace and friendship. She would ruin everything!

Fairtail hung her head. "Without my locket nobody will play or compete fairly," she said.

"That's right, so starting the Games without it would be hopeless," said Queen Aurora. "We're having serious problems right now. Come and see."

She turned towards the shining silver stadium. Aisha and Emily followed, but before they'd gone far, they heard someone crying.

The girls peeped behind a cluster of sweet-smelling dinglebell flowers, and saw a fluffy white bunny. He wore green and white striped shorts, and had enormous blue eyes and silky whiskers.

"A baby pufflebunny!" said Emily.

"And a kitterfly!" said Aisha. A pale gold kitten's lemon-yellow wings flapped as she bounced up and down, looking very cross.

Both creatures were in tears.

"What's wrong?" asked Emily.

The pufflebunny pointed a furry paw at the kitterfly. "We had a go-kart race and Whiskerina cheated! She sent me the wrong way around the Sleeping Willow tree, then called me a loser. She's a cheat!"

Whiskerina's wings flapped so hard she rose off the ground. "I didn't cheat, Billy!"

"You did!" said the pufflebunny.

Aisha patted his quivering paw. "I don't expect she meant to cheat," she said.

Whiskerina dabbed her eyes with a wingtip. "I didn't," she said. "I never cheat." She sniffed, then she sighed. "Well, not normally … but I did today, I admit."

Now Billy and Whiskerina were calmer, Aisha and Emily went to where Queen Aurora was quietly watching with Fairtail.

"You see?" Aurora said. "Without Fairtail's Sportsmanship locket, they can't play fairly."

"And it isn't just the Games it will spoil," Fairtail added. "Nobody will be able to play fairly at anything so it will ruin the whole valley!"

Aurora's mane shimmered as she shook her head. "This will only get worse," she said, "but we must have peace in Enchanted Valley."

Aisha swallowed hard. "Are … are you

saying the only option is to give in to Selena? To give her your crown and make her queen?"

"That's awful!" cried Emily.

Fairtail glanced at Aurora, then said, "We do have a plan to get my locket back, but we can't do it alone. Emily and Aisha, will you help?"

The girls were thrilled. "Of course we will!"

## Chapter Two
# Boardway Park Board Games

Emily and Aisha clambered on to a low, thick branch of a sweetbark tree, and listened as Queen Aurora explained the plan.

"We'll do a practice run-through of part of the Games," she said. "It's the Board Games Tournament."

Emily and Aisha looked at her in surprise.

"Board games?" said Emily. "In a sporting event?"

"Of course! Board games are just as important and fun to play as sports," said Aurora. "Besides," she added, with a twinkle in her eyes, "these are Enchanted Valley board games. They're probably different from the ones you play at home!"

Aisha and Emily squeezed each other's hands. This sounded exciting!

"How will the plan work?" asked Aisha.

Aurora trotted closer and said quietly, "We hope Selena won't realise it's a practice. If she thinks it's a real game,

she'll want to ruin it. That will give us a
chance to get Fairtail's locket back!"

"It's a great plan!" said Emily. "Let's do
it!"

Queen Aurora had to go and protect
her palace in case Selena tried any nasty
tricks to get inside. Brightbold, Quickhoof
and Spiritmane stayed to comfort the
pufflebunny and kitterfly.

"Jump on my back," Fairtail said. "We'll
fly to Boardway Park."

Aisha and Emily adored flying and
loved seeing new parts of Enchanted
Valley! They stood on the branch and
climbed on to the unicorn's back. Emily
buried her hands in Fairtail's mane, which
sparkled like the ocean. Aisha sat behind

with her arms around her friend.

Fairtail leapt into the air. The wind made Emily catch her breath, and she heard Aisha laughing behind her. Emily's fair hair was blowing into Aisha's face, tickling her nose and making her giggle.

As they soared above Enchanted Valley, cross, shouty voices floated up to them. Just below, they were able to make out one, two, three … four! flying pink piggles playing hide-and-seek in the clouds. They looked just like pigs, but they could hover through the air, leaving trails of sparkles behind them.

"Found you, Gigglegrunt!" said the seeker.

Gigglegrunt flew out from behind a

small puff of cloud, looking furious. "You cheated, Twinkletrot! You peeked as you counted!"

"Did not!" said Twinkletrot.

"You did!"

"I didn't mean to. I couldn't help it!" squeaked Twinkletrot.

"Oh dear!" Emily said, her excitement leaving as quickly as it had arrived.

"We must get the locket back, or everyone will cheat at everything!" Aisha cried.

Moments later, Fairtail called, "There's Boardway Park." She swooped down and circled over a clearing. There was a play area with swings and roundabouts of different sizes, but nobody was using it.

Instead, elves, goblins and other creatures were clustered around little tables and chairs. One goblin seemed to be dancing on the daisy-speckled grass. The girls realised he was trying not to tread on a lively group of tiny white birds.

"They're quacklets," Fairtail said as she landed. "If they're not dancing, they're hopping and if they're not hopping, they're playing chase-my-tail!"

The quacklets broke into a fierce, squeaky squabble. The only word Aisha could make out was, "Cheat!"

"Oh dear," she said. "There's no sportsmanship here, either."

An elf tipped over a game board and threw the playing pieces around. He was so cross that his pointed ears turned bright red.

"I didn't cheat," sobbed his friend.

Aisha sighed. "We *really* need that locket."

Fairtail tossed her head. "Here's someone to help us," she said. "It's Buckle the leprechaun. He's the Board Games Master and we've already told him the plan."

A little man in a green suit walked over, swinging his walking stick. He had a ginger beard, and buckles shimmered on his boots, his belt, and even on his green top hat. Even wearing his tall hat he only reached up to the girls' shoulders.

"Ah, Fairtail's brought two smiley

friends!" said Buckle. "That's grand!"

The unicorn introduced the girls, and explained about them helping Queen Aurora.

"That's kind," said Buckle. "Well, Emily and Aisha, I'm in charge of the Boardway

Park games. So let's get started!"

He held the crooked handle of his stick in front of his mouth. "Board game players, gather round." Buckle's voice boomed, his stick working like a megaphone.

A pixie flew over. She had masses of purple curls stuffed under a fluffy nightcap.

"It's Trixie the sleep pixie!" cried Aisha. The girls had met her on a previous adventure.

"Hello, Trixie," said Emily, as the pixie hugged them in turn.

Trixie's nightie had a picture on the front of sleepy lambs jumping over a gate. She looked at the girls with wide purple eyes. "It's lovely to see you again," she said. "I'm playing, too, and so is Hob."

Aisha and Emily turned to see a goblin with a wrinkly green face, who was even smaller than Buckle.

"Hello, Hob!" they called.

The goblin swept off his pointy hat and bowed. His spectacles fell off, but a beautiful phoenix with a crest of orange feathers bent her head to pick them up. Six phoenix chicks clustered around her feet.

"Thanks, Ember," said Hob. "Are you playing?"

"Yes," said the phoenix. She fanned out her flame-like tail. "My chicks have come to see the start."

Emily bent down to the baby phoenixes.
"Have you come to cheer your mum on?"
she asked.

"Yes!" trilled the six. They stood in
a row, wingtip to wingtip. Their tails
swayed from side to side as they chanted.

"Our mum's a win-ner!"

Buckle opened a green box. Inside were some large yellow dice, a pack of circular cards and a folded game board. The playing pieces were top hats, like the leprechaun's, but in different colours. Buckle took out the game board and, with a flick of his wrist, unfolded it.

"Wow!" said Aisha. "It looks just like Enchanted Valley!"

As she spoke, tiny models sprang up on the board. *Pop! Pop! Pop!* There was the queen's palace, the silver stadium and the Pufflebunny Inn.

A glow appeared in the middle of the board.

"What's happening?" cried Emily.

The glow grew into a
tall column of brilliant
light.

"Wow!" said Aisha.

"Keep watching …"
Buckle said.

The dazzling beam
grew as high as a pine

tree, then burst into a great fountain of light. It shone all over the valley, as far as the girls could see.

Emily stared. "What's happened?" she asked, hoping it was something wonderful.

"That magic fountain of light turned the whole of Enchanted Valley into a huge game board," Buckle told her. "That's where you'll be playing!"

The girls were thrilled. This was better than any game they'd ever played before!

The leprechaun tossed a yellow die into the air. It hovered beside him!

"There are no numbers on it," Emily whispered.

"That's strange," Aisha replied. "I

wonder how it works?"

Buckle explained the game as he put the board away. "When you throw the die, you'll learn what to do," he said. "As you travel around the board, collect as many rings as you can find. You'll need the rings at the end of the game. But," he said, looking around at the players, "be careful not to collect the reset ring. That will send you back to the beginning!"

Emily nudged Aisha. "We must remember that."

"What about rules?" asked Hob.

"Ah, the rules, to be sure," said Buckle. "Hmm … Fairtail usually uses her Sportsmanship locket to magically set the rules. She hasn't got her locket, but she'll still explain them, won't you, Fairtail?"

"Gladly!" said the unicorn. "Rule One: take turns to roll the die. Rule Two: no taking shortcuts. Rule Three: no cheating. This one is very important. Players who cheat will be disqualified."

Everyone was excited! Ember's wings twitched, and Hob hopped from one foot to the other. Trixie whizzed around so fast her nightcap flew off, and Fairtail's horn sent out tiny crackling sparks!

The girls could hardly wait!

"It's going to be such fun," said Emily.

"Yes," said Aisha, "but let's remember we're doing this to lure that horrible Selena here. Then we'll have a chance to get Fairtail's locket back."

Just then, lightning streaked across the blue sky, followed by a crash of thunder.

Buckle held on to his top hat. "Wh-what … ?"

Aisha and Emily looked up. A silver unicorn loomed high above them. Her deep blue mane and tail waved wildly and her purple eyes blazed. Sparking hooves crackled as they pawed the air.

"Selena!" cried Emily.

## Chapter Three
# Top Hats and Dice

Even though this was exactly what they'd planned – that their practice game would make Selena appear – the girls couldn't help feeling scared.

Aisha glanced at Buckle and Fairtail. The leprechaun had turned pale, and the unicorn was tossing her head uneasily.

As Selena flew lower, the girls realised
that someone they knew was running
over to greet her.

"It's Grubb the ogre!" said Emily, in
dismay.

When Selena landed, Grubb tumbled over to her. As he scrambled along, his lumpy cheeks wobbled and his flabby ears flapped back and forth.

Trixie, Hob and Ember edged back, but Fairtail and the girls stood their ground.

"Ah, the two silly girls," said Selena, "and the useless unicorn who couldn't keep hold of her locket."

"That's because you stole it," said Fairtail. "Where is it?"

The evil unicorn cackled. "Look at Grubb."

The Sportsmanship locket dangled from the ogre's thick, hairy neck. He laughed. "Geh! Geh!"

"You'll never get the locket back,"

sneered Selena.

"We will," Emily said quietly.

"Ha!" said Selena. "This stupid board game will be a disaster. I'll soon be laughing at all you losers! Grubb?"

The tufty bristles that sprouted from the ogre's chin twitched. "Yes, Your Highness," he said.

"You're going to play with these silly creatures," said Selena. "And because you've got the Sportsmanship locket, you can change the rules."

"Awesome!" said Grubb.

Emily glanced at Aisha. "I don't like the sound of that," she whispered.

Selena's eyes flashed. "Grubb's new rule," she said, "is that no one can cheat ..."

The girls shared a confused glance. *This doesn't sound like Selena*, thought Aisha.

"No one can cheat," Selena continued, "except Grubb. *He* can cheat as much as he likes."

Before anyone could argue, she reared up and flew off, cackling.

Grubb strutted around, looking pleased with himself. "Check out *my* locket!" he said, pointing to where the locket lay on his chest.

Aisha glared at him. "It's *not* your locket, and you know it," she said. "Give it back to Fairtail!"

Grubb scowled. "No way. I never win anything, but that's all about to change now." He laughed. "No one cheats ... No one except *me*!"

Emily turned to Fairtail. "He can't do this!"

But the unicorn said sadly, "He can, with the power of my Sportsmanship locket."

Aisha frowned. "Fine! But he won't have it for long."

"We'll make sure of that!" Emily added.

Buckle looked quite shaken by seeing Selena. He tried to plaster on an encouraging smile. "Ahem … I'd better start the game."

He clapped once. The air in front of him shimmered like sparkling mist. It cleared to reveal a large silver trophy. It was shaped like a bowl supported by three unicorn horns, and it turned slowly in mid-air.

The ogre rubbed his grimy hands together. "There's my prize."

"Not yet!" said Aisha.

"Not ever, if we can help it!" Emily added.

"Ahem," said Buckle. "The trophy will be magically hidden somewhere in Enchanted Valley. The only way to find it is to complete the game. Whoever touches it first will be the winner."

"*My* prize," Grubb said again.

Buckle ignored him. "Don't forget, collecting rings along the way will help you win," he said. "Sometimes you'll find them; sometimes you'll earn them by completing tasks."

He clapped again, and said,

"*Fly away, fly away.*

*Cross the skies.*

*Wait for the winner*

*To claim their prize.*"

The trophy rose into the air. Just before it whooshed away, Grubb pulled the locket and chain over his head and hurled it into the bowl.

He gave a wonky grin. "Now the locket's safe. You stinky girls won't get it because you won't win."

The other players gathered around the girls. Aisha stroked Fairtail's sea-green neck, comforting her.

"What do we do?" asked Trixie.

Hob shrugged. "Play, of course."

Ember nodded. "If we don't play, we can't win."

"And we must win to get the locket back," said Aisha. "There are six of us, so we have six chances of winning. It doesn't matter who comes first, as long as it isn't Grubb. Agreed?"

Everyone nodded nervously. "Agreed!"

Buckle tossed a blue hat to Aisha. It

looked far too small, but as she put it on, it grew until it fitted her head perfectly.

"Your hat's glowing!" said Emily. She put a red one on.

Aisha helped Trixie to jam her yellow hat over her purple curls. Everyone laughed as the pixie's hat grew and grew, until almost all her hair was neatly tucked inside.

Fairtail's white hat even provided slots for her ears. Hob wasn't pleased about having to take his own hat off and wear a pink one.

"It's not pointy," he grumbled.

Grubb got an orange hat, which had to grow a hundred times its size to fit on his massive, lumpy head.

Once they were all wearing their brightly coloured hats, Buckle said, "You are the playing pieces now." He passed out maps. "These will help you find your way around."

Buckle stood back, but as Trixie and

Ember flapped their wings and left the ground, he shouted, "Stop! I almost forgot. No flying. Everyone must walk."

He patted the yellow die, and it bobbed towards Aisha. "Blue hat always starts a new game," he said. "That's why your hat's glowing – it's your turn."

Aisha held the die. "It's blank!" she said.

Buckle grinned and said, "Roll it." So she did.

When the die stopped, everyone was surprised to see it showed a picture!

"It's Flowerdew Garden!" said Emily. "We've been there."

"That's where your first task is," said Buckle. "Go, go, go!"

Grubb lumbered away, followed by

the girls and their friends. As they knew where Flowerdew Garden was, maybe they'd get there before Grubb.

After a moment, Emily cried, "Look! A golden ring!"

It was looped over a tall grass stalk. She ran to take it, but Grubb charged back and pushed her over so he could grab the ring himself.

"Ow!" Emily yelled. "You … you …"

"Cheat!" Aisha shouted, helping Emily up.

The ogre laughed. "I'm allowed to cheat!"

Fairtail sighed. "It's going to be hard to win this game."

Emily and Aisha's eyes met. Fairtail

was right. But if they didn't win, they'd never get the locket back, and no one in Enchanted Valley would ever play fair again. They had very little chance of winning ... but they had to do whatever they could to stop Grubb, or else Selena would become queen of Enchanted Valley.

## Chapter Four
# The Big Flower Challenge

As Aisha and Emily ran down a grassy slope, they spotted little pink clouds popping up from behind a copse of hazelnut trees.

"What's that?" asked Aisha.

The crest on top of Ember's head wobbled as she scurried along. "Mist from the Puffing Lily!" she said. "It only grows in Flowerdew Garden!"

"Then we're nearly there!" cried Emily.

They circled the copse, and saw before them the magical garden, bright with colourful flowers and fruits. Fairtail had to skid to a stop when Buckle appeared in a shower of green sparkles.

Buckle waited until Grubb joined the group, then produced the circular game cards. He handed one to Aisha, saying, "This tells you what to do."

Aisha read it aloud.

"*The garden's full of magic plants*
*With flowers small and tall.*
*One minute's all you have to find*
*The biggest one of all.*"

"Three rings for the winner!" Buckle added. "Ready? GO!"

The friends gathered together. "We must beat Grubb," Emily said, "so do your best!"

Fairtail cantered into the middle of the garden. Trixie flapped her wings and was about to leap into the air, when she clapped her tiny hand to her mouth. "Oops! I almost forgot – no flying!"

Ember dashed in a zigzag pattern, while Hob stomped around, peering left and right.

Aisha found a large yellow fluttercup, but Emily spotted an even larger one at the same time.

"You have it," said Emily, who had just

seen a biggonia smiling up from behind a patch of quietly ticking dandelion clocks.

The girls found Hob sitting beside Buckle. He was clutching a pom-pom carnation the size of a football. Grubb was searching nearby, grunting as his lumbering feet pounded the paths.

Fairtail trotted to Buckle with a parasol pansy that was as big as a frisbee. Then Ember hurtled towards the friends with an enormous silvery flower clamped in her beak.

"A giant moonflower!" said Hob.

"Wow! That's the winner!" said Aisha, but just then, Grubb thundered over and snatched the moonflower from Ember.

"Cheat!" cried Emily.

Hob clutched her arm. "It doesn't matter – look!" he said.

Trixie raced towards them, carrying the biggest sunpower flower anyone had ever seen. Emily reckoned it was as big as the largest family-sized pizza.

"Yay, Trixie! That's a whopper!" yelled Aisha.

Buckle checked his watch. "Five seconds … four … three …"

"There!" said Trixie,

shoving the sunpower flower into the leprechaun's hand.

But as the friends cheered, Trixie's yellow top hat flew off and disappeared into the sky.

"Oh dear," said Buckle. "I'm sorry, but that means Trixie's disqualified. She cheated."

"No!" said Emily. "She wouldn't."

Trixie burst into loud sobs. "I did! I did! I'm sorry!" She wept. "I watered the sunpower flower with the gnomes' magic blooming-can so that it would grow ginormous. I'm so sorry. I don't know why I did it!"

Aisha gently cuddled the weeping pixie. "It was the stolen locket that made you do it," she said.

"As I'm not wearing the locket," added Fairtail, "everyone will cheat sooner or later."

"Trixie, we know you're not really a cheater," said Emily. "Not like Grubb."

The ogre danced a clumsy jig. "Ha! I'm the winner! I get the rings!"

Buckle sighed sadly and said, "Even though Grubb cheated when he stole Ember's flower, he still gets three rings, because he's allowed to cheat." He tapped his hat buckle, and three golden rings flew into Grubb's filthy outstretched hand.

Emily put her hands on her hips in frustration. Aisha frowned.

It was the ogre's turn to throw the die.

He tossed it into a clump of Giggling Grass right by his feet, so nobody else could see it. He bent to look at the location it showed, then charged off.

"Cheat!" Aisha shouted.

"He's got a head start," grumbled Hob.

Emily wasted no time and peered at the dice. She saw a picture of an old oak tree. "Hob! It's your home! Hurry!"

The die floated back to Buckle, and Hob led the friends along a narrow path. "Here's a short cut," he cried. "This way!" He turned off the path and dived between the trees.

"Stop!" Fairtail cried, but she was too late. Hob's pink top hat whipped off his head and disappeared.

The girls stared.

"Of course!" said Emily. "Taking a short cut is cheating. Now Hob's out of the game as well as Trixie."

"I'm sorry!" the goblin said, looking miserable.

"Don't worry," Aisha said kindly. "There are still four of us left." She turned to the others. "Come on! We can still beat Grubb! *And* get that locket."

But with each round, it was looking less and less likely.

## Chapter Five
# Quickie Pix

The four remaining friends used the map to find their way to Hob's house. As they followed a trail lined with pink daisies that smelled of strawberry ice cream, they came across two squabbling little goblins outside a thatched cottage.

"You told Mum you swept the floor

properly," said one. "You cheated. You brushed the dirt under the rug."

"Didn't!"

"You did!"

Aisha shook her head crossly. "If you had your locket you'd put this right in a twinkling."

Fairtail sighed. "If I had my locket, this never would have happened in the first place!"

Aisha stroked the unicorn's mane. "We'll soon get it back," she said.

*I hope so*, Emily thought. She spotted a golden ring dangling from a twig. "Hooray! Another one," she said, tucking it in her pocket.

As they drew near to Hob's home, they

passed a young turtle who was crying quietly as his mum told him off.

"Don't ask your sister to do your fishtory homework," she said. "That's cheating!"

"I didn't mean to," the turtle said with a gulp. "It just came out."

The girls wished they could stop to comfort him, but finding the locket was more important.

Hob's home was reached through a gap in a thick tree trunk. They went inside, down a spiral staircase, through a tunnel into a large cavern. This was Hob's potion workshop. Crystal lights glittered on jars and bottles full of curious ingredients, stacked around his wonky shelves. Buckle was waiting, and Grubb was flopped on a squishy armchair that was far too small for him. It was *very* squished.

"Next is a drawing challenge, called Quickie Pix," Buckle announced. "You'll be in two teams."

Aisha whispered to Emily, "This sounds fun. You're good at drawing and I'm not bad. We'll make a great team!"

Buckle continued. "Aisha will team up with Ember. The other team will be Emily, Fairtail and Grubb."

The girls looked at each other. That wasn't what they wanted.

"The first player of each team gets a card with the name of an object, which they have to draw," Buckle explained. "They must not speak. If their teammates guess what the picture is, the person who draws earns two rings, and the guesser earns one."

Emily pulled Aisha and Fairtail aside. "I won't guess what Grubb draws. If I do, he'll get two gold rings."

Fairtail leaned close. "You must do your best to guess," she whispered. "If you don't, it's cheating, isn't it? You'll be disqualified."

Emily's heart sank. "I suppose so," she sighed. "I don't want to help Grubb, but I'll have to."

"Ready?" asked Buckle. He tapped his green top hat on the floor twice. Two whiteboards on easels sprang up, with marker pens hovering beside them.

Ember was first to draw for her team,
and Grubb for his. Aisha sat on a floor
cushion as the phoenix took the pen in
her wingtip and drew a round shape, then
added two legs. Aisha thought it could be
a bird.

Meanwhile, Grubb clutched the pen
in his dirty fist and began drawing. He

pressed so hard, Emily thought he might carve his picture in the board.

Aisha was sure Ember's picture was a bird. It had lots of tail feathers. She racked her brain for a bird with a fluffy tail. "Ostrich!" she shouted.

Ember shook her head.

"A parrot? A vulture?" Aisha tried.

Ember shook her head again and whispered a few words.

"Peacock!" Aisha shouted.

Immediately Ember's hat vanished. "No!" she cried. "I didn't say the answer. I just said, 'It likes showing off its tail.' I wasn't cheating."

Buckle said, "The rule is no speaking. I'm sorry, Ember, you're disqualified."

Meanwhile, Emily gave a quiet gasp. She'd guessed what Grubb had drawn. "Welly boot," she said in a flat voice.

Grubb nearly exploded with delight. "Two rings! Two rings!" he grunted, as they dropped into his hairy hand.

"Yes, Grubb, you won Quickie Pix," said Buckle sadly, "so you can throw the die to select the final game."

The die floated to the ogre's hand. He rolled it, and everyone bent to see where to go next.

"It looks like trees with colourful flowers," said Aisha. "Where's that?"

Grubb thundered along the tunnel and up the stairs – he clearly knew.

"I think it's Flicker Thicket," Fairtail said. "Let's go!"

They set off. Just outside Hob's home Aisha found a gold ring. "Grubb was in such a hurry he missed it," she said, stuffing the ring in her pocket.

They followed Fairtail down a steep,

stony slope. When the unicorn suddenly stopped, the girls stumbled into her.

"What's up?" asked Emily.

"A ring!" said Fairtail, looking up to where a blue ring dangled from a thin, prickly branch. It was bigger than the gold rings.

"Maybe it counts for more," said Aisha. "Can you reach it?"

Fairtail reared up, and hooked the ring with her horn. As she dropped down, Buckle appeared in a flurry of crackling green sparkles, and the ring vanished.

Buckle shook his head. "Sorry, Fairtail. That was the Reset Ring. You must go back to the beginning again."

"Oh no!" the girls cried.

Fairtail's eyes filled with tears. "Girls, I'm so sorry. I wish I could help you beat Grubb!"

They hugged her velvety neck. "It's not your fault," Aisha said.

"Don't worry," Emily added. "We'll do our best."

"I know you will," said Fairtail. She walked away slowly, head down. "I'm sure you can win."

The girls looked at each other nervously.

"It's just us – to save Enchanted Valley," said Aisha.

"Two girls against an ogre," added Emily.

They didn't want to give up, but they had no idea how they could possibly win. Enchanted Valley would be lost for sure.

## Chapter Six
# Butterfly Ride

Flicker Thicket was a dense mound of
shrubbery. In the centre of the mound
grew a single tree with emerald green
leaves. All the way up the trunk, the leaves
were large and flat. They were dotted
with pink and purple caterpillars, while
dainty butterflies of every colour fluttered

among the branches.

Aisha caught her breath. "I've never seen such a beautiful tree!"

Emily stared. "And all those butterflies too. It's magical!"

A grunt echoed from the thicket. There stood Grubb, tapping his foot. Beside him was Buckle, not smiling.

Aisha glanced anxiously at Emily. "This is it," she said. "Our last chance. We must win if we're to get that locket."

"Ahem," said Buckle. "Your final challenge is a game of Caterpillars and Butterflies. Imagine the tree is the game board. The large flat leaves all the way up the trunk are like the spaces on the board. You roll the die to see how many spaces to move. Have you got that?"

"Yes," said the girls. Grubb grunted.

"Your goal is to get to the top of the tree," said the leprechaun, "and take the trophy."

The girls looked up. The silver trophy hovered just above the very topmost leaf of the tree.

"If you land on a leaf with a butterfly on," Buckle continued, "she will grow big enough to fly you to a higher leaf."

"Wow!" said Aisha and Emily, thrilled.

"If you land on a leaf with a caterpillar, you'll slide down his back to a lower leaf."

"I get it!" said Aisha. "It's like my Snakes and Ladders game at home, but with caterpillars instead of snakes, and butterflies instead of ladders."

Buckle grinned. "Girls! Have you never played Caterpillars and Butterflies before?"

"Never," said Emily.

"Oh, that's good!" Buckle danced a little jig. "That means you get beginner's luck!"

With a flick of his wrist, he produced two four-leafed clovers, one for each of them.

"Ooh, these will give us a better chance of winning!" said Aisha. "Let's tuck them in our hair."

Grubb sneered. "Luck's no good when I can cheat!"

Buckle asked everyone to count their

rings. "That will tell you how many spaces you can move up the tree before this round starts," he explained.

The girls counted. Emily had seven, and Aisha six.

Grubb counted loudly so they could all hear. "Five, six, seven," he said. A moment

or two later, they heard him again.

"Twenty-four, twenty-five, twenty-six ..."

"Hey!" Emily cried. "He's counting his over and over. Grubb, you've got more than us anyway, so why cheat?"

Grubb grinned, showing three grey-green teeth, and said, "Because I can."

Buckle checked how many rings everyone had. "You'll start halfway up the tree, Grubb," he said. "A butterfly will take you."

The ogre ran to jump on to a butterfly. She grew to a huge size, but still squeaked, "Ow!" as he landed on her back. She had to flap hard to carry Grubb to his starting point.

The girls were starting so low down the

trunk they could each easily clamber on to their first leaf.

"It's weird standing on these leaves," said Aisha. "They're very strong." The leaves didn't even waver as the girls hopped up.

Buckle called to the ogre. "Grubb, you won the last game, so you'll roll the die first." He held it out. It floated up until the ogre could snatch it out of the air. He rolled it.

"Four!" he said, and climbed up four spaces, landing on a leaf with a butterfly. He climbed on its back.

"Eek!" she said, and slowly managed to fly Grubb to a higher level.

He flung the die to Emily. She rolled a

three and was just
about to step on a
butterfly leaf when
a thick twig crashed
down, frightening
the butterfly away
before Emily
reached it.

"Ha ha!" she
heard Grubb laugh
from above.

"He's enjoying
himself, the cheat,"
Aisha said grimly.
She rolled a six, and
began climbing. Just
before she reached

her leaf, all the butterflies fluttered up to where Grubb was tossing little golden bobbles around.

"Sorry, girls," Buckle called from below. "Butterflies can't resist honey buds."

Aisha and Emily sighed and gritted their teeth.

Grubb rolled the die and got a three. The girls counted spaces and grinned when they realised Grubb would land on a long caterpillar. But just before he did, he growled at the caterpillar, which immediately turned into a butterfly.

"Bully! Cheat!" shouted Emily.

Grubb carried on, cheating whenever he liked. But when the girls threw six after six, and never landed on a caterpillar, they realised their beginner's luck was working. Soon they were level with the ogre.

As they drew near the treetop and the trophy, a beautiful bluebird with a silvery crest flew down and perched between them.

"I'll help you beat that horrible cheat," she trilled softly. "I'll ask a caterpillar to take you both up to the final leaf, together!"

The girls couldn't believe it. More beginner's luck! "Oh, thank you, bluebird!" Emily whispered.

She looked at Aisha in delight. "We're going to win!"

## Chapter Seven
# Sneaky Selena!

"Bluebird?" Emily asked the silver-crested bluebird. "Please would you ask the caterpillar to take us to the final space?" They were so close to winning she could feel it. They'd defeat Selena and the Games could go ahead as planned. "We just have—"

"Wait!" Aisha said. "I think this might count as cheating."

Emily looked doubtful. "Yes, but … If we can reach the final space, we could quickly grab the trophy. It wouldn't matter how we got it."

Aisha realised what was happening. "*No!*" she said. "It's the locket, don't you see? It's making us want to cheat. We mustn't!"

Emily felt disappointed, but she knew Aisha was right. She turned to the bluebird. "You're so sweet and kind, but we must say *no, thank you*."

The bluebird's feathers fluffed up and faded from blue to silver. Her eyes blazed purple, and she grew and grew. Two legs became four, and with a crash of thunder and a flash of lightning, the bird turned into – Selena!

"You foolish girls," she said. "I nearly tempted you. Well, you're not having that trophy, because I'll get it myself!"

She flew towards the shining cup, but before she reached it, the butterflies left their places and created a fluttering, multi-coloured wall in front of her.

Selena pointed her horn at the butterflies and sent out lightning bolts. But the nimble butterflies dodged the lightning and gathered together again to stop Selena passing through their wall.

Grubb called from his tree, "Oh come on, will you?! I'm getting bored waiting up here!"

Emily shouted back, "But you're winning. Aren't you enjoying it?"

"No," grumbled the ogre. "It's not exciting at all. I thought cheating would be exciting, but it's just boring. I'm winning but it's not fun."

"It's no fun for us, either," said Aisha. "It's not a proper game when one player does whatever they like."

Grubb thought for a moment, then said, "If I stop cheating, will you put down your four-leaf clovers? Then we'll be even."

"No!" screamed Selena. Lightning crackled all around her as she screeched at the ogre. "Cheat! You must cheat!"

The girls weren't sure what to do. "Can we trust Grubb?" Emily whispered.

Aisha shrugged. "He was going to beat

us anyway. We could make him promise."

"OK," said Emily. "Grubb? Do you promise to stop cheating if we get rid of our clovers?"

The ogre waggled his hairy little finger. "Pinky promise."

"OK, it's a deal," said Aisha. She and Emily dropped their clovers down to Buckle.

Aisha glanced up towards the trophy and counted leaves. "Emily, you need a six to reach the top," she said.

Emily felt her heart pounding as she rolled the die and she squeezed her eyes shut, too afraid to look.

"You've thrown a six!" cried Aisha.

"No!" shouted Grubb.

Emily grinned and snapped open her eyes. "Maybe we don't need beginner's luck after all!" she said.

She climbed six spaces, pulling herself up on to one leaf after another. On the final one she found a butterfly with crystal wings. Emily climbed on its back and up they flew.

Aisha cheered as Emily hooked one arm around the treetop and stretched up. She grabbed the trophy and peered inside.

There was the Sportsmanship locket, sparkling in the sunlight. Emily reached in and took it out.

She was overjoyed. "We did it!" she sang out.

Selena swooped towards her. "No!" she screamed.

But the butterflies made their rainbow wall and even though the unicorn tried to leap it, they were too quick. They blocked her way every time.

"Hooray!" cried Aisha. "We won!"

Buckle peered through the branches and gave a thumbs up. "Well done!" he called.

But Grubb's flabby ears drooped, and his bumpy, lumpy face looked sad. "I can't believe I lost my locket," he grumbled.

Selena swooped over to him, her eyes blazing. "It's not your locket," she screamed. "It's *mine*! Get back to my castle – NOW!"

Grubb looked utterly miserable as he clambered down from the tree and lumbered off into the distance.

The furious unicorn circled the thicket. "I still have one more locket," she snarled at the girls. "I'll make sure you *never* get it back. Not unless you make me queen!"

She soared into the air amid claps of thunder and crackling lightning bolts.

The butterfly with crystal wings

fluttered to Emily. "I'll take you to Buckle," she said in a tinkling voice. "You can't climb down with that huge trophy."

"What about Aisha?" Emily asked.

"I'm OK!" Aisha laughed. The caterpillars had joined up, end to end, to make a long pink and purple slide!

Emily's butterfly flew once around Flitter Thicket, to cheers from all the caterpillars and butterflies. With a "Wheee!" from Aisha, they were both down with Buckle.

"Well done," he said, grinning. "You did a grand job."

Aisha and Emily smiled happily.

The game board hovered in front of Buckle once more. As he took it in his

hands, light rushed towards it from every
direction. It tinted everything gold –
butterflies, trees, caterpillars, even Buckle's

top hat! The light gathered in the middle of the board and, as Buckle closed it, the golden glow disappeared. The girls' top hats lost their glow too as they rose into the air and vanished.

Aisha and Emily had done it! They'd won the game and got the locket back.

And they'd done it fairly.

# Chapter Eight
# A Joyful Flight

As the girls grinned and hugged each other, more cheers sounded from behind them.

"Hooray for Emily and Aisha!"

"They won! They won!"

The girls turned to see Hob, Ember and Trixie riding on Fairtail's back as she flew

down to land beside them. Ember's six
chicks were snuggled beneath her wings.
"Emi-ly's the win-ner!" they chanted.

"You saved my Sportsmanship locket,"
said Fairtail. "Thank you."

Emily hung the locket around the
unicorn's neck. Fairtail's horn sparkled
and she tossed her head joyfully.

"Jump on my back, girls," she said. "Hob, too."

They said goodbye to Buckle and mounted the unicorn. Aisha sat with Hob in front and Emily behind as Fairtail soared high into the sky. Ember's chicks clung on to her mane, squealing with joy.

Trixie and Ember swooped around them. They were happy to stretch their wings at last!

"We're going to the stadium," the unicorn called.

As they flew, Emily spotted the young turtle, happily doing his homework. His mum sat quietly beside him, weaving a reed basket. Near the palace, Aisha pointed to where Billy the pufflebunny and Whiskerina the kitterfly were whizzing downhill on their go-karts, laughing happily.

"Your locket's working its magic, Fairtail," she yelled.

"I know!" the unicorn called back. "It's great to hear cheerful voices instead of squabbles!" She dodged a relay race between elves on flying scooters, and just missed the Bat Brigade zooming around a floating obstacle course.

Fairtail landed near where her unicorn friends were practising in the showjumping arena.

"Wow!" said Emily. "This showjumping is much more exciting than where we come from!" There were no fences at all on the course. Instead, as each unicorn cantered up to a flag, they performed elegant aerial stunts.

"It's like ballet in the air," sighed Aisha. "So beautiful."

Queen Aurora and the other Sports and Games Unicorns galloped over.

Emily and Aisha held the trophy

between them and lifted it high in the air.
"We did it!" they cried.

"Thank you so much!" said Aurora.
"You only have to look around to see
how important it is for Fairtail to have
her locket back."

Spiritmane asked anxiously, "You will
help me find my Perseverance locket,
won't you?"

"Of course," said Aisha. "We know the
Enchanted Valley Games can't go ahead
until you're wearing it again."

"It's time for us to leave now," added
Emily. "But we promise to come back."

The girls threw their arms around
Aurora's neck and hugged her, then said
goodbye to their unicorn friends and their

board game partners.

"I'll call for you soon," said the queen. "Watch those keyrings!"

Aisha smiled. "We will!"

Aurora pointed her golden horn towards the girls. Sparkles streamed from it and surrounded them. As they felt their feet leave the ground, the sparkles swirled into a whirl of colour and Enchanted Valley disappeared from sight.

"Bye!" they cried.

Moments later, the sparkles faded and the girls touched down on soft carpet. They were back in the living room of Enchanted Cottage.

Emily grinned. "After that adventure, I'm really looking forward to our afternoon's plans."

"So am I," said Aisha. "Let's have a board games tournament, with all our favourite games! Come on."

They poked their heads into the kitchen.

"Mum, Dad," said Aisha. "Please will you come and play a board games tournament with us?"

"Great idea," said Mrs Khan.

"I'll get some snacks and a jug of mango juice," said Mr Khan.

Soon, they were all sitting around the kitchen table with Aisha's Greedy Goat game board between them.

Mr Khan said, "Before we begin, there's a new rule. Dads get to start five spaces in front of everyone else."

Aisha and Emily burst out laughing. Then they each wagged a finger at him and said sternly, "No cheating!"

The End

Join Emily and Aisha
for more fun in …
# Spiritmane and the Hidden Magic
**Read on for a sneak peek!**

Emily loved school, but she couldn't wait for the weekend to begin. She looked out of the window and sighed. She wished she was already in the park, learning some new football moves from Aisha.

The clock on the classroom wall was almost at three. The second hand counted down. Five, four, three, two …

*Bringggg!* Finally, the bell! Chairs scraped on the floor as everyone scrambled out of their seats.

"Have a lovely weekend, everyone, and don't forget your homework!" called Miss

Mayhew above the noise, as everyone stuffed their pencil cases into their bags.

Emily began to pack away … and then stopped. Where was her favourite pencil? The pink one with the unicorn at the end? It *always* sat at the top of her desk.

Read
# Spiritmane and the Hidden Magic
### to find out what's in store
### for Aisha and Emily!

# Also available

**Book Nine:**

**Book Ten:**

**Book Eleven:**

**Book Twelve:**

## Look out for the next book!

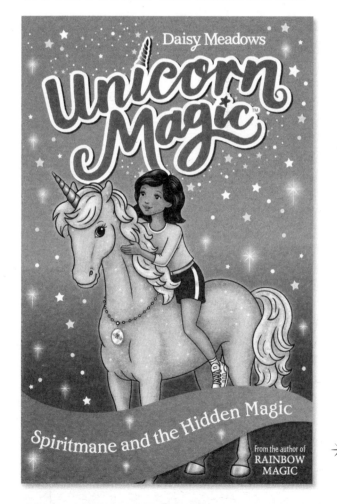

Daisy Meadows

Spiritmane and the Hidden Magic

From the author of
RAINBOW
MAGIC

# Visit
# orchardseriesbooks.co.uk
## for

* ✳ fun activities ✳
* ✳ exclusive content ✳
* ✳ book extracts ✳

## There's something for everyone!

# Spiritmane and the Hidden Magic

## Daisy Meadows

ORCHARD

# For Ruby and Eliza

## Special thanks to Adrian Bott

ORCHARD BOOKS

First published in Great Britain in 2021 by Hodder & Stoughton

3 5 7 9 10 8 6 4 2

Text copyright © 2021 Working Partners Limited
Illustrations © Orchard Books 2021
Series created by Working Partners Limited

A CIP catalogue record for this book is available from the British Library.

ISBN 978 1 40836 624 0

Printed and bound in Great Britain by Clays Ltd, Elcograf S.p.A.

The paper and board used in this book are made from wood from responsible sources.

Orchard Books
An imprint of Hachette Children's Group
Part of Hodder and Stoughton
Carmelite House
50 Victoria Embankment
London EC4Y 0DZ

An Hachette UK Company

www.hachette.co.uk
www.hachettechildrens.co.uk

Contents

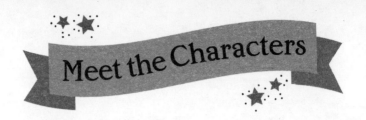
Aisha and Emily are best friends from Spellford Village. Aisha loves sports, whilst Emily's favourite thing is science. But what both girls enjoy more than anything is visiting Enchanted Valley and helping their unicorn friends, who live there.

Quickhoof

The four Sports and Games Unicorns help to make games and competitions fun for everyone. Quickhoof uses her magic locket to help players work well as a team.

Feeling confident in your skills and abilities is so important for sporting success. Brightblaze's magic helps to make sure everyone believes in themselves!

Brightblaze

Games are no fun when players cheat or don't follow the rules. Fairtail's magic locket reminds everyone to play fair!

Fairtail

When things get difficult, Spiritmane's perseverance locket gives sportspeople the strength to face their challenges and succeed.

Spiritmane

Enchanted Cottage

← Golden Palace

An Enchanted Valley lies a twinkle away,
Where beautiful unicorns live, laugh and play
You can visit the mermaids, or go for a ride,
So much fun to be had, but dangers can hide!

Your friends need your help – this is how you know:
A keyring lights up with a magical glow.
Whirled off like a dream, you won't want to leave.
Friendship forever, when you truly believe.

## Chapter One
# School Day Surprise

Emily Turner sat next to her best friend, Aisha Khan, and kicked her heels against her chair. Why did the last few minutes of school always seem to take for ever?

Emily loved school, but she couldn't wait for the weekend to begin. She looked out of the window and sighed.

She wished she was already in the park, learning some new football moves from Aisha.

The clock on the classroom wall was almost at three. The second hand counted down. Five, four, three, two …

*Bringggg!* Finally, the bell! Chairs

scraped on the floor as everyone scrambled out of their seats.

"Have a lovely weekend, everyone, and don't forget your homework!" called Miss Mayhew above the noise, as everyone stuffed their pencil cases back into their bags.

Emily began to pack away … and then stopped. Where was her favourite pencil? The pink one with the unicorn at the end? It *always* sat at the top of her desk. But it wasn't there now.

"Oh no!" she groaned. She quickly checked her pencil case.

"What's wrong?" Aisha asked.

"I've lost my unicorn pencil," Emily said to her friend. "The one you gave me for my birthday!"

Both Emily and Aisha loved unicorns. And they shared a special unicorn secret too.

"Don't worry," Aisha said. "I bet it's just

rolled off the desk."

They peered under the desks and between the chair legs. All the other children were already hurrying out of the classroom, Miss Mayhew following behind.

On the floor, the girls found a hair elastic, a chewing-gum wrapper and plenty of dust, but Emily's unicorn pencil was nowhere to be seen.

"It can't have just vanished into thin air," Aisha said, getting to her feet and looking around.

Emily sighed. "Well, we won't find it now. Let's go home."

At the last moment, she decided to check her pocket. The pencil wasn't there,

but something
inside was shining.

"Aisha,
my keyring's
glowing!" Emily
said.

Aisha pulled her
own keyring out.
"So's mine!"

Both girls
were lucky enough to own beautiful
crystal keyrings in the shape of unicorns.
This was the special secret they shared.
When the keyrings lit up, it meant their
unicorn friend – Queen Aurora – was
calling them. Queen Aurora ruled over
Enchanted Valley, a magical place where

unicorns lived, along with many other strange and wonderful creatures.

Even though it was time for the girls to go home from school, they knew they could travel to Enchanted Valley. In the ordinary world, time stood still while they were away. Still, they didn't want anyone spotting them going off on their adventure!

"We'd better hide," Aisha said. "Miss Mayhew might come back any minute now."

They dashed out of the classroom, looking around. Across the corridor was a supply cupboard where they wouldn't be seen. They ran over and opened the door to scramble inside.

In the dark of the cupboard, Aisha and Emily held up their keyrings and touched the tips of the unicorn horns together.

At once, a whirling spiral of multi-coloured sparkles whooshed up around them. As the rainbow twinkles swirled before their eyes, their feet rose up from the floor. The girls floated in the air and the school cupboard vanished like a mist. The world seemed to hold its breath …

Next moment, the sparkles faded away and their feet sank down again. They were standing on the lush grass of Enchanted Valley. Nearby, on top of a hill, was Queen Aurora's castle, with its four golden towers shaped like unicorn horns. Around it was a moat of blue water.

Right in front of them stood a huge silver stadium. Flags, pennants and ribbons fluttered from poles sticking up from the roof.

"The Enchanted Valley Games!" Emily cried, with a flutter of excitement. "They must be almost ready to start."

The girls knew about the Games from their recent visits to the valley. Creatures

were going to come from all over Enchanted Valley to compete in every event imaginable! Lots of different sports and games were included, from chess to volleyball, and they all had a magical twist. You could play a game of snap against a friendly crocodile, or bounce on magical trampolines that sent you up into the clouds!

Emily and Aisha had been looking forward to the Games, but the unicorns hadn't been able to begin them yet, because of a wicked unicorn called Selena.

"I hope Selena hasn't been causing any more trouble," murmured Aisha as they walked towards the stadium.

Selena had stolen the magical lockets
of the four Sports and Games Unicorns,
and refused to give them back unless
the unicorns made her queen. Until the
lockets were all found and returned,
the Games couldn't begin. The girls
had already helped Quickhoof get her
Teamwork locket, Brightblaze retrieve her
Confidence locket and Fairtail find her
Sportsmanship locket. They knew there
was still one locket left to return.

As they drew closer to the stadium, they
saw a terrible sight. It was being taken
to pieces! A group of badgers in overalls
pushed wheelbarrows, carrying bits of the
stadium away. Magpies took down the
banners. Unicorns and other creatures

packed away all the sports and games
equipment.

"Oh no! I think we've missed the
Games!" Emily wailed.

Aisha pointed. "Look! There's Queen
Aurora," she said. "She'll know what's
going on."

Queen Aurora walked towards them.
Her coat shimmered with all the
beautiful colours of the dawn, but her
head hung and her tail drooped.

"Are we too late for the Games?" Emily asked.

"No," sighed Queen Aurora. "The Games are cancelled. I'm sorry to say that Selena has won."

"What?" both girls cried.

Queen Aurora's eyes brimmed with tears. "I called you here to thank you for helping me so many times. But I won't ask for your help any more. It's all over. After today, I shall rule Enchanted Valley no more. Selena will be queen."

Aisha and Emily looked at one another.

"H-how can you say that?" Aisha stammered. "How can you just give up?"

"I'm sorry," Queen Aurora said. "There's nothing I can do."

Emily grabbed Aisha's arm. "Hold on. Spiritmane's locket is still missing, isn't it? And it's the Perseverance locket – the one that gives you the power to keep going. No wonder Queen Aurora wants to give up!"

"Of course," Aisha said. "She's lost her power to stay determined! We need to find Spiritmane, and fast."

## Chapter Two
# Queen Selena the First

The girls soon caught sight of Spiritmane, with her lavender-coloured body and her creamy mane and tail. She was looking on miserably as the badgers took a golden podium to bits.

"Not much point in having a winners' podium if there aren't going to be any

Games," she sighed.

The three other Sports and Games
Unicorns nodded. Emily recognised
Quickhoof, Brightblaze and Fairtail.

Emily and Aisha ran over to their
friends.

"Spiritmane, it's us! We've come to
help!" called Emily.

"Don't give up. We'll get your locket
back," added Aisha.

"Hmm? Oh, hello," said Spiritmane, giving them a sad smile. "Don't bother trying to find my locket. It's gone for good."

A heap of footballs had been left by the podium. Spiritmane began to nudge them into an open sack. "We won't need these any more," she muttered.

"Oof!" said a squeaky voice from inside the sack. A little hamster tumbled out!

He landed right in front of Emily and Aisha, and blinked. Then he sprang up and dusted himself off. "Hello!" he said, grinning. "Did I vin?"

"Vin?" Aisha asked, puzzled.

"Vin!" the hamster repeated. "Opposite of lose!"

"Er … win what?" said Aisha.

"The hide and seek practice, vot else?" squeaked the hamster.

Emily and Aisha looked at the funny little animal grinning up at them. It was an oddly *pointy* grin. To Emily's surprise, she saw the hamster had two tiny fangs!

"I'm sorry, but you didn't win," Spiritmane told him. "Practice was cancelled. So were the rest of the Games. Everyone's going home."

"Cancelled?" The hamster's face fell. "After I spent so long hiding in that sack? Drat. Vot a shame." He looked up at the girls, and his face lit up again. "Ah! Vhere are my manners? You two must be Aisha and Emily!"

"That's right," said Emily, smiling warmly. "But who are you?"

The little hamster swelled up with pride. "I … am Spike. And I'm a vampster!"

Two tiny bat wings unfurled from Spike's back.

Aisha covered her mouth so she wouldn't giggle. "I'm sorry, but … what's a vampster?"

"A vampster," Spiritmane said, "is a vampire hamster."

"Don't be scared!" Spike said, with a fangy smile. "I only eat blood oranges!"

He vanished back inside the sack of footballs and came out a second later, pulling a bag of blood oranges behind him. "I am a hide and seek champion," he explained. "Sometimes, vhen I need to hide for a long time, I bring a snack along to keep me going. *I vant to suck your blood* ... orange."

He sank his fangs into one and slurped. "Yum. So juicy!"

Aisha and Emily grinned at one another. They were both thinking the same thing: there was nothing *less* scary than the little vampster. He was about as frightening as a cuddly toy!

Spiritmane said, "Spike really *is* the hide and seek champion of Enchanted Valley.

Whether he's hiding or seeking, he just doesn't give up. He's never been beaten!"

"You are too kind, my friend," Spike said. "I just do my best."

Next moment, there was a blinding flash of lightning and a huge *kaboom* of thunder.

In the middle of the stadium appeared a silver unicorn, with a mane and tail of electric blue. She looked at the creatures surrounding her and laughed.

"Selena!" Emily gasped.

"And she's got Grubb with her, as usual," muttered Aisha. Grubb was Selena's grey, lumpy ogre servant.

"Hello, you fools!" jeered Selena. "Oh, look, those two annoying girls are here.

After the locket, are you? You might as
well give up, because you're not getting it
back!" She turned to Aurora. "Of course,
if you make me queen, I might let you
have it ..."

"Very well, Selena," said Queen Aurora,
shaking her head sadly. "You win. Meet
me at the palace at noon and I will hand
over the crown to you."

"At last!" Selena crowed. "Long live Queen Selena the First!"

"No way," said Emily, her hands on her hips.

"*We're* not giving up," said Aisha. "And you'll never be queen."

Selena made a face. "So, you're still trying to stop me?" she said. "Fine. I'll just hide the locket somewhere you will never find it."

"Oh, vonderful!" piped up Spike. "Hide and seek is my favourite game. I like a challenge."

"Spike always wins," said Emily firmly, jutting her chin out at Selena. "And he's on our side."

"Yeah, he's a champion!" said Aisha.

Selena glared at Spike. "A pipsqueak like you, a champion? Well then, game on, you ghoulish gerbil! I'm going to hide this locket. If you can't find it before high noon, the crown is mine. I'll be Queen of Enchanted Valley for ever!"

"I want to hide the locket!" Grubb shouted and stomped his stony foot. "Maybe then I can win something."

Selena rolled her eyes. "Very well,

Grubb! Now, come on. We're leaving."

Grubb grabbed Spike's bag of blood oranges.

"Hey!" yelled Spike.

"Yum!" Grubb said. "Thanks for the treat."

With another crash of thunder and blaze of light, Selena was gone, and Grubb ran off into the distance.

Spike sagged, like a balloon the week after a birthday party. "Ah. On second thoughts … perhaps I can't do this," he said.

"But you're the champion!" Emily said.

"But ve are already halfway through the morning," Spike groaned. "How on earth are ve going to search all of Enchanted Valley before noon? Maybe ve should just give up now."

"He's right, you know," Queen Aurora added gloomily.

Emily whispered to Aisha: "This is all because the Perseverance locket is gone! Even Spike's feeling the effect now."

Aisha nodded. "We've only just arrived, so we're not feeling it yet. But all the creatures in Enchanted Valley have been missing their perseverance for days."

"I bet Spike can still help us, though, even if he doesn't believe it," said Emily.

"Hmm," Aisha said. "Before a football match, our coach always gives us a pep talk. It really helps us stay positive. Maybe I should give one to Spike?"

"Brilliant idea!" Emily grinned.

Aisha bent down. "Hey, Spike? I know you like winning. We all do. But it's not all about winning the game, is it? It's about having a go and doing your best."

"That's right," added Emily. "Every time you play a game, there is a chance you won't win. But if you don't play, you *definitely* won't win."

Spike gave them a little smile. "You may be young, but you show great visdom," he said.

He stood up and spread his wings. "The challenge may be great," he said, "but I, Spike the Vampster, will try my best!"

The girls' pep talk had worked. The game was on!

# Chapter Three
## The Peel Trail

Emily put her arm around Spiritmane's neck. "You should come too," she told her friend.

"I think my locket's gone for ever, and we'll never find it," said Spiritmane sadly. "But I suppose I'd better come with you."

"Velcome to the team!" cheered Spike.

"I think I'll go back to the palace," Queen Aurora said wearily. "I'll say goodbye to it one last time."

"Don't give up, Your Highness!" Aisha urged.

"Yes, you go to the palace and make sure Selena doesn't move herself in," said Emily. "It's still yours!"

Aurora nodded. "For now," she said. She turned and began to walk slowly up the hill towards the palace.

"I can't bear to see Queen Aurora feeling so hopeless. We must find that locket," said Emily.

They headed for the big arched doorway that led out of the stadium. Some banners had been hung up above the door, and a group of kittens with butterfly wings were taking them down.

"Look, kitterflies!" Aisha said, pointing.

"Yes, there's Minky," said Emily, waving to a black and white kitterfly who they had met on a previous adventure.

A little kitterfly with buttercup-yellow wings let go of her banner. She gave a sigh as it fluttered to the ground. "This is taking ages," she said. "Let's just give up."

"Good idea," said Minky. "What's the point of taking all this stuff down, anyway? It'll fall down by itself eventually."

Emily gave Aisha a worried look. "Oh dear. They can't even persevere with giving up!"

"We need to find that locket before things get worse," said Aisha.

"Where should we start looking?" wondered Emily.

"Let's ask the hide and seek champion!" Aisha said. "Spike, where do you think Grubb might be hiding?"

"I always check the most obvious place first," said Spike. "Just in case!"

"I suppose the most obvious place is

right here by the stadium," said Emily.

They all began to search, around the trees, under the benches and along the side of the path. Nobody found anything, until …

"Vait!" Spike narrowed his beady eyes and swooped down on something lying on the ground.

"That looks like peel from a blood orange," Aisha said.

"It is!" Emily said. "But what's it doing out here on the grass?"

Spike frowned. "It looks like one of mine. But I don't peel my oranges, I just sink my fangs into them!"

"Besides, Spike always puts his rubbish in the bin," added Spiritmane.

Aisha snapped her fingers. "I've got it. Grubb must have dropped that orange peel. He stole that big bag of oranges from you, and it's just like him to leave litter lying about on the ground. He must have come this way!"

Spiritmane and Spike looked at one another doubtfully.

Just then, Aisha caught sight of another little piece of peel, lying in the grass up ahead. "Look!"

"That silly ogre's left a trail for us to follow," laughed Emily.

"See? We *can* do this! Come on!" Aisha cried.

The trail of dropped orange peel led away from the stadium, over a green grassy hill and down through a wide, echoing valley. Following the trail, they found a huge ogre footprint, and grinned at one another. They'd catch up with Grubb in no time!

But then they reached a pile of peel, and they couldn't see another piece anywhere.

There was nothing else around, except for a mound of muddy earth that looked a bit like a heap of mashed potatoes covered with gravy.

"What do we do now?!" Aisha cried.

Emily searched around, and her eyes fixed on the mound of mud. It must be a house, she realised, because a wonky door was stuck in the middle of it. Next to the house was a rubbish heap. If it hadn't been for the door, it might have been hard to tell the house from the rubbish.

A wooden sign stood outside the house, with writing scrawled on it in dribbly black paint.

Emily got closer and read the sign.

*NOT Welcome to Grubb's House.*

"Charming!" said Spike, reading it too.

"He must be in there," said Spiritmane. "Let's sneak up quietly."

They crept close. Emily bent down and peered in through a crack in the wall. "I can't see Grubb," she said.

"What about my locket? Can you see it?" Spiritmane asked.

Emily said, "There's something at the back of the burrow, and it's all sparkly!

But it's really dark in there."

Spike flapped up. "I am the only one small enough to get through that crack," he said bravely. "Even if it's all a vaste of time, I must try!"

The little vampster climbed in through the tiny hole. Aisha and Emily held their breath.

Moments later, they heard Spike's muffled voice: "Ooh, it's smelly in here! There's old ogre socks and a mouldy sandvich. "

"Can you see the locket?" Emily called.

The only answer was a rustling noise as Spike rummaged through Grubb's things.

Suddenly, Spike popped out of the crack! On his face was a big grin, and

in his paws was a glittering locket with
a picture of a scroll. "Ta-daaah!" he
squeaked.

"My locket!" gasped Spiritmane.

"Well done, Spike!" the girls cheered.

They hugged
him – very
gently, because
he was so small
– and Spike
puffed up with
pride.

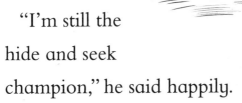

"I'm still the
hide and seek
champion," he said happily.

"That's brilliant," said Aisha, "and better
still, it's not even high noon yet! We've

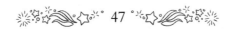

won!"

Emily cried, "Selena won't be queen after all! Long live Queen Aurora!" Her triumphant shout echoed through the land.

"Who's that shouting?" said a gruff voice. From over by the rubbish heap came a groaning, rumbling, grumbling noise, like a whale with a tummy ache. Suddenly, a big boulder stood up.

The boulder glared at them with large round eyes. It wasn't a boulder at all. It was Grubb, disguised as a rock!

"Where did you come from?" he roared. "You must have sneaked right past me!"

He charged at Spike, but the little vampster flew up into the air. "Let's put this locket back where it belongs," he said.

"No!" Grubb shouted, and reached out for Spike.

But Spike's bat wings whirred and he flew over to Spiritmane. She bowed her head. Spike quickly hung the locket around her neck.

"No!" Grubb cried again. "Selena will be furious with me." He sounded very pathetic.

Emily and Aisha watched, smiling, and waited for Spiritmane's magic to return.

But nothing happened. Spiritmane looked just as sad as before.

"Why isn't it working?" murmured Aisha.

"My magic's gone," said Spiritmane in a hollow voice. "It's gone for good. The crown is lost. There's only one thing left to do now."

"What's that?" Emily cried.

Spiritmane sank to the ground, put her head on her hooves and closed her eyes. "Give up."

## Chapter Four
# Selena's Locket Switch

A frown came over Spike's little furry face. "Does this mean I didn't vin after all? I don't understand. I *alvays* vin."

Emily bent down to take a better look at the locket. As she held it in her hand, flaky gold paint rubbed off on her fingers. In fact, now she could see it in the light, it looked like something from a Christmas cracker.

"This isn't Spiritmane's locket at all," she said. "It's a fake!"

Aisha said, "Selena must have given Grubb a fake locket to hide and kept the real locket for herself."

Grubb howled. "Selena tricked me!" He stamped his foot and the ground shook.

"Yes, she did," Emily said.

Grubb sat down on a rock. His bottom lip stuck out. "Why would she do that? I thought she was letting me play hide and seek. But it was all a big lie!"

"I'm sorry, Grubb, but that's what Selena's like," Aisha said. "She tricks people. Even when you think she's on your side."

"Hmm," said Grubb, and rested his huge chin on his fist. He furrowed his brow, deep in thought.

Emily was a little surprised. She'd never seen Grubb look thoughtful before.

Spiritmane shrugged the fake locket off and threw it on to Grubb's enormous rubbish heap. "We've wasted the whole morning looking for a locket that wasn't even real," she said. "The sun's almost overhead, and then it'll be noon. Soon it will be too late!"

"Selena's going to be queen, then. I suppose ve'd better get used to it," said Spike miserably. "I don't expect it'll be much fun. She probably von't let anyone else vin any games."

"No," Grubb said. He heaved a massive sigh. "I wish I'd never helped her in the first place! You girls had the right idea, trying to stop her all the time. I bet there won't be any more games for anyone, except for her."

Emily turned pale. "Aisha," she said. 'I've just had a thought. It's Aurora's magic that brings us here, but if she's not queen any more ...What if we can never come back to Enchanted Valley again?"

Aisha gasped. "You're right! We can

only travel here because of the power of Aurora's friendship. Without that, we won't ever see any of our friends again!"

The thought was like a rain cloud covering up the sun. Emily suddenly felt like giving up.

*That must be because the locket is gone*, she thought. *This is what everyone else is already feeling. Soon I'll be as sad as Spiritmane and Spike.*

"I'm going to miss Enchanted Valley so much," Aisha said, with a trembling voice.

"We hardly knew each other when we first came," Emily said. "But look at us now. Our mums say we're like twins! Enchanted Valley really helped bring us together, didn't it?"

"Yes! But it's not just the two of us, it's everyone else too!" said Aisha. "Aurora and Hob and Pearl, and all the others ... Milo the Moonwolf, and Prism, and Fluffy ... Oh, we've had so many adventures here. And all because we've been making new friends, all the time!"

Bright light suddenly blazed from the girls' pockets. It shone so strongly you could even see it through the fabric!

"Our keyrings?" said Emily. "But …
we're already here in Enchanted Valley.
What's going on?"

They both took out their keyrings
and looked at them. They were glowing,
bright as the morning sun.

"They've never glowed while we were
*in* Enchanted Valley before," Aisha said.

Emily held her friend's hand tight. "It's
a sign from Queen Aurora. It has to be!
She's trying to tell us something!"

The two girls both realised what
Aurora's message had to be.

Aisha said: "Even if it's hopeless …"

And Emily said: "And even if there's no
way to win …"

Together they said, "We'll never give up

on our friendship!"

They hugged one another like they wouldn't ever let go.

"We have to keep fighting," said Aisha.

"And if there's no hope to be found, we'll just have to *make* some," said Emily.

Aisha turned to Spiritmane and Spike. She forced down the despair she could feel. "Come on!" she said brightly. "Why don't we see this as a new game? Us four versus Selena. And the prize is Enchanted Valley!"

"Us *five*!" bellowed Grubb suddenly.

Everyone turned and stared.

Grubb whispered to Spike, "Um … five does come after four, doesn't it?"

Spike nodded. Grubb stood up and came

over to the girls.

"I want to join your team, if you'll have me," he said. "I want to help put things right. It's not too late, is it?"

"Of course you can join us, Grubb!" said Aisha. "We'd be glad to have you!"

"It's *never* too late," added Emily with a grin. "Not when you have your friends by your side."

# Chapter Five
## Quaking Quarry

"So where should we start looking?" Spiritmane asked. And the girls were glad to see she hadn't completely given up yet.

"Hmm," said Emily, looking round. "This is going to be tricky. There's no trail to follow."

"Selena might have left hoof prints,"

suggested Aisha. "And she always makes storm clouds when she flies around, doesn't she? Let's look for both of those."

Emily and Aisha shielded their eyes from the sun as they peered up into the sky. The others carefully searched the ground.

Emily had a sudden thought. "Hey, Grubb? Can you think of anything

Selena might have said about her plan?"

Grubb screwed up his face, frowned hard and scratched his ear. He was clearly thinking very, very hard.

Slowly, he said, "I remember ... Selena asked me how I disguise myself as a rock. I showed her how to do it."

"So how *do* you do it?" Emily asked.

"Well," said Grubb, looking proud of himself, "you find a load of rocks. Then you lie down on the ground, and you sort of ... roll around a bit."

"How does that help?" Spike asked.

"It covers you with dirt and moss!" Grubb explained. "I'm already greyish and a bit lumpy, so I have a head start, you see? Then you curl up into a ball, and keep as still as you can."

Aisha put a finger on her chin. "I wonder … Maybe Selena asked Grubb about his disguise because she wanted to copy it!"

"Could Selena be hiding somewhere in Enchanted Valley, disguised as a rock?" cried Emily.

Spike suddenly became excited. "I think I know where she might be. Follow me!"

Off Spike flew. Grubb followed, thundering through the valley with great bounding strides. Everyone hurried to keep up with them.

As the girls passed underneath the branches of a tree, they heard voices

coming from a nest.

"I don't want to do my flying lessons any more, Mum," piped a tiny voice.

Emily glanced up and saw a baby bluebird peeping over the edge.

"I'm rubbish at flying," the bluebird sighed. "I'll never learn. What's the point in carrying on?"

Further on, Aisha saw smoke curling up

from a little cave mouth in the side of a hill. Out came a small dragon in a white apron, carrying a mixing bowl with a spoon stuck in it.

"What a waste of time!" the dragon cried, and angrily banged the bowl down on a tree stump. "Why should I bother making Rory Firefiddle a birthday cake, anyway? I'll probably just burn it, and he won't want to be my friend any more. I'm giving up."

Emily and Aisha shared a worried glance. "Uh-oh," Emily said. "Things are getting worse."

"People are giving up on everything, not just on sports and games," said Aisha. "We have to get Spiritmane's locket back!"

"Almost there," puffed Grubb. "Just at the top of this big hill ..."

The girls followed him up to the very

top. But what they found there took them by surprise. Instead of soft green grass, the ground dropped away into a great rocky hollow. There were rocks of all shapes, sizes and colours lying around. Some were even gold and silver.

"Vatch out," Spike warned, as they climbed into it. "This is the Quaking Quarry, the rockiest place in the land. If you vanted to hide in a rock disguise, this

is the place to do it. The ground can go a bit vibbly-vobbly sometimes, so be careful how you step."

Aisha and Emily looked out over the quarry, trying to spot any rock that might be Selena in disguise.

"If she is hiding somewhere here, it won't be easy to find her," Aisha agreed.

Spiritmane said, "Selena can use magic, too. So she might have used it to make her disguise even better." She hung her head. "If there even *is* a disguise. She's probably not even here. She could be miles away by now. Look at the sky – it's almost noon. We might as well just give up."

Aisha stroked Spiritmane gently. "No.

We've come this far, and we've nothing to lose by trying just a bit longer."

But as she looked from rock to rock for any sign of Selena, she began to feel hopelessness creeping in. There were just so many rocks!

"I wish the Quaking Quarry would hurry up and quake," Emily said. "If this place was full of rocks tumbling about, I bet Selena would fly out of the way and show herself."

Grubb's face lit up. "Great idea! Everyone, stand back!"

Grubb charged down into the quarry.

Then he started dancing. He jumped and clapped and stomped his huge feet.

"Woohoo!" he yelled. "Rompy stompy!"

He did a back flip and came down hard on his bottom. The ground underneath him began to quake and then the whole quarry started shaking. Emily and Aisha ducked as rocks went tumbling past them.

"Quick!" Spiritmane said. "Climb aboard!"

The girls scrambled on to Spiritmane's back. She leapt into the air, safely out of the way of the flying rocks. Spike fluttered nearby.

The quarry shook harder. Rocks
whizzed back and forth.

"Look!" Emily cried with delight.
"There she is!"

A big silvery rock uncurled itself. It was
Selena!

## Chapter Six
# Friendship Power!

With a panicked screech, Selena shot up
into the air. A boulder crashed down right
on the spot where she'd been a moment
before.

Aisha hugged Spiritmane's neck. "See? I
knew we mustn't give up!"

Selena scowled down at them. Her eyes

flashed with anger. Around her neck hung a sparkling locket with a picture of a scroll on it. "You! I should have known!" she roared.

"My locket!" Silvermane said.

Selena yelled, "You little fools! Why aren't you giving up yet? Can't you see I've already won?"

"Not yet, you haven't!" Emily yelled back.

"And we'll never give up!" Aisha shouted. "Don't you see? You might have stolen the locket's magic, but we've something even more powerful. Our friendship!"

Emily said, "We had it all along, we just didn't realise until now. Look! Grubb's our friend now, too."

"Oh, is he indeed?" Selena snarled. She looked down at Grubb. "I should have known you'd betray me. You're the worst servant I ever had!" Lightning flickered in her eyes as she reared up angrily. "You'll be sorry, you worthless ogre!"

"I'm already sorry!" Grubb shouted, and stamped his foot. "Sorry I ever helped you! You're nothing but a ... a nasty old meanie-pants. I hope you never get to be queen!"

As Selena launched into another angry speech about how hopeless Grubb was, Spike beckoned Emily and Aisha to lean in close. He whispered, "Can you keep

Selena busy?"

"I think so," said Emily. "Why, do you have a plan?"

"Yes!" Spike grinned. "Vhile she's not looking,

I can fly round behind her and vhisk that locket right off her neck!"

Aisha and Emily shared a worried glance. "That sounds really dangerous, Spike," said Aisha.

"If Selena catches you, she'll be furious," added Emily. "Are you sure you want to go through with it?"

"Yes," Spike said bravely. "You vould not give up on your friends, so I shall not give up on mine! Even if it feels like there is no hope, I must do my best."

Spiritmane flew the girls down next to Grubb. Aisha leaned over and whispered into his ear, "We need you to distract Selena so Spike can steal the locket."

Grubb nodded. "Leave it to me. I know

just what to do."

He marched up in front of Selena, threw himself down on the ground and started beating his fists. "It's not fair!" he roared. "You wouldn't even let me hide the real locket!"

"Stop that at once, you silly ogre," Selena snapped. "You'll start another earthquake!"

But the earthquake had already begun

– and it was even bigger than the first one. All around, huge rocks bounced up into the air. Even the boulders at the very top of the quarry started to tumble down. The more Grubb pounded the ground, the more rocks went rolling down.

"Eek!" Selena squealed. She dodged, yelping as the boulders shot past her. Meanwhile, Spike fluttered round behind her with his little bat wings.

Selena was distracted. Spike reached out to snatch the locket. Emily and Aisha held their breath. Closer … closer … almost there …

Just as Spike was about to grab the chain of the locket, Selena turned and stared right at him!

"Oh no!" the girls said together.

Selena narrowed her eyes. There was a sudden, brilliant, silvery-blue flash. With a *boomf*, a little grey storm cloud appeared. And Spike was caught inside it!

The little vampster couldn't move his wings. All he could do was hang helplessly

inside the cloud, while Selena glared at him. "So! Thought you could trick me, did you?" She laughed evilly. "Well, it's nearly noon. Nearly time to crown me as queen!"

Emily and Aisha gulped. It might really all be over now. There seemed no hope left at all. They might as well give up.

## Chapter Seven
## Sticky Attack!

"Silly little meddling vampster!" Selena mocked. "Did you really think it would be this easy to beat me?"

Spike glared back at her. "I don't care how hard it is. Ve *vill* beat you. And I vill never give up!"

Selena threw back her head and

laughed. "Neither will I!"

"And neither will I!" Grubb shouted.

Quick as a flash, he pulled out the
rest of the blood oranges he'd stolen. He
held them up in his big, lumpy fist and
*squeezed*.

*SPLOOSH!* All the juice exploded out
of the oranges at once – and most of it
went over Selena!

"ARGH!" Selena shrieked as the juice dribbled down her face. "Disgusting! Sticky!" She thrashed her head around and screwed her eyes up tight. "My lovely mane's ruined! And now it's in my eye! Ooh, it stings!!"

The storm cloud vanished with a pop. Spike's wings were suddenly free. He swooped down, caught hold of the locket, and whisked it off Selena's neck.

"Give that back!" Selena shouted. "Pesky rodent! Where are you?" Her eyes were still covered with orange juice. "Ouch!"

Spike darted away, leaving Selena helpless and sticky. The little vampster quickly flew to Spiritmane and lowered the locket around her neck.

Spiritmane stood up straight. It was as if the light came back into her eyes.

"Thank you," she whispered.

"Hooray!" Emily and Aisha cheered. Spike beamed, and Grubb happily clapped his huge hands together.

"We did it!" cried Emily.

Aisha looked around, smiling. "Well done, everyone!"

There was a tiny boom of thunder. A black thundercloud appeared over Selena, and began to rain. It washed the juice away, but left her looking like a bedraggled old mop.

"I'll get my revenge on all of you," she growled. "Especially, you, Grubb! I'd make a much better queen than Aurora. You'll see. I'll keep coming back, and one day, I'll win!"

"You know," Spiritmane said thoughtfully, "I usually tell people *not* to give up. But in your case …"

"Give up now!" Aisha and Emily finished.

Everyone laughed except for Selena, who stamped her hoof in fury. Then she flew off into the sky. Thunder grumbled for a moment, then she was gone.

"Follow us, Grubb!" Spiritmane said.

"Why? Where are we going?" Grubb asked.

"The stadium, of course!" Spiritmane said, laughing. "The Enchanted Valley Games are back on."

Moments later, they swept down from the sky towards the stadium. A huge crowd was waving and cheering.

Over the entrance, the kitterflies

were putting a banner back up. "Keep going! We can do it!" said Minky as she struggled to fix her end in place.

The crowd made space for Spiritmane to land and the girls slid off her back. Queen Aurora came bounding up, bright as the dawning sun.

She nuzzled Emily and Aisha fondly. "Thank you for never giving up," she said.

"You've won. Enchanted Valley is safe!"

The girls hugged her, and all the creatures burst into applause.

"Oh! I meant to ask," Emily said. "Back then, just when everything seemed like it couldn't get any worse, our keyrings glowed!"

"It was like a sign that we shouldn't give up," said Aisha. "Was that you, sending us a message?"

Queen Aurora shook her head, and smiled a little knowing smile. "That wasn't *my* magic," she said. "I think it was something else."

"What?" asked the girls.

"The power of friendship," said Aurora. "It has a magic all of its own."

Aisha and Emily held hands. "We promise we'll *never* give up on Enchanted Valley," Emily said.

"Or on our friends," added Aisha.

"Yes, we never could have beaten Selena without Grubb and Spike!" said Spiritmane.

The gathered crowds burst out into wild cheering again. They showered Spike and Grubb with streamers, confetti and flower petals.

Grubb blushed. He went over to Queen Aurora.

"I'm sorry," he said. "I should never have helped Selena."

"That's OK," Queen Aurora said. "You're forgiven!"

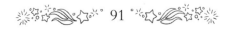

"Am I?" Grubb said. "Wow. I mean …
thank you!"

Queen Aurora turned towards the
stadium. "Come along, everyone. Now we
have all the lockets back, the Enchanted
Valley Games can begin. It's time for the
opening ceremony!"

## Chapter Eight
# The Opening Ceremony Celebration

All the seats in the stadium were full. From all across Enchanted Valley, creatures had come to watch the fun. Aisha and Emily sat in the front row, too excited for words.

Queen Aurora's horn shimmered with

magic, and the sky turned a beautiful
dark blue.

Trumpets blew a fanfare. A single,
brilliant firework shot up and exploded
into a fountain of rainbow colours.
Suddenly, lights blazed all around the
stadium. The green turf in the middle had
been magically shaped into hills, valleys,
mountains and forests, complete with
rivers and lakes, and a very familiar-

looking model palace.

"It's a miniature Enchanted Valley!" Emily cried out.

Dancers came running in from all sides, representing every part of Enchanted Valley. The music changed to a happy jig, then to a swirling symphony, then to an exciting gallop. The girls watched goblins, dragons, mermaids, birds and – of course – unicorns, all putting on a spectacular

show. Spotlights shone on one part of the valley after another.

"They're showing us everything that makes the different places special!" Emily whispered to Aisha.

Ribbons and streamers danced in the air. Fireworks shimmered overhead. Then, after a final tremendous explosion of lights, silence fell.

Queen Aurora walked gracefully into the middle of the stadium. All the other unicorns came and stood with her in a circle.

The queen's horn began to glow. Multi-coloured lights went rippling up and down it. It grew brighter and brighter, lighting up the whole arena.

"I've never seen it shine so much," Aisha whispered.

Aurora leaned in close to the unicorn next to her and touched horns with them. The flaming glow passed from one horn to the other. That unicorn passed it to the next, and so it went on, from horn to horn all around the circle.

The last unicorn of all was a little foal.

She carried the fire up to a plinth, where a large crystal ball rested. She bowed her head and touched her horn to the ball.

The multi-coloured lights leapt into the crystal ball, which lit up and shone like a rainbow sun. The whole stadium was bathed in shimmering beauty. The sky changed back to daylight.

Spike whispered to the girls, "That's the Light of Friendship! It'll stay burning all through the Games. Everyone who sees it vill be reminded of what the Games are really about. Teamvork, confidence, sportsmanship and perseverance. And friendship, of course."

Quickhoof, Brightblaze, Fairtail and Spiritmane lined up in front of the plinth.

With one long blow on their golden
whistles, the Games began!

Emily and Aisha lost count of all the
events they saw. Every time one of their
friends took part, they made sure to
support them. Whether it was Fluffy the
Cloud Puppy tumbling about with the
other Cloud Puppies in a game of sky
rugby, or their mermaid friend Pearl
winning the upstream swimming race,
or Hob the goblin trying his best in a
floating chess match, they cheered and
clapped.

When it was time for the hide and
seek competition, both Spike and Grubb
wanted to take part! All the hiders
sprinted off to different corners of the

arena, while Queen Aurora closed her
eyes and counted.

Spike flew down and landed among the
goodies on the snack table. Aisha frowned
in confusion. "He's meant to be hiding,
not eating," she said.

But then, Spike rolled around in all the
flour and crumbs, and curled up next to
the bread rolls. With his light brown fur,
he looked just like another one!

"He's borrowed Grubb's trick!" laughed
Emily. "How clever."

Meanwhile, Grubb covered himself with
sand to hide in the long-jump pit.

"Ready or not, here I come!" Aurora
called.

Right away, she found a giggling little

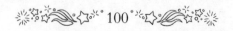

monkey beside her hoof. Then she spotted Hob, lying down beside the winners' podium. She

galloped happily around the stadium, finding more and more creatures.

Soon, only Spike and Grubb were left to find. The girls watched excitedly as Queen Aurora approached the snack table.

"Hmm," she said, bending over the cakes and pastries. "I wonder where they could be?"

Her long mane dangled over Spike.

A moment later Spike burst into giggles and unrolled, sending flour everywhere. "It tickles!" he squeaked.

"Aha!" Queen Aurora said. "Found you!"

"That means Grubb is the winner," Aisha shouted. "Well done, Grubb!"

Grubb sat up in the sandpit. "What? I won? Really?"

"Congratulations!" Spike said. "Vot a brilliant hiding place, my friend. You deserved to vin!"

"But … aren't you sad that you lost?" Grubb asked nervously.

"Not at all!" beamed Spike. "I just love to play games with my friends."

Grubb grinned happily. "That's the

main thing, isn't it?"

Eventually, it was time for the
prizegiving. All the winners stood in line,
and Queen Aurora hung golden medals
around their necks, one by one. An
enormous cheer went up from the crowd.

Then the queen gave Grubb a special
laurel crown and named him Champion
of the Enchanted Valley Games!

"Sometimes the last ones to join the
team are
the ones
who make
the biggest
difference,"
she said with
a smile. "Now,

Aisha and Emily, would you please come up?"

The girls walked over to the winners' podium, a little confused. They hadn't played any of the games – why were they being called up?

Queen Aurora bent down and hung matching golden medals around their necks. "For saving Enchanted Valley," she explained, "and for never giving up!"

The whole stadium burst into applause. The girls looked out at their friends' grateful faces and smiled.

Emily and Aisha took their medals off, and they immediately shrank down into little golden charms. The girls added them to their keyrings along with the rest.

It was time to go home. The girls hugged everybody goodbye.

"See you soon!" called Spike.

"Thanks again," added Grubb.

Aurora's horn glowed with a golden light, and once again the multicoloured sparkles rushed around them. Their feet rose up off the ground …

… and came back down again on the

floor of the stationery cupboard, back at school.

They hurried back into their classroom. The clock on the wall was still at three. No time at all had passed while they'd been in Enchanted Valley. From outside came the bustling sounds of their classmates going home.

"Can we carry on looking for my unicorn pencil for a bit longer?" asked Emily. "I don't want to give up, after all."

"Definitely," Aisha said. "We should persevere!"

They began to search.

A moment later, Emily shouted for joy. "Aisha, look!"

On the classroom wall was a mural,

and parts of it were pink. Emily's unicorn pencil had fallen on to the floor and rolled up against one of the pink parts. Because the pencil was pink too, she hadn't seen it.

"It was camouflaged!" laughed Emily. "Just like Grubb."

"And Spike, all covered in flour," added Aisha.

Both girls smiled to think of their new friends, and all the fun they would have playing together.

They couldn't wait to go back to Enchanted Valley and see them again!

The End

Join Emily and Aisha
for more fun in …
**Sweetblossom
and the New Baby**
Read on for a sneak peek!

Aisha and Emily peeked out of the flap
of their tent into the dark night. They
wore the new onesies that they'd found
laid out last night on their sleeping bags
as a holiday surprise. Both onesies were
covered in a unicorn print. Aisha's had
a silver unicorn horn dangling from her
hood. Emily's had a gold horn.

They'd arrived at Daffodil Dunes
Campsite yesterday afternoon for a
weekend away with Emily's parents. It
was their first time camping and it had
been such fun to sleep in a tiny tent all
by themselves. They'd chattered long
into the night over a midnight feast of

chocolate chip cookies.

This morning's special treat was an exciting one. The four of them had agreed to wake up early to see the sun rise! Outside it was black right now, but they knew that soon the sun would peek over the horizon.

Read
# Sweetblossom and the New Baby
to find out what's in store
for Aisha and Emily!

# Also available

**Book Nine:**

**Book Ten:**

**Book Eleven:**

**Book Twelve:**

## Look out for the next book!

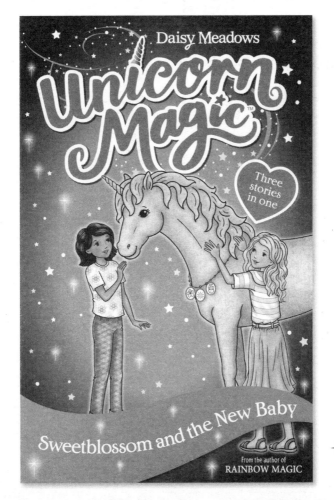